MW01623938

Fever & Slow Hand

A Special 2-in-1 Edition

BOOKS BY MICHELE SLUNG

Murder for Halloween (co-editor)
Hear! Here! Sounds Around the World
Shudder Again: 22 Tales of Sex and Horror
Slow Hand: Women Writing Erotica
I Shudder at Your Touch: 22 Tales of Sex and Horror
The Only Child Book
More Momilies®
The Absent-Minded Professor's Memory Book
Momilies®: As Mother Used to Say
Women's Wiles: An Anthology of Mystery Stories by the Mystery Writers of America
Crime on Her Mind: Fifteen Stories of Female Sleuths from the Victorian Era to the Forties

Fever & Slow Hand

A Special 2-in-1 Edition

EDITED BY MICHELE SLUNG

Perennial

An Imprint of HarperCollins*Publishers*

Published by
HarperCollins Publishers, Inc.
10 East 53rd Street
New York, NY 10022

ISBN: 0-7394-2675-3

Copyright acknowledgments appear on pp. 385

Cover design by Nancy Sabato

Exclusive Introduction for Book Club Members from Michele Slung

What makes a story sexy? And, anyway, what is sexy? Besides, are we talking lust, or are we talking literature? And are the two perhaps mutually exclusive? All I know is that after I published *Slow Hand* and its sequel, *Fever,* many voices clamored to be heard on the subject, and no two reactions were exactly the same.

The truth is, though, that while I'd selected some tales for inclusion believing them to be indisputably hot, others made their way into the books because they carried with them inescapable moments of recognition, or else because they offered glimpses of sensual selves that were simultaneously unfamiliar and unexpectedly right.

Since I was asking would-be contributors only for original stories, this meant I actually *didn't* know what I was looking for until I saw it. And, probably, I was more clear about what I didn't want. All I'm sure of is that, faced with the same several hundred submissions from women writers—a multicultural, varied-age bunch representing most of the fifty states, along with Canada and Great Britain—a different editor would undoubtedly have put together collections that little resembled these two, without being "wrong."

What makes a story sexy? As you've probably intuited, in the end it's thoroughly subjective, and the mere fact of the assembling of the relevant body parts has little to do with it. Yet if one tactical element counted more than any other, as I read through the stories that would become the contents of *Slow Hand* and of *Fever,* that element could be summed up in a single word.

Teasing.

Sexy, for me, meant being kept off balance and held hovering at the edges of satisfaction, then feeling the surprise of a writer's imaginative touches on the way to fictional release. Sexy, for me, meant variety and intimacy and strangeness, and the teasing path through these sensations was the one I preferred to find myself taken on.

So, of course, I hope it's the one you prefer, too.

EXCLUSIVE INTRODUCTION FOR BOOK CLUB MEMBERS FROM MICHAEL MEDVED

Fever

Sensual Stories by Women Writers

EDITED BY MICHELE SLUNG

Perennial
An Imprint of HarperCollins*Publishers*

For Mary Peacock

CONTENTS

FEVER

THE BREAK

By Toby Vallance

She had died that spring. None of us expected it. We knew she was ill, that she suffered and all that, but die? Beattie couldn't die. Not ever. One didn't, you see, in those days, one simply did not. Even the vicar was surprised. For all his baby-faced solemnity he was a man of the world, our vicar; he'd seen grief and relief and excitement and power and that special kind of greed and need and *claiming* you get around death, but never (he confided) had he seen people so shaken and so, what were his words, so in love. We were all young, it must have been that, and people weren't supposed to die, not yet. Anyway, here were the cool, the hip, the unemotional, the usually collected of London's Bohemia prostrating themselves on the muddy Norfolk earth: Roland, never before seen so much as to smile, crumpled completely and leakily sobbed, inconsolable even by the arms of his former mistress, Fanny, now curled around his coat-hanger shoulders; robust and forthright Prue fainted and was led away by Joanna, her rival of years; and Peter, Beattie's walker, seemed to throw himself after the shiny coffin as it was lowered in, wiping his tears on its unrelenting wood. Beattie's parents, who had lived through more of life, looked on with a kind of bewildered resignation (dusting their cheeks with gloved hands) at the scenes around the grave of their daughter. Arms were wrapped around me whose owners I neither knew nor cared for. They pulled me this way and pulled me away, holding me in unwanted grips as part of me left and the earth thudded down on top of the wood.

All the same, there is a kind of highness following a death: There are things to do, people to notify, people to talk to, to discuss it with. One is suddenly important. Roland drove me to his studio for private drinks; Peter rang me daily for two weeks to find out how I was and cried when he heard my voice. Prue brought me white, invalid food from her shop. And Fanny, baffled into wearing something other than her usual black, took me shopping, telling me I should get out, or at least get changed. She confided through her tears that she couldn't imagine either of us, Beattie or I, without the other. To satisfy her need to find me perceptibly altered, or just so that she would leave me alone, I had my ears pierced: three holes punched through each lobe. Morning and night I turned the golden studs, twisting them until blood seeped out and then dabbing at them with sharp, surgical spirit until the flow stopped.

But what do I do when trouble comes along? I don't drink, or talk to people, or eat, or go shopping, or even, usually, get changed. Beattie did all that sort of thing, the woman stuff. I bolt.

I packed up the flat we had shared since college, gave the keys to the neighbor, told the office I needed sick leave, put Sofy in kennels, locked, and left. I left to drift, with the red bandana around my neck, until it all went away. By my going away. I mean, Beattie was home for me, and Beattie had gone and died.

Before I left I went up to the Norfolk graveyard. There was the neat incision in the grass and the trampled clods from our feet where her beautiful head would be. Pushing through the grass, lifting the clods just a little, were the gray-green snouts of daffodils and scillas, the rawer green of crocus buds. At last I cried; not so much, I imagined, from grief but more at the shocking, impertinent indecorousness of it all.

Borophus. Island of spring, of beauty. Persephone's isle. Set in an azure sea warmed by a stream from the Gulf, and the only place in the Med where you can swim in April. Down by the sea its smudged colors, its ochers and terra-cotta and olive greens, give it a kind of shimmer, a kind of blurred, fractional movement, like a heat haze.

"Or is it my eyes?" thought the lady in the large black hat.

Inland, deeper jungle greens of tropical overgrowth pour out of hidden mineral springs over its hills and valleys; perpetual ripeness streams from its secret sources. It is a place without seasons. An island of eternal youth.

She had been coming here three times a year for longer than she would admit to. She always brought books with her, from the spring, autumn, and summer lists, and always she brought a man.

But they were getting so young, she thought, while admiring his sculpted face even in its petulant frown. She had just picked up the phone; there had been the usual bribes, the usual threats, their *under-*

standing; he did what his agent said. And now there he was, scowling prettily into the sun, pretending not to read the book she had chosen for him, waggling his toes in irritation. The lady stared down at him, elegant and jaunty under her hat, and smiled:

"My best feature, my smile. Everyone says."

"She's bigger than me. I mean she's tall. She's vast. She reaches the sky. She towers. She blots out my light, is what I mean," said the smooth-limbed youth to himself. He pushed himself up onto one elbow and lifted his head from the drawing pad with learned insouciance. He didn't have to be here, he told himself; at any time he could be back in the city, in the world, with friends, and admired.

"I hate her," he thought, describing an angry line, "I'm going to have to hump and hump her and I hate her" (with another livid stroke) "and it's the humping and the hating that will give me pleasure. With her hat, her long white legs, that huge mouth, those eyes. I mean she pays me. I drive her. And then I have to hump and hate and hump and hate. Look at me, I can't even look at her; the sunlight crawling into every crack on that plastery face. But then she looks at me with thirsty eyes." The hair on his body was soft, not like fur, like men, but downy like an unformed animal's. He felt every wisp of it as he pushed away the pad, taking up a book instead, and thought, pressing on his swollen lower lip, "I'm going to have to hump her tonight."

I had made a terrible mistake. Everyone was happy here, fat and brown and oiled and grinning, lolling in the early sun as if there were all the time. Stupid of me: One packs one's junk. I could see that it was pretty: the sea, the warm soft sun that couldn't be warm enough for me (nothing too harsh about this island), and food and swimming and all the good things. My ears were starting to heal. But there were people—that rich family getting into a boat, with hampers, and sunshades and bikinis and wraps and a transistor. The elderly pair over there, he smoothing oil onto her rolling brown back. Those children, the heavenly twins, identically dressed as neat as neat can be, muddying their nanny clothes with sand and salt and castles and spades. I grazed my hand on a sharp rock when I took my first swim; it was all wrong for me. The people swarmed and splashed and *smiled* around me and sometimes they stared. That couple, for instance, she of the big hat that hides her face, and the slim man with her—much younger—who's staring at me now. A slight man, with a soft, angelic face. He smiled at me as if he knew me and I found I had smiled back at him. The hat leaned over him and I lost his face and then there he was again, like a sun over the horizon, glowing at me. I bit hard on my cut hand to clean out the wound, and looked away.

The book she'd given him—apparently this place was once Greek. Underneath the stalls, parasols, basket shops, cascading strings of gourds, boutiques, and in between the hotels and guest houses and trattorias, lay a civilization, a city: The square was an agora, that church a temple to Apollo, those paths not arbitrary at all but conforming to an ancient plan. The young man stared from his beach place toward the town, squinting until his eyes blurred and turned tawdry tourists into pagan Greeks, when—"A friend, don't I see a friend? A way out at least." There was a girl just arrived and pale as a librarian. She was walking away, aloof, distracted, a bit gawky, but adventurous too, he guessed from the absurd gypsy bandana at her throat. "A new game to play? Yes, I see a friend all right, a friend in need."

Wasn't she a little weary this year? She stretched her fine legs, elongated her spine, cattishly, sunning and languorous for the world to see. She paraded. But where was the thrill this time with her angry, sculpted young man?

"He could just as well have been chained to me, been on my lead—go there, come back, bring me a drink, my handbag, *oil* me"—this was the game they played of strain and stretch and pull away but never so hard that it hurt. She pushed him, she showed him, she told him repeatedly that she believed in him and he, what shall we say, *companioned* her? She thought of their obedient, tiring nights and yawned. When she looked down at him he scowled again and squinted into the sun, looking away over her shoulder. At last, she was pleased. He was raging more than ever, straining so prettily away. He no longer bored her, but began at last to excite her. He had never *interested* her. Some of his work, perhaps—those three meticulous still lifes. . . .

"Should I have sent him away? Crooked my slender white finger and called him back? Done something?" she was wondering when suddenly she noticed the girl as she walked quickly past, self-conscious and stiff-necked.

"Young enough to be my daughter," thought the lady, "if I weren't so well preserved."

From the coast you could see nothing but fat green hills. But as I walked inland up dusty roads the green became both separate and solid: The smell of the sea, the chatter and fresh breeze faded, giving way to a heavy, tropical silence. I followed a path into the jungle, hung over by sharp, shiny fronds and almost concealed from the sky. The air was dank, and under my feet the ground was creepily soft. Strong, wet leaves brushed against my face and arms; there was the noise of water dripping; the undergrowth rustled as I passed. I ran back into the light, down to the beach and the fresh sea air.

For days after that I didn't budge. The sun gets to you in the end; you can't help yourself. You take the first swim, beach yourself, warm yourself through and through, with the sand on your legs and back and elbows and your eyes closed and that peculiar dark glow under the lids. All around, the noises of children shouting, people walking, the splash of arms through water, leave you in splendid isolation. Then you swim again, beach again, all that; there's a rhythm. I'd hold my arms straight up, stretched out toward the sun, fan open my hands against its light and peer up through my feathered fingers at—

"Your scarf," said the angelic young man, holding out the red spotted kerchief to me. Then, as if embarrassed at his own presumption: "It was blowing away."

I propped myself up on my elbows, smiled up at him reassuringly, thanked him, and could think of nothing else to say. I was both glad of the approach and wished it were all over, so that I could drift and dream again and be nowhere. He was trying to land me.

"You wear it all the time," he persisted and then, caught out by himself again, "except when swimming." He ended with a shyish laugh.

How could I have forgotten the bandana, I wondered, tying it quickly round my neck? Only weeks have passed, how could I?

"It was a gift?" he asked, squatting down athletically on his heels. "From a, from him?" He gave a winning smile.

"From a friend," I said, with treacherous inadequacy, and clutched the ragged scarf to my throat.

"Ah," but he was unsure. I had corrected him; no lover, no him. In his language it should mean that I was available. "Ah, a friend," he echoed foolishly. I looked away.

Standing against the bar, elegant white legs crossed at the ankle, was that lady with the wide black hat. As I looked she turned and in that turn lifted up her face. I gasped. For it was Beattie. Beattie's mouth, Beattie smiling her old sardonic smile at me.

"Perhaps you would like," the man persisted and then, finding in himself a quite forgotten taste and kindness, "to be left alone?"

I remembered myself and apologized to him, for I had been miles away, somewhere else completely. Then I thanked him, glad, finally, of the company.

* * *

She watched them under the brim of her wide black hat—the sculpted, blinkered youth and some young pickup. She knew what he was doing. But it was the girl she fixed on, who held herself to herself, who would not give to him at all but huddled into some private place with spaces around her as one does, as she did herself, in unwelcome crowds. This girl, his little game, was fleshier, rubbery with youth, shining with it, but she had the same sleek hair, the coloring, the same isolation—the breath caught sharply in her throat. She held back her head and smiled up to the sun, in case tears rolled out.

Sometimes a strange place allows you to find yourself. The boatman greeted me in the mornings, the same waiter showed me to my table for meals and now there was this overfriendly young man. Familiarity was stalking me. I would have to leave.

I swam under the sea wall. The turquoise water supported me, but the clear depths dared me to dive further down. I dived, letting the sea take me. Through stinging eyes I saw a shifting sea floor, beckoning vegetable fingers. My lungs began to heave, my chest hurt, ears rang, my head was bursting. Something hard rubbed against me. Eventually I bobbed to the surface, breaking through the waters with a gasp and heaved clean air into my lungs.

"Thank God," came a voice above me, "I was worried."

A shape, dark against the sun, spoke to me; I was blinded and could see only an outline, the long pale legs, the voice with its slight accent. The voice I knew.

"Yes, I thought you'd never get here." There was a laugh in the voice now. I bobbed away under the legs. Long and firm I could begin to form them against the sun into more tangible shapes. A pale hand smoothed oil along the length of the thigh, caressed now one and now the other, up and down and up and down.

I swallowed water, choking down the salty clean sea taste. The hand moved on, up and down, the oil slicking the firm leg to a rounded sheen. The hand lingered, toyed, teased—I put mine onto the sea wall and could feel the warmth of the rock beneath me, the warmth of the bare foot beside me. The foot moved toward my hand, a toe touching my finger, lightly.

"You're bleeding again," said the voice. I looked up into the sun, blinded by the light, up the long, pale oiled legs.

He had begun to draw again. It was one of his most painstaking, one of his labors of love; in fact, it was a plan of the cool, harmonious order that he could now see underneath the violent foliage and cheap baubles of the island. When he looked up for a moment he saw the lady haul the young girl out of the sea as easily as if she were a child. She was doing it to spite him, he was sure of it, to twitch his chain. He turned angrily back to where his city had begun to loom beneath the terra-cotta and leaves. When he looked again they were in the café. She had ordered juice and sweet, colored jellies for the girl who ate and drank with a kind of breathless greed, like a child. The bandana was tied around one hand. The lady took nothing herself, just stared at the girl as her long white hand stroked and stroked her own empty glass.

When he looked down at the lines of his hidden city again he found that his anger, his thwarted spite had gone and that he felt instead a kind of longing, an exquisite and gentle loneliness. He tensed his stomach, flattened his legs and dug himself more deeply into the sand. His body stirred in spite of himself.

I didn't really think I was dead. Only for a minute. Because she looked, she really did, she looked like Beattie. She stood over me, welcoming me, helping me out—

"I thought she had drowned. I thought I had lost her, this young stranger. I panicked. I swanned over—no, I ran, and searched the water, stood there until—and I counted, God, I counted minutes, until she bobbed up again. As she gasped the air so did I. I really thought I had lost her. I led her to the café, bright and light and anodyne, and our moment passed. But she stared at me—I caught her doing it when she thought I didn't notice. Perhaps I have a hair, a smudge, a mark—perhaps I look weird or old."

His obsession grew and filled the last few days. In the afternoons, having been fed by her with plums and dates and the sweet syrups of the island, he would go to the beach to draw. His city now teemed with people, young, ardent, untouched, all of them, and the men and women alike were sleek-haired and shining with youth. In the late afternoons he would walk barefooted into town like one of his pagans and drop into the cool of Apollo's temple or sit for hours in the shade of the agora, while the crowds dimmed around him.

In the evenings they would dine, she starkly elegant in black, clicking her painted fingers to bring waiters with bowls of spiced, creamy dips, dishes of tender local fruits, oiled and skinned and sliced open. She would tell him of other books to read, and places to visit, of pictures to see and to draw, and all the time she held him with her voracious black eyes. Sitting opposite and pinned by her look, he would shift so that he could see the girl in her corner, and smile at the lady, full of secret freedom. And then there were the nights.

On their last night she ordered French champagne. Maroon-suited waiters brought it grinningly. As she filled and refilled him (she took nothing for herself) her hand roved up and down her own empty glass and she fixed on him those burning black eyes. The young man looked away towards the corner by the door: The girl was not at her table that night. She had followed his gaze and now looked down at her painted fingers curling on the edge of the tablecloth. The gesture, full of a kind of shame, stripped her of years more surely than her paint had ever done. He took the bottle from her and let their hands touch when he filled her empty glass. Her eyes now flickered over the empty corner of the room, and her lips compressed into a line of resignation, the crimson stain leaving small pitiful runnels at their edges. She looked down again. As the waiters hovered at their elbows, he studied her: her face, whiter than ever, the creases and cracks of age, harder; the blackened eyes running a little into thicker streaks beneath the eyeline; the hat, the inevitable hat, perched to one side so that the sleek, tight hair peeped out underneath. The waiters had quieted down and formed a murmuring circle around the last of the diners.

The night lapped itself around me like a cat. I sat on the balcony with my robe half open. The wind was lower, the moon swelling in the indigo sky, the air sticky, balmy with a steady beating heat. Music drifted up from the square mixed with voices and chatter from the restaurant, fading to a single violin as the heat thickened and the night trembled around me. For the first time in weeks, was it months, could it be months, I had not thought of, had not thought back. I was drugged. The touch of the stranger had made me high. The air licked about my sunned, stretched limbs, my arms hung gently at my sides, my naked feet danced on the warm rose tiles. The lazy slap of the waves, the murmuring in the trees, the rustle—soft noises filled the air, my throat, my senses. "Where am I?"

He led her to the room they had never shared. She said nothing, told him nothing. He guided her in, sat her down on the bed, then he lifted the black hat from her head, so that her hair hung stiffly about her white cheeks. He stared at her as if he'd never seen her before, biting back his full lower lip, looking at her so intensely that she could not meet his gaze. Then he reached for her hand and hauled her to her feet without a word. He took her into the bathroom and stood her in front of the mirror in a hard light, standing behind her with his hands on her shoulders. Then he began to run water and rinse out a face towel. Watching in the mirror, he began gently to wipe her face. First, he pressed the warm cloth over her mouth, wiping away all the crimson, smudging her chin and cheeks red for a moment and then a bruised, bloodless white. Then, he rubbed the white slakes of powder from her cheeks, leaving her pink and raw in the bright light of the bathroom. And then, moving so gently she could hardly feel him, he washed away the black from her eyes. The lady kept them shut; she was unable to look while the beauty she had so often devoured stripped her of her own. At last he stood behind her, lifted her pale chin, her naked head to the mirror, and commanded her to look.

"All my rage had lifted. I lay down beside her, feeling the heat from her body two inches away. She gasped when I touched her hand. Her eyes were closed tight like a child who would not be seen. I pored over her naked face. The face I'd so raged against and despised, that had held me, was now stripped—of its false whiteness, its blackened lids, and stains—for my greedy gaze. Blindly, her hand reached out for me, flattening itself on my belly. I began to shower that face with kisses while the tears welled under her reddened eyelids.

"Noises seeped out of both of us, muted and full of terror. She cried out when I stroked her lean hip beneath the silken skirt. I touched her pale, bruised face and then began to draw the dark wraps from her. I lifted and opened the warm silk things, putting them to my face before I dropped them, to inhale the scents still held by her empty clothes. Clumsily, she caught my hand and thrust it to her breast and then pulled my head down until my mouth covered her dark nipple, holding my head there. I buried myself in her bosom, enfolding myself, losing myself in its great heaviness. Tasting cool dark cream at first, I felt her change under my busy tongue and moist lips until she grew stiff for me.

" 'Oh,' she cried softly, tears running freely down the scrubbed cheeks.

" 'Oh,' I echoed, my mouth gaping, choking on, drinking in her giving breasts."

In the noise of the night, of the waves, the far-off fading music and murmuring of the trees, I heard "Oh," and a gasp of indrawn breath as near as by my ear, so near that I turned to it, expecting to find a person there. I turned toward the balcony of the next room and watched in the dark, for the door was a little open.

"Oh," I heard again, a man's voice, full and choking. "Oh, God."

The noises love makes: the soft meaningless cries that fill the air, filled, more to the point, my ears, my nose, my mouth. He cried out and I choked; I breathed in his cry. Her sobs, coming now, heaved my breast. There was an enervating pause before a great and terrible sigh as of the life leaving the body, the soul flying up. I could not help myself. I gasped. Abruptly, there was dead silence. I held my breath, high and thwarted, with every nerve straining, the warmth still playing on my stretched body like an instrument.

"She's out there. He poured himself into me, arching over me, quite lost, as I gaped beneath him. My welcoming mouth. Never before, never before—as the tears poured down and he poured inside me, never before had I felt that tugging, that sudden clutching, that quick inner squeezing—and I don't want to, no, stop, I don't want to be naked and lost as, God, as he is. But there is his panting and the drop of his sweat and his agonized cries and all the time my tears and my wet huge mouth—and I can't help it. The clutching and clenching goes right through me now, hurts me, taking me by the scruff as if I were a rag, shaking me.

"He had fallen beside me; we were tangled in juice and hairs and the salt smells of our night. Our fingers matched the tangle of our limbs. I hear the silence and our astonished breath. And then I hear hers—outside, she must be, but as near as he is; just as we finish I hear another sudden intake of breath, a gasp of shock. I *know* it is her.

"We both hear it. I sense from a stiffening beside me that he listens as well. Our breathing changes, is regular, quieter, listening. The noise on the balcony changes—also quieter, and there is the soft pad, less than a noise, of feet creeping towards us. She seeks to hear us; she *wants*. Our hands move together for the first time, twining fiercely around each other. He shifts his leg slightly against mine.

"There is another sound from outside, a chair is gently moved, breath awkwardly held, and then, in spite of itself, panting a little. He tenses briefly beside me. On the balcony the breathing is more regular now, deeper and heavier. There is again less than a noise, a sense, a kind of rubbing of the air, the whirr of cloth moving swiftly and rhythmically through the air. The chair leg scratches briefly against the tiles. But most of all there is the sound of breath as it changes, held now, let out, in spite of itself, heaving.

"His breathing changes and catches. We are all alive with it; the night is full of our discrete breaths. He looks down at me in the dark and reads my mind perfectly. My eyes have widened in acquiescence. Softly, he draws back the curtain covering the long window and eases the doors apart. Together we eye the shape in the reflecting glass—a musician playing, rapt and lost to everything except her music: The head is thrown back, the sleek hair falling free, the robe loose and flowing, legs straddling the chair, and hands, both hands coursing and roving—the stretched body working, busy, frantically playing.

"He's back. We burn up against each other, sides on sides, thighs on burning thighs, every nerve alight. The shape moves and changes, playing for us, faster and more frantic, feverish, the head thrown far back. We close our eyes, hear the sighs, the muffled gasps from out there. His hand begins to play upon my side, my white flank; my hand covers his, covers him. The firm belly, the smooth sides, those small hairs softened by his sweat, my tongue."

I had tilted my chair right back, my heels on the railings; I was taken wholly by the night, the sticky, dripping summer heat, as I dipped and dived. Dividing myself, head back, eyes closed to the night sky, my ears wide open for the answering sounds from next door. I *had* to do this; I *had* to perform.

I thought I was falling, that I was drowning again, and that I was lifted up by kind, strong hands, laid on a warm, hard place. My head remained thrown back and my eyes tight shut; hands, warm and kindly, replaced my own feverish playing; soft fingers unfolded me and held mine firmly down. My mouth was eased open, freed of the scarf I bit on, and a mouth pressed against it, stopping it; a mouth pressed against my other mouth, taking the sea out of me, bringing me into life again. A hard, smooth tongue pried me open and then at last it entered me. I was possessed. And all the time kind hands held me, and other mouths dipped over me with their firm kisses, their own salt, and I drank their other scalding tears.

The sun was already high in the sky. The square was busy with people—the bread buyers, flower sellers, chatterers, already about their tasks. "Peter," I wrote, "meet me. Collect Sofy and meet me. Take me home."

I saw that couple checking out of the hotel, the tall woman, the slender youth. He carried a small attaché case and her hat; he opened the car door for her and held her elbow briefly to guide her in. He said something to her and then slid easily into the front seat. Without hesitating for a second, as if attached by some invisible direct beam, she turned around and looked directly up into my eyes. I was held there until she got in behind him and I could watch their two heads, one sleek and dark, the other soft and fair, as he drove the car out of the square. I would sit for a few more minutes on the balcony before clearing up my things and checking out myself; my bandana, in a tight scrumpled ball, had fallen between the railings onto the adjacent balcony. I felt my naked throat.

"Later," I thought, "later."

AUTHOR'S NOTE

My story is about loss and the recovery from loss. It charts a journey from grief and other entrapments to a sort of liberation and celebration of the senses. I hope that somewhere there's an island like Borophus.

MARIAN'S EARS

By Susan St. Aubin

When Joe Turner came into Hal's office cubicle and started complaining about his ears, Hal could only see Marian's ears, small and pink as shells, slightly peaked at the top like elf's ears, a very different organ from Joe's fleshy, hairy protuberances. Joe stuck his little finger in one ear and wiggled it around.

"Plugged," he said, "completely plugged. What do you think?"

Hal thought of Marian's pink shells. "See a doctor," he suggested, shrugging at his computer screen while he scrolled up a menu. Joe melted out of his vision into the next cubicle, his voice fading to a mutter.

Marian was the only woman Hal knew who still had unpierced ears. Even his mother had had gold studs nailed through her earlobes in a department store one Saturday afternoon. His wife, Evelyn, had three holes in each ear, two in each lobe and one on each side, where she wore two gold rings that stuck out at angles from her head.

Hal first discovered the secret of Marian's ears when he touched them after dinner one Sunday while they were sitting at the card table at the foot of her bed in the center of her one-room apartment. He reached both arms across the table and gently stroked down from their peaked tips to their small lobes, connected to her jaw instead of hanging loose like most people's did.

She shivered, her hands flying up as though she wanted to push him away, but she stopped and breathed deeply as he moved his fingertips across the lobes onto her cheeks. He'd never seen such a reaction, and started to move his fingers back to her ears again.

"No," she said, putting her hands on his.

Later, in bed, physiology was turned upside down. Instead of reaching between her legs, his fingers went for her ears. She reached up, turned off the lamp beside the bed, and let him stroke the rims, the nearly fleshless lobes, the delicate peaks at the tips. With his tongue he explored one ear's orifice, trying to remember names for those inner convolutions. Labyrinth. Cochlea. Coiled shells.

Marian moaned beneath him, her pulsing ears warm. He bet himself they were red, the way they were when he embarrassed her or made her laugh. When he turned on the light, she sat up, crying out "no" as her hands jumped to her ears.

"You know I don't like the light on!" Her face was flushed. When he took her hands away from her ears, her hair fell over them. She was panting and her forehead was sweaty. He brushed her hair aside but her quick hands were on those ears before he could see a thing, so he kissed her on the mouth, turned off the light, and pulled her back down on the bed. She sighed as he traced the outer rim of her right ear, this time with his tongue, circling slowly into the labyrinth while his fingers stroked her other ear. Her breathing became deeper and faster in time with the rhythm of his tongue and fingers. He put a little finger in each of her ears, tickling the invisible hairs there until Marian gasped and shuddered, then sobbed, "Don't ever tell anyone this, I couldn't bear to have people know."

He paused. "Know what?" he asked, as though he hadn't noticed a thing.

At work he hid medical books about ears in his desk, furtively taking them out when no one was looking. Earlobes have few nerve endings, he read. That's why doctors take blood samples from children's ears, because they won't feel it. Hah, he thought, like baby boys don't feel a thing when their foreskins are peeled off. But when he touched his own ears, he found them strangely numb compared to his face.

She's a secret pervert, he thought. That's why this cool and doll-like girl excites me. Everyone's got some strange sexual button, and I've found hers.

At home in bed with Evelyn, Hal read about ears while she studied the books on French cooking the head chef at Chouette whose apprentice she was, had recommended. She licked her lips as she turned the pages, but those full, pink lips had temporarily lost their charm for him. He turned back to his own book and read that there are many myths about ears. Wrinkled earlobes, for example, have long been thought to indicate problems in the heart or circulatory system, but, of course, wrinkling of the skin is as common in old age as various heart problems.

Hal reached up to finger his earlobes, which felt perfectly smooth. Even though, as his book said, cause and effect cannot be presumed, he thought he'd take a closer look in the mirror sometime when Evelyn wasn't around to laugh at him. Connected lobes, he read, are a recessive trait in which the lobes, like Marian's, meet the jaw instead of hanging loose. He wondered if ear orgasms could be a recessive predilection, but there was no mention of sex.

He planned his next date with Marian on Friday. Evelyn worked at Chouette mostly on the weekends: Fridays, Saturdays, and Sundays were the big days; they were closed on Mondays and Tuesdays. Evelyn sometimes spent Friday night with her sister, who lived a block away from the restaurant. It gave them a chance to get caught up, she said. He reached over and stroked Evelyn's earlobe. Without all her rings, her ears looked delicate and damaged, slightly bruised around the holes. He wondered how much it hurt to have the holes done, if even now it was ever painful to wear earrings.

Evelyn dropped her book and lay back with her eyes closed. He continued stroking, his smallest finger moving slowly to the secret and unseen part of her ear. He was more aroused than Evelyn, who breathed lightly, as though asleep. She moved one hand across his thigh to his hardening penis; while her other hand moved his fingers from her ear to her breast.

"Don't you like that?" he whispered.

"Like what?"

He flicked his tongue into her ear and whispered, "cochlea," loving the sound of the word and the sensation of entrapment that whispering it gave his tongue.

Evelyn laughed. "That tickles! What are you doing?"

"Some people's ears are very sensitive," he said.

He wanted to tell her. There was no reason why he shouldn't; they'd both had lovers before, but unimportant lovers they could laugh about together, like her friend George from New York with his pierced left nipple who tried to talk her into piercing her right nipple so they'd be mirror images. Hal was afraid that if Marian wasn't his secret, he'd be in danger of losing her. Evelyn's laugh could sometimes kill like a frost; she would be capable of making him think Marian's mysterious ears were silly.

She kissed him on the mouth, then slid her mouth down his body to kiss him where Marian never would. "I guess everyone's different," she murmured as her lips sucked his cock into the labyrinth of her mouth. He thought how the human body, especially the female body, was a series of labyrinths tunneling to an unknown center.

The next day at noon, he walked six blocks to the school where Marian taught and stood behind a tree just outside the chain link fence. In dark glasses, with the collar of his jacket turned up, he watched her play a circle game with a group of children. They all moved right, then left, singing a song whose words he couldn't catch because their voices were so high-pitched. One of the first signs of aging, he remembered, was a loss of hearing at higher decibels.

Marian's hair covered her ears except when the wind blew it back to reveal their tips, glowing red with the cold. He pulled his face further back into his collar, enjoying the role of voyeur. Once she looked in his direction but didn't seem to recognize him. Surely someone will call the police, he thought. Maybe Marian will when she goes back inside. A squad car will pull up and take me away at Marian's command. His heart beat faster. When no one came to get him after she took her class inside, he went back to work feeling light-headed with freedom. On his way into the office, he bought a bag of pork rinds from a machine in the lobby and ate them as he rode up the escalator.

Friday morning Evelyn kissed him, saying she'd be back early the next day.

"Early enough to get back in bed, if you're there," she whispered.

"I will be," he answered, glad he wouldn't miss Evelyn's Saturday morning seduction, glad Marian didn't like him to spend the night because she was afraid someone might see him leave in the morning—a neighbor or even her landlady.

Hal thought surely one of those watchful people would notice how the lights always went off for hours when he visited, even though no one left the apartment. He and Evelyn would laugh together about something like that, but when he mentioned it to Marian in an attempt to get her to leave just one light on, she didn't understand.

"We could be doing all sorts of things in the dark. We could be watching television in the dark. Having the lights on doesn't mean anything because you always want to do it with the lights on." She reached across him to switch off the lamp on his side of the bed.

Evelyn always liked the lights on and so did Hal because he wanted to see her vaginal lips turn a dark lipstick pink, her breasts rise and tighten and her face flush as dark pink as those inner lips when she came. Even though there was something exciting about scuffling around in the dark, he often wondered what Marian looked like in her secret inner parts, beyond the quick flash of pink lips and lavender interior before she pulled her legs together on the rare times they made love in daylight. There was more to life than ears, he thought.

Friday night after work he climbed the stairs to Marian's apartment, an image of her ears before him. Through the window he could see across the room into the former closet that was her kitchen. Everything seemed to be on a child's scale: miniature gas stove, sink, and counter, with cabinets packed beneath and above. An uncurtained square of window was in the center of the upper cupboards. She was grating cheese, her ears hidden by her hair, which was pulled over them in two loose pigtails. When she came to the door he lifted one to kiss the ear beneath it, but she ducked away and went back to the counter where she was arranging lasagna noodles in a baking dish between layers of cheese and sauce, like weaving a basket, he thought.

"I'm sure Evelyn makes this much better," she said. "I just use my mother's old recipe; it's probably not even really the way Italians do it."

"Evelyn doesn't cook Italian so far," he assured her. "Only French."

While her hands were occupied he pulled the ribbon holding one pigtail, then the other, loosening the silky light brown hair and smoothing it behind her ears in her usual style.

"No," she said, pulling her hair back over her pure, unadorned ears. "Not yet. Wait."

While the lasagna baked they sat side by side on her bed, his arms around her shoulders. They listened to the soft, unidentifiable music she liked, which, when he asked, always turned out to be something like Japanese flute concertos, or instrumental whale songs, or wind chimes played by musicians he'd never heard of. When he brought tapes of Talking Heads or Elvis Costello, she'd listen for a few minutes, then cover her ears.

Once she said, "This isn't very relaxing, is it?"

"Relaxation isn't the point," he answered, but when she looked blankly at him, he realized that, for her, it was.

He leaned his head on her shoulder, sniffing her ear through her hair, getting his nose right inside the vestibule, smelling a scent like dying roses, like rain, like dust. She pushed him away to go check the lasagna.

While they ate, she kept smoothing her hair over her ears with her free hand. Hal thought her hair looked like a helmet pulled down like that, or a nun's wimple. Later, in the dark, he hoped to penetrate that wall of silky hair to free Marian's ears.

"No," she hissed as his fingers felt for her ears. "It's too much, I can't take that much."

"That much what?" he asked.

She mumbled something that sounded like "pleasure."

"What?" he whispered. "What?"

"Nothing," she said. She guided his hand between her legs to her less certain arena of pleasure. He stroked and stroked with his fingers, then entered her, stroking from deep inside, and had his orgasm because he couldn't wait forever for something like that electric reaction she'd had when he touched her ears. He kept trying to sneak his fingers up to them to see what that zap would feel like inside her, but she kept pushing his hands away.

Late at night, walking down the stairs, he watched the clear, cold stars in the wet sea of the sky and thought, she'll stay the same, always hanging like that at the brink of the universe. It'll never be more than this. He sighed as he unlocked his car door, glad he still had Evelyn, his earthly love.

"Did you ever think of piercing your ears?" Hal asked Marian one winter afternoon when they were hiking. She stopped suddenly on the trail as though she'd seen a snake.

"Pierce?" she asked, turning around to face him. Her ears were hidden under the two navy blue mounds of her earmuffs.

"People do that." He laughed at her.

"I don't usually wear jewelry," she sniffed as she walked quickly on ahead.

They came to a meadow with new green grass already poking up beneath the dead grass of last summer. It was almost warm in the sun. They sat facing each other on two large rocks, their hands on their knees.

These hikes were a Sunday afternoon ritual because Evelyn was usually at Chouette from ten in the morning until midnight, doing brunch and dinner. He put his hand on Marian's knees while she looked at a distant ridge through her binoculars, then reached up and slowly removed her earmuffs. Her hair dropped over her ears as she lowered her binoculars to stare at him, the irises of her eyes quickly narrowing in the light.

"Not here," she whispered, turning and raising the binoculars to her eyes again.

"Where?" he whispered. "When?"

She pretended not to hear him.

Back at her apartment she made a vegetable soup, nervously consulting a book called *101 Quick Recipes* that looked old enough to have belonged to her mother. As Hal lay on the bed and watched her work, he imagined these were the simple recipes she was raised on, a contrast to Evelyn's mastery of thousands of sauces and ways to perform fellatio, none of them easy.

Marian frowned. "I'll bet Evelyn would never use *canned* stock," she said, adding chopped carrots, celery, and turnips, and then a can of tomatoes. She crushed dried basil and oregano between her fingers. He loved the smell of herbs on Evelyn's hands when she came home from Chouette, some as simple as sage or tarragon, and others he couldn't identify, not even when she named them.

"Fennel?" he'd ask. "Chervil?"

Marian washed her hands, drying them on a kitchen towel so immaculate it looked new, though he'd seen it often in the past year hanging beside her sink.

"Your soup smells wonderful. Come sit down here while it cooks." When she crossed the room, he took her hands and sniffed the rose scent of her soap, then tried to pull her down to the bed, but she leaned toward the pot on the stove.

"It doesn't have meat in it," she apologized.

When he finally managed to pull her down beside him, she sat stiffly, smoothing back her hair with one hand, while he held the other.

"I don't eat meat half the time," he said. "Evelyn's studying eggs now, so we eat a lot of soufflés, and casserole things with cheese and vegetables. I don't miss meat."

He was staring ravenously at the ears that held back her hair. He was touched she'd bared her ears for him; he thought of telling her he missed them more than meat, but knew she wouldn't understand. He pulled her closer and circled the rims of her ears with his fingers. When she let her eyes shut, he watched the lids pulse and flicker with her breathing. He lowered his tongue to one ear, nudging aside his own finger, thinking she'd never notice the difference, but she opened her eyes at once.

"The soup! It's boiling, it's not supposed to boil!" She shot off the bed to turn it down.

The soup was done. "Overdone," she moaned as she ladled it into bowls.

Hal rolled off the bed to sit opposite Marian at the card table. For him the soup was perfect: the vegetables and noodles well done but not soggy, the broth clear. He even thought Evelyn might approve because she had an appreciation for simplicity as well as variety. He'd seen her open cans. He told Marian the soup was good, but lack of perfection made her sullen. She sipped, frowning, ignoring his slurps and murmurs of appreciation, so soon he was quiet, too.

She got up to put on a tape, something with flutes, and then sat down again. When a noodle, curled like an ear, floated to the surface of his broth, he sucked it up silently from his spoon, letting it slide around his tongue before he chewed and swallowed.

After dinner Marian did the dishes while he drowsed on the bed, listening to the flutes. When Evelyn cooked he did the dishes because she told him chefs were above that, a division of labor that seemed fair to him. He usually did them early in the morning while he listened to the birds at the feeder just outside the window. He realized those flutes carrying on above the clink of the dishes in Marian's miniature sink were someone's idea of bird calls. All wrong, of course; real birds were never that melodiously annoying.

He opened his eyes when he heard the water gurgle out of the sink. Marian dried her hands, then moved through the room turning off lights until she stood beside him.

"Are you asleep?" she asked.

He could see her by the light of the winter moon shining through the high window of her closet kitchen. Her head was bent; the hair fell forward, occluding her ears. She sat on the bed beside him. He reached behind her hair to massage the rims of her ears.

"I have to ask you something," she whispered in his ear while moving his hands off hers. "I have to tell you your obsession with ears bothers me."

"My obsession?"

She lay on her back, arranging her hair over her ears. "It's not normal," she said.

"They're your ears," he answered, "so if you want to call them abnormal that's fine with me."

"It's not my ears," she said, "it's you, always touching them. If you'd just leave them alone, I'd be fine."

"But you like it." He sat up and turned on the light. "I can tell how much you like it. You *come* when I touch your ears."

"I do not." She sat up, her face pink.

He grabbed her hair to hold it off her glowing ears. "Ah hah! See these ears?"

"Hal, please! Turn out the light."

In the moonlight he pulled off her clothes, then stroked her breasts and belly down to her clit, which he took in his mouth and sucked like a nipple while one finger stroked inside her, feeling distant pulsations get stronger. The instant when he knew she'd say, as she often did, that's enough, I've had enough, he lifted his free hand to her ear, stroking from rim to lobe until she rocked beneath him like a boat on a rough ocean, waves lapping and pushing against the finger he still held inside her.

"No, oh, no!" she cried, then lay very still. "Why do you keep doing that with my ears?"

"It's sex," he answered. "I thought you'd like it, I thought that's what we were doing here."

"I don't like it like this," she said. "I don't like to go that far."

When he turned on the light her face was still as pink and swollen as he was sure her inner parts were, as well as her ears, now covered by her damp hair.

"I personally like going as far as I can." He was beginning to feel like a perverted missionary of sex, trying to explain himself to the unheathen. Right now he wanted to be in bed with Evelyn, on the road to eternity, holding her vibrator inside her and nibbling gently at her thighs just the way she wasn't afraid to tell him she liked. Evelyn's way was more ordinary, not quite the challenge Marian presented.

"Maybe I'm just not ready," Marian said.

"Ready for what?"

"I don't know. Men. A lover."

"Ears?" he asked. "You mean you're not ready for ears?"

"I don't see what ears have to do with anything," she said, covering hers with her hands.

He looked at her closely, but she wasn't laughing or lying.

"I guess it's your bad luck you met a man who appreciates ears."

His sarcasm went over her.

"I can't see being into just one thing, that's all," she said. "It's so narrow. What about my legs, my breasts, the things most men like? Why are you so exclusive? When I make love I want all my body parts included, and my mind. All of me."

He stopped listening and kissed her nose, her lips, her fingertips.

"That's nice," she murmured. "You can be so nice."

* * *

He was glad to get home to Evelyn, who was sitting up in bed reading a book on Asian cooking. She wore a black cotton gown with cut out embroidered places all around the low neckline. He could see her flesh moving as she breathed.

"Branching out?" he asked. She never could stick to one thing for long; France to Vietnam seemed like a natural culinary progression.

She looked up. "Have you eaten? I brought back some spinach quiche if you want it."

"I ate." He stretched out on the bed beside her.

She returned her attention to her book, but stroked his hair with one hand until he was nearly asleep.

"Get under the covers," she whispered. She was wearing nothing now, the black gown in a heap beside the bed. He took her breasts in both hands as she kissed him and climbed on top. He liked being seduced for a change. She fit his cock into herself like a cork and began to ride him. His thumbs found her clit, pressing the way he knew she liked. She squeezed his earlobes between her fingers to match his rhythm. This was a sensation he scarcely noticed, like a fly buzzing. He grabbed her around the waist to pull her down harder while he rose up, coming. Every nerve in both their bodies centered between their legs in sparkling points of electricity. Evelyn fell forward on him, her hands on his senseless ears.

Next morning he lifted one of his medical texts to read in bed, carefully so he wouldn't wake Evelyn. In the dim light behind the shades, he read that there may be some truth to the old wives' tale that wrinkled earlobes mean a person is likely to develop heart trouble, because wrinkling of the skin in the extremities can be a sign of poor circulation. A weakening heart doesn't pump enough blood, so the skin withers.

He slid out of bed to go to the bathroom, leaving the open book on his pillow. In the mirror he inspected his ears: the lobes were large, fleshy, and wrinkled, especially the right ear, the side he slept on. When he turned on the light to have a closer look, he discovered even more lines. His ears were criss-crossed with white and red lines. He massaged his right lobe to improve the circulation, but when he dropped his hand his ear was still wrinkled. He thought of Marian's small, smooth, nearly fleshless lobes, and his heart lurched against his ribs. Was there anything at all to her except ears? He really couldn't see the rest of Marian in his mind. She was right: He was obsessed.

When he came back into the bedroom, Evelyn was paging through his book. She looked up, yawning, and asked, "So, are ears the doorway to the soul? The cochlear passage to the northwest corners of the heart?"

He sat down on the bed beside her.

"Well," he said, "I just noticed my ears are wrinkled. They say that might be an early sign of heart failure."

She laughed, turning the pages of the book. "Where? Where does it say anything like that? Anyway, you're thirty-five, so it should be normal to have a few wrinkles. Look—there's one at the corner of your mouth now. And look at your forehead."

She sat up and pointed. He slapped his forehead with mock horror. Soon they were both laughing.

"They're all bullshit anyway, those medical books," she told him. "What could ears possibly mean? Ears are nothing."

Evelyn could only say that because she didn't know Marian, and if Hal had his way, she never would. He was a man who could tell his girlfriend all about his wonderful wife, to whom he could say nothing about that girlfriend for fear of his own confusion. As he laughed harder he suspected that straight through to his weakening heart and his immortal soul, he was as insensitive as his ears.

AUTHOR'S NOTE

It continues to amaze me that most people, sometimes even other writers, assume that fiction is fact, or, at the very least, based on real events. Often, what I write may be the truth in some philosophic sense, but it certainly isn't fact. Like most creative people, I'm a chronic liar. That's what's fun about writing—the moral and legal injunction to tell the truth can be relaxed. So, to answer the question I'm frequently asked, especially, it seems, about my erotic writing, the answer is no, none of this really happened. I must confess, I lied—and not only that, I had a great time doing it.

QUEER

By Elizabeth Clarke

I admit I saw Anderson first. He served me a cup of coffee in Donut World. This place is a charming example of Only in America. Permanently sticky yellow Formica, waxy doughnuts under lights in a glass case, and a big sign on the wall: 30 MINUTE TIME LIMIT. NO LOITERING WITHOUT PURCHASE. Suddenly you've left San Francisco and stumbled into East Jesus, West Virginia. Free refills? My ass.

Someone had succeeded in mortally wounding the coffeemaker in the dressing room and I needed caffeine to see me through the ten P.M. to three A.M. shift. Donut World was practically across the street from the theater where I danced, the Cherry Pit. When I walked in, it was occupied by two cops scarfing crullers in a corner booth and a fiftyish hippie zoning out on the fluorescent lights. And Anderson.

Tufts of ragged black hair stuck out from under the paper Donut World hat and the yellow Donut World smock was unzipped to show a T-shirt featuring a skeletal mariachi band. There was a silver ring through his left nostril and another through his right eyebrow. More in his earlobes. He was leaning against the counter smoking a cigarette, tapping ringed fingers against the Formica.

Like Miranda said, retrospect always wears rose-tinted glasses. It's hard to remember, *really*, what you thought the first time you met someone who later became your lover. When they ask, you tell them your clit started throbbing instantly, of course.

Actually, I thought he was probably gay.

That was why my clit started throbbing. Aside from him just being gorgeous, with those big brown eyes. Faggots get me wet. Even when I'm attracted to straight boys, they're femmy little girly-boys. Boys with doe eyes, long delicate fingers, smooth skin that a few days without shaving only makes more tender and bitable. Much later I told him this and he said *he* thought I was probably a dyke.

He handed me my change. On the Donut World nametag, he had neatly lettered "Peasant." I hiked my backpack (full of wig and high heels and makeup) more comfortably on my shoulder and smiled at him. And I picked up my coffee and I went to work.

What did you expect? For me to fuck him on the counter?

It took three weeks of shy smiles and coffee before I even asked him his name. I had a feeling it wasn't really Peasant. And then it was another few days before I stopped in at Donut World after a six-hour late-night dance shift.

I had a severe case of wig-head and I hadn't bothered to take off my stage makeup. Just another Threat to Society on her way home from work. I was tired and I felt gnawed and ugly; my mouth was coated with sour fur. If Dante had wanted to portray an accurate vision of Purgatory, he would have had his sinners endlessly working a peep show at two in the morning on a Tuesday.

"Here." Anderson took one look and poured me a cup of coffee. "On the house." He looked slightly embarrassed at using a dumb-ass phrase like "on the house." "The profit margin on this is obscene."

We were the only two people in the place. Outside, crack-heads maintained shuffling curbside vigils. Cabs and police cars prowled the street. Alone together, Anderson and I smiled at each other across the counter. There was no warm bakery smell; it was more industrial-grade floor cleaner and stale cigarette smoke.

"Are you hungry? The muffins probably won't kill you."

"Thanks. I'm starving." I avoided chewing the gummed lipstick off my bottom lip. I was positive my breath was hideous. "Sit down with me?"

For half a second I waited for him to claw an escape tunnel through the linoleum. But he smiled. "Sure."

He helped himself to coffee and a jelly-filled and came around the counter, shucking the smock and hat and tossing them onto an empty chair as soon as he set down his bakery treats. This time his T-shirt had a picture of Mickey Mouse. He had a silver chain with a couple of fishing swivels and a Chinese coin, and four Fimo beads on a piece of what looked like dental floss.

We slid into one of the yellow booths. He lit a cigarette.

Awkward eye contact. I switched my gaze down into my cup. What I was thinking was, what do I want from this guy? And after that, what does this guy want from me?

I didn't know Anderson well enough yet to know that the only time he really got talkative was when he was stoned—which was unfortunate, since then all I wanted to do was watch "Star Trek," get my cunt eaten, and go to sleep. We must have sat there for an hour, making halting, shy smalltalk, trading stories about our jobs, our families, laughing more than things called for, the usual dancing around what we were both really thinking but weren't yet sure the other was thinking. Sometimes, despite its clumsiness, its awkwardness, its rich potential for mistakes, rejection, disaster, those hours or minutes (or months or years) when attraction moves from the potential to the actual, the brief space of time when things are still unspoken and unacted upon, when the air between you is heavily charged with the possibility of sex that *might not* happen . . . that's the time that often turns me on the most, and the time that I sometimes wish I could prolong. As my eyes met Anderson's with less hesitation and his stare grew more intense, my heart was already beating faster. Back when women were expected to Wait until they were married or at least engaged, I wonder if they could appreciate anticipation in quite the same way.

Here's a fun fact about straight boys. When I tell them I'm bisexual they (first of all) get a blistering hard-on and (second of all) think I want to hear every sexual thought they've ever had, or not, about other males, down to sleepover wrestling matches at age nine. Miranda said the same thing happened to her all the time. Don't get me wrong, I think boys with boys is hot, and my most recent issue of *Mandate* already has lube stains on it. But these guys think it's some kind of hip pickup, proving how cool and open-minded yet aggressively heterosexual they are. Snore.

When I mentioned my ex-girlfriend and the conversation turned to sexual matters (at last), Anderson said, "Yeah, I'm pretty much only interested in other queers whether they're men or women. It gets old having straight girls tell me they've thought about it and all but they just don't think they could handle eating pussy and besides what if the other girl was prettier than them."

"I usually get guys telling me they could fuck another guy, if they were horny enough, but not feel romantic toward them," I said.

We laughed and when we stopped laughing we looked at each other and there it was. You know the look.

The table was too wide for us to kiss, and it would have been awkward for one of us to get up and come around. But our hands met among the litter of cups and napkins, cold fingers knotting, our rings clicking together.

Our coffee was down to tepid dregs. "I need to close up," Anderson said. "How are you getting home?"

Should I invite him back to my place or suggest we go to his? And how do we get there, and does either of us have a pressing engagement before noon . . . I had all my supplies right by my bed; latex, lube, toys, but I also had a month's worth of laundry turning into a science project on the floor and two housemates, one of whom was my sister Patrice, always sadistically happy to do a morning bed check, plus she and Ron both got up at seven in the morning to go to school or work and could only eat breakfast to James Brown. Loud. On the other hand, I really needed a shower and men are terrible about having clean towels and an extra toothbrush.

He was probably making the same calculations. I picked at the rim of my cup. White Styrofoam with a yellow-and-red Donut World logo. Half-moons of lipstick. "This late I usually take a cab," I said.

"I'll close up," he said.

We went to my place.

I took off my makeup with baby oil while Anderson used the bathroom. I don't care about anyone seeing me with wet hair, no makeup, whatever, but the actual process of makeup removal, that incredibly attractive black oily smearing, is something I prefer to save until I know them a little better.

He came into the room and shut the door behind him. I could see him reflected in my mirror.

I dropped the oily Kleenex into the trash as I turned. "Just ignore the mess. I really need to do laundry." At least I wasn't scurrying around to straighten up. Are we just plain doomed to turn into our mothers?

"What mess?" He was still standing in the doorway.

I hesitated, decided there was no point in playing coy, and said, "I need to take a shower. Do you want to?"

"Sure." He stepped over a drift of Frederick's of Hollywood catalogues, porn magazines, unanswered mail, garter belts with sweat-crusted stockings clipped into them, to kneel at my feet, and he started unlacing my combat boots.

When he'd pulled off my boots and socks, me holding onto his shoulders for balance, he stood up and I kissed him. The first kiss: another area fraught with the potential for disappointment. I relaxed into Anderson's body with delight. His lips were generous. His jaw was rough with stubble. My face would be raw in the morning. My last few lovers had been women and I was surrounded by hard, thin boy body, boy smell of cigarettes and coffee and sweat.

I started to reach under my dress to pull off my leggings and Anderson took my hands. "I want to."

He pulled off the leggings, stood up and unzipped the dress, pulled it off over my head. The front clasp of my bra took him a while to figure out but he finally got it open. I put my arms around him, standing there, him dressed and me in my flowered underpants, goosepimpling from cold and lust, gnawing the tender curves of neck and shoulder and earlobe, while he squeezed my ass. I could feel him hard against me through his jeans. Briefly, I remembered kissing some boy goodnight with enough distance between our pelvises to build a skating rink, afraid to open my eyes and glance down—oh, my God, what if, you know, and I *see it?*—as if the looming monolith of an erection would burn me to ashes like Semele before Zeus in his full thunder god regalia.

We changed. I slid my palm across his butt and up his thigh to press against the swell; just letting him know I'd noticed. He jumped and I laughed. I pinched his nipple through the cotton of his T-shirt and found a piece of metal inserted through it.

Anderson went down on his knees to take off my underwear. "Very nice. I like the purple flowers." He smiled up at me, the thin nylon around my knees, and kissed my belly. The little blood left in my brain slammed downward.

I pulled him up. I unlaced his boots. I peeled off his socks. Pulled his T-shirt over his head, carefully not catching it on pierced nose or ears or eyebrow. I sucked on the barbell and the nipple containing it, ran fingernails down his back, complimented him on the intricate band rendered in black around his upper arm. He complimented me on the large purple orchid blooming between my shoulder blades. I unbuttoned his jeans.

Time and experience have made me much more relaxed around this moment, the final unveiling. When I'd pulled down his underwear I licked the insides of his thighs, complimented him on the tattoo of Calvin and Hobbes frolicking on his calf, kissed him from navel to pubic hair, before I put my hands on him, traced the tip of my tongue around his balls, up the shaft of his cock. He gripped my shoulder, the other hand gently rippling the close-shorn back of my head. A clear drop of pre-come glistened at the tip. I wanted to lick it off, taste him salty-sweet as a tear. Why couldn't I have been a slut in the seventies, when the worst thing around was penicillin-resistant gonorrhea? I got him the rest of the way out of his ripped black 501's and tossed his boxers across the room to nestle up with my dress. "Shower?"

"Right."

open and swell until I was nothing but a pulse, nothing but pounding blood. Then I hauled him up by the hair, his chin slick with saliva, wadded up the dam, and put him on his back.

I got a condom from the bedside table, out of the litter of matchbooks and ballpoint pens and tumbled stones. I've learned a few good tricks in the sex industry. Putting on a condom with my mouth, which I do on dildos at work, is a fairly simple one, but always a crowd pleaser. Anderson was duly impressed. He had a beautiful cock and I told him so. I see a couple hundred dicks a day and some of them would make you a vegetarian.

Anderson's wasn't the biggest I'd ever seen—and who cares—but far from disappointing and sculpted as perfectly as a Rodin bronze. I worked on him with my mouth, bit and kissed the insides of his thighs, sucked his balls, sucked his cock, my hand around the base, holding the condom in place and my fingers playing in his pubic hair.

"Good?" I asked, surfacing for air.

He nodded, somewhat out of breath.

"Hand me a glove and the lube."

He watched me pull the glove on. I touched his nipples, traced the line of dark hair down from his navel. Latex against skin. "Is this okay?" He nodded. Plenty of lube on my fingers and gently worked one, then two into him.

"Good?"

And it was good.

I took him in my mouth again and sucked slowly while I fucked his ass. Slow, careful, so I wouldn't hurt him. Such intimate contact, Anderson completely vulnerable to hands and teeth. His hands clenched, unclenched. His mouth was open. My tongue traced the tender ridge of his head. A third finger slid in without a struggle. He'd done this before.

"Lily—"

I stopped sucking him and looked up with my fingers still inside him. "Yes?"

"Get on top of me and fuck me."

I stripped the glove off; it joined the plastic wrap in the trashcan by the bed. On all fours I moved up the length of his body, breasts rubbing thighs, belly, chest. I bit his nipple softly and he yelped.

I rubbed the head of his cock between the wet, open inner petals, wanting him in me, enjoying teasing myself as much as I enjoyed teasing him. "Does that feel good? Hmm? Yes? Do you want that?"

"God—"

Anderson thrust his hips up, attempted to grab my ass and push me down onto him. I moved just out of range and pinned his wrists over his head. His look of frustration was damned amusing, considering how much bigger than me he was.

"Now don't you move."

He was getting incoherent. I was thoroughly enjoying myself. Again rubbing his cock against my clit, which was swollen like a grape. Just barely took in the head, quickly, enough to torture. My muscles were tense, clenched, waiting ready to come.

"What do you want?" I purred in his ear.

"I—God—Lily, fuck me."

That was what I wanted to hear. I slid down onto him, all of him inside me, perfect, tight around him, flowing like oil.

"God, you feel good. I want to stay like this forever." I kissed him, stuck my tongue catlike into his mouth.

"Okay."

We moved in slow motion, drawing it out. I didn't want to come; it was too good. Every motion huge, making me struggle for breath. Suspended. I lost any concept of time. His arms around me, his hands on my ass, his breath in my ear. We drifted in that place until I jerked myself back and sat up, still straddling him.

"Anderson."

"Uh?"

"Would this be a good time to ask what you're doing tomorrow after work?"

"Uh . . . this?"

"Good. Me too." I disengaged from him and rolled onto my stomach.

He took the clue. I got on my knees, elbows and chin in my Raggedy Ann pillow, and Anderson behind me. With one hand on my back he eased his cock to the mouth of my vagina and I rocked back, swallowing all of him, forcing breath out of him in a small surprised explosion.

Anderson grabbed my hips. "Uh-uh, girlie, now *you* hold still." He held my hips and fucked me, fucked me hard, sound of his tight boy belly slapping my ass, sound of rough breathing turning into a continuous groan, skin slapping skin, slamming all the way up to my cervix, almost hurting, please don't let him stop—

Supporting my weight on one elbow smashed into Raggedy Ann's face, I reached down to rub my clit and the sounds I was making doubled. Too late now to worry about the housemates.

"Yeah, come on, make yourself come, let me hear you . . ."

I was yelling now, clit huge and slippery, moving with Anderson, my ass in the air slamming back onto him as hard as I could, babbling an incoherent rosary. My muscles tightened, contracted, hovered for an agonizing heartbeat and then I was soaring. I couldn't have stopped it if I'd wanted to, face buried in the pillow, I mean really yelling, everything exploding into colors and stars and I came all the way from the soles of my feet. Dimly in the midst of it I was aware of Anderson coming, his fingers dug into either side of my ass. He collapsed, still inside me, across my back.

It was a while before we could move.

When he was capable, Anderson disposed of the condom and lay down beside me, facing me. Our sweat had begun to cool and we got under the covers.

"I don't think I've ever come together with somebody the first time."

"I hardly ever have at all." I burrowed my face into the curve of his collarbone.

Outside, the sky was streaked with pink. Two birds sang back and forth.

"I think I need a shower," I mumbled into Anderson's neck.

"I need a cigarette."

"I'm hungry."

He got up and got his pack of Camels out of his leather jacket (I watched his butt as he crossed the room and his quietly resting penis as he returned) and smoked sitting up in bed, using an unwashed coffee cup as an ashtray. I curled up on my side and watched him, the motion of his hands, the curls of smoke.

"Are you sleepy?" he asked.

"Not really."

"Me either."

"I wish we had a car. We could go up to Twin Peaks and watch the sunrise." I'd done that with a woman I dated when I first moved to the city. Morning never tasted so good, let me tell you.

"Too cold anyway." He inhaled, and knocked ash into the cup.

In the end we concluded that doing anything at all was too damn much trouble, and we went to sleep. I dreamed vaguely of music that, in the dream, had a very important and perfectly obvious meaning but that faded away and could not be recalled when I tried to translate it into words.

AUTHOR'S NOTE

In my own writing, the line between "porn" and "erotica" is blurry, at best; it doesn't have a lot to do with whether or not or how many times I use the words “cunt” or “fuck” or whether or not the characters love each other. I generally write about people living in “voluntary exile” (my favorite self-serving term) from the societal mainstream, and I have some crazy notion about acting as a representative voice to let everyone else know that my ability to love and care and feel and think didn’t leak out of my eyebrow piercing.

WEDDING NIGHT

By Francesca Ross

A woman was singing a lovely lilting song, a familiar melody with unfamiliar words. There was a cool cloth on his forehead, a cool hand on his cheek. And nothing hurt anymore. Brennan turned his head so his mouth brushed the palm touching him. He heard the woman's quick, indrawn breath, and her song broke off, and he knew a moment's sorrow. Then paradoxically rough fingers grazed his lips. A string-player, he thought, opening his mouth, tasting the callus at the tip of one finger before the hand withdrew to the safety of his chest.

"Open your eyes," she said. Her voice was stern but shimmered with a low note of laughter. "If you are well enough for that, you are well enough to look at us too. Minna," she called to someone else, and he heard the swish of silken fabric across the floor, and another hand, this one entirely soft, touched his cheek, drew the cloth from his forehead.

The soft one whispered a question in the dialect of the song. The reply was in the same dialect, an odd, sibilant blend of tones and syllables. Then he was alone again with the singer. "Minna will get the others," she told him, and he understood that, as he had understood her first remark. She was now speaking Dorran, the language common to the cities—not his language, but the primary one of the western principalities, the language he had spoken since he left his home fifteen years before. She spoke slowly, cautiously, fluent but uncertain. "Come now, sir, open your eyes. You'll want to see us before you decide."

"Before I decide?" His voice was rusty but still his own, and his eyes worked also. They showed him a half-lit room, a window open to a light evening breeze, three purple moons in a slight arc in the sky outside. I am very far from home, he realized, but that was nothing new, and this room was a more pleasant exile than he had known before.

"Before you decide to take us to wife."

He jerked his head to see her; the movement made him dizzy, but he took fistfuls of the coverlet and focused on the woman until the vertigo disappeared. She was sitting in a chair beside the bed, her hand still on his bare chest. She was a Dorran, he thought; she had the glossy dark curls, the slightly slanted eyes, the winged brows of that warrior race—and so, like him, she was very far from home. Take her to wife. No. Take us to wife.

Then the door opened and the room echoed with women. The candlelight flickered over their light, flowing garments, their fair, untrussed hair, their smooth, ivory faces. Two whispered at the door; a third, taller than they, with the strong stern bearing of a captain, came up behind the singer.

"These are my sister-wives. Celie." The singer tilted her head toward the tall one. "Minna." That was the soft one, near the foot of the bed, one of the whisperers, bending her head shyly. She was tiny, ethereal, blonde, angelic. "And Dacie." The other blonde whisperer wasn't so shy; she gave him a smile so brilliant he had to close his eyes. "And I am Rica."

He had traveled long, voyaged far before this. He had fought off mountain-worshipers and barbarians, escaped cannibals and head-traders. But he must have lost some fight he didn't remember—"Am I in the endworld?"

Rica laughed as she translated this to the others. The two younger women giggled, but Celie, the elder, called to them sharply and they quieted. Rica said, her voice still quavering with laughter, "No, quiello." Quiello—it was a lover's word. Did she know that, this Dorran girl, so far from home? "This is Tyne." An island kingdom, remote in a remote ocean. "Your ship foundered yestere'en on the rocks on the north cape. Do you remember?"

Suddenly he remembered—a long voyage, the stirrings of mutiny, the gale winds, the sight of land ahead. He turned his head and stared out into the darkness, the moons swimming into a single misty arc while he gathered his voice to ask, "The others?"

"We found none." Rica made a quiet request, and the soft one, the one in silks, Minna, left. There was silence then, except for the women's soft breathing and his own, more harsh. Rica's hand stroked his chest, her fingers each in its own position, a musician's pattern. He closed his eyes hard, concentrating on that, hearing the chords she was shaping even as she must be hearing them too, shaping another traditional lulling melody he remembered from his childhood.

Minna came back; Rica's hand left him. "We found this on the shore near your hand. It is yours, I think."

He opened his eyes. She was standing now, holding what was left of his guitar, the body caved in, the strings dangling. His words choked in his throat, and he held out his hand. She laid the guitar on his chest, and he took hold of its neck, rubbing his thumb on the rough strings, his fingers along the slick varnish, the jagged edge of the break. "It's broken," he whispered.

"You can fix it. I can help you."

For a moment he let the grief grab him, strangle him. The guitar destroyed. Sixty men dead. All the music stilled.

Celie spoke finally, a cool voice, the voice of calm, and though he understood none of the words, he let it calm him. To Rica, however, it was a command of some sort, a call to order. She took his hand from the guitar, gave the instrument back to Minna, and said, "Can you sit up? Dacie, come."

With the help of the two women, he sat up, propped on pillows, more in control of himself now that he could hold his head up. To escape the memory of the broken guitar, the broken ship, he said, "What did you mean, before? About—about taking you to wife."

"We lost our husband. A year ago. We must have another." Rica sat down again, smoothed the coverlet over him, took his hand. Her strange slanted eyes were alight in the dimness. "We thought you might—you are very far from your land, you know. We do not attempt the sea, and ships come seldom. Yours was the first in two years. If you must stay here, we thought—we thought you might stay with us. As husband."

"But I—" Then the reality of his situation broke over him. His shipmates were lost, all of them, in a single night. But he could not think of that; it would drive him mad, and he couldn't go mad. He was six months' voyage from the rest of the world, lost and alone on this rocky island. He might never be able to leave, to return to his home—

She was offering him another home, if her words, so unthinkable, were true. That was what she meant, that he could live here, in this cliff-house. It was a saving thought, oh, this offer she made, a shelter from the storm. He could rest here, in this house of women, if in truth they wanted him . . . Then he thought of that broken guitar, the lost ship. He had two professions, and they were both lost to him now. Hot shame coursed through him. "I couldn't support you. And there are four of you. You would need four men, not one."

"Oh, I'd forgotten. You haven't the same custom, in the West, do you? We have one husband for several wives here. It is best."

"Best?" He pressed his head back against the pillows, his gaze intent on her, searching for some key to all this in her exotic, familiar face. "Why best?"

"We have so few men. More baby girls are born, many more. We don't know why. It is not the same in the West, is it?"

"No." There had been twelve children in his family, twelve who lived, anyway, seven boys and five girls. He was the final, drawing his first breath as his mother, exhausted, drew her last. It was women, grown women, who were rare in his land. "More women than men?"

"So we must have several women to bear children from each man. And the men—they are not long-lived."

Her long lashes swept down to hide her expression, but he knew. She was thinking of that husband, the one they lost. Something hot rose in him. He wondered if this was jealousy.

"You are strong. You survived the shipwreck; you are awake now and your mind is quick." She smiled at him. "Even as you slept you sang ballads. Dorran marches, Fadeen love songs. You are a good man."

"How do you know?" He leaned toward her, almost persuaded by the certainty in her voice.

"You are a musician." Her hand sought his, found the telltale roughness on his fingers. Her other hand cupped his cheek, her thumb sliding over his mouth, and she smiled. "And very beautiful. Beauty and music are goodnesses. We would be fortunate to have those in a husband." When he started to protest, she covered his lips with her thumb. "You needn't think of supporting us. We have our own work, a family concern. You will be our husband, give us love, stand father to the three children we have, and give us other children. That is all you need do. We know you can do that. We know that you are entire—and entirely healthy."

"How do you know that?"

She smiled, and slipped her hand down his chest under the coverlet. For the first time he realized he was naked. Her hand, rough and gentle, brushed the line of hair down his belly, and to his dismay he found that was enough to stir him. He was a young man, and he had long been without a woman, and there were women, beautiful women, all around him.

"But—four wives. It is wrong." The edicts of a long-abandoned faith pricked him, but then, along with that, came the quickening. Four wives . . .

"It is our way here. We should not survive otherwise. We share our home, and our husband's bed."

"All at once?"

The words were out before he could call them back. Rica drew away, and he was sorry. Then she laughed, glancing back at her sister-wives but apparently deciding not to translate that. "One at a time, you wicked boy. A night for each, and then each again other nights."

He knew the barest bit of disappointment, then the vision she described opened for him, and he fell back against the pillows, knowing this must be a dream, a dying man's dream before death.

But her hand on his belly was real, rough here and smooth there, and so was his anguish when it withdrew and she rose at Celie's voice. Celie called to the others, and the women gathered near the door, holding hands, talking in low voices, though he wouldn't have understood them anyway. Then Rica detached herself from the rest, and came back toward the bed, and the others left, Dacie lingering to flash him another radiant smile before closing the door behind her.

"Can you try to get up?"

It was too late now to plead modesty. He swung his bare legs over the side of the bed, and using her shoulder as a crutch, he stood. He was predictably light-headed, but he gripped her shoulder hard until the dizziness went away. He heard her stifled gasp, and immediately released her. "I am sorry. I didn't mean to hurt you."

"No, no, I did not regard it. Come, walk with me to the window. It is too dark to see the water, but you will hear it."

At the window he took great swallows of the cool sea air, and as she must have known, the familiarness calmed him. He was very near the sea, near enough to hear the steady ebb and flow, the crash of the waves against the rocks, the calls of the swooping seabirds. And he was well enough, only a slight ringing in his ears—concussion, probably—and an ache in his chest to remind him of the shipwreck and what was lost to him now forever.

Forever. He would likely never again see his home.

He dropped down onto the cold stone sill, less weary now than waiting. Rica was watching him, waiting also, and he returned her gaze, studying her wild, lovely face. She was as foreign as he in this land of Tyne, and she had made it her home, this warrior girl.

"You are Dorran, aren't you? How came you here?"

She must know how expressive her dark eyes were, for her long lashes swept down again, casting shadows on her cheeks. "My mother brought me years ago, when I was a girl. Then she died. Celie's family took me in." There was a wealth of secrets hidden under that sweep of lashes, in those dark exotic eyes. But when she looked up at him, her expression was teasing, tantalizing. "I was chosen, of us all, to persuade you to stay. Will you let me try?"

She did not touch him then, but he had felt her caress before and felt it again, a memory brushing his loins, and the alienness, the uncertainty, the grief ebbed away. "You may try."

But she slid away from his embrace, a slender elusive form leaving him in the dimness. "Wait there," she said, and he was alone again, entirely bereft in the cool night air.

She returned, her hair tumbled over some new, flowing gown, gossamer like the candlelight—a nightdress, made for seduction. But she was not yet to be his. She brought with her a varnished tub dragged by two girls, serving girls to judge by their sober dress and deferential air. They were plain compared to the blonde and dark sister-wives, and he wondered if the foreign Rica would have shared their fate had she not such quicksilver beauty. One of the girls glanced up at him as she pushed the tub into the corner, her eyes wide, a gasp hovering on her lips. But a sharp word from Rica had her scurrying out after the other one, out into the hall that lay behind that thick, sheltering door.

"They have never seen a man like this, you see," Rica said, and he felt her admiration warm on him. "And you are so lovely a man . . ."

The girls were back with jugs of steaming water; he was to bathe, he realized, and was glad of it, running his hand through his hair, stiff with saltwater. He must make himself ready to be her lover, worthy to be her lover, if that was what she wanted of him.

But Rica did not leave him alone, as he expected. She helped him climb into the water, knelt beside the tub, took the sponge from his hand. "Just rest," she murmured, a hand on his chest.

So he lay back, all sybarite now, breathing in the fragrance of her perfume, of the flowers she had scattered in the water. He understood none of this, why he was here, why he had survived, why these women wanted him. But he had ever been a fatalist, and accepted this comfort as he had all his life accepted sorrow, with stoicism, with hope.

As she drew the sponge in a lazy circuit over his body, Rica sang softly that slow, sweet song from their childhoods. He sang with her, but in his own language, as he had heard his father sing it so long ago. She fell silent, and then, to his amazement, she began to echo his words, hesitant over the gentle rhythms of the ancient Eirenn tongue, as if they came from deepest memory.

Their voices joined in the quiet night, hers a throaty contralto, his deeper and fuller, and the joining seemed to him so aching with promise, with desire, with something so close to joy that the song faltered as longing closed his throat.

In his anguish she became brisk, scooping up water in her cupped hands and letting it pour over his head, caressing the tension from his temples and jaw, tangling her soapy fingers in his hair. "Such lovely red curls," she murmured. "Who are your people? Not Dorran."

"Eirenn."

It was a small country, on the western edge of the west, poor and rocky and obscure. But she nodded. "Your music, of course. We had a troubadour, when I was a child. He taught me that song. Oh, I knew the Dorran words. But he taught me the Eirenn verses. I had forgotten, till you sang them."

Only the elite Dorran families had Eirenn troubadours, who held themselves high and their talent priceless. "Who are you, Dorran?" She had the grace of a princess, even on her knees beside him, even serving him.

She only shook her head, took his hand, pulled him to his feet. He took the heavy, woolly towel and wrapped it around his waist, bemused by the half-revealed secrets of this woman. She left him there, but returned almost immediately with a tray of food, and he knew a sharp, sudden hunger that drove out any other thoughts.

They sat cross-legged on the bed, the tray in front of them, and though he protested she insisted on feeding him by hand. "This is what we do for our husband," she told him, nudging his mouth open with an anglaberry. As soon as he swallowed it, she kissed him, her tongue tracing his lips and slipping inside, sweet as the berry it chased.

There was bread and cream and kisses, and bites of savories and the tug of her teeth on his lip. There were goblets of wine and the cup of her silk-covered breast warm in his hand. There was a sleek slide of chocolate down his throat, and the sleek slide of her legs over his: a meal so sensuous, so sating, that he thought he could never eat again without her hand at his lips.

But then, a neat chatelaine, she gathered all the crumbs and empty glasses and linens onto the tray and put it outside the door. He rose from the bed, meeting her in the middle of the room, his impatient hands slipping through the fastenings on her loose robe to the slender waist underneath. She let him revel in the satiny texture of her skin, the sweet curve of her hip, for just a minute. Then she detached his hands and stepped back. "We Tynan women are taught to please our men. Let me show you. It is the only way I know to make love."

He was almost mindless with frustration, but grudgingly he nodded, and she turned slightly to undo her gown. She let it slip from her shoulders; she was naked underneath, golden in the candlelight. By sheer force of will, he kept his arms at his sides as she came to him, warm and silken against him. She stood on tiptoe to kiss him, and then, generous, she let him kiss her, his tongue sliding across her full lower lip, tasting the sweetness of the wine they had shared, the sweetness of her. His arousal rose, pressing against her thighs; she moaned softly, deep in her throat, and closed her eyes as he kissed her neck, the hollow of her throat, the valley between her breasts. When his hands slid over her waist, down her hips, cupping her derriere, she came aware again. "No," she murmured. "Let me. *My* pleasure is pleasing you."

He had no time to object, for she was slipping down his body, her breasts brushing against his belly, his thighs. She went to her knees before him, her head bent, her dark hair spilling over her face. She laid her cheek against his erection, and his breath caught in his throat. He was all hard, searching desire, a question in need of an answer, and he found it in her lips, tentative, sweet, in her delicious murmuring moan, in the teasing tug of her mouth slipping over and back, back and forth.

When he could bear it no longer, he withdrew from her, slid down her body, knelt with her, stifled her protest with a kiss, tasted himself on her tongue. He pulled away, breathless. "I am not used to this, to being loved so. Let me, now. Let me love you. I know how to do that."

Her answer was a sigh, a lingering kiss, a hand that crept round his back and pulled him closer. He cupped her derriere in both hands, lifting her slightly so that he could slide between her thighs, his erection pulsing against the soft damp heat there. He slid back and forth, across but not in, and she gripped her thighs tight around him, her dark, intense eyes softening, hazing, as the sensation flowed from him to her, and all through her. Her head fell back; he kissed her throat, traced with his tongue the clear sweep of her jaw, the delicate bow of her mouth, echoing the gentle thrust and ebb of his arousal against hers.

"Please," she whispered against his mouth, and he laid her down gently on the rough carpet, covering her against the chill with his body. With a sense of waiting, a half-held breath, he entered her, paused there to listen to her quickened breathing, to his own, joining there until he could no longer hear himself apart from her. She closed her eyes, waiting, waiting, and finally they began to move together, in point, in counterpoint, in harmony again.

A symphonic swelling into a hush, then breaking free a stringed melody, a single, ever-changing note soaring against the silence, up and up aching, intense, sweet like the curve of her breast, the curve of her cheek, like the cling of her mouth on his, of her body on his.

And then, almost too late, the note broke, dissolved, a shatter, a shimmer of sound, and he broke with it, with her, dissolving into her, into the elusive hidden essence of her song.

Gradually the hush receded, left him there listening again, hearing her quiet breath, his own, separate again amid the night noises. What joy to lie there, still entangled with her, to feel her stirring sensuously under him, to imagine this always . . . two lost souls, cast up on this shore, finding home.

"Do you know," she whispered, her tongue flicking at his ear, "why I was chosen to persuade you?"

"Because you are the best."

"Oh, no." She laughed, a rippling breath on his neck. "Oh, no. I came here so late, I was never properly trained. See what I did with you, slip off into my own pleasure, when I should think only of yours—"

Somewhere here was an answer to a question he had never known to ask. "It is the same, isn't it? The pleasure, the joy? It is both ours."

She glanced up at him, a slanted look through those shadowy lashes. "We are neither of us Tynan, or we would not think that. No. I was chosen, quiello, not because I am the best. Because I am the worst. The clumsiest, the laziest, the most distracted. The least adept at the arts of love."

Then she spoke aloud the thought that half-formed in his mind. "Imagine what the others are like."

He couldn't help himself. He loved her madly, entirely, but he couldn't help himself. He thought of Minna, the little fair beauty, all demure delicacy, of Dacie with her bold radiance, of the serene Celie. One by one by one, and then Rica again.

There had been women in his life before, intermittent loving, an occasional spell of peace, a few moments of sweet passion and tenderness. But these were never enough, always just an interlude, a transitory occurrence ever longed for and soon forgotten. He had wandered the world an orphan, alone in life as he had been alone at birth, and he had imagined that solitude was his destiny, and music his only solace. But now he was offered another destiny, one that was his for the believing. He had only to say yes, and this was his: the trust, the meaning, the women, the loving. Rica.

"I will always love you best," he whispered.

She pressed her fingers against his lips, closed her eyes tight, slowed her breathing until she could speak. "This is my home. Yours too, if you will take it. And this is our way, to share. You must not choose, or prefer, do you see? Or we will not know peace."

She opened her eyes; they glowed dark and brilliant and fierce. "So you must never say that, never." Then, softly, "Except to me, in the dark. Never, never to another." Then fierce again. "Say it now."

And he did, laughing, taking her in his arms, sitting up with her in his lap, cradling her like a babe, singing it softly like a love song. "I will always love you best. Always, always, always best. Always always always you."

AUTHOR'S NOTE

As the working mother of two small children, I've often declared, "I need a wife!" So far, no one's volunteered. When a science fiction writer friend let me read a story about "her" universe—a place where each woman is allowed more than one husband—the prospect of two or more male egos just didn't appeal. "What I'd prefer," I told her, "is an extra wife or two." "Wedding Night" was the result of this exchange.

AN HONEST TRANSACTION

By Marion Callen

At 7:30 A.M. on May 14, Mavis Fletcher returned to bed to sip her first cup of Earl Grey tea. With a frown that was half concentration, half disapproval, she surveyed, through the open bedroom door, the small suite of rooms that was her sole capital asset. "This will not do. Not any longer. I need space and elegance and a view of a well-kept garden. I need tall trees and birdsong. I have let things go for too long."

She made a brief entry in her diary. "53rd Birthday. Four cards; one from John and Nancy, one from Mr. Myers, two from the girls at work. Decided to give a month's notice and pursue my destiny."

She swung out of bed and made a tour of her tiny, tidy kingdom as though a removal van were already at the door and she about to step delicately into a waiting taxi. She returned to her diary and made a list: "Phase 1—Reconnoiter.

A) Buy *The Lady*
B) Prepare a c.v.
C) Find an agency to handle short-term lease of flat (preferably to single, professional woman)
D) Purchase interview outfit."

As an afterthought, she added, "and 3 sets of matching underwear (lingerie, not M & S)."

She boiled and ate a celebratory egg and went to work. The shock of her announcement gave the manager such acute dyspepsia that he swallowed half a box of antacid tablets before lunchtime and had to cancel his late afternoon round of golf. In spite of his agitation, Mavis was serene in her purpose and composed all the letters her employer had not the heart to tackle before typing out an immaculate curriculum vitae. Her skills in organization and administration were beautifully balanced by evening classes in Cordon Bleu Cookery, Jams and Preserves, First Aid (certificated), Choral Singing, Flower Arranging and Assorted Crafts. Leaving the office at five o'clock with ten photocopies in her bag she felt well-satisfied. Even if she had known when Father was alive that one day she would be applying for a post as housekeeper, she could not have chosen a more suitable cluster of interests to develop, and Mr. Myers's despondency would not prevent him from supplying an admirable reference.

Forty-eight days and three interviews later, Mavis was unpacking two modest-sized suitcases in the first-floor bedroom of a large country vicarage. As she moved about, she watched her reflection in the long mirror of the wardrobe, the triple mirror of the dressing table, and the oval mirror over the handsome, bow-fronted, mahogany chest of drawers. Not bad at all. An agreeable face; neat, compact figure inside a well-fitting dress; deft, economical movements and the haircut in the West End had been worth every penny. Setting the last personal item, her new, softly chiming alarm clock, on the bedside table, she pushed open the casement window to admire the tranquil view: well-tended lawn and borders, mature trees full of songbirds, a small orchard, and the stooped back of the twice-weekly gardener in the vegetable plot. She could see enough ripening soft fruit to make summer puddings galore; gooseberry crumbles, strawberry shortbread, raspberry pavlovas, and a shelf full of vermilion and claret-colored jams to last into the winter. From her first sight of the Reverend Michael's spare frame as he waited for her in the lane outside the railway halt, propped against his aging Riley, she knew that he had not been properly fed since his wife's demise ten months earlier.

But she would change all that. Gathering speed, her imagination conjured up a beautiful, tan-flanked, golden-eyed cow browsing in the meadow beyond the garden wall and herself, in an apron and floppy cotton hat, sitting on a three-legged stool to milk it night and morning. Fresh, frothy milk to churn into butter; cream for the scones at afternoon tea; a row of soft cheeses on plaited straw mats—she realized she was extremely hungry and that, if she did not stop daydreaming and go down to take stock of the immense kitchen with its walk-in pantry and cold store with marble shelves, her first attempt at producing a meal would be an overdue disaster. And she must remember to rein in her appetite also, or the trim figure she had been admiring would outstrip its new outfits.

By ten-thirty, Mavis was exhausted. The journey to Suffolk with its three changes of train, the preparing of supper in a different kitchen and listening to the history of the parish narrated by a widower who was as starved of conversation as he was of good cooking left her with little energy for her diary. She wrote, "The way to a man's heart . . ." and immediately fell asleep.

"Phase 2—Infiltration" started with the laundry, which Mavis hung out each morning. In between clumps of short, gray socks and solid, ribbed-cotton male undergarments she planted her flower-sprigged camisoles and French knickers. White shirt alternated with pastel blouse; dark trousers with cream, eight-gored skirt. "Summer is a-cumen in," hummed Mavis, hearing a cuckoo in the wood at the bottom of the valley. She stood back to take pleasure in the billowing line full of washing; the way a lacy, dove-gray brassiere entwined and danced around the out-flung arm of a manly shirt. And if the vicar should happen to glance up from his letter writing to the bishop, at the desk in the study window behind her, might not he be thinking that she, too, made a pleasing picture as she stood with the wicker laundry basket tucked against her hip and her apron pulled tight around the waist undistorted by childbearing and over her generous bosom?

Other domestic conjoinings took place. Their Wellingtons stood side by side in the back porch, outdoor coats hung from adjacent pegs, and their two black umbrellas were so alike that each frequently took the other's by mistake. The Reverend Michael, now urging her to call him "just Michael, please," had apologized for what he called the lack of en-suite facilities for her, but the intimacy of a shared bathroom suited Mavis's purpose. On the window ledge her row of matching floral toiletries confronted his modest duo of shaving mug and talcum, their flannels overlapped on the bath rack, and two bath towels, one dark blue, the other fluffy pink, nestled up to each other on the narrow heated rail. On a Sunday evening four weeks after her arrival, Mavis made another cryptic entry in her diary, a catch phrase remembered from her youth: "Softlee, softlee, catchee monkee." Phase 3—Settlement was about to begin.

On her next afternoon off, Mavis borrowed a bicycle and pedaled to the public library in the small market town four miles to the west. She spent two profitable hours in the reference section and emerged with several pages of handwritten notes: a well-rehearsed list of the names of major crime writers and outlines of the plots of their chief successes. A detour to the bookshop to buy the latest paperback P. D. James, five minutes in the haberdasher's next door to collect the darning materials that were the ostensible reason for her trip, and she was ready to cycle home, singing alternately "Praise to the Holiest" and "All things bright and beautiful" as she dipped and soared along the country lanes.

After a light Saturday night supper of poached salmon, new potatoes with mint, and a well-turned green salad, followed by a crème brulée, the two sat in companionable silence, Michael reading through his notes for the next day's sermon, Mavis turning the pages of the new *Radio Times*.

"Oh!" She gave a little hoot of delighted astonishment. "Sunday evening! Another Dorothy Sayers on the television. Starting at nine P.M., so Evensong will be well over. *And* it's filmed on location in Suffolk. Won't that be a treat?"

She waited. Michael scratched his ear with the pencil end and looked at the mutual pile of fish bones on the serving dish. He said, thoughtfully, "That old black-and-white portable in your sitting room won't do justice to the scenery. I think you should join me downstairs. I hadn't realized you shared my passion for detective stories."

"Thank you," replied Mavis, "I should like that. And, come the winter, it should save a little on the heating costs." Immediately she regretted the last comment. Wishing to appear frugal, she feared she had been presumptuous.

But she had not and, thereafter, evenings were shared in the large, comfortable sitting room with French windows leading to the terrace and a view of the terra-cotta urns filled with geraniums and trailing lobelia and of the heron that occasionally visited the fish pond. Mavis experienced many a frisson of excitement as, without looking up from her book or her sewing, she sensed the vicar's eyes turn with ever-increasing frequency in her direction, traveling slowly from her ankles to her hips and breasts. He sometimes opened his mouth as if to speak and then sighed and said nothing. One evening he sat down briefly on the arm of her chair to look at the *Radio Times* she was holding, and she smelled the attractive odor of washed shirt and clean male body. Before going to bed, she made a brief entry in her now rarely touched diary. Influenced by a recent rereading of *Tale of Two Cities*, she wrote, "The Storming of the Bastille cannot be far away."

* * *

And she was right. The very next evening, after an exhausting supper of lasagna, followed by fresh fruit salad and homemade chocolate eclairs, Michael dozed off in his armchair. Mavis sat in the deepening twilight, unwilling to disturb him by switching on the lights and enjoying the rare opportunity to gaze openly at her vicar, who was, one could say, almost handsome and certainly what her mother called "a fine figure of a man."

Suddenly, he sat bolt upright, opened his eyes, and said, "Sarah?" Without his glasses and still half-asleep, he had mistaken her for his wife. He rose, took a step forward, tripped over the book that he had laid beside his feet, and fell heavily onto the carpet. Instantly she was on her knees, helping him to sit up. Naturally, she drew his head to her bosom and naturally stroked his neck and made little soothing noises.

"There, there, my dear. Where does it hurt?"

"I think it's my ankle, my right ankle," he said. "I do apologize."

"Just sit where you are," said Mavis, "I have witch hazel and a bandage in my room. I'll be with you in one minute."

When she returned with a bowl of water, a towel, and her first-aid kit, he had pulled himself up into the armchair and was lying back with his eyes closed, looking pale. She set a low stool before him and rested his slippered foot on her thigh. And if, in the course of the sock removal, the foot bathing, and the tender application of a cool bandage to the twisted ankle, her breasts brushed the tips of his toes or his heel slipped down toward her groin, neither of them appeared to notice it. However, by the time she had finished, the vicar had a slight flush in his cheeks and a brightness in his eye, and she detected a tiny sigh of regret when she replaced the injured foot beside its healthy partner.

"That feels good," said Michael, not sure to what he was referring. "My father's father was a shoemaker," she said, to ease his embarrassment. "He taught us all to take care of our feet. I think I should bathe the other one, or you will be lopsided."

"That would be . . . nice," he said, struggling for a suitable adjective.

"Good," said Mavis, thankful that she had decided to put on the suspender belt and stockings for an experimental wearing.

Naturally, it was impossible to keep her knees pinned together as she smoothed talcum powder between his toes, or to prevent her skirt from riding up over her thighs. Naturally he could not resist slipping a hand into the enticing divide between her breasts, or easing the buttons through the button-holes of her charming *V*-necked blouse. Summer clothing is easily removed, and a chaise longue makes an excellent impromptu substitute for a bed, although they did move to the bedroom later, when they had discussed details such as the length of the engagement and who would officiate at the wedding ceremony.

While Mavis collected a few essentials from her room, Michael stretched out comfortably on his back in the roomy double space and addressed his dead wife, somewhere beyond the foot of the bed. "Your plan was an inspiration, Sarah," he said softly. "You knew the stipend would not run to a housekeeper's salary indefinitely." And he turned over to wait for his new fiancée.

AUTHOR'S NOTE

With this story, I wished to widen our current perceptions of the erotic. Like most of the characters I find myself writing about, Mavis is neither gifted nor glamorous—at least, not in the conventional sense. She has, however, reached a moment in her life when change is imperative.

LILITH

By Francine Falk

A stick of sandalwood incense smoldered in a bronze burner, its filament of sweetly pungent smoke curling and shifting in a soft breeze that now and then wafted in from the open bedroom window. A fragrance like sex, thought Mona. Lying on the bed, she inhaled deeply and sighed, stretching her long, thin legs. She was nude, nude and waiting for a phone call—for words that would waft her to a temporary heaven the way the breeze . . .

Her languid thoughts were interrupted by the jangling of the phone; before the second ring, she eagerly reached for the receiver, cradling it between her ear and a hollow in the pillow.

"Were you waiting for me?" asked a husky female voice.

"Yes," answered Mona, and when she heard the tension in her own voice—the telltale note of desire—she blushed. "Yes," she repeated, the warmth of her embarrassment increasing her ardor.

"I knew you would be. I love it that you lie there naked—primed—waiting for my call. You are naked, aren't you, my sweet?"

Mona's chuckle was like the throb of a cello. "Buck naked, ma petite." She delighted in their use of silly, extravagant endearments.

"Good," cooed her unseen friend. "Mona—even your name is sensuous. Describe your body to me in detail. Gaze at it, scrutinize it closely. I want you to get turned on by the sight, as though you were someone else. Do that for me, Mona. Make me see it."

"I can't. I'd feel so—I don't know—narcissistic."

"Why must we always equate self-appreciation with narcissism?" The voice had taken on an assertive, pontificating tone. "I think women need to focus more attention on themselves—in every way, and without a sense of guilt; it's guilt that trips us up every time. We need to erase it from our lives, we need to reclaim ourselves and our right to happiness and . . ."

Mona shifted on the bed, stretched her legs, and let loose a massive sigh. "Is this going to turn into a sociopolitical lecture or are you going to . . ." She paused, searching for words to clearly yet elegantly state the activity they engaged in almost every afternoon.

The friend whom she had never met laughed a velvet laugh. "Or am I going to . . . what?"

". . . do your stuff."

"I love it when you're blunt. You're turning me on, you know."

"I'm glad," said Mona, warmly. "What about you—are you naked?"

"Yes—except for a long string of pearls."

"A nice touch. Do me a favor."

"Anything, puss. I'll do anything you want. I have no shame. I'm your slut, your slave."

It was a playful abasement but heady nonetheless, and Mona squirmed. Finally, she was able to collect herself enough to issue a request. "What I would like is for you to take the pearls and drag them slowly along your crotch."

"As you wish." There was a pause.

Glancing absently about the room, Mona found that her attention kept returning to the oval-framed picture that hung opposite her four-poster bed; it was a Victorian fashion plate showing two delicate, doll-like women hidden under layers of frilly, bell-shaped skirts and crinolines. They seemed to be watching her—sly, knowing expressions on their otherwise prim faces. Mona stuck out her tongue at them and averted her eyes.

"The beads feel smooth and bumpy. Oh, yes," murmured the voice. There was a long, lush sigh. "I'm holding an end of the necklace in each hand as I glide it along my lower regions—my knees bent in a most obscene position. Can you picture it?"

"Yes—I can almost feel it, in fact." Of its own accord, Mona's hand drifted down and wedged itself against her slippery, satin folds—her thumb softly and rhythmically mashing against a clit that had become an alert and throbbing nub. "Mmm," she murmured, "tell me more."

"Now and then, a bead or two lodges in my quim and ass. I pull them out—slowly. It's an exquisite sensation." The words flowed like syrup, the speaker sounding drugged with ecstasy, as Mona began to savor the pulses of heat now flowing through her own body.

"You're tempting me to get up and go hunt for *my* pearls, but I'm feeling much too lazy. I'll just use my hands." And as she said this, two fingers slid into her hungry channel, then skimmed down her perineum to probe at the tightness of her twitching anus. They were avid explorers, those fingers—wicked, determined. "I'm hot and slimy," Mona informed her friend. "Mmmm, what you do to me."

There was a chuckle on the other end. "We're animals, aren't we?"

"Like two bulls in heat," she agreed.

"An apt metaphor—though the gender's wrong. Tell me what you're doing to yourself, my horny lady."

"What do you want me to do?" asked Mona. "Just name it."

"I can't. The phone lines would melt."

"Let me describe myself, then, as best I can—even at the risk of sounding narcissistic. You see what you've done to me—I'm no longer the modest and demure young woman I was at the start of this exchange."

"Good," said her lover.

"Well, first off, I note that my nipples are about the size and color of pencil erasers. And I sport a mammoth muff—a noticeable contrast to my narrow hips and coltish legs."

"The body of a pubescent tomboy. I'm drooling."

"I'm twenty-seven," said Mona. "That's postpubescent, I would say."

"What I would love more than anything right now is to probe you with my tongue."

Mona shivered.

"Tell me what you're doing this very second."

"Right now, I'm batting at my clit."

"So am I," said her friend. "Let me hear you come. I'm ready."

This request was all Mona needed to be catapulted into heaven. A yelp, a moan—and as her invisible lover climaxed with her, the sounds were echoed in the receiver that still lay pressed against her ear.

"My god," said the voice, "I came like the end of the world."

"It was an apocalypse for me as well."

"Tomorrow?" breathed her friend.

"Yes. Oh, no—wait, I can't. The painters are coming tomorrow. Damn. Make it Friday."

"Friday, then. Sweet dreams, my Mona."

"Wait—before you hang up—tell me your name. Please. It's not fair that for all these weeks you've known my name but I don't know yours." It was a plea Mona had made several times before.

"I told you, I don't like my name. Anyway, I prefer it this way. We can feel secure and totally uninhibited—totally. Besides, you once said yourself that it's extremely titillating—the strangeness, the anonymity."

"Yes, I know, and I agree, but, well, fair is fair. You're one up on me."

"All right—how about a compromise. *You* name me. Any name you like."

Mona pulled at a loose thread on the bedspread while considering the matter. "It's not the same, you know."

"It's the best I can do. Believe me, I have a really hideous name. I'd prefer you didn't know it."

"Poor baby." Mona wound the thread around her finger and yanked, grateful that the spread did not unravel. "Well, how about Lilith, then? I like the legendary sound of it; it seems to suit you."

"Lilith," said the woman, testing it. "It's lovely. Lilith it is."

"Bye, Lilith."

"Bye-bye, Mona. We'll be in touch." She giggled.

"Wait a second."

"What?"

"What we do—is that what they mean by 'oral sex'?"

"Very funny. Bye, now."

"Bye."

Reluctantly, Mona scooted off the bed and began to gather up her discarded clothing—jeans, wrinkled blouse, scuffed loafers, thick socks; while doing so, she briefly experienced the strange feeling that she was picking up the worn, mismatched pieces of herself. Since leaving her teaching job to pursue a writing career, a course that so far was proving unsuccessful, she had often felt that way—disused, even scruffy.

The Victorian ladies on the wall seemed to mock her. They, at least, fit their place and time and even now were suited to the quaint decor surrounding them. Mona, on the other hand, felt that she was neither fish nor flesh nor good red herring.

The words "double life" flashed into her consciousness. She studiously ignored them, and went about tidying the bed—replumping the pillows, pulling the white chenille spread taut so that no one could ever guess what glorious self-abandon had taken place there.

The sweet delirium had begun innocently enough. It was not deliberate on either of their parts; it had simply happened, which made it seem all the more magical to Mona.

In an effort to launch an informal poetry workshop, she had posted notices on the bulletin boards at the local colleges, and among the calls that trickled in was one from a friendly, vibrant-sounding woman with whom she had struck up an immediate rapport—the kind of instant camaraderie she hadn't experienced since high school.

Within minutes, they found themselves joking, laughing, philosophizing, griping. That simple request for information stretched into a gab fest lasting for over two hours, and after they had hung up, Mona went about with a sense of exhilaration that persisted throughout the remainder of the day. Later she realized she'd failed to get the woman's name.

The very next day they were on the phone again, reveling in the pleasure of newfound affinity. The conversation turned to the topic of sex—their turn-ons, turn-offs—until gradually, in what seemed a natural development, they found themselves making verbal love to one another. This time Mona remembered to ask the woman's name, but by then she would not reveal it. Nor her phone number. And, not surprisingly, she never appeared at the workshops.

"You have me at a definite disadvantage," Mona had complained.

"I know, my sweet. But I'm a coward. Maybe someday."

So far, that "someday" had not arrived. The unseen Lilith was still in the control seat, so to speak; Mona could only wait for the calls; she could not initiate them. At times, she rather enjoyed that aspect of the situation, but more often she felt hurt and vexed by the imbalance. And "Lilith" remained a beloved stranger, a phantom she could neither see nor touch.

She folded the towel and returned it to the bottom drawer of the nightstand. The "fuck-towel," Norman called it. Mona stared at the scrolled mahogany drawer for a moment while absently fingering a zit that was forming on her chin. Such an earthy, practical man—an ordinary Joe. She had called him that once and he had gotten pretty steamed; in fact, he had sulked for two whole days.

For the hundredth time Mona wondered how he'd react were he to learn of her afternoon delights. Outrage or titillation? Poor Norman. What he would probably feel was desolation. He would think he'd failed her sexually or at least romantically. He must never know, she decided. Never.

That evening for supper she fixed spaghetti and meatballs, his favorite. Later, she lay on the four-poster bed, the towel underneath her, while he plunged his rampant cylinder of flesh in and out, in and out, like a machine. She smiled limply, and when his face crinkled and he grunted, she emitted an authentic-sounding moan, and he kissed her lips, then rolled over and quickly fell asleep. The ladies on the wall appeared to sneer. They knew her secrets.

* * *

Friday morning, hours before the anticipated phone call, Mona became a prey to certain longings; her soft cleft throbbed and grew moist; her face was warm; she was feeling restless and distracted.

But she didn't masturbate. Not alone—that would be cheating. It really would seem that way, she thought—like infidelity.

Odd. She realized suddenly that she seldom felt that she was cheating on Norman. Funny.

"It'll have to be a quickie," said Lilith in a silken drawl. "My brother just called to tell me he'll be here in about a half-hour. He has a paper that's due out tomorrow and he wants to use my computer."

Mona pouted, scratched at a large mosquito bite on her knee, wrapped the coiled phone cord around her finger.

"Mona?"

"Yes, I'm here. I hate feeling rushed."

"Consider it a challenge, honey-love. You start."

"Tell me about yourself."

There was a pause. "I'm tall and slender. My breasts . . ."

"That's not what I mean. Tell me, you know, what you do, or fill me in on your past or something. Tell me about yourself."

"I can't." Mona heard the drag in the woman's voice. Sadness? Exasperation?

"I think I'm in love with you." Mona found that she was holding her breath, and she expelled it with a quivering sound.

"You know that I'm married."

"Yes, I do know that."

"We have to keep it this way," explained Lilith, in the pleasant but firm tone of a headmistress. "And it's not just because it's more exciting. It's safer, for both of us. I don't think either of us wants this to get out of hand. I mean, we don't want to screw up our lives over this or hurt anyone, now, do we?"

"I don't care anymore." Mona sat up in bed, excitement creeping into her voice. She gestured with her free hand. "I want to soar. You're the one who's always talking about freedom and eliminating guilt and how women should feel they have the right to happiness and fulfillment."

"Now you're lecturing me. That's a switch. I deserve it, though, I suppose." Her voice sank. "I'm a hypocrite and a coward."

"No, you're not," said Mona earnestly. "You're, well, it's understandable, I guess."

"Listen," said Lilith, "I better get going. Ron'll be here soon. I'll call you."

"When?"

"Soon. Tomorrow, if I can."

After they hung up it occurred to Mona that Lilith had not really responded to her declaration of love. She felt her stomach tighten.

She glanced around, not really seeing anything. The heavy, acrid smell of paint hung in the room. Incense and open windows had failed to dispel it.

Rapt, Mona sat on the edge of her bed, staring at the sleek beige phone, willing it to ring. She was attempting to summon Lilith telepathically, if she could—commanding her with the force of her thoughts to call.

It wasn't working. Three weeks had gone by since the last brief exchange. "I shouldn't have pressed her," thought Mona, berating herself. Her anguish was lavish, all-consuming. Slumping, she took a deep breath and gazed out the window at the green park across the street. There was no breeze, and the motionless, closely spaced trees had an artificial look. Somewhere in the white, neutral sky a pale sun was lurking.

She was very sweet to Norman that evening—solicitous, charming, attentive. He responded in kind. At one point, he even made her laugh. He was really a good man, she thought. And he loved her so.

"You can't have everything," she thought. She was sure Lilith would agree, despite all her assertions to the contrary. Maybe that was why she'd decided to end the affair—she was being mature and realistic.

The next day, the sun was out in full force; the sky was a piercing blue; the trees rustled. Mona was sitting on a bench in the park, watching a robin that was hopping and strutting about with a small worm dangling from its beak. The bird suddenly flew off, and as she raised her eyes to follow its flight, she spotted the figure of a woman who was standing motionless some distance away. Mona received the distinct impression that the woman had been watching her for some time.

She squinted, trying to discern her features, but the woman was standing in the shadow of a large oak, making it difficult to see her clearly. With a start, Mona realized suddenly who the woman was, and she slowly rose and took a few steps forward. The woman remained stationary and continued to watch her steadily and without expression.

She had a handsome, regal face with dark, liquid eyes, chiseled lips, black brows. Although fairly young, she emanated a serenity and self-assurance that verged on hauteur. The eyes were sultry, the body lean, statuesque.

Mona approached within five feet of her and still the woman didn't move. For several moments they stared at each other, locked in a wordless and profound communication. Then the woman turned suddenly and strode off, as though feeling some dreadful enchantment. Mona refrained from calling out; she loved her enough to respect her uncertainty, her fear of complete surrender.

The next afternoon the phone began ringing gaily, insistently, and Mona scurried up the stairs to the bedroom. She knew who was calling.

"I'm sorry if I worried you," said Lilith. "I had to take a break and sort things out."

"Tell me all about it." Mona felt suspended, no clear thought or emotion stirring in her; she merely waited.

"I want us back the way we were. Maybe someday I'll have the courage for more than that. Take me back, Mona. I missed us. I do love you. I'm sure about that much, at least."

"That was you I saw in the park, wasn't it?"

"I don't know what you mean." There was mirth in her voice.

"Go ahead and tease me if you want," said Mona, "but I know it was you, even though you'll never admit to it. You're quite beautiful, by the way."

"Thank you. So are you."

"Oh, really?" said Mona with an exultant laugh. "And *how* do you know that?"

"I can tell by your voice and manner. I'm very sensitive, you know."

"And very stubborn," added Mona.

"And sexy?"

"Very sexy."

"I know. So are you. Make love to me."

Mona nestled lower into the pillows and exhaled a rapturous sigh. "Softly press two fingers against your secret folds and pretend that they're my lips . . ."

"Yes, my butterfly—anything you want."

And as Mona continued with her elaborate and delicately lewd instructions, she could hear and feel the mounting passion of Lilith; and as she fondled her own warm flesh, seeping its excess of pleasure, she saw the face of the woman in the park—an image of hope and desire that she knew would remain with her forever.

AUTHOR'S NOTE

For many women—at least for those who, like myself, are somewhat inhibited—the idea of anonymous sex is very freeing. Although the affair between the two women in the story involves the safest of safe sex—no physical contact—both find it thrilling. I also wanted to explore just what constitutes infidelity. Do desire, fantasy, and verbal love play alone, even if they culminate in climax, count as cheating?

SHOES

By Lawanda Powell

Girlfriend, I don't believe in spendin no whole lotta money on no shoes. And even if I did, that ain't no reason to keep 'em locked up. So what am I doin with this here box? See, I got to explain how it is with me and Russell.

I had been knowin him for a long time. Always did like him. Not like that. I just liked to keep his company. Russell had somethin about him that drawed me to him. He one of these men that like women. I mean, really like 'em, not just for foolin with, but to be friends with and joke around and laugh with. Russell and me went out lots of times and spent the whole night laughin bout one thang and then anotha. Couldn't remember the next day bout what, just that we had a good time.

Well, one night I was up to Marguerite's. You know that place where Gilbert's band plays. Gilbert was wailin on his sax and, girl, we was ballin. Everybody was all dressed up. I had on my purple dress with the gold threads and the turquoise flowers. You know, the one with the ruffles around the hem and the back out. Lookin good. All the mens was posin around like peacocks and all the women was flouncin round like peahens tryin to be noticed.

You know I thought I was too cute to be standin around with the rest of those heffas. I mean those men's heads was big enough without me addin to they adoration. So I took to standin by myself at the bar facin the door so I could see whoever was comin in. That's how I happened to see Russell.

Now, in all the time I spent with him, I never thought of Russell in any way more than as a friend. So you know I was not ready for what happened next. And while I know why I stay with him, for the life of me, I cain't figure out what made me get started. I mean he ain't much to look at, bald and short, but that night, I'm here to tell you, that man was fine!!

It was hot outside and he had his jacket slung over his shoulder when he walked in so I could see everythang he had. His shirt was fittin him real close, and I could see every muscle in his chest. When he turned around, I could see how his pants cupped his behind. And, right off, I knew just how it would feel if it was my hands on his naked behind 'stead of his draws. Just thinkin about it gave me a thrill that started in my coochee and spread up and out so far he must have felt it too. Cause he looked up, and, girl, our eyes met, and right then we both knew that we was gon' get it on.

Now, don't get me wrong, we didn't just like that run off and do it. We worked up to it. First he had to pretend he didn't see me. And so did I. But you know I knew where he was every minute of the time. I saw him talkin to Rosalee and the way she was rubbin his thigh. I saw how that huzzy Greta Mae was lettin her titties brush up on him tryin to pretend she didn't know it was happenin. All the women was flockin to him. It was like he was a chocolate ice cream cone and they all wanted a lick. That's all right, I said to myself. They was just warmin him up for me.

He finally worked his way round to me and asked me to dance. The band was playin somethin whiney and slow and we pulled up real close to each other and started grindin. Chile, I hadn't done no grindin since I was in high school. I had forgot how good it felt. He had his thigh rubbin between my legs, rubbin and rubbin in time to the music. I could feel his thang get hard and his breath hot on my neck. Breath hot and soundin like he had asthma or somethin. I like that. Listenin to a man breathe hard and knowin he's doin it 'cause of the way I make him feel. Makes me hot.

His hands was strokin the middle of my bare back and I was holdin tight onto his shoulders tryin to keep myself from grabbin his behind and everythang else 'cause after all I was in public and I don't do that stuff where folks can see me. Girl, that man was gettin to me.

Now, that's how we got started. And we gon' stay together, too. Cause we know just what the other one likes. Russell know how to touch me. He got hands that know when to be rough and when to be soft. He knows I like him to grab my behind real firm and make it move so the stroke is right. He know how to touch my nipples just so, makin me want to scream out his name. But I don't, 'cause his mouth, his lips sweet like candy, is over mine, and for me to scream out, he'd have to move 'em. So I moan. Only real low, so I can hear him breathe. I love to hear him breathe.

And I know what he likes. Russell likes me to wear shoes. Not just any shoes. He likes me to wear mules. You know, those shoes with the toe out, and no straps, and four-inch heels. I remember how I found out. He gave me some money and told me to buy a pair of shoes. I went out and bought this pair of black pumps I had been eyein for about a month. When he saw 'em, he was mad. He grabbed me up, took me to the store, picked up a pair of mules and told me that the next time he sent me to buy some shoes these were what I was supposed to come back with. Now, sometimes he sends me and sometimes he comes home with a pair. I got 'em in every color. You can look over there in the closet and see 'em if you want to.

Anyway, we bought those shoes, went home, and he showed me what to do. I got all dressed up, shoes and all. And then I stripped til I didn't have on nothin but those shoes. Russell watched the whole time, his thang gettin stiff as a baseball bat and him breathin heavy. That was some of the best lovin I ever had.

Now, any time I see him with a pair, I know what to expect. I know we gon' do us some real good lovin, that he gon' last a real long time. I put on those shoes and nothin else. Parade around, throwin my hips everywhichway while Russell lays on the bed watchin me. All the time I watch him out the corner of my eye, likin to see his thang jumpin up and down and hearin him breathe.

But you didn't ask me bout all that. You want to know about this here pair of shoes and this lockbox. I already said I don't pay no money for no shoes, but one Easter I saw this pretty pair of white slingback pumps with the toe out that was just what I needed to go with my new suit. They cost way more than I usually pay, but they was so pretty, I bought 'em anyway. Come the day I wanted to wear 'em, I couldn't find 'em nowhere. Somethin told me to check the closet where we keep my special shoes, and there they were. No longer fit to wear except in the privacy of my bedroom. That man had cut the straps off!!

So now when I buy toe-out, slingback pumps, I lock 'em up in this here box. That way, girlfriend, I keeps my shoes and my lovin in good shape.

AUTHOR'S NOTE

The incident of the cut shoe straps is true: It happened to someone else. I first heard it in a hotel room where a group of women were discussing men's preferences in sex. We laughed at all the stories and, for this one, had to be picked up off the floor. But the more I thought about how we laughed, the more I thought about how vulnerable we are when we reveal our sexual preferences and how hurt and humiliated our partners would be if they knew how we'd laughed. Then I started thinking about the power there is in knowing what pleases our partners. What a turn-on, this power! Yet I also had to wonder how much of our sexual behavior is engineered solely to maintain this power and its feeling.

A SLOW FREIGHT

By Phaedra Greenwood

When I fell out of a twenty-one-year marriage back into the singles meat market, I made three rules for myself: No one-night stands, no married men, and if I'm going to go to bed with some guy, he at least has to love me. The last part was trickier than it seemed.

It was summer in North Carolina. The radio said the heat index was going up to 105. I worked in the darkroom all morning and then felt so sleepy I lay down for a nap. I woke up longing to be outside lying in the grass with Sam, looking into his cat-green eyes. He hadn't called or sent me a letter all week. He had told me he'd be busy this weekend. Maybe he even had a date. The first time he'd taken my hand, I'd gently pulled away. "I'm fifty and you're thirty-three," I reminded him. "So why even start?"

A couple of days later I got a letter saying, "I'm not a hit-and-run artist, but you're wise to protect yourself by setting limits rather than diving in head first with your eyes closed as you have in the past. But about the difference in our ages, you must resist the urge to 'protect' me from myself, as you tried to do the other night. I felt humiliated and diminished by it. We're both adults. This is the only ground rule I insist on as we open these emotional negotiations. Someday I would like to have a wife and family. My wife will probably be closer to my age than you are, but that's a long way off. What I am ready for now is an emotional, growing relationship with a woman."

I wrote back, apologizing, but said I thought almost any woman would prefer that a man move slowly so they could both savor each step. I included an article about human courtship that showed how we tend to follow a pattern as prescribed as the dance of mating birds. I was surprised and gratified when he started using these steps on *me*, sending me flowers and poetry. I loved having a friend to hike with, someone who needed the quiet forest paths as much as I did. But the closer we got, the more Sam's cheek twitched up in a nervous squint. Then he withdrew.

Now I was halfway out the door when the phone rang. Sam's voice resonated with a deeper note, and I resonated with it. "I have to see you."

"Okay."

"I wasn't going to do this," he said.

"Me neither."

"We have to stay out in public so things won't get out of hand."

"Okay." His AIDS test was negative, but I had to wait for my six-month test until September. We arranged to meet in the parking lot at the art museum in half an hour.

I took a quick shower, patted myself dry, and rubbed some lotion on my arms. Fifty years old, and my body still felt good, but I noticed the fine wrinkles on the backs of my hands and a couple of age spots. No makeup today, I decided. We've been dating for three months. If he's really my friend, it's time for him to see me as I am. I slid into my shorts and a tank top. All my bras were in the wash—the hell with it.

I raced over there. I was fifteen minutes early. I climbed the green mound of the hill where I could view the whole parking lot. In the distance I heard the sharp wail of a train as it sped by. In two months I'd be on one headed west. And not have tasted Sam? I didn't want to get locked into another long-term relationship, but I was curious about where this might go. I wanted to give it a full breadth.

At last he pulled his Toyota into a space below. He got out and locked it. The sun struck the gold wire of his glasses as he squinted in the direction of the museum. That squint went right to my heart; sometimes he seemed like an old man. He was tall and walked stoop-shouldered. There's your Lancelot, I thought, following him along the crest of the hill. At last he looked up. "Terry?"

I waved and skipped down the slope into his arms. He laughed and hugged me, then gave me a letter he'd just written. I flopped down on the grass to read it and in a second he was lying beside me.

The letter said, "Terry, you are so funny, strange, magnetic, and erotic. I have to have you. Let's be pals. Let's walk in the woods. Let's be artists. Let's get it on. Your pal, Sam."

"Have to, eh?" I laughed. "What about my test?"

"There are lots of other things we can do. We don't want to skip any steps, right? Restraint heightens the passion. I just read that."

He took off his glasses. Without them his face looked wider, more boyish; when he smiled, two dimples appeared. He braced his foot against the bottom of mine and kissed me. "Sometimes I draw back," he said, wiping his mouth, "because your mouth is too wet. You want it moist—enough to make a good seal."

"How you go on."

People were walking by, glancing at us surreptitiously. He swung one leg over me and kissed me into the ground. I was coming unglued. "I want to get on top of you," he said.

"Not here."

"Can I look down your shirt?"

"All right." I sat up. He pulled my top out with one finger and peered at my breasts.

"I can't see without my glasses." I snorted.

"I'd like to give it to you, just the way you want it," he said, breathing in my ear. "Fall asleep, wake up, do it again. Fall asleep, wake up. Do it again."

"Can you *do* that?" I asked, surprised.

"I don't know. But I have a very vivid imagination. You don't realize how inexperienced I am. The last date I had was a year ago. She slid down on my couch as we were kissing. I was thinking, Oh, now I'm supposed to feel her breasts? Okay. I guess. I hardly knew her. Just when I was beginning to relax and think I might be able to perform, she jumped up and said she had to go shopping."

"How humiliating."

"My shrink says I'm afraid of women."

"Sex is less scary when you feel some affection."

"I don't really know what love is."

"Neither do I."

"But I read somewhere that people need to be touched about twelve times a day. Let's go to the park where we can feel each other up."

"Not your apartment?"

"I'm not ready for that. We might do something wild."

We drove to the park. The landscape was heat-blasted; a gray haze hung above the highway. We strolled down a path to a picnic table and paused to admire a huge oak tree, the muscular roots, the spread of the branches. Cyclists spun by on the path and disappeared into the woods. I sat on the tabletop and he stood in front of me.

"May I touch your breasts?" he whispered.

"Okaaay."

He leaned toward me and slowly massaged my breasts. "Were they once less floppy?"

"Sure. Bigger, too. Wish I had the body I had at thirty-three. I'd wow you. I was really beautiful."

"You're really beautiful right now. I like how your breasts fit in my hands—like perfectly shaped fruits. Can I spread your legs apart?"

"You're so outrageous!"

He took my ankles and spread my legs. "Can I kiss your crotch?"

I shivered. "Okay."

He glanced around, then bent over and thrust his head between my legs. I felt the pressure of his mouth on my pubic bone. My pants were wet.

We got up and wandered down the path that led to the river. The woods were dry and still. I watched a trickle of sweat start from under his hairline and run into the folds of his neck. I wanted to lick it. At last we bumbled down the hill and saw Maple Creek sparkling through the trees. We paused to listen to the woodthrush as it dropped liquid notes, one by one, into the leafy coolness. In this loop of the river the water was so still and clear you could see all the way to the bottom. The clay banks made the whole river look red. Young maple trees arched over the water, lime-green leaves reflected against the burnt sienna bottom, their spiky shadows clearly outlined on the sand. "Wish I'd brought my camera!"

"Do you see those little fish in the shadow of that rock?" he said. He was standing so close I could feel the heat radiating off his skin, smell his sweat. I took off my shoes, while he stood on the bank, his face pink with the heat, slapping at a horsefly. I waded into the water, hesitated, then launched myself flat out. I rolled onto my back and paddled a few strokes. Suddenly, my whole body felt refreshed. "God, this is nice!" My nipples swelled against my tank top. Sam knelt and unlaced his boots. He waded in, sat down, sighed, and closed his eyes. I paddled up beside him and leaned back on my hands, silky water soothing my shoulders. His eyelids were a delicate lavender. His body hair came in three colors: red, black, and blond. Every red hair of his stubbled cheek glowed in the sun, but when he turned his face into the shadow, the blond ones stood out. The folds of his blue shirt were molded to his shoulder.

He opened his eyes and turned his mouth to mine. "Try this," he said. With the tip of his tongue, he pressed something into my mouth. Sweet and sour. I took it out and looked at it. A Jolly Rancher. We shared the candy back and forth, tongue to tongue, until it was gone and we were both out of breath.

It took forever to get back to the car. Fireflies winked phosphorous yellow in the blackness between the trees. The car door was still warm from the sun. I leaned back against it. He made a sucking noise with tongue and teeth. "Wanton woman." He fell in slow-motion against me, pressing me with the full weight of his chest and thighs and soft belly, taking my whole mouth in his. The top of my head was buzzing. I panted and pressed back.

"You're so delicious!"

"Have we skipped anything? What's next?" He led my hand rather forcefully to the bulge in his pants. I caressed it through the fabric.

"This is building trust," I said, "taking the scare out of it. But you'd better be careful. I'm relentless when aroused."

A pair of headlights caught us and we sprang apart. "Well," he said, folding his arms, "what do you think of the economy?"

"It sucks." We guffawed.

"I'm beginning to have real feelings for you," he said.

"I hope so!"

"I'm so lecherous."

"That's healthy."

"It takes such a long time to get to know someone," he said. "What is love, anyway?"

"A warm feeling in your chest."

"Just that?"

"Yes. No."

"Are you hoping if I go to bed with you, I'll fall in love?" he said.

"No. I'm hoping someday Miss Wonderful will parachute into your life. Meanwhile . . ."

"I want us to stay connected, no matter what happens," he said.

I ran my fingers down the valley of his spine and up under his shirt. His skin was cool, silky. I couldn't get enough of him. "We're good together," I said, stroking his arm. He nodded. "I'm sorry you had so little touching in your marriage. I'd like to take you home, take off all your clothes, give you a full massage and then make love to you." I burrowed my nose into his furry neck.

"Let's."

"I'm embarrassed."

"About what?"

"The train. It runs right behind my apartment."

"I've always had a thing about trains," I said. "Take me home. I just want to hold you. I don't care if we make it or not."

* * *

He put on Santana, lit a candle, then gently undressed me. My arms were stiff at my sides, bolstering my breasts. In the candlelight the stretch marks won't show. But what about the hysterectomy scar? Oh well . . .

"Where do you get off having such an outrageous body at your age?" he said. I gave him a faint grin.

"I dance. And roller skate." I lay face down on his bed and he gave me the massage, just exactly the way I wanted it, pressing into my neck and the sore places around my shoulderblades with strong thumbs, slowly loosening my muscles, his total attention in his hands. He massaged me from my scalp down to the arches of my feet till my whole body tingled. His hands were so large that together they spanned my back. His palms were hot and molded to my curves as they slid around and around, up and down my arms, across my bottom, down my legs.

He flopped down beside me and looked into my eyes. "That's it."

"Aren't we going to make love?"

"Something's not connecting . . ." He was still wearing his jockeys. I ran my fingers gently over the lump that just fit my hand. It stirred like a sleeping animal. I reached inside his shorts and brushed the back of my hand across his belly. I tugged at the elastic.

"Why don't you take these off?" He grinned, embarrassed.

"Can I leave my socks on?" I nodded. The hair that curled up out of his groin was reddish gold in the candlelight. I moved down and kissed his expanding flesh. I licked the blue rivers of veins. His penis pulsed and lifted toward my mouth, seeking heat. The tip was the shape of a ginger leaf and the tiny wrinkles fled beneath my tongue until it shone red and silky. I closed my mouth over the whole shaft, gently sucked and flitted my tongue over the cap until he let out an "ahhhh!" I caught his liquid in the palm of my hand. His toes twitched, he sank down on me and lay still, but I was panting and wet.

In the distance a long wail rose and rose. "It's the cry of the wild train," he said. "About to come right through the kitchen."

"Waaah . . . wa . . . wa . . . waaaaahhhhh . . ." The wavering note flattened, fanned, and broke into two notes, one high and one low, echoing back and forth between the buildings and trees.

"Nothing like a slow freight," he said, pinning me with his heavy thigh. "My turn." He kissed my breasts and my belly and opened my legs. "I did learn something in college," he said. His agile fingers explored my crevices. His tongue circled my nipple and his long finger slid into me.

Now came a deep rumble as the train hurtled toward us, a surge of power, tons of rolling metal, a bell clanging, a squeaking of wood and banging of metal. I felt the engine throbbing in my chest like another heartbeat. Then the click-pause, click-pause, click-pause, of the wheels vibrating through me. "My god!" It went on and on and on.

"Take your time," he said. "I'm with you. I'm enjoying this." I trembled and rocked under his relentless hand, lifting my hips to meet him, till I cried out and came.

In a swirl of air, the train was gone and the woods settled slowly back into stillness. His eyelashes brushed my cheek. One eye looked into mine.

"I don't know which I love more," he said, "you or the Norfolk Southern."

I laughed and kissed his neck. "Neither do I."

AUTHOR'S NOTE

I have always loved trains, the dark journey that takes us out of ourselves into worlds we never imagined. Like Millay, "There isn't a train I wouldn't take, no matter where it's going."

THE NIGHT MARE

By Susan Dooley

Her father picked up the quill and made the entry in the family bible. "Hannah m. William Eaton, May 14, 1692." Marry in May / rue the day. But Will had insisted. Now her father was reaching for her hand, giving her over to the stout, middle-aged man whose sudden, relieved smile showed the brown stumps of teeth that marred his mouth.

"She has to marry someone," her mother had argued when her father had protested the union. Hannah had agreed. She had to marry someone.

Will tugged at her hand, pulling her toward the door, not seeing the cup of cider her father held out. Ill luck. Ill-mannered. Ill. Hannah fought a fog of dizziness and jerked her hand away. Surprised, Will turned, and then he saw the cup. He drank it down quickly, his mind on the rising wail of a child. A second shrill voice had joined the first. Five months since Anne had died. Five months of listening to his children cry. He wanted his new wife at home.

That morning Hannah's father had driven the farm cart to Will's house and unloaded Hannah's spinning wheel and the dovetailed chest he had made to hold her linens. They stood now where he had left them, pushed against one wall of the low-ceilinged room. The house was smaller than the one where Hannah had grown up. There was only this room, with the bed in the corner, a table and stools, and a loft where the children slept.

As they stepped through the door, three-year-old Natty asleep in her arms, and Lem, five, riding on his father's back, she saw a bunch of wild roses in a jug on the table. She was touched that Will had bothered, but it was Abby who danced in front of them, pointing, "See! See what I got thee."

It was seven-year-old Abby who helped her boil the beans and the salt pork for dinner, while Will sat outside. It was Abby who, when dinner was done, pushed her brothers up the ladder to the loft. Will had gone outside again, leaving Hannah alone to open the chest and take out her nightdress, to climb into the big bed. Hannah lay with her eyes closed, listening to the deep twang of the frogs in the pond. Fiddle frogs. Joining them, playing its sweetness through her mind, was the memory of Thomas's flute.

They had lain like this in her parents' house, the bundling board making a small wall between them, the heavy quilt shutting out the cold and wrapping them together with their whispered plans.

She heard the door open, heard the soft huff of Will's breath as he blew out the candles, and felt the heave of the bed as he settled beside her. Hannah felt his hand touch her leg through the heavy linen of her nightdress. Then he was pulling the cloth up around her waist, shoving at the bulk of it, pushing it aside as he rubbed his hand up her leg, across her stomach, until it rested on her breast, closing, opening, squeezing tight, letting go. He was like a cat kneading a quilt, Hannah thought, rigid under his touch. He had begun to make quick gasps, and with his other hand he pulled at one of her legs, opening her up, spreading her apart. Hannah pulled her legs back together, but now Will was on top of her, using his legs and his knees to hold her open, poking at her with his hardness. He was beating against her, thudding up against bone and unyielding flesh, trying to force his way inside. He found the opening and she felt herself give way with a rip of pain and a dragging of flesh as he pushed himself in and out, beating, beating, beating until he moaned and shuddered and brought himself to a stop. She felt the full weight of him, sinking down on her, burying her in the softness of the bed, making it difficult for her to breathe. She bucked her hips, trying to make him move. Then she wiggled sideways, inching her way out from under him. As she escaped he gave a great breath that slid into a small, whinnying snore.

Hannah wanted to get up and wash away the stickiness between her legs, but she was afraid to move. By closing her eyes and keeping her hands at her side she could avoid contact with Will's unfamiliar shape. She could pretend that the warmth and the weight next to her was Thomas. Thomas come back.

His eyes were gray as the slick, slatey sea, laughing at her when he bent over to stroke her cheek. The first time he had touched her. She was thirteen, gathering shore greens for supper. He was sitting on a rock, mending his net with long wooden needles. He had come from England to live with his uncle, he said, and offered to show her a patch where the wild blackberries had just come ripe. They had eaten all that they picked, and he had laughed at the way her lips had turned purple from the juice. It was when her skirt had gotten caught in the brambles that he had first touched her, lifting a hand to cup her chin, tracing a rough finger along the line of her cheek, lightly, mockingly touching her purple mouth.

Abby pushed the treadle of the spinning wheel with her toe, touched a finger to the wheel, setting it in motion. At seven she should have learned to spin, but for months her mother had lain sick in bed. Now Hannah dragged the wheel outdoors under the elm tree that shadowed the yard and sent Abby inside for the stool. Holding the young girl on her lap, Hannah guided her foot to the wheel, held the small hands inside her own as she showed Abby how to take the greasy fleece, comb the fibers so that they lay in one direction, and then feed them into the gulping mouth of the ravenous wheel. The child spun out a long, thick lump of yarn, looked at the fine thread that was wound around Hannah's spindle, and began to cry. "It takes time to learn," said Hannah, and then remembered what her own mother had done when, at five, Hannah had first been set at the wheel. "We will save this, Abby, as my mother saved mine. Would it please thee to see the first thread that I ever spun?"

Abby nodded. Hannah found the crude, lumpy rope at the bottom of her chest, under the linens, lying next to the flute Thomas had left behind.

The flute played in her dream that night and brought Thomas with it. It was the first time she had seen him since he had gone away. "I'm sorry," she said, looking into his gray eyes. "I never meant for thee to go." He smiled. "I never meant to," he said. Hannah was glad he was back, glad that awful night was forgiven. She had been fifteen and her father had accepted that she and Thomas would wed. When Thomas came on the winter evenings, the two were left alone in the big room where the fire threw shadows on the wall. They were allowed to lie together in the bed, warming each other under the quilt, as long as the board lay between them. Thomas had become adept at unbuttoning her bodice from his side of the board, at rubbing the nipples on her breasts between his thumb and forefinger until they grew hard and Hannah felt the pleasurable heat spread between her legs. That night, when her parents began to snore in the next room, Thomas had wickedly moved the board.

"We are on our honor, Thomas," Hannah had reminded him, but he had ignored her, sliding his hand under her dress, under the heavy petticoat and up her leg until his palm rested on the rounded mound of hair. He stopped his rubbing when Hannah protested, but he kept his hand there, warming her with a flush of desire. "Sin," she had hissed at him, but he had begun again, rubbing the heel of his hand gently against her, bringing her a surge of pleasure. His mouth had moved to her breast and for the first time he had taken the nipple between his lips, licking the hardness with his tongue. Hannah wanted him to keep touching her forever but, instead, she had sent him away.

"We pledged our word," she had said, making him leave the warmth of the bed. She never thought he would go home by boat. The wind was too high. Hannah pitied Thomas the long, cold walk along the shore, but she thought of the danger to their souls and she could not let him stay.

It was late afternoon of the following day when his uncle came. The canoe had washed ashore. Thomas had not come home. Turning her back on all of them, she had rested her head on the chimney piece. Level with her eyes was Thomas's flute, lying where he had left it.

The weather had turned warm and dry. Will had gone off to Apple Island with the other men to fish for cod. He would be gone several weeks while they pulled the nets and hung the fish to dry, storing them in barrels for the winter.

Lem was playing with Natty in the tall grass, making the baby giggle by blowing puffs of seedy dandelions up into the air. Abby had dragged the bag of seed corn from the cowshed and now Hannah was showing her how to plant. Wrinkling her nose, Hannah picked up one of the dead fish they had found on the beach and buried it, firming the soil on top and pushing the shriveled yellow corn seeds into the center of the mounded earth. She took a handful of red-speckled beans out of her apron pocket, and, using her thumb, pushed them one at a time into the dirt around the mound. "When the vines come up, they'll climb the corn," she explained to the watching child. Hannah felt happier with Will gone, teaching Abby, picking up Natty when he cried and feeling his soft, sobbing breath tickle the nape of her neck.

Evenings were long in June's lingering light, and after the children had climbed up to the loft, Hannah took her knitting outside. The lilacs had begun to bloom. Their sweet scent reminded her of how Thomas had once come to call, his arms so overburdened with the purple blooms they spilled out behind him in a fragrant trail. From that night on, as soon as the children were in bed, Hannah hid herself in sleep.

Thomas was riding a mare with a coat so black it was patched with blue. How strange, thought Hannah. Thomas had never owned a horse. Seeing her surprise, he laughed, caught hold of her, and swung her up behind him. Hannah tried to tell him that she had thought he was dead, but the horse stamped and fidgeted and Thomas didn't hear. Hannah gave up trying to talk and wrapped her arms around his waist, rubbing her cheek against his back and pressing hard against him, feeling the warmth of him through his shirt. Thomas kicked hard, and the mare jumped. Hannah tightened her hold, but the mare did not jolt back to land. She kept flying higher and higher, soaring over the tops of the spruce trees, out over the rocky shore, up and up until she finally brought her hoofs down among the scattered stars.

When they landed, they were on a strip of wet, dark sand curled with silver where the waves rolled in. Thomas slid to the ground and began to play his flute. "You left it behind," Hannah said, amazed that he should still have it. But Thomas shook his head and smiled at her. Holding it up to his mouth, he blew a few false notes and then began to play a soft, rollicking song, dancing toward Hannah, his feet shooting sprays of sand onto her skirt. She laughed at him, grabbing up her skirt and giving it a shake, sliding off the horse and letting her own dance keep pacc with his. Hands at her side, she danced in front of Thomas, moving faster and faster with the music until she looked down and realized that she had danced the buttons off her bodice. Her breasts were bouncing bare under Thomas's delighted eyes. Hannah danced forward, letting her breasts come within inches of Thomas's chest, then she darted back, her feet kicking up mussel shells and tangles of rockweed. Her bodice had slipped down off her shoulders, leaving her naked to the waist, and she shivered with pleasure as the sea breeze touched her skin. "It is wicked," she told Thomas, but he shook his head. His clothes had come loose, too, and she saw him grow hard as they danced. He danced closer, teasing her, letting his cock brush her skirt.

Her skirt was gone. She and Thomas were naked, their feet stamping prints in the sand. Then they were lying together as they used to do, and he had come into her, not like Will, hard and hurtful, but gently pushing pleasure into the place between her legs. He put both his hands around her buttocks, holding her tight against him as he rolled over on the sand. "Sit up," he said, and she sat astride him, looking into the dark mist of his eyes. "Like a horse," she said, rocking herself atop him, feeling a sweep of warmth. "I am riding thee like a horse."

She woke hard, dropped back onto the bed from a far height. The cock was crowing, and the geese were making a shrill complaint. She felt heavy and stunned all that day, her mind slipping back to the beach where she and Thomas had lain. It began to rain shortly before supper, and she used the weather as an excuse to send the children to bed. She pulled the quilt over her own head and closed her eyes, seeking sleep.

She stayed in bed for a week, dreaming and languorous, ignoring Abby's frightened questions, irritated when Natty tried to climb into bed next to her and cuddle inside her arms. With her eyes closed, she held onto the night, held onto Thomas who was somewhere nearby, waiting for the descent of darkness. When Abby had fed the children and they had climbed up to the loft, Hannah would feel the floorboards shake. The mare would trot into the room and Thomas would reach down his hand, pulling back the covers and pulling her up out of bed. "I have two mounts," he teased her, the second night he came. "I ride my mare and I ride my mistress Hannah." Later he had had her kneel on the silver sand and had come into her from behind, fluttering his fingers over the nipples of her breasts as he drew himself in and out. Hannah was happy to please him, to have her desire bring him back from the waves that had washed him away.

On Saturday, Abby gave up trying to rouse Hannah. She walked the road until she found the house where she had seen her father wed. When she returned, she brought Hannah's mother with her. Tea of raspberry leaves and tea of vervain. Her mother stayed by her side, making Hannah sip the warm drinks. That night it was her mother's body that bulked in the bed next to hers.

On Sunday they all went to the meetinghouse, Lem and Abby walking solemnly ahead, Natty trying to wiggle away from her arms. There were people Hannah had never seen before. If she had not been so sleepy she would have wondered at the unfamiliar crowd, at the murmur of voices that should have been stilled in prayer.

"Satan is among us!" The words came as a bellow of rage. The Reverend Winthrop stood in front of the congregation, his words shocking them into silence. The rumors from Salem were true.

Later, when Hannah tried to remember what he had said, all she could recall was that if you flung a witch into water, she would not sink. That there was an ointment that enabled them to fly through the night. Smallage, wolfbane. She couldn't remember what else. And then, "With a strange and sudden music, they fell into a magical dance, full of preposterous change."

Hannah was afraid to sleep. Not Thomas, but an incubus. Satan had seized her soul and she was sick with shame at the pleasures she had felt. That night, she did not climb into the big bed. She took her stool outside and kept herself awake by praying in the dank night air.

For three nights Hannah sat outside. She slept only in the light of day, while Abby sat nearby practicing at the wheel and Natty curled inside the curve of her arm. She tried to shame herself by thinking of Tituba, the slave-witch. Flying through the night, as she had done. Dancing to the devil's tune, as she had done. She thought of the loss of Thomas and it hurt to breathe.

She slept. Abby, frightened of what was happening to Hannah, did not wake her. She fed Natty and Lem beans and biscuits from last night's supper and helped them up the ladder to bed. Alone, exhausted from her nightly vigils, Hannah drifted deeper and deeper into sleep. It was not the noise of the horse's hoofs that woke her this time but Thomas's hands, pushing against her shoulders, rocking her gently awake. She opened her eyes and saw his face. He looked so sad. "How can thou doubt me, Hannah? Do thou not recall? 'If two be one, as surely thou and I, / How stayest thou there, whilst I in heaven lye?' "

"In Ipswich, not in heaven," Hannah corrected, remembering the poem and sure now that it was Thomas before her, repeating the lines he had used to bid her farewell. She was light with joy at his return, giddy at the mistake that had led her to think him the devil. They rode this night to the blackberry patch where they had first met, and he placed the juicy pips one by one upon her tongue. Then he kissed the sticky sweetness of her mouth, letting his tongue travel along the edge of her lips, licking her clean. When he pulled back, she leaned toward him, letting her own tongue etch the outline of his mouth, a tool to retain forever the image of his lips. With her mouth on his, tongues touching, they breathed their souls to one. If he were to pull away, thought Hannah, my life would run with him, draining away on the ground. With their mouths still touching, they slipped slowly down to where soft green moss made a springy cushion of the earth.

Thomas touched the top button on her bodice and her dress disappeared. Hannah felt his mouth smile against hers. He was proud of his trick. She smiled back, and pressed her forefinger against the front of his shirt, making his clothes vanish as well. What a clever pair we are, thought Hannah, as he rubbed his nakedness against her. The wind of the ride had loosened her hair and Thomas delicately brushed the strands away from her eyes. He traced her mouth, then let his fingers memorize her breasts, her stomach, the soft place where her thighs came together in a mound of silky hair. His fingers drifted past the opening, teasing her with their nearness, but he continued down the length of her until his finger stroked the sole of her foot.

Then, slowly, he was moving his hand up her calf, warming the soft skin of her inner thigh, letting his fingers find a home in the place between her legs. Hannah was edgy with pleasure by the time he came to her. She closed her eyes, still seeing his face floating in the darkness of her desire as he loosed his life inside her.

There were things one could do. A knife laid under the foot of the bed. A horseshoe over the door. Satan banished, or would it be Thomas she kept at bay?

Will would come back and lie between her and the night mare. There would be no more danger. No more delight.

Hannah dreaded the day of Will's return. Still more, she dreaded the day when she might feel life quicken inside her, might feel the kick of a small, cloven hoof.

When the children had gone to sleep, Hannah walked down to the shore where, earlier that week, she had seen a canoe. The wind had begun to rise and she had to use the paddle as a pole, pushing away from the rocks. Wind and tide tied her to shore, and her shoulders ached with the effort to push out to sea. Then the wind dropped and the tide turned. She was free. As she began to paddle, she heard a faint whickering. She had known Thomas would find her, the night mare dancing toward her on the darkened water.

"Let us sleep in thine arms, and awake in thy kingdom," she whispered to God or to Thomas as she felt herself lifted out of the boat and folded into the familiar warmth of his body. Safe now, she let her hands find their way beneath his shirt, her lips breathing life into the nape of his neck. Thomas turned and smiled. He held up one hand to show her he still had the flute whose soft, sweet notes Hannah could faintly hear, drifting across the water.

AUTHOR'S NOTE

I wanted to write about guilt and found it hard to do so in a contemporary setting. How do you write about the way love can break down your boundaries when sexual satisfaction is considered a right and eating dessert a sin?

G.T.T. (GONE TO TEXAS)

By L. M. Lippman

She does not admit it now, but Cameron came to Texas for a man. With a man, her college boyfriend. It seemed to solve so much, on that gray March afternoon, when Paul announced he had one of those teaching jobs that wasn't really a teaching job. If she went with him, she wouldn't have to think about what she might do, or who she might be, or if she should be with him at all. Those questions could be postponed, just a little while longer. Cameron saw her life as a cloth to be laid out for a picnic on a beautiful but windy day. Having a place to live it, San Antonio, would anchor the first corner. The others would follow.

"It's like the Peace Corps but in a public school!" Paul had told Cameron excitedly, and she tried not to listen to the part of her mind off in the corner, evaluating him. It was a part of her mind that seemed to be getting louder recently. It was hard to imagine they would last, in any city. Still, as spring stalled out somewhere south of Boston, Cameron found herself checking the San Antonio temperatures in the *Globe*'s weather tables. Seventy degrees, 80 degrees and, just once, a high of 87 degrees. To Cameron, who was pale and thin, with blood pressure so low she fell into near-swoons if she stood up too quickly, it had an undeniable appeal. She found herself eager to hear Paul's impressions after he visited his school in April, during some citywide revel known simply as Fiesta. She found that a wonderful conceit—a party so big it was simply called Party. Paul told her people ate turkey legs in the streets, waving them around as if they were Latino versions of Henry the VIII. There were four parades—three through the streets, one on the shallow river that wound through downtown. Better yet, the entire city smelled like La Choza, their favorite cheap restaurant.

"Fiesta is bigger than Mardi Gras," he told her, sounding faintly like a brochure for the Chamber of Commerce. Bigger, better, grander, hotter—Paul's vocabulary had already been corrupted by Texas, Cameron noted. Still, she was pleased when he rolled a dyed egg toward her across the Formica table. They were in their kitchen, the warmest room because it had only one outside wall, which faced on a narrow courtyard. Here, Cameron could prop her always cold feet on the radiator and keep her back to the space heater, while Paul brought her cup after cup of hot tea.

"They call them *cascarones*," he said, as she examined the egg, dyed an uneven blue, its tip shaved off and replaced by a thin piece of pink tissue. Then, to her dismay, he took the egg from her and smashed it against her head, just above her left ear. Tiny pieces of confetti—blue, pink, turquoise, red, gold, silver—scattered through her hair and spilled across the table. She liked the effect but was annoyed he had broken her egg.

"You can't save it," Paul said, laughing at her. "The whole point of a *cascarón* is breaking it."

He had brought her salsa, too. Mild, medium, hot. It was important, Paul said, that they learn to eat the hottest kind. They didn't want to be gringos or, worse, *bolillos*—white bread. Cameron noticed his "r" rolled like a runaway train; he hit the double "l" diphthong like someone biting off a piece of beef jerky. Her own Spanish was far more fluent, yet prim and contained. She considered it in bad taste to speak a foreign language too familiarly.

Paul poured a sample of each salsa into their Four Corner snack trays, found in an overpriced consignment shop they loved. They had been able to afford the gilt-edged squares only because Utah was chipped and Arizona was missing. Paul handed Cameron a tortilla chip—this, too, from San Antonio, he told her, one of its many fine local tortilla factories—and she whisked it through each sample, her sinuses clearing for the first time in weeks. Paul's forehead began to sweat on medium and the hot made him wheeze, inhaling a chip's sharp corner. Cameron had to pound him on the back to dislodge it. She had known they would not last. Now she found herself wondering how long Paul would last on his own. In San Antonio, in teaching, in any place that was not Boston and college. She could not buttress him. She suspected no single person, or place, ever could.

He gave San Antonio six months, not even the entire school year. For him, it was over before she got there. Paul flew down in early

August. Cameron followed ten weeks later, arriving just before Halloween in the ancient Toyota whose ownership was no longer clear, and found him surprisingly pale and fragile. Haunted. In fitting Gothic style, there was even a streak of gray in his left sideburn.

"You look . . . distinguished," she said, after considering and rejecting several other adjectives.

Paul muttered that the city was unlivable, more like an outpost of Mexico than the U.S. of A. He actually said "the U.S. of A," as if he were one of those military types who retired to San Antonio, the kind of people who called talk radio shows. He said he was stuck with an ESL class—English as a Second Language—that was twice as much work, because you had to translate everything, which was ridiculous, immersion was obviously the way to go, hadn't anyone here heard of "Hunger of Memory"? The phones went out when it rained, he said, and innocent-looking streets filled with water, sweeping people away. So why did they call them low-water crossings? Weren't they highwater crossings? And these red bumps on his arm, he asked her, was that heat rash?

Cameron, unsure how to respond to this rush of words after four days and almost forty hours on the road, simply said: "What about that all-night taco stand you told me about?" That produced another rush, about how the classic Mexican diet was really very healthy, but Texas had perverted it, with too much cheese and sour cream. He had especially harsh words for avocados—"All fat, even if it is a monosaturate!"—but he finally took her to Taco Cabana.

On the patio there, a *tostada compuesta* and *carne guisada* taco in front of her, Cameron lifted her thin shoulders, enjoying the harmless breeze eddying around her. She was warm, her food was hot. Across the street, a mechanized billboard spilled forth a neverending circle of white bread slices. Butterkrust. She felt very white herself, almost larval, surrounded by so many wonderful hues of brown skin. But no one seemed to hold it against her. She would buy a Guatemalan belt, the woven kind she had seen back East. And she wanted one of those T-shirts with the tinted photographs of old cowgirls. As for cowboy boots, she was already wearing a pair, purchased on a detour through a town called Rosebud. She stretched out her legs, admiring the dove-gray boots, with white and navy insets. She felt like one of those outlaws in the nineteenth century who scrawled "G.T.T." on the door—Gone To Texas—and disappeared into their new lives. Or the men who flocked to the Alamo to fight and die, although they had no real stake in the future of Texas. That was it—she was Davy Crockett.

As Cameron fell in love with San Antonio, Paul's hatred of it grew.

Whatever had spooked him in August stayed with him throughout the sweet, mild winter, a time of achingly blue skies and balmy temperatures. When spring break came, he announced he needed to take a little trip alone. To Nepal. For Cameron, the hardest part was trying not to be too happy. She was fond of him, in the way that one feels affection for any significant part of your life that is about to end. Graduation had brought out the same nostalgic twinge—and the same firm desire to see it all done. She helped him pack, checked to see if he needed any booster shots, didn't quibble when she saw him take T-shirts and soft, worn polos she knew were hers. They said goodbye at the airport, surrounded by rich Mexicans carrying bags from weekend shopping sprees at Saks and Marshall Fields. Cameron tried not to rush the farewell. They even kissed, for old time's sake. Then she drove to a nearby taco stand, one that served beer. When a plane flew overhead, she lifted her Pearl Light in salute, and watched, telling herself it was her past vanishing on the Northeast horizon, although she could not know if it were Paul's plane. Paul ended up in Nepal and a distant corner of Cameron's memory, where he existed solely as someone she called "my college boyfriend." San Antonio was hers now, hers alone.

She quickly forgot Paul had found the perfect apartment, just one big room on the top floor of an old mansion, with stained glass windows facing east and west, French doors to the south, and a tiny deck on the north. And she seldom recalled it was he who had seen the ad that led to her job, working at a small foundation that underwrote folk art exhibits and local artists. History had always been particularly malleable here, she knew. Some of the best stories were true—Colonel Travis drawing a line with his saber, daring the Alamo defenders to cross it, separating the men from the boys. Some, like the legend of Emily Morgan, the beautiful slave who made Santa Anna late for San Jacinto, appeared to have little basis in fact. It made no difference, Texans stood by them all. Cameron especially admired the Daughters of the Republic of Texas, the keepers of the Alamo, who steadfastly withstood any attempt to disrupt their myths.

It was an old city, at once wilder and stuffier than any place she had known back East. The Anglos still ruled, especially the old German families. The city's aristocrats were so sure of themselves that they crowned each other during Fiesta. Then the daughters of the finest families traveled through the city on flatbed trailers, so the citizenry could admire the embroidered-and-beaded trains on their $10,000 court costumes. And at the "coronation," the girls bowed to the King of the Order of the Alamo by sticking one leg out directly behind them, then pressing their foreheads to the floor. Most needed an escort's hand to rise again, but an occasional princess or duchess, her thigh muscles tightened by years of horseback riding or soccer, rose of her own accord, drawing an ovation from the audience in the municipal auditorium. Cameron went, just to see this, then practiced the curtsy at home, giving up after she toppled over and bruised her forehead. She would never be a duchess.

At work, the Vaca Naranja Foundation, she served at the pleasure of a board of retired duchesses. She was a go-between, the buffer between them and the artists they patronized. Yes, patronized was the perfect word. The president of the board, a banker's wife who had endowed the foundation and named it, more or less, for the University of Texas mascot, liked to tell Cameron: "I think those Day of the Dead figures are just precious." Or, "Do you think you could tell that woman who makes the puppets to put a little more pink in their costumes? I think that would look *darling*." Cameron claimed she forwarded the requests, but they always seemed to get lost in translation.

It was hard enough just to get the Latina artists to take the pitifully small amounts of money offered. She would sit across from, say, Beatriz Villarreal, trying to convince her that the $350 stipend was free and clear, a way for her to buy paste for the *papier-mâché* monsters she made under the pecan tree in her backyard. Or she would drive all the way to Hondo, just to sneak up to Josefina Cisneros's mailbox and leave a certified check to cover the costs of the paint she used on her bleach-bottle versions of various saints. It was a wonderful life. Then August came, and she began to understand what might have dimmed Paul's pleasure in San Antonio.

It was hot, of course, and had been hot since April. The city, like a slow-baking oven, gathered more and more heat with each week. Cameron was stoic at first, almost smug, telling people it was no different from the humid summers back East. She was even rather proud of not having a working air conditioner in her car. At day's end, when the seat belt left a wet sash along her clothing, she felt as if she had been decorated for bravery in the world's oldest battle, the struggle against the elements. Then August began and soon she was stripped of her medals.

In August, San Antonio was hotter still, a seeming impossibility. Meanwhile, the city's interiors seemed to get colder and colder, as if it were written somewhere that inside and outside must be equally inhospitable. Even the air conditioner in her apartment could not be controlled; no matter how she fiddled with the little dials, it roared forth with a blast of too-cold air. She was reduced to wearing socks to bed. And that was before August.

In the daytime, she wore even more clothing. Slips, cardigans, pantyhose, things she had left behind in grade school. But you needed them indoors here. Then she would step outside, and her pores would seal beneath her nylons as if she were the gilded woman in *Goldfinger*. Or perhaps it was more like some cheesy science fiction movie, where one lived beneath a bubble dome and was cautioned never to enter the Forbidden Zone that lay beyond, so beautiful and enticing. She moved quickly through the outdoors, from home to car to work and back again. She felt as if she were scuttling through some war-torn city where gunfire might erupt. She carried the necessary supplies—dark glasses, diet soda, an elastic band to whisk the hair off her neck—and kept her head low.

And there was no end in sight, no cool breeze promising an imminent change, no hope that Labor Day was anything but a Monday. This was August's true cruelty here. People went to the Coast, to wade in the flat, warm waters of the Gulf and drive on the tar-flecked beaches. Cameron, used to the Atlantic, could not bear to look at it, much less swim in it. Nearer by, people drove to New Braunfels and rented inner tubes for floating down the icy Gruene River. The river froze one's backside, while the sun baked the front. Or they drove to Austin to swim at Barton Springs, a quarry that was never above 63 degrees. People sat on the lawn until it was unbearable, then surrendered to the frigid water. There was no modulation here, Cameron noted in disgust, just extremes. August stretched out before her, taking up September and, she feared, the early part of October. She felt like a runner who had trained for a ten-kilometer race only to find it was ten miles. Her only relief came in Mexican restaurants and *taquerías*, where hot food and iced tea, or cold beer and margaritas, combined to make her feel neither hot nor cold, but like Goldilocks at Little Bear's plate, just right.

She sensed it was her golden locks—really more of an ashy blonde—that drew Jesse to her. Or perhaps it was her appetite. She felt him before she saw him, sneaking up behind her in Los Arcos, where she was eating the no. 12 dinner. Two chicken enchiladas, a crispy taco, a gordita, beans, rice, and a basket of flour tortillas. It was the meal she ate everywhere, and everywhere it was served with the same warning: **"Don'touchtheplateisveryhot."** Yet the person who served it often carried it in bare hands, suggesting the plate was not so hot after all. Cameron, noticing they gave her mild salsa, suspected they thought she was a lightweight. She ate more to compensate, wiping the plate clean with a lard-light tortilla. This is what she was doing when Jesse crept up behind her.

"Cálmate, la flaquita rubia," he said, touching her elbow. Tex-Mex for: Calm down, skinny blonde. Cameron turned, let her narrow eyes take him in. Slender, with the long, tight muscles of a marathon runner, the profile of an Aztec, and skin the color of flan. Brown eyes, of course, and black hair, with color so true that light couldn't penetrate. His Spanish had a precise, fussy edge, as if he were mocking her, or himself. He wore jeans and a clean, white T-shirt, stretched tight across his chest. He could have been a lowrider, a *vato*. Or he could have been one of those new-and-improved Mexicans, who want to grow up to be JFK or the mayor of San Antonio. Impossible to tell, and not important. If Cameron wasn't sure she liked him, she knew she liked the way he looked.

"I'll show you someplace where you can eat your fill." He put money on the table, more than enough to pay her bill, and Cameron, knowing only what his fingertips felt like, followed him from the restaurant. She still had a tiny crescent of beans on her left cheek, a refried dimple.

She followed him as if he were Juan Seguin, sent from the Alamo in the dark of night to bring help for the 180 or so who remained there. She followed him as if he were Zapata and she, a Mexican farmer ready for a revolution. She followed him for the simple promise of a bigger, better taco, and it seemed to her the history of Texas, of the world, of time, was based on nothing more than the desire for more.

He led her through the streets of the West Side, supposedly a dangerous place. They walked past piles of rubber tires, past *botánicas* and *farmacías*, through Alazan-Apache Courts. Even the housing projects sounded exotic here, Cameron thought.

They found a festival. There was always a festival in San Antonio. Fiesta, the one that had so charmed Paul, started the season, but another followed every weekend, increasingly obscure in origin and purpose. By August, they didn't even bother to name them anymore. The disc jockeys on the Spanish radio stations simply said: *"Venga al Mercado, para más cerveza y comida."* ("Come to El Mercado—or the park, or the convention center, or the River Walk—for more beer and food.")

Smoke from a hundred grills hung over Eureste Park. An accordion dueled with a saxophone. In front of a makeshift stage, people danced the polka and the merengue. No one seemed to notice it was at least 95 degrees, even at eight o'clock. By daring to move, to dance, they staved off the heat, beers clutched in their hands, sloshing over their feet.

Jesse guided her through the crowds with his fist in the small of her back, hard enough for her to imagine a bruise starting on her knobby spine. "Our Lady of Sorrows," he said, and it seemed mystical, thrilling, ominous. Then she realized he was simply referring to the church booth whose tacos he preferred.

A girl with skinny legs and a round belly leaned across the plywood counter until it bowed dangerously. "TACO, TACO, TACO, TACO!" she bellowed. "Make your own! No skimpin' on the fixins'! Guacamole *and* borracho beans!" She was a good advertisement; she looked like she had eaten a few tacos in her time.

Cameron held a tortilla on her fingertips, large as a Frisbee. She spooned in skirt steak, grilled green onions, *pico de gallo*, guacamole, and still it stretched out, larger and whiter than ever. She added a little bit more of everything, folded it in half, took a bite, and the guacamole overflowed down her shirt, leaving a yellow-green stain. Jesse licked the overflow from her chin and neck, and eagerly she licked him back, although there was nothing to taste on him, not yet. It was the hottest part of the day, but Jesse pressed a bottle of beer against her neck, and she felt as if she were standing in a stiff breeze somewhere along the Atlantic coast. Braced, cooled, refreshed.

Cameron thought of the poster that hung in her boss's office at Vaca Naranja: *El noche cuando viene el hombre con las patas del gallo*. The night when the man with the chicken feet came. If a woman danced with that man, she belonged to the devil. Cameron looked down at Jesse's feet but saw only black Chuck Taylors. Paul had worn those, too, and if she knew anything about Paul, it was that he wasn't the devil.

She thought they might dance, although she had no idea how to approximate the moves she saw. And she felt plain among the women, dressed and made-up, so obviously anticipating the Saturday night they were having. Cameron wore a baggy T-shirt and baggier shorts; her hair stuck out of the back of her head in a straggly ponytail. She wanted to tell them she understood their culture, that she had a degree in Central American studies, that she understood their accented Spanish, so unlike anything she had ever heard in a classroom. She wanted to announce that she could, with a little warning, look pretty good herself. She wanted to put on some mascara and lipstick. But Jesse—had he told her his name, or did she simply bestow it upon him—had other plans. As suddenly as he had brought her here, he took her away, past the *farmacías* and the *botánicas*, past the pile of tires, through Alazan-Apache Courts, ending up at a dark green Lexus, its steering wheel locked with The Club.

She guessed that they were stealing the car and, somewhat dreamily, accepted it as inevitable. She was more surprised when Jesse produced a key, opened the door, and removed the red metal bar from the wheel. "Where do you live?" he asked, and that was more surprising still, for she thought he was, if not the man with the chicken feet, if not the devil, then someone equally dangerous and omniscient. She told him how to get to her apartment. It was the last thing she would have to tell him.

In her apartment, where there were no walls, just area leading to area, it was easy to go from the front door to the bed, with only a few detours in between. But Jesse didn't hurry. While Cameron lay on her soft mattress, staring at the ceiling and trying to remember if she were drinking or dreaming, he found a cognac bottle and two jelly glasses and pulled a chair up to the bed. For a long time, he seemed content just to look at her.

"Show me your stomach," he said, in English or Spanish, she was no longer sure what language they were speaking. At any rate, she did as he asked, pulling her shirt up and shorts down, baring the very white expanse of her belly.

"It still goes in," he said, marveling. He walked over to the bed and held his hands over it as if it were a fire that would warm him. "All that food, and it still goes *in*."

Feeling cold, exposed, she tried to move beneath the covers, but he caught her by the ankle. He snaked his hand up the wide leg of her shorts, and held her there, testing her, taking her pulse. His palm was the perfect temperature, like a bottle of milk tested on your mother's wrist. She felt something she had forgotten: the sensation of being warm, yet not hot, of being cool, yet not cold. She was wet, but she wasn't sweating. He squeezed and she felt her own steady pulse, her blood rushing toward that one point.

Next to the bed, in the window, the air conditioner roared. She could hear it, but she no longer felt the cold blasts of air that had driven her mad all summer, driving her beneath the blankets, only to surface again at three A.M. sweaty and disoriented. The air was still now, but not stagnant, more like the first breeze she had ever felt here. Cameron saw the Butterkrust billboard in her mind, but now it was her body falling forward on the plate, then circling around again.

Her shirt came off, but she did not flinch. He hovered over her, her own bubble, protecting her. He kept his hand between her legs, then fastened his mouth on her breast. Everything was the same perfect temperature, there was no variation. She felt as if she were suspended in amber liquid, ready to be fossilized for whatever future archaeologist wished to excavate her. She felt like a fly dipped in honey. Her muscles worked without her, taking her nowhere. Her legs slapped against his hips, her arms circled his neck. When had his clothes come off? When had the rest of hers? Except for her white crew socks, she was quite naked.

He showed himself to her with a shy pride. "It's like a churro, isn't it?" he said, and the light brown length of him did remind her of the pastries sold at Mexican bakeries. She ran her tongue along it, expecting to taste bits of sugar still clinging to him, but found a different sweetness, more like molasses cookies, or butterscotch brownies.

He began to push inside her, and this felt better still, just a shade warmer than his hands and mouth. Then he stopped abruptly, pulling back, and she heard her own cry, a banshee wail, echoing around them. Her legs boxed his hips as if she were boxing his ears. Bad boy. Bad boy.

But all he wanted to do was remove her socks. She waited, sure this part of her must still be cold, that blood could never reach those distant extremities. He would be disgusted, he would be repelled, and she would be left alone, too cold and too hot, all at once. It was only when he pressed his lips against the arch that she realized her feet were no longer cold. Nor was her nose, nor her fingertips. She felt like a lizard on a rock, or the Cameron who once sat in a Boston kitchen, drinking cup after cup of tea. Warmth became heat, but so gradually that it felt good, natural. And they could face the heat, without air conditioning or icy water or an inner tube to float them down the river. He took her temperature, finding it just a degree hotter with each thrust, until she felt as if she had finally equaled the record high of the day, of the month, of the summer.

She crawled on top of him, determined to make him sweat, indifferent to her too-full belly. She should be ill, she knew, or at least stupefied from her day of overindulgence and extremes. Yet all she noticed was the perfection of the climate—the mechanized breeze washing over them, their mouths swollen as if they had been sucking the salted rims of margaritas all day. Hip to hip, thigh to thigh, they smacked together, and she waited for the hideous tearing sound that comes when perspiring bodies collided in the heat. It never came, they moved easily as two dolphins, twins floating in their mother's belly. From this perspective, she saw how similar their bodies were. Straight, tall, slim. His legs were as long as hers; his ribs winked at her through brown skin. She wanted to get closer still, allowing no space, no air, no breeze, nothing between them. She wrapped herself around as tightly as she could, allowing no movement at all. And it was in the stillness that she felt it, a long rippling sensation that she wanted him to feel, too. She placed his hand back where it had started, so he could feel the pulse again. Stronger, steadier. Hot. And the world settled back into its separate spheres. It was August again.

"A Latin lover," she thought, as the chill crept in. Viva Zapata. Or was she thinking of Santa Anna, so besotted with sex that he showed up late for the battle of San Jacinto, guaranteeing Texas's victory? Time was back in focus, but she could no longer remember her history. The future suddenly seemed near and sharp, and the present was all too fleeting. She could feel August slipping away from her, see the fall's first blue norther massed on the horizon. Shivering, Cameron tucked her feet beneath Jesse, as if he were a radiator she once knew. The mechanized breath of the air conditioner raised goosebumps on her back. It was not that different, after all, from floating down the icy Gruene River or diving into a quarry. Surviving a San Antonio summer, it seemed, was just a matter of finding which extreme worked best for you.

AUTHOR'S NOTE

I hate heat. I hate adjectives like "steamy" and "sultry," which remind me of swamps. But more than this, I hate air conditioning. Only cheap motel rooms, which feel, already, as if they have no connection to the outside world, are improved by air conditioning—but that's another story.

CLIMACTERIC

By I. Buguise

I've been avoiding him for the past three months. Taking the tube at a different time. Waiting till nine-thirty when I know he's already left. Not buying the newspaper on the corner. Not taking the rubbish out. He might walk past. I can't bear the thought of running into him. I can't bear the thought of not running into him. Especially in the morning. That's the hardest time.

It worked. For three months I haven't thought of him. I went to the office. I made dinner. I slept with my husband—never pretending he was someone else. I coped. Well, sort of. And, then yesterday I saw him again. Oh, God. I was coming out the door and he was standing on the pavement, talking to the postman. I walked toward them. It was difficult. I sucked my stomach muscles in. Stood up straight. Dropped my shoulders. Sucked my cheeks in. Held my chin up. Tried to make my double chin disappear. Tried to make myself not look fifty-five years old. It doesn't work. I feel so ugly. So ravaged by time. No one will notice me. No one wants me. My legs were wobbling and my face was trying to organize its friendly-muscles expression. Christ, I'm a walking timebomb. But I made it. The postman smiled and walked off. We were alone. I looked him in the eyes. I always do that. That's the hardest part. His eyes are really the only remarkable feature he has. The rest is just regular middle-aged, probably paunchy, middle-class man. Why does this happen?

He stares back. Very few men can do that. Most of them look away.

"Hi," I say, trying to look composed, feeling shattered. My mind is a pressure cooker.

"Where have you been?" he asks as he walks toward me, starting to come closer. Oh, God. Is he going to embrace me? Why? Does he really miss me when I'm not around? Is this all in my mind? He's looking at me. Not through me. But right at me. I pull back. I stiffen. He holds back. He senses my tension. He must. It's so obvious. He's nervous. No, it's not just my imagination. I'm not making this up. He must feel something. Why else would he notice I haven't been around? He must have missed me. That's clear. Is he scared of contact? Maybe just as scared as I am? Does he want contact? Just as much as I do? I can't talk. I know I have my vague, blank look on. I try not to slouch. I don't want my double chin to appear.

"Where have you been?" he asks again.

"Hiding out. Hiding and working. Working really hard. What's new with you?"

"Nothing. Same as ever."

Don't ask him where he's been. Pretend you haven't noticed the absence. Does he know I avoid him so that I can put some order in my life? Does he know I'm obsessed with him? I know I'm about to ramble. I know I'm about to start saying things that won't make sense. I better leave. That's it. That's all there is to it. Be casual. Be normal. Look him in the eye and say bye. Get out of here. Hurry.

"Bye. See you later." I go back inside, crawl into bed with my husband.

And now I have another conversation, another posture for my fantasies. I'll spend the next few weeks playing with these words, with his meaning behind these words, with his movements. I won't be able to concentrate on anything else. I'll resent any intrusion into my thoughts. I'll be bitchy and mean to my husband, to the kids. My work will suffer. The people I work with will find me distracted and uncertain. No decisions will be made. Oh sure, decisions will be made but only insofar as they don't distract from my thoughts and his comings and goings. He'll be sitting on my head directing my every movement. I'll be out on the street all the time now. I'll be looking for him. I'll consider everything I say and do and hope he approves of my thoughts and actions. I can't stop thinking about him again. I sit in front of the telly. The news is on. I can't concentrate. Is he watching the nine o'clock or the ten o'clock news? I better watch both. I don't want to miss any of his experiences. Did he watch the program on ferrets? Did he read the article on Hemingway? Does he like Hemingway? Does he like the films better than the novels? Does he go to the movies? Did he see *Damage*? Did he think about me when he saw Jeremy Irons fucking his brains out? I couldn't stop thinking about him. My crotch was zooming off into clitoral fling land. Christ. I don't even know if he goes to the movies.

It's not as though my life is lacking in luster. It's even exciting most of the time. I have everything I want. Even more. Lots of travel. Great house. Great kids. Loving husband. I even have great sex. It's just that I want him. No. I don't. I want him to want me.

When I'm not working, I'm thinking about him. No. I'm thinking about him when I work. I think about him all the time. How I can meet him, what we will say, what our first kiss will be like, how we will get in bed, how we will get out of bed. I'm obsessed with what kind of sex he likes. Is he slow? Is he gentle? What does he smell like? Does he sweat? Is he selfish? Does he care about the woman he's with? Does he want to satisfy her? Oh, God. I don't mean her. I mean me. Does he want to satisfy me? Does he like to kiss? I mean, does he really enjoy it? Not just do it to get to another stage? What position does he favor? I don't care. I don't care. I just want him. I've got lots of scenarios in my mind. They often get tangled up so that the end product doesn't make much sense.

And then today we meet again on the street, this time near where we both work. Two days in a row. I can't stand it. Yeah. We even work near each other. I didn't do that on purpose. I had my job first. It's lunchtime.

I walk down Crumble Street. See him approaching. I pretend I don't see him. Either he's pretending he doesn't see me or he really doesn't see me. I've got to do something quickly or my chance will be lost. What can I say? Say something intelligent, slightly sarcastic. Sarcasm is the best. It will make me sound nonchalant yet knowing. I look up and say "Hi. What are you doing here?" So much for brilliance. That was pretty trite.

"Joanna!" he exclaims. He seems pleased to see me. Is it just a pleased-nice-to-see-an-acquaintance face or is it a finally-we-meet-and-end-up-in-bed face? I don't know. I'm concentrating on staring into his eyes. I don't want anything to ruin this. Do I make the first move? Is that too forward? Can two people, male and female, meet on the street and have lunch? Is it allowed? Will he think ill of me? Does he want this as much as I do? Does he ever fantasize about me? Maybe he's shy and he can't make the first move. He's not shy. Don't be silly. I've got nothing to lose.

"What are you doing here?" he says. Do I read friend in his eyes? Is it maybe even lust? Is he nervous? God. I'm so nervous I can't think? Didn't I just ask him what he was doing here? Why is he asking me the same question and not answering mine? Is this a good sign? Is he just as nervous as I am? Or is he just being polite? Oh, God. Quick, answer him. Don't let him move. Don't let him get away.

Putting on a bored expression, I say, "Getting out of the office and getting something to eat. I'm famished." Maybe my expression was too bored. Now, do I ask him to eat with me? Oh, no, I can't put the words eat and me in the same sentence. I'd faint with pain and embarrassment. I can't say dine. That isn't me. I make fun of people who say dine. What do I say? I know. I know. I can say, "Do you want to have lunch?" No. What if he says no. I couldn't bear it. My hands are shaking. Can he see it? He isn't shaking. He's totally composed. He doesn't know what is going through my brain. I'm just fantasizing. He just thinks of me as an acquaintance. He has no idea. So there's no problem. I can ask him because he won't think it forward or rude. No, no, I'll wait for him to say something. Ask him. Control yourself and ask him. Get the words out. It's OK. He's only human. No, he isn't. That's the problem. I see him as superhuman. No, he isn't. There's nothing special about him. He eats, drinks, and sleeps like everyone else. I know. Imagine him snoring or worrying about prostrate cancer. That will make it easier. He probably has hemorrhoids. That should help. Just visualize him sitting on the toilet and it will be easier. OK. Go.

"I like this street. There's this cheap Indian restaurant over there. I go there whenever I want to run away from work and relax," I reply. I know he likes Indian food. He told me that before. Oh, shit. I've told him I eat here before and he has never said, "Let's meet there. It's right by my office." So. He doesn't want to eat with me. Oh, God. There are those two words in the same sentence again. He doesn't want to spend time with me. He only thinks of me as a dumpy, slightly ditsy middle-aged crone. I don't know what to say now. He hasn't said anything. He hasn't put his hand on my shoulder and steered me toward the restaurant. He's going to go away. I know it. What can I say to make him stay longer? To make this accidental meeting something special? Something we will both remember. Don't say anything corny. Don't mess it up. Keep looking him in the eyes. It's getting harder. It's his eyes. I know. Pretend they aren't staring back. Pretend he has a stye. Oh, don't be stupid. He doesn't have a stye.

It isn't going to work. I'm sure he doesn't have hemorrhoids. And he probably doesn't snore. My legs are wobbling again. Not my legs, really. But my crotch. Oh, my God. I just felt his hand on my breast. I can't stand it. I've got to sit down. I've got to lie down. I've got to hold him. Those lips. Oh, no. I can't look at his lips. His lips are more sensual than his eyes. I never thought about that before. Now there're two things

I have to focus on looking at and not looking at. Thinking about them, looking at them.

I lie down. He lies next to me. Suddenly we have no clothes on. We are drowning in a pool of feathers. His body is firm. Not flabby. Not the body of a middle-aged man. We are holding each other. Not tightly. Just gently. We are rocking. Touching each other. Softly. Everywhere. Our lips meet. They touch softly and then harder. We can't stop kissing. I can't open my eyes. I can't breathe. He rubs his leg against mine. I breathe in his smell. It is the smell of sex. Clean and newly born, fresh, scrubbed. I taste toothpaste. I feel muscles, strong and knowledgeable. I hear moans. I sit up. I climb on top of him. Put him inside me. Easily. He slips in easily. I sigh. I move up and down, over and over. I open my eyes. His are closed. Well, really half-closed. His tongue moves gently over his own teeth. I want that tongue in my mouth, not his. I want his taste in my mouth. I lean down and place my lips on his. Our mouths meet again. I don't want to let go. I want to feel this forever. I see apple orchards and sun and hear rushing streams from my youth. From the sex I used to know. From the past I want to relive. I am young and supple again. I have no ties. Total freedom. Lust and innocent pleasure. Moaning, he comes inside me. I can feel him spilling out of me. It is warm and clean. Again, there is the fresh, scrubbed scent of birth. I'm pleased and satisfied. But, I want more. I want to devour him. I want to be devoured. I don't want this to stop.

"Where's this restaurant?" I hear his words through a fog and a tunnel. Are they coming from him? I can't answer him. I don't know what he's talking about. What restaurant?

"Is it the one on the corner?" he asks, still looking into my eyes. His mouth is moving. I can't see his tongue. I don't feel his hand on my heart.

"Yeah. Yeah. The one over there on the other side of the street, next to the lighting shop. They have a lunch special. As much as you can eat for five pounds. Quite good." Well, is he coming or isn't he? Doesn't he understand this is my way of inviting him? Doesn't he realize we've just made love? Doesn't he know the colors and smells and sights are so much more vibrant now? Can't he feel the electric current running from my thoughts through his veins? How much longer can I live with this?

"We'll have to go there sometime," he says.

When, when? Now. Right now. Let's go now. We can make love under the table. On top of the table. Against the door. Anywhere. I don't care. I'll do anything. Just come inside me. I'll climb on top of you.

You can slide in. No one will know. I don't care where. Let's just do it.

"Yeah. I need a good curry to get me through the day every once in a while," I say.

"Enjoy your meal," he says as he walks off in the other direction. I stand there alone. Does he know I'm not moving? He's not looking back. He's forgotten me. I no longer exist. I can't leave this spot. We made love here. He lay inside me. He came inside me. I was free. There was no pressure, no pain. How can he just walk off and leave me? Did he mean it when he said, "We must go there sometime"? Was he just being friendly? Did he mean just the two of us? Is he still thinking about me?

AUTHOR'S NOTE

This story is part of an ongoing set of narratives. I find myself especially drawn to women whose dramas involve growing old, unwanted, and unloved.

WHERE THE CYPRESS PAINTS THE SKY

By Laurel Gross

The land stretches flat and brown as a piece of toast, then lifts into peaks overlooking the sea.

She is thinking how Dali painted the landscape of his native Catalonia as the contours of a woman—the tan mounds of burnt hills the breasts, the valley between them extending into flatness until a slight rise of belly, and then the lowlands, pressed between the thighs.

But maneuvering her rented Fiat further along a scratch of red earth, not in Dali's Spain but in Greece, she is seeing the face of a man she once knew on this island. For a moment, she can feel his presence, hot on the seat next to her. But it is only the sun.

A little edge of earth is all that separates her from a spill into the sea, a reminder of how quickly the end can come. The way things turn out is not always up to you, it takes luck too . . . even as a child she knew that, skipping over the cracks in sidewalks, just in case . . .

The grip of the stick shift feels unnatural. She's never gotten used to it, all the adjustments you have to make in a manually driven car. The automatic is what she craves. Automatic—that was how it was when she met the man whose imagined presence still seems so real to her. The way she fell for him was instantaneous.

Fall.

It is a long way down to the sea. Others have slipped from paths just like this. The twisted carcasses of metal sprout foliage in neglected meadows and cliffsides. But she is cautious, wary, careful. A planner. She makes lists. Lists are her salvation. She makes a mental one now, running down an inventory of the stuff she has lugged across the sea and crammed into the tiny Fiat—her Nikons, their wardrobe of lenses, tripods, film, flashes.

She is well equipped, prepared for anything.

Anything—except the old feelings that rush up at her as fast as hairpin turns in the road. It is amazing how much you can feel . . . for a dead man.

The landscape has triggered feelings she'd thought were buried. But they are fresh as plowed earth.

The earth that here is red as an open wound.

Again she sees how close to the edge she is. Her hand wavers. He used to do the driving along these foreign roads.

It's a relief to see the path widen, the tall cypresses signaling that she is on the right road. There must be a dozen of them. Giant feathered arrows pointing to the sky. Or fingers in prayer: supple, swayed, steepled.

He had taught her to see like that. One thing always changing into another. Trees . . . arrows . . . fingers.

The drop to the sea vanishes. Secure enough to lean her head out of the window, she swallows the fresh scent of lemon from the groves stretching out in a field with no boundaries. On the other side, the tangled tops of olive trees scrub the sky like brushes.

A paved drive leads to a cool white villa. Sleek to the ground, everything about it reads privacy, and a discreet plaque identifies the place as "a distinguished hotel of the world."

Outside, a young man shields his eyes from the noon glare. He looks like a dark paper cutout against the white. A sailor on the lookout for land. Getting closer, perhaps he is not quite so young. But he is a good number of years younger than she.

She is one year shy of forty, and feeling older.

He motions for her to leave the car right there. She pulls up, cuts the engine, and almost steps out before realizing that she isn't wearing shoes.

A heel pokes out from under the passenger seat. The rubber floor is grainy with sand. She scrapes the straggler out. The other comes easily. But, swollen from the heat, her feet resist the leather. Suddenly she's Cinderella's ugly sister anxiously stuffing a clumsy foot into a rejecting shoe.

The Greek is still there. Something self-possessed and gracious about him suggests he is not the bellman.

The gravel rearranges itself underfoot as the spiky heels dig in.

They're so impractical on this terrain, making it hard to retrieve your land legs. And yet it feels sexy the way they break the arch, forcing you to hold your belly in when you walk.

"Kaliméra," says the Greek, reaching for her hand.

She had forgotten how beautiful a language it was. It had been a long time since she'd heard it spoken like this on its own turf—an utterly different species from the harsh voices shouting food orders in Greek diners.

"You may call me Stathis. I am the proprietor here."

His hair curls tight around the head like one of the statues in a museum. He is fair for a Greek.

"Claire Winter," she says.

"Yes, I know. I recognize you from your photograph."

What photograph?

The portrait on the back of her book on Alaska, he says. A guest had sent it after hearing him confide that he had "always wanted to see snow." So it seemed "fortuitous, like an omen" when her letter arrived saying that she was coming to photograph his island for a book on Greece.

And so he is definitely not the bellman, this receiver of gifts, but the owner of the island's best hotel.

It occurs to her that this Stathis had been waiting for her all along. Does he wait outside for all of the guests?

But she is a curiosity. Someone to greet.

And she has made snow real to him.

He leads her into shade. A white hall sparkles with the colorful chips of mosaics. The floor like a picture shattered and put back together. Blue sea swirls, and a dolphin encircled in the center by a ring of shells. The room, evoking a royal residence from an earlier time.

"Perhaps you have time for lunch before you start?"

Is he inviting me? she thinks. She's not sure, but he might be. Then again, maybe not. But Greeks are friendly, hospitable, there's no harm in it. "Yes," she says. "After I've stored my gear away. I can't live without my cameras."

"Your cameras? Oh, yes. Of course." He gives her such an endearing smile, she suspects he almost pities her for being so intimately attached to so much baggage. She almost expects him to say, "Life without love, or children? Impossible. But cameras?"

She may be stereotyping him. He is so Greek, so handsome. She looks away. It's one thing to stare through the camera, but doing the same thing with your eyes alone reveals too much.

She doesn't usually react to people this way. But these islands, they can work on you in strange ways. You can come with the best intentions, to work, for instance, but soon you are staring out to sea . . .

Even the dedicated loner will be wishing there was someone standing beside him, someone whose eyes will follow as he points out something on the horizon.

She thinks, I've been here five minutes, and I'm almost forgetting my cameras.

But her host has not. "We'll put your things in my office. They'll be safe there. Nobody can get in there but me," he says.

His hands are like roots. Brown and firm against the white tablecloth. His fingers lean toward hers.

"You've been to Greece before?"

"A long time ago." She doesn't volunteer more.

"You will know, then, what you wish to photograph?"

"I have some ideas. But I'll look around, see what strikes me."

"So you can be—how do you say—spontaneous?"

"Spontaneity's highly overrated."

She gets the feeling the stranger senses more about her than she admits. She would give anything to be able to live in the moment instead of being fed by memory or anticipation, but that is a talent that eludes her. Surprisingly, the idea that the hotelier may have some insight doesn't make her feel uncomfortable.

Instead of contributing further to conversation, he swishes the wine in its glass. The sun glows through it, stamping a ruby reflection on the damask.

Spontaneity. She'd given in to impulse. Once. It had been the most joyful and the most treacherous time of her life. It was just like Theodorakis had said. One thing's always capable of changing into another. Joy and pain, how closely they were linked. How one flowed back into the other.

First, his exquisite presence expanding to fill her like a fertile womb, and then, all that transformed into torturous absence when he returned to his family and his wife.

Life is fluid, he'd say. Like the clay he molded. He hated it when it was time to set anything to bronze. "By then—it's a dead thing," he'd say, his fingertips still throbbing to mold the clay. To destroy and build again.

That's why he'd never go to museums or galleries to see his sculptures. "It's a funeral," he'd say.

How many times she'd found him inspecting some "finished" object that, despite its beauty, didn't please him. In an instant, he'd pummel its features back to pulp.

But she doesn't share any of this with the stranger who now challenges her solitude from across the table. Stathis refills her wine glass without being asked, as if he has known her for a long time and is sure she will drink it.

She lifts the hard edge of the cup to her mouth. It feels like some kind of assent. She doesn't usually drink in the afternoon, especially when she's planning to work. But this is so pleasant, and she hasn't been near the sea in a long time.

The sea, which has always been seductive, the way it reaches out to you with its sounds and enfolding layers of greens and blues.

The terrace where they've been dining overlooks the water like the deck of a ship. It's mystical, the way Greece can be, and she half expects a mermaid to jump up and greet them. But then she is reminded how fickle the sea can be. How it can change at any moment and swallow up great ships, devouring those who love it most. The Greeks know its double-edged nature so well they put a message on their money warning about it.

Her companion softly calls something to the waiter, and a plate of fruits and pastries appears. Yet still they sit in silence.

A famous radio host once told her, don't feel you have to fill the empty space with words. There has to be room to breathe. "Sometimes the best part comes in the silence." Instinctively, she follows that advice now.

The honey from the pastries sticks to her fingers. She licks them like a child. Stathis pulls on one of his curls. It springs back into place. A nervous gesture? Or a flirtation? He delicately peels an apple, cuts the pulp into thin slices. Bites one of the half-moon shapes he has neatly arranged like a series of mirror images on the plate. She can almost taste the juice.

How many times in your life are you aware of the sound of your own breathing? Of another person's? These things preoccupy her.

These, punctuated by a crossfire of bird cries. The soft step of the waiter. The chime of a china plate. The pines shuffling their needles.

She watches him take some slivers of cheese and arrange them on their plates as if they were the petals of a pale flower.

"You eat like an artist," she says. The words ring so strong in the quiet that she imagines she hears them twice—once for real, and then again as an echo.

But they do not offend. "Growing up in a house full of chaos, you learn to appreciate order," he says. There's an edge in his voice, but he softens it. "My mother was something of a decorator, so I suppose that could've rubbed off. I wouldn't call it art."

"And your father?"

"What people call 'a great man.' Rich, famous—but difficult to share. It was a rare moment we spent alone. I spent half my life craving his attention. The rest trying to be different. As a result, I couldn't be more reliable or more responsive to children and animals. But in some ways, we were a lot alike."

"Like how?"

"We both couldn't eat potatoes without ketchup."

"Everybody likes ketchup on their fries."

"Only in America."

He places his fork down gently, so it doesn't ring against the rim of the dish. Such genteel, impeccable manners—his father must have been a brute.

It's funny how one thing breeds another, how people yearn for what they don't have. People who endure long winters dream of Greece and the sun, while Greeks count snowflakes in their sleep.

"What about you?"

"What about me?"

"Your family."

"I'm not married."

"I meant your parents."

"Like anybody else's."

Stathis is too polite to press. She's grateful, although he would probably understand. Like his, her father was elusive.

A man with money for opera tickets but not for rent, he went on trips alone. Looking for work, he said, but he never once came back employed. His postcards could have been icons, the way she prayed over them, scrutinizing the glossy images and bland messages for hidden meanings, while her mother sought solace in sleep.

But she doesn't invite that conversation. Instead they watch the waiter scrape crumbs from the tablecloth onto the edge of a broad silver spade. The job is accomplished with amazing grace.

"Would you like anything else?" Stathis asks.

Only to sit here in this spot and do nothing.

Instead, she politely says, "No, thank you," in a Greek voice she had forgotten she had. *"Ohi, efharistó."*

Words from another life.

"So you know some Greek?"

"Only a little."

He looks at her as if he suspects she knows more. But again, he doesn't push. "Shall I show you your room, then?" he says.

She nods and follows.

Her eyes shoot around the room like a camera. Wherever she goes, she needs to know exactly where she is in relation to what's around. This, she sees quickly, is a splendid room. The sea makes itself available through a wall of glass. Such a wide-angled, inspiring view that, even with the best equipment, and on a good day, it would be tough to capture it in a photograph.

The double bed is cloaked in a canopy of pale netting hanging down from its slender posts like a veil. A bed made for dreaming.

"Is it satisfactory?" he asks, putting his hands in his pockets, disturbing the smooth line of his tan trousers.

With his hotelier's instinct, she suspects he must already know the answer. But she is moved to say something in Greek, anyway, about how special the place feels. Yet the vocabulary is lost to her. She nods and moves toward the window, with its floor-to-ceiling exposure of the sea. Edging the terrace on the other side of the glass, purple clematis clings to the bushes of plump pink azaleas, making it seem as if the plant bears two fruits.

The transparent panel of the terrace door glides aside easily. The sea fizzes like seltzer poured into a glass. Something irresistible about it. The way it laps toward you, and then away.

Theodorakis—not seen through the camera now but in the bare eye of memory. Theodorakis in his mountain studio, his thick hands glazed with damp clay. He lifts a finger to rub his face, leaving an ashen scar on the jaw. Color in the blue of the sky through the wide white archway carved out of a wall in this high place, where he works under a cathedral ceiling until sunset.

"You've been hurt," Stathis says.

She is almost startled to hear him speak, as if he and not Theodorakis is the figment of her imagining. But he is standing so close, this Stathis, that she can almost feel the scratch of his starched shirt on her bare arm.

"I'm all right," she says, reflexively searching her arm for scrapes.

"Not that. In the past. Someone hurt you, very badly?"

She should be repelled by such intimations from a stranger, but she is not offended by this beautiful man, standing with her so near to the sea.

He puts his hand on her shoulder. She doesn't shake it off.

It feels natural, as if she's known the touch before.

There is a thin sheet of air between them. He does nothing to enlarge it. Does he sense the acceptance in her?

And then, she knows the answer, because his hand is pressing the point where the straps of the sundress cross the back. She leans toward him. Not a decision, really. More like an involuntary movement. A plant to light.

And then, the soft, moist flesh of his cheek—smooth as a boy's who has never needed to shave—is hard against hers. The skin of a wild fruit. Her lips are pressed against it.

And then her mouth opens, his tongue assaults the softness, and she feels the loosening of the joints. Especially in the gut, and downward, there's a fierce rushing of blood . . .

The inside of his mouth . . . amazingly, it suits her taste, and there is a sweetness to his scent, especially around the warm expanse of his throat, that tells her she is lost.

Scent is key to sexual attraction. You can't go to bed with someone whose smell repels you. Everything follows from there. Theodorakis was exactly right—the smell and flavor of an exotic, refreshing fruit, sweet but not cloying. And now this boylike man delves into her, and the scent, the taste, is right. The brain says don't give in to impulse. But her breasts are packed against his chest and he is growing larger between her legs, crushing out any air remaining between them.

She hasn't felt this urgency for anyone—not since Theodorakis. Theodorakis again. Nostalgia, not for David, with whom she's just ended a nine-year marriage, but for the ghost of a man she hasn't seen in ten—no, twelve—years.

Did David ever sense the intrusion? Somehow, this acquaintance of just a few hours does. Grasping her head by the cheekbones, Stathis demands an inspection of her eyes. He reminds her of herself looking through the camera. The object that, no matter what beneficence of light and position, eludes her capture.

"Are you sure that you want to?" he says.

He wants to be sure . . . Why does it matter to him? It's a rare man who thinks to ask what a woman wants. And even if they do wonder, she expects they'll say nothing. Maybe this one's a thoughtful lover, one who only wants a willing partner. Someone who doesn't play the ambiguities. He may have the face of a conquering Alexander but no wish to subjugate. And maybe he wants assurance that he is wanted. Maybe he is just as capable of becoming the wounded one.

"That other thing, it's over." She is amazed that she is talking about

Theodorakis. After so many years, and so simply, he has drifted back to his place in the past.

So now there are only two of them in the room. And she realizes that with David, there must have always been three. Me and my two men. The husband and the man who would not leave his wife for her when she was single.

"I can't risk my sons," the Greek had said. She respected his not being able to bear separation from his children, although she never did really understand why he couldn't be a father and have her too. What she later suspected was that, in midlife, he could not risk a known life for the new.

But risk or not, she is ready to move ahead.

"Take off your shirt," she says, stunned by her pleasure in being so direct.

Her fingers chase his as they hurry to release the tiny buttons through the slits in the stiff fabric. Now, quickly, there is only skin. Stathis, his bronze chest glistening, puts his hand on her breast. It swells. She is surprised how out of control she is. No. She is in control. She is doing what she wants.

Silently, he slips the straps off her shoulders, touches the other breast. The tip stands up, burning a little. She is reminded how the unfinished limbs of Theodorakis's earth-mother sculptures expanded, magically, roundly, under his hand.

Now she is the dead clay coming to life.

She has forgotten what it was like . . . the sensations of her own body. Will her figure be sleek enough from its once-a-week jog? Stathis has that firm flesh that, at a certain age, comes with little effort. It was once like that for her. But it doesn't seem to matter to him as he nudges his way along the crease of the breasts where they fold over chest.

He is so young, and yet it is as if there is some ancient understanding between them. Their bodies fit so well together, like molded parts of the same figure. She can't draw away. She doesn't even want to. Her mind warns that acting impulsively can so easily end in disappointment, but she is biting the rim of his ear like it's an apricot, and . . .

"I want you," she says, feeling his penis bore into her, despite the fabric that separates their lower halves.

"Did you ever notice how everything in Greece moves more slowly than in the rest of the world?" he says. "It's how we eat, it's how we move, how we—"

He tosses her onto the white bed, anchors her firmly against the coverlet, and unspools her from the crumple of the linen dress. Her panties are gone fast, it's as if they were never there. His touch is so penetrating, so lingering—it's like he's writing on her skin with a pen.

He is searing her everywhere—licking her under the armpits and behind the ears and between the deep valleys that link the toes. Even the tender skin that creases behind the bone of the knees has been found. Everywhere but that place men usually seek to go first, hardly taking the time to explore the other territories that might benefit from careful handling.

"Come inside me," she says, awed at her greed.

"There is time for everything."

The phrase "hurry up, it's time" pops into her head. Is that a line from a poem? But remembering the radio broadcaster's advice, she does not fill the silence. "There is time for everything," her new lover just said. So why not place some trust in him?

He pelts her with kisses and tiny bites, his headful of uncontrollable curls adding to the sensation with their tickle. Now it's the satin smoothness of his penis, dangling free, that writes on her. Her hand darts for it. He catches it. "Think only of yourself," he says.

And then, finally, he is between her legs. Hands or lips, after a while she doesn't know which, only that she is soaked as a squashed fruit whose skin the heat has caused to burst. The permission he has given her is freeing her to indulge in sensations in a way she has only been able to achieve alone, in her bed, with the help of an electrical appliance that she is suddenly not ashamed to admit using—not just in between the times when men wanted to have their way with her but on other occasions, when she wanted to have her own way with herself.

The double-gated lips of her lower mouth start to embrace him. And then his mouth is on her own, and she pleads, in muffled cries, that he come fully inside her. But the pulsing has already started, and she's seeing spots before her eyes, like after the camera flashes. Bright pink spots dangling in the particles of air—reflecting, she thinks, the hot spot igniting between her thighs.

Orange-red now, that round smudge of light she sometimes sees when she does this to herself, greedily orchestrating her sensations while lying on her back, her legs splayed in the position for giving birth, the light from the overhead bedroom fixture reflecting pinkish through her tightly clenched eyelids—the way the glare of the sun burns through the lids you've sealed for a bit of respite on a hot day.

And then it's the pink fire of the lower limbs she sees, fanned by that hard nub that causes her delicate membrane to pulse into a slow burning.

But there's no need for appliances now, and she thinks, how handy this man would be in a blackout. No socket, no plugs needed for this electricity.

And then she's reminded of David—how he could never do this for her. And she thinks how unfortunate it was there was only one man who could—until now.

And how, maybe, finally, she is allowing this for herself.

And then the focus of brain and body is again on the pink spot, which she sees as a projection of her own blood rushing through the purpled lips that guard the entrance to the womb, and which now, praise the lord, are screaming, for the man to enter.

And finally, he obeys.

"There's something I want to show you," Stathis tells her, after they have lain together for a long while. They pile on their clothes and enter the tight quarters of his white Volvo. For a quarter-hour they journey up along one of the steep hills edging the sea that define the island's landscape. Sometimes, while adjusting the clutch, his hand brushes her knee, causing her to feel a sting of intense pleasure. Since their route is crossed by high-pitched roads and trenched with valleys, he must make these adjustments often. She revels in such scrapes of his hand.

Another slide, this time into low land pinked with thyme and prickly with rosemary. They seesaw up again, on a path that seems somehow familiar, though many of the roads here look alike.

Terra-cotta stones keep the edges of the terraced farmlands clinging to the hillsides from tumbling over. More tall cypresses, black-blue as raven feathers.

A sheer rise of red earth.

The path here, etched in dirt, is too narrow for a car to pass through. They go on foot, tackling a series of stone steps overgrown with island herbs.

"The front road's being worked on," he says, apologizing for the unruly landscape. "I live up this way."

"Just you, and your smile?"

He seems pleased that she cares to know. "Just me, and the constellations."

"I thought Greeks married young."

"After seeing my parents, I decided not to rush."

They trudge on. And then, suddenly, she sees it—the wide white archway of the house she once thought would be her home.

The breath freezes in her jaw. An instant chill, like when you're eating ice cream and your teeth sting because it's too much cold too fast.

The sharp slap of more than déjà vu, as more evidence that she has been here before reveals itself. The singular sapphire swirls of the pool where she once clocked laps. The chipless blue glaze of Mediterranean sprawled beneath the dry crust of cliff. The broad stretch of sky framed in the white archway of the villa's showcase room.

This room just as it was, with its high white ceilings, vaulted as in the island's whitewashed churches. But the furniture is different. He used it as a studio because it got the best light, but in this incarnation it's fashionably decorated, with a low banquette of indigo, green, and yellow pillow squares neatly laid out in a row like Chiclets and white leather chairs and sofas soft as sponges. The floor is now a sea of alternating swirls of mosaic blues and yellows.

A camera crew from *Architectural Digest* could come right in and start snapping—but it all has a friendly, lived-in air.

She supposes the house must have been sold after Theodorakis's death—the only thing that could have caused him to abandon the potential of its perfect light. And for an instant, the revelation wounds. After all, he did not find it *impossible* to shed her company. But she sees her host is watching her intently.

"I used to know the man who lived here," she explains.

"Did you?"

Only for a second, she sees one last flash of Theodorakis's bearish figure up on a hammock of white canvas that billows in the breeze like a sail. "He was a very talented artist. A sculptor."

"I know," says her lover. "I am his son."

AUTHOR'S NOTE

I've always been fascinated by islands. There's nothing more seductive than a scratch of earth surrounded by sea, cut off from the mainstream, with its own distinctive personality. The right island can bring out aspects of ourselves of which we're not conscious, and, somehow, the intimacy and smallness of an island give perspective to the larger things of life.

LOVE IN THE WAX MUSEUM

By Nancy Holder

Mae West, Michael Jackson, and that new one, that country singer. Bonnie thought it very charming of her nephew, Jay, to think of taking her and Clara to the wax museum and to ask every twenty minutes or so if they were tired. Of course they were—they were old ladies—but they denied it in one voice, "No, no, not at all," on the off chance that saying so might dull his pleasure. And they were born of a generation when a man's pleasure should not, under any circumstance, be dulled.

Clara was hiding a yawn behind her fist; her gaze slid toward Bonnie and she grinned an apology. But there was amusement there too, in her eyes, so dark against her white, crepey skin. She walked with a slight hunch these days, slowing down. It seemed as if less than a year had passed since they'd first met instead of decades.

Jay's wife, Alyssa, touched Bonnie's arm and pointed at a mannequin dressed like Batman. That young man, that one with the weak chin. Bonnie nodded appreciatively as Alyssa said, "I almost got a part in the first one." Alyssa was an actress; she was beautiful, luminescent like the statues around them. As firm. Bonnie had never looked that way in her life.

When she was young, once she realized she was a lesbian, she thought she would become exotic, a brittle New York art-lesbian in a black turtleneck, chignon, and stiletto heels. Smoking and painting, a highball in one hand while her lover, in a beret, played the bongos.

Growing up on lesbian prison-warden movies, she knew she was not like *that*.

What she had failed to realize until later was that she was a small-town girl growing up in a small town, and she would grow into a small-town lesbian. She would hide herself amid church socials until she became the kind of woman who went to church socials, clucked her teeth at profanity, and bought pastel pantsuits and sensible and very ugly shoes to wear on her big trip to Los Angeles to visit her nephew.

Clara tapped her shoulder as Alyssa walked on. She whispered, "Do you think they'll be very hurt if we skip the Chamber of Horrors?"

"They've probably been here a million times. Taking all the out-of-towners." All at once she was depressed. She felt dowdy. Their neighbors back home had warned them about the superficiality of Los Angeles, but she liked it here. The sun was golden, the people clever, ambitious, and attractive. Their affectations made her envious. They opened up themselves, their lives; as they said, they "went for it." Exposing your dreams, wearing your heart on your sleeve. How could that be superficial?

Sometimes Bonnie used to imagine that she and Clara would move to the desert, two Georgia O'Keeffe's, and grow their hair long and gray and beautiful. In the twilight they would sit by the window because there would be no air conditioning, and Clara would brush her hair, and a bird would sing in the hushed, graceful silver-ending day.

In the wax museum, her group were beckoning her to move on. Clint Eastwood, Kevin Costner, that young, flat-chested actress—there were so many these days, so many, who were more boyish than any dyke of her day. Androgyny was stylish. Not so in her time. She lifted a brow at the munificent waxen breasts of Sophia Loren, Liz Taylor. They had looked great in black turtlenecks and stiletto heels.

Now the gift shop. Clara was looking for something to buy, not because she particularly wanted to. Bonnie watched as she picked up salt and pepper sets, spoon rests, scarves with the faces of movie stars printed on them. For the folks back home. To show Jay that she wanted to remember having come here. Clara was a bookkeeper and played bridge; Bonnie worked for the water district and had never gotten the hang of bidding and given up after a while because she made Clara lose. They knew people talked about them, although their public behavior never betrayed a thing.

Alyssa said brightly, "This is cute, Clara." She dangled a coffee cup from her thumb. Bonnie couldn't see it clearly from where she stood. Clara didn't like it, but she made nice noises and took it from the young woman's smooth hand. Alyssa smiled and turned away. Clara examined the cup and put it down rather absently. She looked tired.

"Are you getting hungry?" Jay asked, startling Bonnie.

"My, yes, I am." That was an answer that would bring him pleasure.

On the way home the kids—as Bonnie thought of them—couldn't bear the thought of missing one last sight for the day. They assured Bonnie and Clara that it was "on the way," but it seemed they drove and drove and drove. Bonnie had begun to doze; she jerked as Alyssa said, "Here we are!"

The Range Rover overlooked the city of Los Angeles, glassy structures like silvery mirages sparkling in the sunset. Incandescent, magical, brimming with possibility. Bonnie caught her breath and imagined herself describing this moment to the folks back home. She would not do it justice. She would use ordinary words, and they would see something ordinary. Her throat was tight with emotion. The city was so vast, filled to bursting with young dreamers.

Clara's hand brushed hers, just so; Jay had gay friends who probably held hands in public, perhaps even kissed. Wore those T-shirts with slogans and attended rallies. Still, she did not take Clara's hand, and she knew Clara did not expect her to.

Bonnie wondered if Clara felt the same regret, the same longing, for all the untapped . . . extremity they might have experienced. If she, too, felt as ridiculous as a character in an old Carol Burnett skit.

"The sun's this bright because of all the smog," Jay said. He put his hand on Bonnie's shoulder. "Kind of a downer, huh."

Bonnie smiled for him. The knowledge made no difference; it was still an exquisite sight.

"You must be worn out," Alyssa said.

"No, not really." Bonnie traded glances with Clara. They both smiled.

Dinner at Jay's pleasant stucco house was fish and new potatoes. And asparagus, always very pricey in the middle of Texas. Everything was wonderful and fresh. There was wine. When they sat down to the colorfully set table, Clara had murmured, "Oh, my," impressed in her subdued way. Bonnie was glad Alyssa wasn't some kind of health-food nut, had known when she met her that she wasn't. She was an utterly charming woman, and Jay clearly adored her. Jay worked at NBC as a cameraman. Not too glamorous, but a good union job. He was happy, and he owned his own home. He knew movie and TV stars, and tomorrow he was going to introduce her and Clara to some of them.

"Have some more wine, Aunt Bonnie." Jay filled her glass even though it was more than half full.

Clara said, "Me, too," holding hers up in a coquettish way. Women of their generation often flirted with men as a matter of course. It was a way of flattering them, smoothing their way. Their mothers taught them to do it, and how to do it; it was no trouble, and Bonnie didn't understand why the young women of today resented it. It was simply common courtesy, a social grace that cost one nothing.

Alyssa understood that; now she was bringing in a cheesecake she had bought at a bakery because it was Jay's favorite. His eyes were warm with gratitude and desire. Bonnie's gaze ticked toward Clara, whose head was bent. She had white hair now. It had been rich and brown when they had met. Bonnie felt a tinge of remorse, as if she herself should have prevented the change from happening.

Alyssa cut the cake, Jay poured Amaretto for everyone in cunning little liqueur glasses, and Bonnie realized that there was no reason for her to be unhappy, depressed, or sad, and that it was actually rather selfish of her to let herself go on like this when Jay and Alyssa were trying so hard to entertain her.

"Here's to my two aunts," Jay said warmly, raising his glass. "It's so great to have you here."

Bonnie got teary, murmured something about being so glad to be there, and meant it. She tossed off her Amaretto and poured herself another glass. Jay said, "All right, Aunt Bonnie!" and laughed. For a wild moment she thought about asking him if he had any marijuana, but it was beyond her even to joke about it.

"Oh, God, I forgot the chocolate sauce!" Alyssa said, jumping from her chair. "Jay loves chocolate sauce on his cheesecake." She hurried toward the kitchen.

"It's in the bedroom," Jay called. Clara guffawed, caught herself, saw Bonnie, and chortled as she tipped back her glass. Jay said, "Sorry," but he didn't mean it. Everyone was giddy. Outside the crickets were scraping, the city lights were sparkling, and it was wonderful to be in the superficial city of Los Angeles.

Jay showed them bloopers of some of the shows on NBC. Bonnie didn't watch much television and didn't know the actors, but their awkwardness and fluffed lines were amusing. Clara was braying like a horse, pointing and laughing, holding out her glass for more Amaretto. She was having a wonderful time, and Bonnie thought she had never loved her more than in that moment.

Then it was bedtime, and there was no fuss or confusion: Alyssa showed them to a guest bedroom dominated by a huge king-sized bed. There was a black and gray quilt on it, very modern and elegant, and at least six pillows.

"You have your own bathroom," Alyssa pointed out. There was a vase of fresh roses on the black lacquer bureau, a florist card that read "Welcome!" Tears sprang to her eyes at the thoughtfulness, the opulence. Alyssa kissed them each on the cheek and they were alone.

Clara flopped onto the bed and sighed. "I'm floating. Your nephew is wonderful. And his wife." She patted the bed and said slyly, "Turn on the radio, dear." It was their code. Even at home alone, they turned on the radio.

"I need a shower," Bonnie said.

"You don't." Clara half-turned her head and eyed her. "You smell good. Like wine."

Bonnie sat on the bed and began unbuckling her sandals. She saw the veins on the backs of her hands, her knuckles, gnarled from arthritis. She thought of Alyssa's hands, of the hands of the mannequins in the museum.

"Where are you?" Clara asked, and Bonnie jerked, realizing she had stopped taking off her sandals. She hurried with the left one and began on the right. Clara waited.

"Oh, I . . ." She shrugged. "Everyone here is so . . . nice, don't you think? Alyssa's very lovely. Pretty enough to be in that museum."

"Nice buns," Clara said, snickering at herself. They never talked like that about other women. She said, "Firm as wax."

"Yes." They should have come here, Bonnie thought fiercely. As soon as they had found each other, they should have flown here like witches on brooms, goddesses of the wind. She in her late thirties, Clara on the other side of forty—they would still have been young enough for Los Angeles. Maybe they would have become actresses or opened up an art gallery. Something fabulous would have happened to them.

Clara rolled up to a sitting position and turned the radio on. It was an easy-listening station; they were playing the theme song to a movie they had rented back home. Bonnie couldn't remember the name, but it had made them both cry romantic tears.

Then Clara reached for Bonnie and murmured, "Come here, old thing," and laid her on the bed. Bonnie began to protest; she wasn't in the mood. She was tired and she wanted a shower. No, that wasn't it. She was old and she thought she might need a shower. She couldn't imagine Clara actually desiring her. All their years of lovemaking were distant from her now, as if she had only dreamed them; as if Clara were merely a friend who had had a little too much to drink.

Clara kissed her cheek, the hollow of her eye, her forehead. She clasped Bonnie's shoulder and cupped the side of her face. Her gentleness loosened Bonnie's muscles; she was so tense. Slacken and loosen as Clara helped her undress—dowdy jacket, blouse, slacks—until she lay in Clara's arms in her underthings.

"Oh, Bon." Clara kissed her mouth. Bonnie felt her lips part; she was becoming warm and languid and easy. Everything was sliding away, rolling away, like heated wax. It was all leaving her as Clara guided and manipulated her body. Her breasts, her stomach, the cleft between her legs that Clara kneaded, shaped, reshaped.

They used to wonder what they would do if either of them decided she needed a man. A penis, to be exact. Shyly, they'd purchased what was called in those days a marital aid. Now they called it a dildo, a very ugly word. Bonnie and Clara had never had any quarrel with men; they had simply preferred women.

Now Clara's fingers were a penis that slipped into Bonnie, and her vagina became molten. Liquid and malleable, golden and good, clear wax, pearlescent, excitingly unformed. Images flashed through her mind—what could have been, what they might have been.

New York and black turtlenecks.

French lesbians.

Movie lesbians with huge breasts.

She pulled herself against Clara, whispering, "Make me into what you want," with an urgency she had never heard in her own voice before. Saying her name, "Clara Clara Clara Clara," as if she had never spoken it before. Making it become the name of a famous woman, a brittle woman, the sexiest woman in the world, Clara Bardot Clara. Bonnie's hands ran over Clara's face, cupped her breasts as Clara undressed herself with one hand while she slipped her fingers into Bonnie's vagina and caressed her labia. "Clara Clara Clara Clara."

And Clara's answer, "Bonnie," was full of desire and love and need, but questions, too. Bonnie let herself forget that she had questions; she let herself forget that she was from a small town in Texas. All she remembered was that she was in Los Angeles with the woman she loved. She rose up and over Clara, parting her legs, and kissed her there because Clara loved it so. Her love, her dear love who smelled everywhere of wine and, yes, of wax; melting beneath Bonnie's burning adoration.

In delicious amnesia, they rode together along sensations that thickened and pulsed, pulled harder, harder; Clara climaxed and Bonnie held her buttocks to make her go further. As if in shame Clara pushed at

Bonnie's shoulders; she always did. It was like a small battle that Bonnie forced her to win.

Then it was Bonnie's turn, and she shook her head and cradled herself against Clara instead, loving the urge in her body to finish it off, savoring the fact that she herself wasn't yet satisfied. Clara was panting, and that was so sexy and wonderful; and Bonnie wanted more than anything to be with her. Usually Bonnie drifted away into fantasy before she came, feeling distanced from the woman she loved. As if she were watching a movie, all alone. Preferable to coming now was staying in the moment with Clara, who didn't understand but did in bed whatever Bonnie wanted.

Bonnie's body quieted, although it did not rest. Her reality began to rush back in—her Texas dowdiness, the ordinariness of knitting and bridge and clerical tasks. The things they could have been, and had.

She lay so still that Clara whispered carefully, "Bon? You asleep?"

Tears spilled down Bonnie's cheeks; she didn't answer. Clara kissed the top of her head and settled into a more comfortable position. After a few minutes, Bonnie said, "I'm not asleep."

"Don't you want to come?"

Bonnie hesitated. "I . . . I want to do . . ." She took a breath, let it out. "I want to do something different tomorrow."

Clara cupped her breast. "Like what?"

"Not sexwise. I want . . ." She raised her eyes and Clara saw the tears. She was clearly surprised, concerned. She started to say something. Bonnie made a little moue of apology; if she didn't know better, she'd say it was her hormones. "I want . . ."

Clara regarded her. "What's wrong, Bon-bon?"

"I want to get a tattoo. Or something." Bonnie shrugged. That was all wrong. That wasn't what she wanted. Now Clara would say something like "land's sake!" and that would thoroughly depress her.

"Or something?" Clara kissed her breast. "What something?"

"I want . . ." Bonnie put her hand on Clara's neck. So many years of pillow talk. More tears spilled down her cheeks.

Clara got off the bed. "Come on." She grabbed Bonnie's hand and pulled her up. "Come on." To her feet.

Clara urged her to the door; she opened it and bounded into the hall. Looked in the direction of Jay and Alyssa's bedroom, gave Bonnie's hand a shake, and dashed toward the living room.

"Clara!" Bonnie whispered, shocked.

Clara giggled girlishly. Their feet made padding noises on the carpet as they went into the living room. Clara grabbed up the bottle of Amaretto and changed direction, toward the back yard.

She opened the screen door. They stood naked in the cooler air, both slightly out of breath, their hands clasped.

Below them, Los Angeles lights spread in all directions, a brilliant, vast wonderland. Cars crowded the freeway lanes, speeding; the moon was one more energetic current that glowed and charged and recharged the landscape with its potential.

Crickets chirped above the susurration of the traffic. An owl hooted.

In the moonlight, Clara was a glowing, pale figure, a perfect being of indescribable beauty. Her drooping tummy and breasts, her pudgy thighs, amazingly wonderful. She was the patron goddess of Los Angeles.

Clara took a swig of Amaretto and handed the bottle to Bonnie. She said, "We'll go in their Jacuzzi," and pointed to the wooden structure surrounding it, on a small slab of concrete to the left of the house beside a row of oleanders.

"Now?"

Clara let go of her hand and found the controls. Red lights glowed beneath the surface; soon the water bubbled and roiled. Clara climbed the two steps to the top of the structure and stepped in. She sat down and sighed delightedly. "Oh, you'll just melt," she said.

Bonnie followed. She put one foot in, the other. What would they do if Jay appeared?

Clara reached for her, rosy and wrinkled and from a small town in Texas. Bonnie went to her: two buck-naked old ladies—broads!—in the hot tub, sharing a bottle of booze.

"Is this something different?" Clara's hands were everywhere, her mouth, everywhere; Bonnie got excited but found herself right beside Clara, with Clara, not leaving; the place beside Clara, in Clara were the most glamorous, dreamlike places, magical places Clara had never taken her before. Where old lovers know, and understand, and perhaps don't even realize they do, which makes it all the more fraught with chances for another visit, and another, and a lifetime of them: Potential. Extremity.

Seized opportunity.

If Jay showed up, they'd all just laugh.

"Yes," Bonnie whispered gratefully as her vagina gathered and pulsed and began to contract.

"I'm glad, hon. It was such a long day."

That wasn't it. Or maybe it was. Bonnie kissed Clara, their lips melting together as they swirled and flew among the lights and dreams of Los Angeles, their kisses like reflections in the hot, flowing pool of waxy, clear love, of Texas and bridge, of *them*.

AUTHOR'S NOTE

To Dixie Barnum-Scrivener and Alan Scrivener, who took me to the wax museum. And to Claudia O'Keefe, who gave me the directions.

AUTHOR'S NOTE

Being a native Californian, I'm one of those people who loves L.A. and all the strange and semireal dreams that are spun there. It is my own dream that my desire for sensual and erotic pleasures, like Bonnie and Clara's, will last my lifetime.

YARN

By Jenny Diski

For the purposes of the story, I never had a name. I was always just the daughter of a miller, and then later the Queen—meaning Mrs. King. But us millers' daughters have names, like everyone else, though the archetype makers would have you think different, even in a story such as this, where naming names is the name of the game.

Well, I bloodywell had a name and have one still—excuse the language, not suited to a Queen, I know, but, once a miller's daughter, always a fucking miller's daughter, I say. My name, I can reveal, was, and still is, Claraminda Griselda. The first confabulation of a name being an indication of the florid hopes my father had for his own flesh and blood to raise him up above his natural station in life (a hope rather surprisingly granted, now that he's been elevated, as the father of a Queen must be, to an earldom); the second name my father once heard in a tale told in the local inn by some accountant fellow called Chaser, or Chooser, or Chancer, or something, who fancied himself as more than just an ordinary customs and excise man. My father, the recently elevated earl, told me he had liked the sound of Griselda, and that the story the tax man told had held out great promise for the bearer of that name, who, though she had her troubles, came out well settled in the end.

However, not wishing to antagonize the rest of the village children (my father already having alienated us from our neighbors, on account of his comical fantasies and highfalutin ways), I called myself the rather simpler Clary, and even now, though the King has all the pretensions of a miller and insists on having my full name on documents of state, I think of myself as plain Queen Clary.

I spent my childhood in a miasma of flour dust; no matter how my mother wiped and washed while she lived, it was always possible to write my name with my finger in the film on every surface. Naturally or, rather, unnaturally, my father insisted I go to the village school to learn to read. So while most of my contemporaries were productive elements of their household—carrying water, carding wool, pumping bellows—I sat in school, alone except for the children of better families than ours, who would not talk to a mere miller's daughter, learning my letters, and what to do with them. I could not see what such an excess of learning achieved, apart from being able to write my name on stools and tables and windowsills.

Of course, the price of his flour reflected the extraordinary expense my father had in the raising of a mere daughter, so we weren't very popular on that account, either. There were plenty of people who passed through our village with tales of the price of a sack of flour just a few miles away. I say a few miles, but each one of them might have been a continent for most of the villagers, with their broken-down nags and rickety carts, and then only if fortune had smiled on them and the brigands kept away. It goes to show—me saying *a few* miles—the way you get used to a new station in life. What would a dozen miles be to me, with all the resources of the stables and a choice of exquisitely crafted carriages at my disposal? If I ever used them, that is. As for brigands: I should be so lucky.

So I grew up in a flour-pale house where even our eyelashes were dusted with pulverized wheat and rye, and learned, in readiness for the future in my pompous father's head, to read. Even now, in my mind's ear, I can hear his bellowing baritone carrying through the air from the mill next door to our cottage.

I care for nobody
No, not I
And nobody cares for me.

They were the truest words that ever came from a man's lips.

So we weren't a very popular little family, and I spent a good deal of time on my own. Often, I'd sit in a corner watching my father at work. Not from any admiration of him, but with fascination at the process he carried out. The two great granite grinding stones were turned by two pairs of donkeys at opposite sides of the stones, going 'round and 'round very slowly as if once they had tried to catch each other up but had finally tired out and, realizing they never would manage it, had slowed forever down to a dull and hopeless plod. Actually, there was a series of donkeys—they didn't last long, my father being mean with feed and generous with their work hours. I never cared for them much, they seemed so depressed. What interested me was the process they set and kept in action.

My father tipped grain into the hopper and it trickled down, like the sand in the hourglass in my husband, the King's, countinghouse, between the great stones that turned, thanks to the will-less motion of the donkeys, and crushed the grain into a gritty powder. I think it was the relentlessness of the process that fascinated me. 'Round and 'round, and on and on. Grain in at the top, flour out at the bottom. An endless process for the endless need of the village for bread. Those grinding stones were at the secret heart of all our lives. Whether they liked it or not, the villagers had need of my father and his mill. No one could manage without bread, and those who had fallen on bad times were obliged to go cap in hand to my father and ask for time to pay for the sacks of flour they could not do without.

He always obliged, but not very obligingly. There are two ways of having people in your debt. You can make it easy, taking the long view that everyone has periods of difficulty but also other times that are not so hard, and treat your creditors as if they were yourself at a different stage of fortune, so that people know when better times come they can take an extra chicken or whatever and the debtor will rejoice with them in their improved fortune. And there is the other way—my father's way. Everyone in the village owed him at one time or another, and he never let them forget it. He would mark the names of those who couldn't pay him on a slate with exaggerated care, listening with relish to the screech it made. Other people's hard luck made him feel richer, not just in what they owed him but in some more mysterious way, as if every degree by which someone else was down pushed him up in his own esteem. "They can't do without me," he would say, booming with self-satisfaction. Then he'd burst into the old chorus

I care for nobody
No, not I
And nobody cares for me.

It was a song of triumph. And although the last line was as true as true could be, it didn't worry him. It made him feel bigger and more important in some twisted way to know that nobody, including his daughter, *did* care for him.

I never had much time for my father, and my mother for the handful of years I knew her was too preoccupied with drudgery and not getting on the wrong side of him to make much impact on me beyond pity for her lot. She died very quietly, apparently of nothing more than lack of will to live. She faded away, as if each day proved that there was little and increasingly less to live for.

So I was a solitary child. I watched the stones grinding and listened to the rhythm they made as the slight hollows and bumps in the granite altered the pitch. *Strraagga graast, scrummm, scrummm. Straagga grasst, scrummm scrummm.* It inhabited my dreams, that beat, becoming as much a part of me as my own heart's rhythm. And I was content in spite of my loveless surroundings. Somehow, the perpetual circling of the stones seemed to me very like the shape and movement of the world itself. The village, bread, work, children seemed to have a pattern I knew, for all the ups and downs of fortune, to be a good solid pattern. I felt a rightness about how things were, about all the circles that were drawn by each family and each village with the millstones grinding out the rhythm of being alive. And my father, for all his foolish pomposity and grandiose notions, could not help but provide the certainty as he ground the grain around which life made its circles.

Only once, while I was growing up, did the circle pattern fail. A blight on the crops, who knew why, one year, and for a while the grinding stones were silenced. There was no grain to mill, and it was as if my own heart had halted, the silence was so ominous. It was, that time, a localized problem, however, and soon enough grain was brought in from the outside world, and the stones began their *strraagga graast, scrummm scrummm* once again. It was a warning to me, though. That pattern, so close to life itself, was not immutable. The vital circles could be halted. It was a useful lesson to learn.

Of course, the King was nowhere to be seen during that time of hardship. It was not his way to go abroad among his people unless he was certain of their loyalty and affection. And no one in the village doubted that the King had enough grain stored away to get him through difficult times. However, once the millstones were doing their work, he passed through our village in a grand, triumphant ride, as if the return of the stuff of life was his doing. People lifted their heads as he passed, magnificent on his great white horse, weighted down with plumes and tapestries. They bobbed a curtsy or a brief bow, while he nodded graciously at them. No one took much notice. The King was not part of village life, except inasmuch as he taxed and tithed us. No one hated him, he was too remote, too irrelevant for that. They simply saw him as a fabulous creature passing through their byways.

Except my father, of course. He bowed and scraped so much that the King thought him his finest subject and actually dismounted and demanded to be taken on a tour of his miller's mill. Oh, my father obliged, with such obsequiousness that I thought I might vomit. I suppose the honor was too much for his miserable mind. At any rate, that is some kind of explanation for what happened next. My father entirely lost his head, faced with the condescending attention of his liege lord. It was never entirely true that he cared for *nobody*. For the rich and powerful he cared, it seemed, beyond his own sanity and both our well-being.

My father called me to him, hissing out of the corner of his mouth while blathering to His Majesty, who was about to remount and go on his way, back to the relative warmth and comfort of his castle.

"Sire! Sire!," he said, bowing and scraping, while from the other side of his smiling face he summoned me. "Where are you, girl? Come here! Come *here!*"

"Sire, may I introduce you . . . she's just coming . . . here in a moment . . . to, yes, here she is" ("Straighten your dress, girl!") ". . . my daughter, Your Majesty. My daughter, Claraminda Griselda."

My father held me in front of him by my shoulders, his fingers digging into my flesh in his excitement. The King looked at me and smiled a vague, royal smile. Frankly, I wasn't the prettiest girl a King had ever laid eyes on. Not *ugly*, you understand, but nothing really special. He was again about to turn and go when my agitated father, seeing no light in His Majesty's eyes, let out a strangulated sound, a screech not unlike the sound of a creditor's name being marked on the slate.

"Your *Majesty*!"

The King turned at the urgency of his cry. My father now had to think up the rest of the sentence. But thinking isn't a good description of what he did.

"Your Majesty, this is no ordinary girl. No mere miller's daughter, Sire. No, she is a remarkable child. Not just dutiful and clever, though she is that, of course, but something more, much, much more."

We all waited to see how my father would complete his babblings. I supposed madness mixed with insatiable greed came to the rescue.

"This child, this young woman, Your Majesty . . . has an extraordinary gift . . . given to no one else. You see, Sire, she can . . . she has the ability . . . gained from God himself, it must have been . . . she can . . . spin . . . straw into gold."

There was an astonished silence while my father stared at the King, his eyes bugging almost out of his head as he himself heard the preposterous thing he had said. Everyone else looked at him; the King, myself, the whole retinue. I thought for a moment that the King was going to have my father arrested for ridiculousness, but when I dragged my eyes away from my demented creator and took in His Majesty, I saw his expression change from disbelief at what he was hearing to something very like my father's when someone came to him to put themselves deeply in his debt. I saw the King's eyes glaze over with lust at the idea of monstrous wealth and power.

"Your Majesty," I said, trying to think of something to excuse my father and prevent him from being thrown into the country's deepest, blackest dungeon for the rest of his life. I did not love my father, but still I felt that the blood between us was enough to want to try and salvage his life.

"Be quiet, girl!" my father shouted, though he needn't have bothered; I couldn't think of a thing to say that might mitigate the nonsense he had spoken.

His Majesty turned his head to me, and the former complete lack of interest in the plain miller's daughter was transformed, as if my fairy godmother had waved a wand and made me the most exquisite maiden in the land. I immediately understood my position, and a shiver of despair ran through me. I was locked between the gaze of two avaricious men, both of whom saw me as the means vastly to improve his own standing. What hope had I, imprisoned between the hungry stares of father and King? It was as if a sentence of death had already been pronounced on me, before His Majesty ever said a word.

"Is that so, Miller?" the King finally said, never taking his eyes off me for a second. "Straw into gold, you say?"

A look of fear crossed my father's face, as for the first time he realized what would happen to him (never mind me, of course) when his ludicrous boast was proved to be a lie.

"Your Maj—" he began, but what could he say to retrieve the situation? The words had flown from his mouth and nothing would make them unsaid.

Funnily enough, the King did not think to ask me about my unusual skill. Nobody thought to say anything to me at all. You could see the King wavering between his eagerness for such a thing to be true, because if so, he would be the beneficiary of a treasure beyond the dreams even of Kings, and the thought that he was being made a fool of. There was nothing he liked less than people trying to make a fool of him; just the idea put him into an executionary frame of mind. You could see him weighing up the benefits and the risks of believing my father. You might say that my father's story was so preposterous that no one could give a second's credence to what he said. But that would be to underestimate the power of greed. Our future, my father's and mine, hung in the balance, as the seconds passed. Our very lives depended on the King being as avid a greedy fool as my father. It was all we could hope for.

The King stared dangerously at my father when he spoke again.

"Well, let us see, Miller, what wonders this daughter of yours can perform. I will take her to my castle, and if she can indeed turn straw into gold, then I will marry her. If not, the pair of you will die so that the world can see I am not a monarch to be fooled with."

Now, it has probably crossed your mind that it's a damn strange thing for a girl to become a wife purely on the grounds of being able to spin straw into gold. She could become your bank, yes, but why a wife? Of course, it has to do with the needs of the structure within which we were all of us imprisoned—the story. That's how it goes in this corner of the narrative world; the prize for doing the impossible is to become the wife of a King. Nothing to be done about that. Not even the fact that I cherished the idea of this particular King for my husband as much as I cherished the idea of my father being my father. But we have no choice, characters such as us. Nor could I, given my lack of regard for His Majesty, decide to sit in his palace and flatly refuse to change his straw into gold (if I could have done so, which obviously common sense would tell you I couldn't), preferring to die than live out a miserable life as Queen. Like the circular life of the village, I was caught up in a pattern, though this pattern was a great deal less to my liking than the everyday life of the world I inhabited.

My father threw a desperate look at me as I rode away, perched on the back of some flunky's horse, as if begging me not to let him down now that his life depended on me. Brilliant! All I had to do to keep us both alive was spin straw into gold. Why hadn't he made up something *really* difficult for me to accomplish? In fact, it seemed to me that straw into gold might be relatively easy; all I'd have to do was join the ranks of magicians and alchemists and tinker with potions of this and that, and perhaps, given a lifetime of esoteric study and all the luck in this world and the next, come up with the philosopher's stone to realize my father's boast and achieve the King's dreams. The real problem facing me, however, was a great deal more fundamental: I didn't know one end of a spinning wheel from another. I'd been far too busy being prepared at school for my social climbing to learn anything useful like how to spin. I was, quite frankly, absolutely useless with my hands.

I was installed in an out-of-the-way room in the castle. Up everlasting winding stairs, to a room at the top of a turret. Since it was circular, it had commanding views of the whole area. I suppose looking down on the world I had previously been a part of was what my father had intended for me, but, quite honestly, I had other things on my mind than the view.

Half the room, a semicircle as it were, was filled with a great mound of straw; the other half was empty except for a spinning wheel, and me standing staring at it. The deal was, I spin all the straw into gold by morning, or else. Some deal. Also, I knew my way around stories of this kind, being of them as well as in them. I knew as well as anyone about the rule of three. Once never does in this kind of tale, and I was certain that I'd have to perform my miracle times three. Frankly, it didn't matter this time, since I couldn't do what I had to do, anyway. But in general, it's a most dispiriting law. Knowing you have to do everything three times takes the sense of achievement away before you've even started. One might be thrilled to have done something brave or clever or impossible the first time, but knowing you have to do it twice more takes immediate gratification away. Even having three wishes loses its charm. You can be sure you'll get one of them wrong and lose the benefit of the other two.

However, that was all rather theoretical as I stood in the turret room, staring at the spinning wheel and not having the faintest idea how it worked. I grant you, it was an interesting piece of psychology, worrying about not knowing how the spinning wheel worked, as though if I'd known everything would be all right. But if you're going to die, you have to pinpoint a single, simple reason. The fact that I didn't know how to turn straw into gold seemed an absurd reason for dying, so I transferred it all on to the spinning wheel. It seemed more acceptable somehow to die because I didn't know how to do the simplest, rather than the most difficult, thing.

The question I held in my mind was: Did I really mind about dying and leaving a world where fathers and kings (and, it ought to be said, ineffectual mothers) caused one to be in such a predicament? Put that way, my fate seemed less unacceptable. Still, I was young, barely fourteen, and I had not used up all my optimism about what might lie ahead for me. So, quite honestly, I was not entirely reconciled to my forthcoming fate.

I perched on the wooden stool attached to the spinning wheel and identified a sticking-up thing in front of me as a spindle. That's education for you. What I was supposed to do with it, I had no idea, but I knew it by name. I pushed the wheel around listlessly, listening to its wobble and creak with growing interest. It had in some way a relationship to the pattern of sound made by my father's grinding stones. Not surprising, really, both being circular and designed to go 'round and 'round. The rhythm was a comfort to me. By morning, and the end of my life, I thought, I'd be quite consoled.

I can't say how long I'd been doing that when I heard a gratingly high-pitched voice coming from behind me.

"Quite a pickle you're in, isn't it?"

And there, of course, was a skinny little man with a most unpleasant leer on his wrinkled, disagreeable face. Well, I don't need to tell you that he said he could help me, but there would be a price. My ring, I said. All right, he said. And he set to work.

But knowledge is a terrible thing. How could I be delighted with my magical escape when I knew that tomorrow the same scenario would occur, and that the night after that I would have run out of ornaments to barter with? Yes, yes, I thought, so the room is filled with gold where there had been straw, but was I really any better off? At best I would become the Queen of this King, and what kind of compensation would that be for my suffering and anxiety? Riches, power, even, if I played my cards right. Nice frocks and servants to take care of them, but I had an intuition that all those things would pall before long, and when they did I would *still* be married to a pig of a man whom I disliked almost as much as my father.

On the third night, in the unwavering way these stories have, I'd promised the firstborn of my marriage. Things will sort themselves out, I thought, in the way things do. And I concluded it was, on balance, better to be alive than dead. More opportunity.

And then the marriage, the wedding, the raising of my father to his earldom, the wedding night. Each of those events, and in particular the latter, filled me with disgust. Best leave it at that. Suffice it to say that kings do not necessarily carry their royalty into the bedroom. Once the fur and finery were off I might as well have been at it with the local shepherd boy. As a matter of fact, having been at it with the local shepherd boy for several months before my new life began, I can tell you I missed him that night—and for a good few thereafter.

That shepherd boy was no slouch in the carnal knowledge and skills of love department, and he taught me a thing or two, but His Majesty had such a depressing effect on me I could not bring myself to practice any of the interesting tricks I had learned. Eventually, my Lord and Master tired of plowing into me while I lay there limp, with nothing more than my fists clenched, and went on to entertain himself with some of the likelier lasses from the village (all of whom, it must be said, had also learned everything they knew from that delightful young shepherd—how he had learned these things, I wouldn't like to say, but I wager the sheep could tell a tale or two if they had the power of speech).

Nine months later, as sure as fairy tales are fairy tales, I gave birth to a young son and heir to the throne. Huge celebrations, and the return of the wizened little man. Now, I wasn't all that attached to my offspring. Frankly, I would have given him away—I hardly ever saw him in any case, he was nannied and wet-nursed and kept in isolated splendor in the nursery wing of the castle. But I didn't fancy explaining to the King that I'd swapped his son for a load of old hay, even though he would have had only his own greed to blame for it.

"Very well, then," said the little old man, predictably. "I will give you a chance. If you can guess my name within three . . ."

"Oh, please," I interrupted. "Don't you get tired of this nonsense? Guess my name. Three days. And what would you want with a baby, anyway? Listen, I have an alternative suggestion."

He was not pleased to have been stopped in mid-cliché. He stood staring at me open-mouthed and was, I'm sure, about to ignore what I said altogether and simply carry on with his preprogrammed deal. I daresay he was unable to consider even the possibility of an alternative. I carried on before he could.

"I've got a better idea. More interesting for both of us. Why don't you give me three days to make *you* forget your name?"

He was flabbergasted, and screwed up his face in confusion, trying to think out this new angle on an old story.

"But . . ." he sputtered eventually. "That's not the way it's done. You have to discover my name. You've got to find it out. Names. It's about names."

"But actually it's not very interesting, is it? All that happens is that I send out my servants who creep about and listen in doorways, and eventually—though granted at the last minute—you can be sure one of them will come across you in a wood cackling your name to yourself in premature self-congratulation, and the game will be up. What's clever or amusing about that? A rich and powerful woman uses her servants to find something out. Big deal. Now, what I'm suggesting is another thing altogether. Think of how difficult it is to make a person forget his name. Especially someone with as rare and interesting a name as I'm sure yours must be."

Still bemused, he scratched his head.

"How would you do that?"

I smiled at him.

I'd better explain something about myself. Just as I wasn't your archetypal beauty of a miller's daughter, I also did not have the same hankerings after pretty golden princes as my peers were universally supposed to have. Don't ask me why. A matter of personal taste. The King, as handsome as a former fairy tale prince must be once he's stopped being a frog, left me cold. I had always been attracted to—how can I put it?—the unusual. The shepherd boy was no one's idea of an Adonis; he suffered badly from the aftereffects of chicken pox and had a body that at best could be called weedy. But once he did the things he did, I came to love each and every crater on his pallid cheeks and lay in my bed at night entertaining myself with visions of his skinny thighs and unmanly, thin, rounded shoulders. It's fascinating how human desire can find all manner of things exciting once it's been given a push in the right direction. Beauty, muscularity, height, and thick manes of hair didn't do a thing for me. There it was. Apart from the pockmarked shepherd, I had had another regular liaison with the girl at the dairy—a blowsy, bulbous, ruddy-cheeked creature, bovine like her charges but as lusty and lewd as any you might hope to meet in a cowshed while collecting the milk in the early dawn. I did not know what to call what the two of us did in the hay together every morning, but I enjoyed it no end, and our frolics added nicely to the detail I was accumulating with my shepherd lad. My tastes were, therefore, catholic, and desire was to me to be found where it may. I did not dismiss the possibility of lascivious, unlawfully wedded bliss with someone simply because they did not conform to the current form of beauty dictated by our fairy tale existence.

The little man, as stringy as a newborn foal and half my height, with a face so wrinkled that his wrinkles had wrinkles, intrigued me. All that nervous energy, hopping about from one foot to another, his wide, thin lips all aquiver, and violent, cornflower-blue, stark-staring eyes. Everybody has something about them that can be found attractive.

"Come here," I said. "I've got something to show you."

For the statutory three nights he came to my queenly bedroom, and I did indeed show him such things as he'd never even dreamed about. Each morning, at dawn, he'd stagger from my royal room, moaning and murmuring things to himself as if he were trying to lodge impossible truths in his brain. I used and passed on everything I'd learned during my glorious times with the shepherd and the dairymaid, and the scrawny, twisted little man trembled and mewed, night after long, slow night, with the results of my expertise. Each morning, as he limped, his muscles wrenched and ragged, away from my bed, I stopped him and asked him: "Little man, what is your name?"

On the first morning he stopped his muttering and turned achingly toward me on the bed with a wild look in his eye. After a moment of enormous effort, he managed to raise his voice enough so that I could hear what he said.

"My name . . ." he croaked. "My name is . . . Rumpelstilts—"

And then his eyes went vague as something disappeared into the mist that was his mind. I smiled and said how much I was looking forward to the coming night.

On the second morning, I asked him the same question as he was leaving. Again, he turned, but this time it took much longer to bring the words out into the world.

"My name . . . my name . . . is . . . my name is . . . Rumple—"

And he fell silent. I bid him a warm good-day.

On the third morning, he was barely able to reach the door, his thin little legs were shaking so much. Great sighs came from him as each foot touched the floor and sent a shuddering memory of bliss and agony shooting through him.

"Little man, what is your name?" I asked him gently.

A strange, almost strangulated sound came from his depths and stuck fast in his throat. His mouth worked and his eyes rolled while he quivered from head to foot, as if every ounce of himself were involved in the effort to think what I could possibly mean by my words. But nothing came.

"What is your name?" I said again.

But the little man had given up, and merely shook his head in wonder and confusion as he disappeared from my room, like a shadow slipping beneath a door.

And so my life is just as my father had dreamed. I am a rich and powerful woman. The Queen of all and everything. I am respected, even revered for my wisdom and carefully considered decisions. The King, these days, is too busy to attend to matters of state, so I make sure that everything runs well and for the benefit of all the people. My father, the *arriviste* Earl, assists the King in his neverending task, so he also doesn't have much time to visit his royal daughter or attend to the mill, and I have placed it in the safe and talented hands of the shepherd boy, who says it makes a nice change from tending sheep. In order to maintain this satisfactory state of affairs, I arrange for the turret room with the spinning wheel (I still have not learned how to use it—just as well, considering the risk and result of pricking one's finger on the spindle, in a world such as ours) to be filled every day with straw-spun gold.

So the King is in his countinghouse most of the time, these days, along with my father, counting out his money. There's so much to count, I'm afraid they will never get to the end of it. And while they are thus engaged, I run the country, dispensing just law and keeping the millstones grinding and all the necessary circles turning. And for entertainment? For entertainment, I have my milk delivered fresh to the castle every morning, and at night I summon my little man from his day's spinning, and, over and over again, make him forget his name.

AUTHOR'S NOTE

This is a story about circles and cycles, with a raging perversity at the center.

A DISH FOR THE GODS

By Kay Kemp

My mother went to graduate school in English and became a feminist at an awkward time for me. I was sixteen and falling in love regularly. She went to seminars, fell in thrall to the feminist critics, and came home boiling with rage: "Look at the way all the poets made women into comestibles! Who needs this 'dish for the gods'? There's no end to it: Her *milk-white* skin, her *cherry* lips, her *tender* flesh. We're positively masticated by these guys—look at this one, 'Spearmint Girl with the Wrigley Eyes.' Huh! Eat or be eaten, I say."

She cooked well but it was never easy. Her lips did not drop as honeycomb, nor was her mouth as smooth as oil as she stood over the stove counting the seconds to stir the chocolate sauce. She cursed the pastry when it stuck to the rolling pin. Nothing came naturally: She measured everything, she never guessed, she never tasted, she never experimented. And always she fulminated over her labors, savagely gnawing on her lower lip, her eyes dark with resentment.

Her bravura collapsed, however, when she served my father. The roast beef may have been the same tawny red, like a pair of penny loafers, but sometimes he waved it away.

"How many times have I told you, a flat platter, please! I can't carve on a platter that's concave!!"

We didn't eat potatoes because my father thought they were pig food, but there were always three vegetables—broccoli, carrots or cauliflower, and a salad composed of a few leaves of lettuce, transparent slices of radish, and two strips of purple cabbage, maybe, in fluted wooden bowls bought on a trip to Hawaii. Dessert was heated chocolate sauce over ice cream or nonexistent.

If my mother pulled this off without spilling on a burner or smoking up the oven or scorching one of her stainless steel pans, she was relieved. They both hated cooking smells. She sat down to eat, but her face stayed in knots of tension as she chewed.

I had probably just come in from necking to the breaking point in the front seat of the car, pants down, bra unhooked, my boyfriend poised over me, his cock buried in my belly, him dripping, me dripping, gasping, "We can't, we can't!" No doubt I'd ridden home in the car with my face in his lap. I'd watch my mother and father eating and try to imagine them making love.

How trying it must have been for them both! I couldn't see my mother enjoying all that finger dipping and licking, the yeasty smells, the smoke, the heat. And you never knew how it was going to turn out! As for my father, if it wasn't served up flat he'd get mad. It must have been no fun, no fun at all.

As it happened I married a nudist. Not a card-carrying member, just a man who likes to walk around the house with his clothes off. He's been known to go out and fetch the paper off the front porch that way, which was a problem when we lived in the city. Now we have no near neighbors: We moved up to our cottage, where I grow strawberries.

The strawberries are finished; it's August now. My husband drives up from the city Friday night. He likes to shop at the market first thing that morning. In his business suit he runs from farmer's stand to farmer's stand, hearing them boast, watching them fondle their produce. Then he puts all the food he buys in bags in his car and goes to work for half a day (he's in hospitality). At three, he jumps in the car full of warm eggplant, softening Brie, baguettes, and new potatoes.

When I meet him at the marina the food is at the critical stage. We drive the boat full throttle to the cottage and rush up the dock with the lettuce, the green, red, and yellow peppers, the croissants in their buttered bag, whiskered corn on the cob, first apples so hard they explode at your bite, the trembling beige eggs. We stash it all in the cooler, the fridge, and the baskets that we hang on pulleys from the ceiling so the mice won't get them.

Then we pour ourselves drinks and sit in the declining sun on the screened-in porch. Last night I made guacamole with an avocado that had survived the week. We sipped and we dipped our tortilla chips in the soft green mash. I never eat like this when he's not here. Food tastes better when I look at this man. My husband is big and there's nothing faint about his intake.

We ran our fingers around the rim of the bowl and sucked them.

He pretended innocence as I took him by the hand and led him into the little bedroom we have up here, which is only large enough for the bed and a few hooks for clothes on the walls. We have to fall over forward to get onto the bed. There was a wind blowing and the faded chintz curtains flew over us like a shower of petals.

We started kissing hungrily, as we always do. It's a long week when he's gone. His mouth is wide and he sucks as if he could take me all in. Then I get on top of him and gather his lips in mine. I love the way they crush up against his teeth, the wet of his mouth that seems to run from them. He bought those concord grapes today, the ones that are meant for making wine. His concord lips are velvety, crushable, slightly sour, and stain purple the harder you press.

While we're kissing we're wriggling to get as close as we can on that large, soft old bed, and out of the angle of that last searching beam of the sun, which pierces the western window. He hitches me up against him, and I run my hands over his back, his neck, his head, down the back of his thighs. I get my hands on his belt as soon as I can without seeming greedy. I just love to undo it and get my hand inside his pants.

By this time—and it has taken some time—we've rolled around enough so that he's erect, all tangled in there in the opening of his shorts, and my hand goes in and there is this great, warm, bristling, satiny root vegetable that pulsates in my palm. Perhaps it is a yam, one of those long ones with hair and eyes, a vegetable so rich I want to taste it, so febrile I want to cool it. I have a whole lot of places where I want to take it in, but that's for later.

I run my hand down its length to feel, at the place it springs from, the hard, sour plums in their furry sac. I hardly touch them at all—when they're cool like this it's best not to. Later they'll be hot and soft.

I actually enjoy the awkward business of pulling our wrappers off. Now we can see what we've bought, taking away the sticky plastic, the manmade markings, and finally bringing it into the light of our own home, getting our hands on it. Sometimes we don't quite remove the last tie but are so tempted we begin before we're bare.

Shirts we push up. Pants we untangle from ankles. I can separate my legs now and I'm kneeling over him while I undo my bra and let my apples spill over his face. They're Empress, the best for eating raw, rose on the outside, very white flesh. He goes for them, takes in as much as he can in his mouth. His lips go as black as eggplant meanwhile, his neck flushes, and his hands become white and his cock goes purple with blood. Under his skin, you can see all the juices begin to run.

He can take nearly a whole apple in his mouth, and does, and pretends to bite, but doesn't, then lets the full part slip out and nibbles daintily on the nipple. He bobs for a while, catching one and letting it go. We play that game. I'm the water, too, moving up and down, teasing his teeth. He's trying to sink his teeth in, get a purchase on me. Meanwhile I can feel that root vegetable test and try my thighs and my belly.

When I can't stop myself any longer I roll off him, turn, and take the yam between my two hands, rolling it slowly and bringing the tip up to my lips. He is over me now, and he has his hands on my pelvis bones. My belly goes concave as he presses those two horns, handles, really, and lifts my hips like a two-handed cup from which he can drink the sweet, warm, white milk of my pelvis.

But he doesn't drink, not yet. His lips graze the inside of my thighs, those straight white stalks, he takes a nip here and here and here, moving up, yes, it is like eating a cob of corn. So hungry now I can't stop, I take him between my lips and make circles with my tongue. I dip him in and out gently until he responds and moves a little more, and I know he's too distracted for more corn.

My thirst is overwhelming, and now I'm drinking his wine, and finally he too finds the narrow mouth of the cup buried in the folds of linen. All the fine food in the world is lost without wine.

We're calmer when we turn again to face each other, and we take a little time to look at the feast we have. The sun is sinking fast beyond the window, and before it goes it gives a boost of pink to our cheeks, our bruised lips.

The finest meal is nothing without music. Now I am wearing him across my front, like a cello between my legs, off at an angle over my shoulder. But this cello is reversed, its strings are toward me, they run through me, from crease to clavicle. I have my arms around the neck of the instrument, I let my hands play over the white swell of his hips. He moves up and down, sideways. The sounds that begin to flow are not mine or his but both of ours.

I lie here on my back and hold the white back of this man and follow with my body the undulations he makes. I find the crease between his white loaves of bread, I even find those plums I saved before, which are different now, they're soft, they slide inside their sac and they are warm as life. I run my hands from the back of his neck—his face is buried somewhere over there in the pillow—along his spine, and down his legs. I feel the pressing within and my mouth yearns for one more thing to take in. I fasten on his shoulder, mouth the flesh there, feel the muscles working under the skin.

You are my nourishment, my food, I tell him.

And then it's over. The stained remnants of our feast are cast with abandon across the bed. The silence of fulfillment is soft as twilight.

Already I'm thinking about what we'll have for dinner. Before long he'll get up naked and light the gas barbecue, standing on the front porch where the whole bay could see, if it had eyes. It will be dark by the time we dine on his market offerings. The end of the meal will be my strawberries, so small and ripe and sweet they run without sugar.

AUTHOR'S NOTE

Of the two lusts, desire is more elusive than hunger. Too frequently these days we hear about those arid phases of our lives when we are dead to sexual desire, when we must seek out the bizarre and the dangerous in order to reawaken a longing, which, in truth, has always been there. I wanted to write about the sort of desire that is kindled as easily and as naturally as the passion for delicious food. "Mouth-watering" is the word that comes to mind, the one I wish to attach to this story.

LAST TANGO IN GENEVA

By Jacqueline Ariail

It was 1973. Geneva. Our honeymoon—though neither of us was so sentimental as to call it that. A working honeymoon, at least for Barry. He had a conference in Naples; in Geneva, there was an Institute to visit. Capelle, it was called. A few cities we threw in for pleasure: Florence before Geneva; Paris, after. But it's Geneva I remember best.

We stayed in a guest house in the Commune de Carouge, a suburb on a hill outside the city. We had a private bedroom; we shared a kitchen and bath with another guest. The ferocious Madame Vicquerat was our *propriétaire*: a petite woman, with perfectly coiffed black hair. She wore old-lady flowered dresses and a demure half-apron, though she was not old. She was brusque in her dealings with us, nearly inhospitable, and Barry and I wondered aloud together why she bothered to take in boarders, except, of course, for the money.

She kept the place immaculate, and at every turn there were signs, penned by Madame. In the kitchen, above the counter, hung two hooks, and above each hook hung a small hand-lettered sign: *essuie-mains*, hand towel; *torchon*, dish towel. In the bathroom, over the john: *Prière de tirer la chasse d'eau*, please flush. Above the light switch in our room: *Prière d'éteindre les lumières*, please put out the lights. And in every room, including the large upstairs hall, onto which the guest rooms opened, *Défense de fumer*.

Our room was at the back of the house; it had a French door onto a tiny balcony that overlooked the garden. Our fellow boarder—a red-haired man, an American—had the room across the hall from ours. I watched him on the afternoon we arrived from behind the lace that covered the French door. I was putting our things away—Barry had gone out for a few groceries—when I heard some commotion outside. Opening the door a little, I saw the boarder emerge from the woods and enter the gate of Madame Vicquerat's garden. He had a red beard as well, a close-trimmed one. It was Madame who was shouting, as he walked toward the house, and it took me a minute to understand what she was saying as she came into view, waving her arms at him. *"Et le jardin—interdit—aux pensionnaires."* The garden—forbidden—to guests. He stopped and stared at her. He was tall and thin. He pulled his glasses off and rubbed his eyes wearily—he looked bemused, then he said something quietly in French. Madame Vicquerat was not satisfied; she gestured at the gate behind him and pointed along the edge of her garden to a path outside the fence. He turned and went out the gate, and I watched him walk along the path with a wry smile on his lips. He went to the front of the house. The door closed behind him, and I heard his footfall on the steps.

I stuck my head out of our door as he got to the landing. *"Liberté, égalité, et le jardin,"* I said.

"Mais oui," he told me, as he went into his room.

The Europeans, it seemed, had a penchant for single beds, even in rooms meant for coupling. Often these rested a foot apart; sometimes they were pushed together; always there was a gap where the frames met but the mattresses didn't. Our beds in Madame Vicquerat's room were no exception. They stood with a corridor between them. So Barry would visit me, but without the sexual charge you'd expect a single, narrow bed to elicit. Our lovemaking that summer was no different from what it had been in my dormitory room or in Barry's apartment: It was too quick, too hard, too quick. Before I knew it, he was gone, back to his own narrow bed, asleep. I didn't have the words to protest. I didn't know how to ask for more. I was young then, and he was so much older.

Silently, I resented his not lying in bed with me all night, not coming to lie with me in the morning. He was up early. I'd wake to the sounds of him making coffee for the two of us in the kitchen below. Our fellow boarder—the intruder in the garden—seemed always to sleep late. We never met him in the kitchen. Hearing Barry's morning noises, I'd get up and dress and go down like a dutiful wife to share coffee and bread in Madame Vicquerat's spotless kitchen. When he left for the day, I'd wave from the door, then go back upstairs to read Henry Miller. I carried *The Tropic of Cancer* with me that summer. *The Tropic of Cancer* and George Eliot's *Daniel Deronda*—unlikely bedfellows. I was supposed to be making notes for my dissertation, which I actually did some mornings, after my rendezvous with Miller. I sat at a small writing table across from the separate beds. On the wall behind the table, from the ceiling down to the floor—where, if I stretched my legs out, I could touch it with my feet—hung an enormous snakeskin. I suppose it was a boa constrictor's. At its widest, which was about at eye level, it was a good eight inches. Sitting at that table, trying to take notes but catching myself staring at that dry, speckled skin, drove me out every morning into the quiet streets of Carouge. We were on the edge of a forest. Madame's fenced garden backed up against a thick copse of trees. Nearly every other house on the street had a front fence of some kind—a high stone wall, or wire strung between heavy round posts, curling over forbiddingly. Dogs barked as you passed. Mourning doves cooed. They reminded me of home.

I walked a lot that summer. In every city we visited, I walked, and walked again, stopping in shops, stopping in museums. Sometimes I'd lunch in a small café. I told myself that it was an adventure, but, in truth, I was lonely and bored. I wanted company; I wanted affection. I bought pastry or fruit at the end of the morning and, following an afternoon stint of notetaking before the snakeskin, made myself coffee and had my treat, with my back to the beds and the table, and the lace-covered door onto the balcony flung open to the garden and the woods.

On one such desultory day I wandered out of the Promenade des Bastions with its grim statues of the Protestant reformers and over to the Rue de la Cité. There were people, lots of people. Up ahead I saw a marquee and on it *Le Dernier Tango à Paris*. I went in to the cool dark of the theater and watched Brando fuck Maria Schneider. Watched Schneider unzip her jeans and reach her hand in to make herself come, rolling giddily onto the bare wood floor. And suddenly it struck me: If Barry couldn't please me, if I couldn't tell him how to please me, I could please myself.

I went out of the darkness into the harsh afternoon light, thinking, how could she shoot him? thinking, I'd take the streetcar back to Carouge. I wasn't meeting Barry until seven, at a restaurant near the Capelle. The afternoon stretched invitingly ahead. I stopped at a little market before I caught the streetcar and bought some luscious red strawberries. They smelled so good. In Madame Vicquerat's kitchen, I washed them, leaving the stems on, putting them in a shallow white porcelain bowl. I took them upstairs and set them on the writing table. I opened the French door onto the balcony. The afternoon was hot; there was hardly a breeze. The whole room smelled of strawberries. They made the room come to life; they made the snakeskin less sinister. They were lovely.

Then I went to the bed, propped the pillows against the headboard, and lay back on them, pulling my shirt out from my jeans, reaching a hand under and up to my breasts, rubbing them gently. It was the newness of it that excited me—this possibility of pleasing myself. I unzipped my jeans and reached inside. They were still too tight and I wriggled my hips out, aching for my own touch. It was lovely, this gentle probing with my fingers between my swollen lips. I took my hand away. It was too good not to prolong. I pulled my shirt off, reached around and unfastened my bra and let it slide from my shoulders. I wet my fingers with my own saliva and circled my nipples, first one and then the other, while the ache grew. I rolled onto my stomach, up on my knees, pulling the pillow down, brushing just the tips of my nipples on the cool cotton, and with my fingers once again—not needing any saliva now—rubbing my spot, gently at first, then harder and harder, and my hips moving, as they were never inclined to move with Barry, in slow waves, back and forth, with my ass in the air, my breasts against the pillow, until with each twitch of pleasure, each rocking motion, my legs widened and spread, my ass touched the sheet, and I came, moaning, sinking, spreading myself wide onto the bed.

I teased Barry over dinner that night about working too hard. He was in no mood to be teased.

"All day," he said, "I've been trying to understand the makeup of this virus. And nothing." He threw up his hands. "Nothing."

I murmured sympathetically.

"It's not the same for you," he told me. "You can spend the day reading and writing and actually get somewhere."

"Yes," I said, "I suppose I can."

We walked back from the restaurant in silence and were growled at by several dogs along the way. A German shepherd barked and ran at us and leapt against the crisscrossed wire of its owner's fence.

"I bought strawberries," I told Barry as we let ourselves in. "I saved them for you. They're in the fridge. You won't believe how beautiful they are, how good they smell."

"No, thanks. I'm bushed. I'm going to bed. You have some, though."

"I already have."

The *minutier* went out just as we reached the landing, and I noticed a narrow slit of light beneath the door of the red-haired boarder. After our door closed, his opened; and I heard his footsteps on the stairs. I sat on my bed, fidgeting for no good reason while Barry took off his clothes. He was handsome and hairy. I loved to run my hand over the thick curly dark hair that covered his back and his chest. When he got into bed, I leaned across the space that separated us and kissed his forehead. "I'm going downstairs," I said.

When I got to the kitchen, I found the red-haired boarder standing at the open refrigerator, admiring my strawberries.

"Go ahead," I said. "Have some."

He turned, startled, but then he smiled. "They're gorgeous."

"What's your name?" I asked him.

"Alan. What's yours?"

"Laura. Too bad we don't have any cream."

"Ah, but we do." He reached into the fridge and produced a small carton, then took the bowl of strawberries and set it on the table between us. He poured the cream on. I got spoons from the drawer.

"I don't think we need those," he said. He held a strawberry, glistening with cream, to my lips. We sat at the table and fed each other strawberries as if we were old lovers. And when we'd finished them off, he got up and set the white bowl with all our discarded stems in the sink. "Let's leave that for Madame, shall we?"

"I saw your encounter with her from my window. The garden is forbidden," I said, laughing. I felt giddy. "You were very gracious," I told him.

He leaned against the sink. "And you have good taste," he said.

I went to the sink to wash my hands as he crossed to the door. Our arms brushed. It was like a charge of static on a crisp winter's day—only nicer. It made my stomach dip.

He was in the doorway, leaning against the jamb. "Night, night," he said. And if I hadn't been a newly married woman, I would have followed him to his room.

When I came down the next morning to the aroma of Barry's coffee, he told me that he was going overnight to a lab in Lucerne, where someone else had a lead on his virus. He looked sheepish. "I forgot to tell you last night. Jurg is taking me. He said it'd be better if we stayed overnight. Do you want to come? There's a wonderful bridge in Lucerne. A covered bridge with paintings inside."

"No. You go. I've gotten into a rhythm here. Walking, working. It's fine."

"I'll be back in the afternoon. We could go to a movie."

After Barry left, I didn't know what I wanted to do: read, walk, get into bed. I opted for my usual routine minus Henry Miller, whom I thought I might save for the afternoon. Walking into the city, I decided I'd buy myself a dress. There was a shop I'd noticed a few days ago, with vivid, bright things in the window—in particular, a maroon dress with a wonderful batik pattern. I walked in, asked to try it on, and liked it immediately. It had slender straps and a low, scooped neckline that showed my shoulders. There were buttons all the way down the front, from the fitted bodice and waist to the full, long skirt.

"I'll take it," I told the smiling clerk. "May I wear it?"

"Oh, oui." She cut the tags off for me, put my shirt and jeans in a bag.

I walked out feeling good and went back to the same open market I'd visited the day before. There were raspberries today, big ones, and small oval purple plums. I bought some of each.

From the bottom of the street, I saw a small knot of people outside Madame Vicquerat's house, heard shouting voices, a dog barking. A car with a flashing light was parked at the curb. They were all at the formal front entrance, standing under the eaves on the wide stone steps. Alan was there, his red hair bright in the afternoon sun. He did not look happy. He bent down just as I drew closer, putting his hand to the bare calf of his leg. Madame Vicquerat's voice rose above all the others. There were two policemen and a man with a German shepherd, straining at its leash.

When I came up, the policemen were laughing and Madame Vicquerat was arguing, in furious French, with the man with the dog.

"What happened?" I asked Alan.

"I was bitten."

"Let me see it."

He was holding a crumpled, bloody handkerchief to the bite. He took his hand away, and I winced at the wound. It was deep. It had to be painful.

"What are they arguing about?"

"Whether the dog should be impounded. The police think I'm an idiot for having her call them."

"Let them argue," I said. "Let me take care of that."

I led him inside and up the stairs and into my room, closing the door behind us. Barry's socks, which I'd washed the day before, hung over the radiator near the French door. I made him sit on my bed.

"I don't know why I'm shaking," Alan said.

"I do. I would be, if I'd just been bitten by that dog."

"I really didn't see him coming. That sounds silly, I know. But I heard him barking and thought he was inside the fence. Do you know the one I mean—the wire one?"

I nodded. "Hold your leg out."

He had on khaki shorts that came to just above his knees. "You wouldn't have been much better off in pants," I said.

"I know."

"Here's a clean handkerchief. Keep holding it there. I'll get some soap and water." I propped the pillows from Barry's bed and mine behind him.

He eased himself back and stretched his leg on the bed. "I'll bloody her damn duvet," he said.

"So you will."

When I came back with a small bowl of water, soap, and a clean towel, he was smiling.

"You're taking awfully good care of me."

I smiled back. "I'm happy to. This isn't going to be fun," I said.

It was still bleeding. I tossed the handkerchief aside, dipped the towel in the warm water and wrung it out, then pressed it against the bite. I held it there for a long time and ran my other hand up and down the front of his leg to distract him. His skin was smooth, and the hair on his legs was fine, a light blondish-red.

"That feels nice."

"It's to make up for what's next, which probably won't feel nice. I think it's time I cleaned it."

He nodded. "Go ahead."

I rubbed some soap on the towel and swabbed the wound as gently as I could.

His muscles tensed.

"This may need stitches."

"Oh no," he said. "No doctor's office. No hospital. I've had enough of Swiss authority. We'll use adhesive tape if we have to."

"I'm nearly done."

I had my free hand on the back of his leg just below his knee as I dabbed at the wound with the soapy towel. "Do you run?" I asked him.

"Yes. Why? Do you?"

"One at a time, please. I'm concentrating here. Because you have wonderfully strong calf muscles. And yes, I do."

"Have you run here in Geneva?"

"No. There're too many dogs."

We both laughed.

"I've got good old American Bactine in my toiletry bag, but I don't have the kind of bandage this needs. Let's see what Madame has."

"Find out, if you can, what's happening to the dog."

He was lying with his legs slightly apart, one arm across his chest and his eyes closed behind his glasses, when I came back with the bandage. His hair was mussed; he looked very attractive.

"This is going to sting," I said quietly, and he sat up and opened his eyes. He turned his leg toward me and I looked at the smooth white inside of his thigh. I squirted the Bactine on.

"That hurts."

It seeped into the wound and went running in little rivulets down to his ankle. I dried his skin with the towel and put the bandage on.

When I finished, my hands were trembling.

He saw that they were and took both of them in his. When he looked at me, I saw his eyes register the snakeskin behind me on the wall.

"What the hell is that?"

"You mean you don't have one? I figured it was Madame Vicquerat's reminder to her boarders that this *is* a Protestant city. Knox, Calvin, original sin. Actually, I hate it."

"Let's take it down," he said. "Stuff it in the closet."

"There is no closet."

"In the wardrobe, then."

"I don't know why I never thought of that."

"Because you're too gracious a guest," he said. He started to get up.

"Don't," I told him. "I'll do it." I climbed from the chair onto the table and took the snakeskin off its hook. Holding it in my hands, touching it, made it less menacing. I rolled it loosely and set it in the wardrobe atop Barry's suitcase.

"Better?" he asked.

"Much." I sat at the foot of the bed. "Oh—the dog *will* be impounded. That's why the owner was so incensed. Madame Vicquerat says the police want to speak to you again, but I told her not tonight. I said you didn't want to see anyone tonight."

"Thank you."

"You're welcome." I looked at him for a moment, then bent my head to his leg and kissed him gently just above the newly dressed wound. When I raised my head to look at him again, he took his glasses off with a quick, impatient tug that made me want him. Then he reached for me and pulled me toward him on the bed, up between his spread legs.

He kissed my hands first, both of them. "How can I thank you?" he asked.

"You have," I told him, "you are."

He touched my hair and my face, tracing the line of my cheekbone, and I put my hand on the back of his neck, at his hairline. His hair was thick and a little wiry. I could push my fingers into it.

Then we kissed—a long, slow, exploratory kiss that relaxed us both.

"Where's your husband?" he asked.

"In Lucerne for the night."

"Good," he said and kissed me again.

Then he drew back and looked at me. "This is what you want?" he asked.

"Yes."

"Tell me," he said, "tell me what you'd like."

"I'd like you to unbutton me." I scooted up on my knees, pulling my dress out from under me. He sat up, against the headboard. First he kissed my face, then my neck, and just above my breasts where the dress began.

"It's a pretty dress," he said, as he started to unbutton it, kissing me as each button came undone.

How delicious it was to feel the dress come open, to feel myself open, slowly, to him. I had no bra on. When he'd opened the buttons down to my waist and my breasts just showed, he reached in with his tongue and licked them.

"Keep going," I said.

He unbuttoned every button with the same measured calm, licking his way down. And I unbuttoned his shirt as well, pushing it off his shoulders and down over his arms. When my dress was completely open, he slipped it off and smiled at me, and I felt as I had never in my life felt before, desirous and desired.

I lay on my back and he ran his hands over me, down my arms, over my breasts, across my stomach, as he pulled at my underpants. I wiggled out of them.

"How did you get skin so soft?" he asked.

"It's a gift from the gods," I told him. "Like you are."

I unzipped his shorts then, and we took care to pull them gently over the leg with the bite.

Beneath *his* underwear, he was hard and ready. I touched him, cupping my hand to his crotch, feeling his hard penis, his soft balls. Then I reached inside, holding him, stroking him, as he pulled his briefs off, and we were naked on the narrow bed together.

"This is what I want," I said.

It was twilight. The last light of the day filtered through the lace on the door. We pushed the bunched-up duvet out from under us. It fell off the bed.

He kneeled over me, caressing my breasts with his hands, kissing them again. And with his fingers, he touched me where I was so wet and ready.

I reached for his penis, but he took my hand away. "Not yet," he said. "It's your turn first."

He ran his tongue across my belly, then spread my legs wide and put his mouth to my hot, wet, full lips and licked me there, flicking his tongue back and forth till I couldn't stand it.

"Stop. Please stop. And come inside. That's what I'd like. It's what I want. For you to come inside me."

I pulled him up. He stretched out over me, and now it was my turn to run my hands over his chest as he leaned on his elbows. To reach around and feel his taut ass, to put my hands in the deep hollows just inside his hip bones. I guided his penis to me, and the sensation of him pushing in and moving—not deeply, not yet—inside me was the most exquisite thing I've ever known.

"Now," I said, "come in now." And he did, all the way, and we moved together, slowly, and then faster and faster in quick inevitable waves of hot, lovely motion until we both were open and spent and done.

"Don't move," I said. "Stay where you are." I took my hands from his back and felt the sheet on either side of us. We were perfectly centered in Madame Vicquerat's narrow bed. I smiled.

"Now you can move," I said. And he slid down beside me, tucking his arm beneath my head, gathering me to him.

"I want to sleep like this," I said.

"So do I."

With his free hand, he fished on the floor for the duvet and pulled it over us.

"I don't want to think about tomorrow."

"Don't," he said, "just sleep."

And I did. And I remember that in the morning, in the first light, we lay together quietly on that narrow bed and listened to the mourning doves coo in the forbidden garden.

AUTHOR'S NOTE

I started to write this story without giving the man and woman in it names, calling them simply "he" and "she." Then I realized that they had actually been with me a long time; in fact, they are the main characters in the novel I'm currently working on. Only Alan, the man bitten by the dog, is new—as new as the heroine's sexual awakening.

POLISHING MY SKIN

By Nazneen Sheikh

They have come for me. Two women carrying wicker baskets covered with cloth and a small charcoal brazier. My mother and sisters have left. All my mother whispered into my ear was "let them prepare you." This time it is a gentle entreaty quite unlike her usual stern maternal injunctions. This time her gaze softens as she strokes back the strands of hair sculpted across my forehead. I am startled because in the shining depths of her brown eyes I see the iris ringing out as though it is trying to contain something that smolders . . . unfurls inside. I have never seen this expression in my mother's eyes before, and I move closer to her, but she has turned away and moves beyond the door. I am left with the two women who have already shut the door to the bathhouse in my grandmother's ancestral home.

The wedding is five hours away and the city of Lahore scorches under a July sun. Not here, though, in this plaster and tile room equipped with water faucets mounted above a tiled bathing trough. I have heard about this bathhouse since I was a child. All the women of the family have come here before their weddings to be "prepared." When they are viewed many hours later as brides, each one shimmers with an uncanny luminosity that we all know is nothing to do with cosmetics. No one shares the secret and nothing is ever discussed. Now it is my turn, and I can hardly wait. I am not like the other women. I am my mother's wayward daughter who has lived in the West and is not a virgin. The man I have chosen to marry is much older than me and a Hispanic American. I have brought him to my father's home so we can have a traditional wedding. This is the land of soft women with hard yet resilient minds. So I am here not to indulge my mother but to satisfy my curiosity. My favorite aunt has guessed it, though; she looked at me with a diamond winking in her pierced nostril and said, "The West cannot teach you the mysteries of the East." Her comment is clichéd and outmoded, yet I am ensnared. I grew up surrounded by these women who had husbands chosen for them. Educated women, who managed to escape abroad for prized vacations with their husbands so that they could get their hair permed in Paris and pick up shoes in Rome. Their conversations were dotted with anecdotes of their husbands, children, tailors, and maid servants. Some of them held political debates and exercised intellectual freedom in unique ways, but they never spoke about sex or desire, let alone their orgasms, and their fantasies. It was their lot, I had decided, and nothing whatsoever to do with me. I had my hair cut at Vidal Sassoon and poured myself into denim and offered my body to men I desired. My only innate female vanity is to envelop myself in rose-scented fragrances.

The two women are busy removing objects from the baskets. The older one moves slowly, giving instructions to the younger one, who is plump and given to giggling. They are professionals in the rituals of their trade, which has been passed along from mother to daughter. The items they use are indigenous, organically grown, dried, and then pounded in primitive mortar and pestle and finally stored in delicate earthenware vessels. I am told to remove my clothes. The older woman makes this request as casual as asking for the time. The younger one pulls down a *charpai* that is leaning against one wall. It is the traditional hemp woven bed bolstered by four wooden legs. The legs are ornately carved and painted in lurid colors. As I step out of my clothes, the younger woman covers the bed with a white cotton sheet. I am naked in front of two other women who are fully clothed. The older woman looks at my body, and a smile plays across her lips. I am convinced she is taking some sort of inventory. Then she puts a hand on my shoulder and pivots me around. I almost stumble, but she holds my waist to steady me. The palms of her hand are soft, and I feel as though a silken sash is holding me in place. She is behind me now and I know that some sort of examination of my back is being conducted without my being touched. She steps out from behind me and leads me to the bed. In that minute and a half I am made aware that some transformation of my body is imminent, and I instinctively trust my benefactress.

Silk, she says, looming over me, as I lie on the bed knotted with anticipatory tension, is always packed in tobacco leaves. But when we take it out, it is silk. I can make you into a river of silk and he will never want to cross to the other side. I will turn you into the milky flesh of the green almond, which he will hold in his mouth without ever swallowing. I can do without machines what they can never do in America. Amused, I gaze up at her face and nod. Then she deftly adds: It may hurt a little. Plump and giggling Safia hands her strips of muslin coated with heated brown sugar and lemon juice. It starts from my ankles, the primitive depilatory process. The sticky heated embrace of the cloth, the quick caramelizing on the skin, and the sharp yank. A three-tiered process in which I go through a contracting, relaxing dance of my own. The discomfort is minimal. Silk and pearls, croons the woman, moving upward to my knees, deforesting my skin, making me truly naked. Defoliating, deforesting . . . denuding. Like some lyrical poetess, she hums with similes and metaphors. Then she takes my hand and trails the fingertips across one of my thighs. This is his hand, she whispers, these are his fingers. All you will have to do is look into his eyes and you will feel your own skin. I am instantly catapulted into the heavy-lidded gazes of Eastern men gazing from old portraits. Were all those smoldering orbs reflecting the opalescent skins of their hairless women? Was this the reason perhaps that women were hidden, veiled, and closeted from the eyes of men? How quickly would the warring instincts of their men be derailed by images of desire. All those pear-shaped Mughal women with complexions the color of yellowing clotted cream had kept this secret buried. But I return again to this century and this room, where I sense that, although something else is about to begin, I am not certain if my hazel-eyed lover with his sensuous smile will attain the mystery of the East in his arms tonight.

Now this, she says, tapping my pubic mound, is like a ball of wool. What will he say when he gets here? There isn't any way to tell her how my soon-to-be-husband separates with almost surgical delicacy all the strands of the ball of wool. How the anticipation of the moment as he deliberately prolongs finding my clitoral bud is also one of the more enthralling aspects of our lovemaking. You pant, he always chuckles, like a little animal. I say, record them, I want to hear these pants of mine. These half-breaths drawn out from my primeval self where I am neither human nor animal yet miraculously sensate. But a strip of muslin is already settling into place, and the following yank ricochets with a stinging pain that shocks me into silence. It is repeated three more times, and when it is over I discover a new sensorial receptor in my body. Now, says the woman, helping me up to a sitting position, we will polish your skin. I glance down between my legs, seeing a continuous line of skin and the pale flesh rise of my pelvic mound a freshly revealed contour. I know I suddenly want a full-length mirror in order to pose for a moment like the heavy-hipped women of Botticelli and Titian.

Plump Safia's giggles hiccup softly in the room, and the gleam of approval mirrored in the older woman's eyes makes me rise slowly. I walk like a piece of statuary toward the bathing area. I walk like Cleopatra, Nefertiti, but most of all I walk like the Mughal Empress Nur Jehan, who hunted tigers and created Attar of Rose. I sit on the wooden stool placed in the sunken area near the taps, and as I reach toward a faucet, a hand encircles my wrist. It is the older woman, holding a clay jar in the crook of one arm. I am told to extend my arms and be still. There is more to come. The pale yellow paste is rubbed into my entire body and massaged vigorously. The base is turmeric, I am told. The other ingredients have names I cannot even pronounce. The movements of their supple fingers are circular. Both women work on my body as if they are polishing a metal object. I know for the first time how the skin folds over my elbow and how it disappears into a dimple behind my knee. How the spill of my stomach is guarded on either side by the angular thrust of my pelvic bones. Where the weight of my breasts create a niche in my midriff and how far my navel is embedded in my stomach. Every protrusion, each folded crevice is sought out and attended to.

Safia now turns on the water and collects it in a bucket, which she pours over my body. The older woman removes the paste with a coarse loofah. Each section of my cleaned body draws a satisfied murmur from the older woman, and I, who have suddenly been gifted with this polished and tingling skin, am overwhelmed by the desire to rub myself like a cat against the fold of a curtain, the leg of a chair, and most of all the softly crisping hair on my lover's chest. My breasts begin to stiffen, and I cannot be certain if the liquid between my legs is water or my own sex juices. A heaviness, almost a languor, roots me to the wooden stool. When my feet are lifted one at a time and scrubbed with another paste, this one abrasive, I know that I will insist his tongue pay homage to every inch of this glistening nudity I call my body. When I am finished I feel ready to jump into a car and reach the hotel room, where he lies, waiting for his foreign wedding to begin. I don't want to cover myself with the stiff gold tissue outfit that has been stitched for me. I don't want the heavy, encrusted gold jewelry to pinch my throat and earlobes. I just want my nipples sucked into hard pellets and his sweet hard cock riding high inside. I want the women now to disappear.

The older woman is rubbing my American shampoo into my wet hair. She sniffs at the mouth of the bottle once in curiosity and then the second time in obvious disdain. Yet she sees the warning in my eyes, so she works a lather in my hair. After Safia has poured the cool well water through it eight or nine times, I become aware of a hissing sound and a fragrance rising around us. It is coming from the small iron brazier that is lying close to one end of the bed. I inhale deeply, just the way you do with marijuana. It is sandalwood, pure with its almost sickly sweet draw, coiling through the bathhouse. I am motioned toward the bed and told to lie down. Now, says the older woman, I will rub oil into your body; you will carry its fragrance through the first night into the second. I am eased up toward the edge of the bed so my hair hangs over the edge. Safia, positioned behind me on the floor, uses a fan to push the heated, fragrant smoke through my shoulder-length hair. Her fingers are parting my hair, coiling strands around and around. My head feels warm and cool simultaneously. I long to smell it, inhale the sandalwood, but I can't as yet; the older woman is massaging my feet with slippery hands. Jasmine oil, she says to me. It is the lightest and the most delicate of all flowers. It is better in the heat, she adds. When you perspire, even your sweat will be scented.

Where is my lover, says my perfumed skin, I want him to ride me like a centaur in the heat of Lahore, pounding his haunches into mine, making me slippery with scented sweat. You will put it between your legs, yourself, she requests politely, this high priestess of flesh . . . this polisher of skin. Into my cupped palm she pours some oil, light as water, and I am dabbing between my legs around the lips, cautiously, toward the bud and then around the soft sides. I cannot go further because there is music pounding in my skull entirely made up of a palpitating state of desire. I want to escape this room and end this drawn-out erotic exercise where I have felt the power of my femininity only filtered through the ritual of this most exquisite of toilettes. This preparation which my mother had slipped into the chaos of my East/West marriage had been done only to remind me of the reverence paid to the act of love. Now the legions of Eastern women, shrouded by their stultifying conventions, assume a new aura for me. Their silence is understandable. They have memorized the ultimate sex manual, not with the aid of text or illustration but rather through the most conscious examination of their own bodies.

You, says the older woman, massaging my earlobes with jasmine oil, may wish to have something to drink. We give it to the younger brides. She had guessed, this polisher of skin, this titillator of nerve endings, that I had come back from the land of free and easy women. I am interested; I normally see things to the end. I sit up on the bed like a column of incense. Hair of sandalwood and body of jasmine, ready to swallow the libation of the moment. It is offered by giggling Safia in a metal glass. I am drinking milk with ground almonds, laced with powdered cardamom. It is cool, with a bit of an aftertaste. Nothing comes to mind. The older woman watches me intently. I drain the glass and wonder how much time has passed. Will anyone remember to collect me from this place? Safia brings the pile of fresh clothes for me to wear home. I am stepping into them slowly when I realize that my body has lost some contact with the outer edge of reality. I am floating in etherized form. There is no substance to my limbs as a series of minute explosions press out the unconscious tension that has always pulsed inside.

You are not even waiting now, whispers the older woman, as she leads me toward the door. You are in the moment, and what you have drunk heightens it so that it does not end even when you have taken him.

Much later, when a monsoon-like torrent cools the night and we lie in the flower-strewn debris of this great white bed and I am covered by the blanket of his limbs and he whispers, You are in my nostrils, in my hair . . . aah, the feel of you . . . I can hear the older woman wearing the face of Ikbal recite:

> It must be known, this world of scent and sheen,
> They must be plucked, the roses in the dene;
> Yet do not close thine eyes upon the Self,
> Within thy soul a thing is to be seen.

AUTHOR'S NOTE

I wrote this story because I wished to put women from the East and the West into the great white bed together. When the face of a Moroccan or Bengali woman peers out from a shrouded form, her sisters in Boston or Toronto conjure up images of deprivation and oppression. But the kaleidoscope needs to be tilted so that the celebration of erotic power is not stifled by geography. In the culture in which I was raised, the physical act of love becomes a form of worship, and at this altar the most glittering and precious offerings are our bodies.

VALENTINE'S DAY IN JAIL

By Susan Musgrave

Western wind when will thou blow?
The small rain down can rain.
Christ that my love were in my arms
And I in my bed again.

ANON.

The bus dropped me in the heart of town, across from the funeral parlor, where a sign in the window read, "Closed for the Season."

"No one dies much this time of year?" I asked, making small talk with the taxi driver taking me the rest of the way to the prison. "Not if they do it around here," he replied, and then asked me if I minded if he smoked.

Before I could answer, he lit one and blew the smoke out his window. I sat in the back watching rain streak the windshield as he talked about the justice system and how "sickos like drug dealers" should be shot to save taxpayers' money. He must have thought I worked at the prison because he kept glancing in the rearview mirror, waiting for me to agree. I explained I was visiting a convicted marijuana smuggler, a Colombian, doing life, that it might even be love. He apologized, saying he should have kept his trap shut. He said there must be one heck of a lucky guy waiting for me inside, that all he'd ever wanted was a soft girl in his bed every night, and all he'd ever been was disappointed.

I looked away into the mountains above the distant town of Hope, the snowy ridges few had ever set foot on, and tried to picture what

Angel, the lucky man, might be doing at this moment. I imagined him lying on his bunk, staring up at the dull green institutional gloss on his ceiling, with not even a crack or a ridge he could use as landmarks.

"So when's the honeymoon?" the driver pressed. The window had steamed up, and he wiped a little space with his hand. "You going to escape? Go someplace tropical? Swimming pool, palm trees, hula-hula. You wish, huh?"

We rounded a bend at the northern end of the valley, and Toombs Penitentiary came into view. All that separated it from its sister prison, Toombs Penitentiary for Women, was the Corrections Mountain View Cemetery. Both prisons were cut off from the world by mountains so high their western flanks were always in shadow.

I'd met Angel when I visited both prisons, and the adjoining cemetery, a year ago. I had just begun free-lancing and hoped to cover the story behind the high rate of inmate suicides over Christmas. "No one but the law ever wanted them when they were alive, and now *no one* wants them," an official told me, indicating the forlorn tract of land, overgrown with scagweed, where the unclaimed bodies of lifers were laid to rest. Escape risks, he said, were even buried in leg irons.

My driver let me off in the parking lot, a hundred yards from the front gate, and wished me luck. "You know, you make me jealous," he said. "You get to go in there and be all lovey-dovey while I go back to work." I paid him and stood for a moment watching him drive away, then turned to face the prison.

The heavy gold watch on my wrist told me it was 12:45, and I had to stand outside in the rain, waiting, until the big hand on the clock inside gave its single digit salute to the sky. Then the guard buzzed me in. I waited some more as he went through my handbag, taking apart my fountain pen and getting ink all over his hands. I was allowed to take in with me a tube of mascara and lipstick, but not the lozenges that Xaviera Hollander, the *Penthouse* columnist, had recommended as a prelude to oral sex.

"Leave these in there," he said, pointing me toward a metal locker. "And this, too." He held up the loose tampon he'd found at the bottom of my bag. "Security measure," he said. "An inmate could suicide himself by choking on one."

He repacked my handbag, saying they would supply me with a substitute if I needed it. "The matron will see you next," he said, pointing to a door marked NO EXIT. On the other side of the door I could hear a woman protesting.

I sat on a hard chair and waited. Angel's sister emerged, with the red-faced matron, Miss Horis, behind her. Consuelo, which was her current alias, had told me to trust her—she could hide *anything*. Why wouldn't I trust a woman who had smuggled herself and three kilos of cocaine into the country so she could pay her brother's legal fees, and be near him? Angel told me, too, she had once smuggled a grenade in her vagina into Bella Vista prison in Colombia. The condom she'd offered to carry for me today seemed like small beer in comparison.

"Miserable enough out there for you?" Miss Horis asked, sighing as she ushered me into the NO EXIT room, then telling me to remove my coat, suit, blouse, underthings, and "all other personal items." Naked, I placed both feet firmly in the middle of the mirror.

"Straddle the mirror, please, one foot on either side. That's it. Now relax, and cough twice."

I coughed, and Miss Horis peered in the mirror, then asked me to lift my breasts one at a time, before opening my mouth where she checked under my tongue. "Enjoy Valentine's Day," she said, as she left me to get dressed again.

She hadn't mentioned the watch—obviously meant for a man's wrist. I got dressed again and she popped her head in the door a moment later, offering me a sanitary napkin to replace the seized tampon. I shook my head no. No inmate, evidently, had yet thought of trying to suffocate himself with a Kotex.

Once inside the Visiting Room I headed for the washroom, where I found Consuelo fighting with her hair. A sign informing visitors that there was No Necking, Petting, Fondling, Embracing, Tickling, Slapping, Pinching, or Biting Permitted During Visits was posted above the condom machine (foreplay might be prohibited, the machine's presence seemed to suggest, but fucking was not). Today the machine bore another warning: "Sorry. Out of Order." The word "Sorry" had been crossed out.

I turned to Consuelo for the condom she was supposed to smuggle in for me, but she held out her empty hands. "I had to swallow it," she said. "That woman she wanted to look me in the mouth." She said Angel and I should get married so we would be approved for private visits. But Angel and I weren't waiting for approval. Today our names were at the top of a clandestine list for a different kind of private visit—the unsanctioned kind. I borrowed Consuelo's comb and dragged it through my own damp tangles.

At half-past one, Mr. Saygrover, the Visitors and Communications officer, led us into a hallway painted the same avocado green as the outside of the prison. He nodded to the young guard in control of the first of the iron-barred gates blocking our passageway, and the heavy steel doors parted on their runners. We crossed five more identical barriers before reaching the gymnasium.

I could see the men pressed up against the last gate, awaiting their visitors. All were dressed in green shirts and pressed trousers the same shade as the prison walls. The ritual had been the same ever since I first started visiting Angel—the men standing behind the barrier waiting and waving, and the women approaching, awkwardly, looking at one another for reassurance, like girls at a junior high "turnabout" sockhop. The closer we got, the longer it seemed to take the guards to open the barriers. A female guard with sweat stains in the armpits of her uniform opened the last gate. Janis Joplin's voice came rasping out of two coffin-sized speakers strapped high on the gymnasium wall. She didn't need to tell anyone here how freedom was only another word for nothing left to lose.

The gym was decorated with red balloons and white streamers. The streamers had been affixed from corner to corner the night before and had lost their elasticity. A prison sculptor's *papier-mâché* heart, trapped in barbed wire, lay on display next to the Coke machine, which was also "Out of Order."

Visitors found seats around the long banquet tables, each one laden with the institution's version of hors d'oeuvres: mini-sizzlers on toothpicks, rolled cold cuts, radishes that had been sculpted to look like roses too terrified to open, a pyramid of mystery-meat sandwiches and plates of heart-shaped cookies baked by prisoners in the kitchen. My eyes moved from table to table, searching. Angel sat upright on a metal chair, arms folded across his chest. Our eyes locked. He stood up.

Nothing had changed. He didn't speak. I couldn't. He had a smile bittersweet as a pill for the sick at heart, a pair of lips you wanted to lick under a mustache that would keep you from getting close enough, and sad night eyes. His hair was straight and black and today he wore it tied back in a ponytail. In my last letter I'd written, "Tie your hair back so it won't get in the way. I want to see my juice all over your face."

Angel pulled two chairs together so we could sit facing one another, and he leaned forward and put both his arms around my neck. "I'm always afraid I'll never see you again, that you won't come back," he said, breaking the silence. "I'm afraid you might find me—too available."

I laughed as I cupped his dark face in my hands. "I wouldn't call any man doing life behind bars *too available*." His moustache, smelling of the red-hot cinnamon hearts he sucked every time I visited to hide the smell of the dark tobacco on his breath, scoured my upper lip. More than his smile or his eyes, I think it was his smell that attracted me most the first time we met, like the air before a storm, long before there is any visible sign of it.

"You look thin," I said, sitting back in my chair. "Are you getting everything you need?" Angel sat back, too, straightening the sheet that served as a tablecloth. He picked up an orange and poked his finger into its navel.

"I'm getting your letters every day. And you're here. What more do I need?" He kissed me, but I pulled away. "And you?" he asked.

I needed privacy. I wanted to be with Angel, alone. We'd had one chance, at the Christmas social, to spend five minutes in the toilet stall of the men's lavatory, but I needed more time than that to fondle him, embrace, tickle, neck, pet, slap, pinch, and bite—it was all I had thought about since we'd met. I pictured him alone every night in his cell, penis erect and shining, sad as tinsel at an unattended party. When we were together I was aware of how close he stayed beside me and how every time we brushed against one another I felt a shiver of something long lost stirring inside me, the same longing I'd felt for a brown-eyed boy in the fifth grade, my last painful crush before the crash of puberty.

I'd been afraid, too, I told Angel, afraid I had "gone too far." In my last letter I'd quoted Kurt Vonnegut, who said the only task remaining for a writer in the twentieth century was to describe a blow-job artistically. I told Angel I'd rather *show* him a blow-job than write about it, then went on to discuss the calorie count in a mouthful of sperm (one swallow contained thirty-two different chemicals, including vitamin C, vitamin B12, fructose, sulphur, zinc, copper, potassium, calcium, and other healthy things). I said I had a One-a-Day Multiple Vitamin habit but figured I could give these up if he were willing to have oral sex once a day.

Angel told me "far" was the only place worth going, and he kissed me again. This time I didn't stop him. He shifted on the hard chair, adjusting the bulge that strained to break out of his trousers. I squirmed on the warm metal, forcing my knees together, my sex swollen, struggling to escape. I caught two guards staring at us; I nudged Angel and we pushed back from one another. Angel held my hand underneath the table, stroking it with his thumb. "I haven't been in the yard yet today," he said, after a silence. We'd been having the same thought. Out there we might be alone. "How is it, outside? The weather?"

"Wet," I said, taking a heart-shaped cookie and breaking it in half. Angel took the other half from my hands, and I watched it shrink under his mustache. "Raining."

"Good," he said. "Let's walk."

We had the yard to ourselves, almost. Two guards in a patrol vehicle slowed to look us over as we stopped to watch a pregnant doe browsing on the thick grasses outside the perimeter fence. It was the same spot, Angel said, where a half-blind bear had been shot in the autumn. Angel said the guards had fired warning shots at her, but she kept coming back. A handful of yellow-and-purple cartridge shells lay in the wet grass.

"She couldn't see well enough to get away while she had a chance?" I asked.

"Few see that well," said Angel, and when he looked at me this time I saw, in the gleam of his shadowy eyes, a depth of wanting that promised heaven.

We kept to a well-worn trail Angel called the warning track. Walking, we lifted our faces to scale the double high-wire fences but stayed well inside the dead line, the line beyond which any prisoner would be shot. Angel pointed to where a man had been picked off by the tower guard "before his hands were even bloodied by the razor wire."

I squinted up through the rain, beyond the gun towers, to the sky. Angel slid his hand in under my thin coat, cupping my breasts, milking my nipples between his thumb and forefinger, and I felt the wet silk of my panties sticking to me where I was open, and a thin seam of silk rubbing back and forth across my clitoris with every step. But Angel, his faraway eyes on the towers, seemed to have scaled the high-wire fences and left me behind. Then, as we rounded a bend in the warning track, he said someday he would take me so high, so far up in the Andes, nobody, not even God, could stare down at us.

"You're dreaming." I screwed up my face at him. I didn't need to say it out loud: "You're stuck in here doing life." Angel knew my thinking.

"Life can be shorter than you expect," he said. Then he looked at me and laughed, in a way.

I laughed, too, but pulled him closer. For now this was good enough.

When the call came over the loudspeaker to clear the yard we went back inside, elbowing our way through a cluster of guards who'd been checking us out from the door. We sat in our wet clothes holding each other and waiting as more guards pinned two sheets together to make a screen on the gymnasium wall. The Inmate Committee had planned to show *Carmen* before the food was served. Angel whispered what he wanted me to do when the lights dimmed, but now, without the condom for protection, and surveillance from every corner of the room, my heart started looking for an emergency exit. I told Angel we had too much to lose, including our visits. But then the lights went down, he lifted the hem of the tablecloth with his foot, and pushed me under.

Beneath the table, in a private world, I sat hugging my knees, feeling lost and uncomfortable. The Inmate Committee, in charge of all forms of entertainment, had transformed the space under the table into a low-ceilinged motel room. We had a foam mattress, two arsenic-green blankets, and a pillow, upon which someone had placed a long-stemmed rose. My mouth felt dry. How was I going to give Angel that blow-job? I longed for those lozenges and thought about the editor from *Elle* who'd phoned a few months ago asking for reminiscences of "my most embarrassing sexual encounter" for their Valentine's Day issue. I'd been unable to come up with anything, but now, as I sat composing the story in my head, I concluded a guard must have seen me and apprehended Angel. I would be forced to wait it out under the table until such time as they chose to humiliate me publicly; precisely the ending I needed for my date from hell for *Elle*.

I felt a hand go over my eyes, then (the smell of him!) Angel began kissing me all over my face and head, sniffing my hair along the part line. When he took his hands away from my eyes I saw he was wearing dry clothes.

"I went back to my house to change," he said, laughing, taking off his jacket and draping it over my shoulders. "Your dress is soaked," he said. "Wear this, too." He began to unbutton his shirt.

He peeled back the blanket, gave me his dry shirt, and made me get under the covers. I told him he was the first man I'd been to bed with who tried to make me put more clothes *on*, and he told me I was the first woman who could make him hard and make him laugh at the same time. He wanted to know if all Canadian women could do that, and I said as far as I knew there'd never been a poll.

We kept our voices low. The room, too, grew quiet, as the credits began to roll. "Are you sure this is safe?" I whispered. "What if a guard saw us?"

"No one saw us," he said, as he pulled off his undershirt. For the first time I saw the hollow place in his chest. It looked as if his heart had been excavated, like the ruin I once visited in the remote Yucatán. Everything of value had been dug out and taken away. Only a pit remained, which, over the years, had been reclaimed by the jungle.

"I was born with this . . ." He took my hand, curled it into a fist, and placed it in the little hollow. "My mother used to say by the time I died it would have filled up with the tears she would shed for me during her lifetime."

I laid my head on the pillow, waiting for the table to be pulled out from over us. It took an effort of love to get in the mood, staring up at the words PROPERTY OF CORRECTIONS CANADA MORGUE stamped on the underside of the table. I shut my eyes tight as Angel picked apart the rose, then laid the cool crimson petals on my eyelids.

"You're not like any woman I've ever known," he said, pressing his nose in my armpit and edging one finger under the elastic of my bra.

"What's that like?" I shook the petals away.

"Uuuummmmmmmm," was all he said. I wanted to undo his zipper and take his cock in my mouth, but something made me hold back, an old memory, perhaps, of my first "most embarrassing date" in the old boathouse smelling of high tide, fish, and water rats. I was twelve and Dick Wolfe (not his real name, but close) showed me how to light a banana slug on fire, how it would melt into a pool of sticky stuff if you had the right touch. Then he undid his pants, and I remember it looked so eager, so trusting, as he said "put your mouth on it," and when he came I thought I'd cut him with my tooth, the crooked one my parents could never afford to have fixed. I believed I had a mouthful of his blood but did the polite thing, I thought, and swallowed it. "I've cut you," I said, thinking we'd have to go to the hospital and how was I going to explain cutting a boy "down there"? Then he said, his brown eyes more open to me than ever, "That wasn't blood, sweetheart."

"It's been a long time," Angel said, as I lay still, dreaming, half-listening to someone at our table tuning a guitar. My arm was going to sleep, and I shifted position. The movie had begun, and the man who'd been tuning his guitar began strumming on it so passionately that Angel and I could no longer talk. Then the projector shut down and the lights went back on. The voices up above us grew louder, as if an argument were taking place.

"Something's up," said Angel. "It sounds like there's a problem with the projector."

"The lights have come on," I said. "How are we going to get out of here without someone seeing us? What sort of person will they think I am?"

"No one is going to blame you," Angel said. "The guards will just think I corrupted you. They think all inmates are criminals."

He put his arms around me as if to reassure me. Then he saw the watch I was wearing and asked if it was a gift. He didn't say "from another man," but I could hear it in his question. I unstrapped it from my wrist and said yes, a gift for him. It was guaranteed to be shockproof and never to lose time.

"I've never owned a watch that didn't break down," he said. "I think watches get nervous being on my wrist."

I pushed him back so I could move my pillow away from the end of the table, where a pair of knees was invading our love nest.

"This one comes with a lifetime warranty," I said.

Angel settled his body back alongside mine and blew a strand of hair out of my face. He shifted again so his chin rested on my shoulder-blade. The person with the intruding knees began tapping his feet and calling for more music.

It was growing stuffier under the table, and neither of us had enough legroom. But I'd waited long enough: I slipped my arms out of my dress, pulled him close to me, and kissed him, for a long time. It didn't matter that up above us there was a world of men and women arguing and laughing. (The film, I learned, leaving the social, had turned out to be *Carne*, sado-masochistic pornography, not *Carmen* the opera, and the guards axed the show.) We were alone in the new world of our flesh, and the occasional appearance of the toe of a running shoe under the hem of the tablecloth, or a hand slapping the tabletop, no longer felt like an intrusion.

"But will you still respect me after this?" I smiled.

He took my hand and guided it to his cock. "My respect for you knows no limits."

I unzipped his trousers. Erotic texts from ancient India claim there is a definite relationship between the size of an erect penis and the destiny of its owner. The possessors of thin penises would be very lucky, those with long ones were fated to be poor, those with short ones could become rulers of the land, and males with thick penises were doomed always to be unhappy.

For now, I was destined to make Angel happy. I began licking the end of his cock, which was already swollen. I thought it was going to burst as my tongue busied itself.

"I'm going to die," he said. When I looked up at his face, across the nut-brown expanse of his body, he smiled back, that slow smile, and I took his cock in both my hands. I could barely get my fingers around it. Its head had a ruddy glow and was grinning. It glistened. I kissed it. Sniffed it. Sucked it hard, taking as much of it into my mouth as I could, then licking it again, making a lot of noise while I sucked and licked.

"I'll come if you keep doing that," he said.

Then he pulled me up so I lay next to him and reached inside my panties. He said my cunt nuzzled up to his hand like a horse's soft mouth when you feed it sugar. He moved down between my legs, pulling my panties aside, sliding one finger inside me, sliding it out, sliding two fingers in, then sliding them out, then sliding three fingers in. I arched my back, spreading my legs wider to give him better access, and he tugged gently upward on my pubic hair, baring my clitoris. Then he began licking me, slowly, teasingly, moving in small circles with his lips and tongue, his kisses falling on me, gentle as the scent of rain in a lemon grove. My body strained against his face, and when he looked up at me, his skin was alive with my juices.

I sat up and pulled him down on top of me.

"I don't have any protection," he said.

There are some exquisite moments from which we are not meant to be protected. I slid him inside me, achingly. I had never had anything so hard inside me. I held my breath as he kept coming into me, we were breathing and then not breathing in unison, and I brought his hand up to my mouth to cover it, suppress any sound, and then I began sucking his fingers, one at a time, then two at a time, then three. His fingers tasted of salt, of my own sweat and juices. "Suck," he said, and pushed into me, harder still, as if by trying he could disappear up inside me and escape forever into the rich orchid darkness of my womb. When he came his face became contorted as if it hurt him to come so hard, then we lay quietly for a while, and then he began licking me again, making me come with his own come, with his tongue, his lips, and his fingertips. I cried when I came, and doubled up, curling into myself. He began kissing me, from my toes up along my legs and the insides of my thighs, over my belly and breasts, up my neck and onto my face and in my hair. He said this was his way of kissing me hello and goodbye at the same time.

Afterward as I lay on a bed of bruised rose petals, licking the drops of sweat that had rolled down his chest and collected in the hollow above his heart, Angel said coming inside me was like coming on velvet rails. And later when we'd crawled out from under the table and were standing alone once more in the slanting rain, we kissed again. We kissed as if to seal our fate, to finish a life together we hadn't even begun.

Years ago, on an island in the tropics, I had been lured from my bed in the night by the air pregnant with the scent of vanilla. I found giant cauldronlike cactus flowers opening in the moonlight and thousands of tiny sphinx moths fluttering from one pod to another. In the morning, when I came to show them to a friend, the flowers had disappeared.

I missed the next visit because I had a deadline to meet (a piece about these cactus flowers that bloom one night a year, conduct their whole sex lives, and vanish by dawn) and the one after that because the prison was locked down. There'd been a stabbing, and a hostage-taking, and rumblings of a hunger strike. I wrote to Angel, concerned about his health. He wrote back, worried about mine. He hoped I wasn't pregnant, for though he liked the idea—that way part of him had already escaped for good—he didn't want to leave me with a burden.

Angel must have sensed it: Visits weren't the only thing I'd missed that month. I made a doctor's appointment. In the evening I tried to phone Angel, but good news was not enough of a reason to bring an inmate to the phone. I asked to book a Special Visit to see him the next day. An officer informed me that Special Visits were granted for death or bereavement only. So I had to save my news until I could sit across from Angel in the Visiting Room and touch his face, let him take my hand under the table and stroke it with his thumb.

But the next time I saw Angel, he was in the news. "Two men are dead after today's daring escape attempt from Toombs Penitentiary" was all I heard; my heart began to pound to the staccato beat of a police helicopter, a throaty thwap thwap thwapping. I moved closer to the screen and turned up the sound. "Earlier this afternoon two Colombian nationals tried to climb aboard a waiting helicopter that had landed in the prison yard . . ." There was a shot of the dead line where Angel and I had walked, then a file-photo closeup of his face.

"*Life can be shorter than you expect.*" Consuelo and I rode the bus to the prison in the rain. She said Angel hadn't confided in me, hadn't been able to tell me about his escape plan, out of respect . . . *my respect for you knows no limits* . . . but that he'd been insistent: He would send for me when it was safe. My good news—that I wasn't pregnant—seemed like sad news now. All of him had escaped for good.

Mr. Saygrover asked Consuelo to sign for Angel's property, which fit in a gray plastic suitcase. Consuelo looked inside, then handed it to me. Angel, she said, would have wanted me to have everything. He had left his battered *Pocket Oxford*, a key chain with no keys, a toothbrush, an unopened bag of Cheetos, and $2.37 in change. And, he had left me. So much for respect!

A service took place in the prison chapel. A handful of fellow inmates gathered to pay their last respects, the chaplain mumbled a few words and asked us to pray. Consuelo said Angel wouldn't have wanted hymns, so she sang a song from their childhood, "*Si me han de matar, que me matan de una vez*": "If they're going to kill me tomorrow, they might as well kill me right now."

I wanted, for a moment, to kill him, myself, all over again, until I saw him lying that still in his gray Styrofoam coffin. I tried to hold one of his hands—awkward because of the handcuffs—then stroked one of his thumbs instead. He wore the watch. I could hear it ticking.

I moved my hands down over his body, saying hello to Angel, saying goodbye. And when I felt the leg irons at his ankles, I wanted to rip open his shirt and let my tears collect in the hollow place in his chest.

But I didn't weep. Through the bars of the chapel window I watched the slow rain falling on the fake-fur trim of the guards' brown jackets, and thought how lonely it would be, how cold and cramped the earth Angel was going into. In this world, I knew, there was an unending supply of sorrow, and the heart could always make room for more.

AUTHOR'S NOTE

Romantic love flourishes when there is intense passion along with a monumental impediment to its fulfillment. Erotic love, even more so. This story is drawn in part from my relationship with Stephen, my life partner, whom I met in 1984. He was then serving a twenty-one-year sentence for gold robbery, and in prison he'd begun a novel, which I was asked to read. I began to edit it and fell in love with his main character, then with Stephen himself.

Slow Hand

Slow Hand

Women Writing Erotica

EDITED BY MICHELE SLUNG

HarperCollins*Publishers*

This one is Trin's, with love

And therewithal Criseyde anoon he kistė;

Of which, certeyn, she feltė no dis-easė.

And thus seyde he: 'Now woldė God I wistė,

Mine hertė sweetė, how I yow might pleasė.'

FROM *TROILUS AND CRISEYDE*, BY GEOFFREY CHAUCER

I want to write a book of erotic short stories.

MADONNA, QUOTED IN THE *WASHINGTON POST*

CONTENTS

Slow Hand

IN THE PRICK OF TIME

By Susan Dooley

We admire some stories for the dazzle of their artifice; others, however, may win our hearts with their naturalness. Susan Dooley's "In the Prick of Time" embodies, I think, everything that is splendid about being a Grown-Up Woman, yet it reminds us also that we are the sum of our experiences, that our sensuality can grow and flourish only if we accept and nurture it.

"Too fat."

The mirror was an old one, its oak frame holding glass that was wavy and dappled with dark spots. It could distort image, she thought, just as earlier she had muttered about how her jeans had shrunk in the wash.

"Too fat," this time she sighed and accepted it.

"Just right." He had come up behind her in the bathroom where she stood, her body still wet from the shower. He put his arms around her and nuzzled his face into her neck. She watched in the mirror as he slid one hand up her body and cupped her breast. He played with her nipple, running a finger back and forth until the flesh hardened beneath his hand. Then he moved until he was between her and the mirror. She watched as the back of his head ducked forward and felt the slight pressure as his mouth began a soft sucking at her breast.

The man in the mirror curved his hand over her hip. His fingers pressed in for a minute and then continued on until he had shoved his hand between her legs. She could feel his tongue teasing the inside of her mouth, and she felt a warmth and an urgency even as she watched, detached, the two strangers who slid awkwardly to the floor and began to press themselves together in the shifting light.

She could no longer see the mirror. There was only the pressure of him, hip to hip, tongue to tongue, as he pushed himself inside of her.

The telephone rang.

She tried to ignore it, but both of them had gone still, waiting for it to stop. The noise had broken their connection, and though they rocked together for a minute more, she felt him ebbing away.

Mary raised herself on an elbow. In the wavy glass she saw two people who had passed their moment of passion. The woman had wet hair. The man had on his shoes.

"What are you writing?"

"An erotic memoir," she said, turning around and placing the flat of her hand on the front of his jeans. She felt him move at her touch, and she smiled up at him. "I'm going to call it *In the Prick of Time*."

She was sitting at the long pine table, having cleared a small space between a stack of books and a large gray cat, and was writing out the grocery list. He put one hand on her shoulder and leaned forward to read what she had written.

"Oatmeal?" he asked. "I thought this was supposed to be erotic."

"Well, it's not the *most* erotic thing I could think of," she conceded, wiggling her eyebrows in what she hoped was a Groucho Marx leer. "But once a long time ago I stood and watched a pot of oatmeal boil for ten minutes. It was a very sensual experience. Voluptuous. It sort of . . ." She was remembering that time when she had eaten oatmeal six days a week, saving all her money to have one glorious meal on the seventh, and of how she had often gotten mesmerized by the sight of the bubbling oatmeal. "It sort of erupts at you. Oatmeal has orgasms."

"You must have been a very cheap date," he said, going to the refrigerator to see what other erotic treats were on offer.

"Do you remember oleo orgies?" he asked, having found a piece of lemon pound cake.

"Did you ever go to one?" She put her pen down and turned expectantly—the magician about to pull a rabbit out of his past.

"Once in Ohio when I was in graduate school. It wasn't oleo. It was some vegetable oil in a bottle, and we all got a little drunk and then smoked pot for courage. Then we took off our clothes. Except Nancy. We were still married then, and she insisted on keeping her underpants on. Everyone else looked innocent. Nancy in her underpants looked like a very dirty girl.

"We sat in a circle, willy nilly, except you couldn't sit next to the person you came with.

"The man giving the party went around the circle, pouring out handfuls of oil. He made it a priestly act. We began rubbing the oil on each other. I was sitting next to a woman with incredible breasts and a beautiful tan. I put my head in her lap so I could look up and watch the light gleam on her skin. She leaned over to rub oil on my chest and I caught her breast in my mouth to suck it. It tasted strange—almonds, vanilla—I can't remember except that made it even more erotic.

"She didn't seem to mind, but she didn't seem aroused either. She kept rubbing me with oil in a very efficient fashion, and all around us everyone was doing the same thing. Suddenly I started to laugh. I felt like a leg of lamb.

"Everyone else began to laugh too, and the girl whose lap I was on would give these great hee-haws and my head would bounce up and down. It was silly, but at the same time it was very erotic."

"What ever happened to her?" Mary asked. Her voice had gone cool.

"To who?" asked Paul.

"The woman you were bouncing about on."

He looked at her curiously. "I have no idea. I never even knew her name."

He got up. "I'm going into town. Do you want anything? Oatmeal?" He bent over and rubbed his chin against the top of her head and was gone.

She heard the rough cough of the car's motor and watched Paul back the old station wagon out of the driveway. When she was sure he was gone, she pulled a fresh piece of paper off the pad and wrote his name.

"Paul."

She tried to think what it was exactly that made her want him. Rationally, there were only so many spots the hand could touch, so many places the tongue could lick, and that made fucking finite in its possibilities.

Why was it that somehow lovers were not?

She folded the paper with Paul's name and set it aside. Then she began again:

"Herbert."

An erotic memoir should begin at the beginning. In the prick of time, when that first tentative tickle had come from the unlikely Herbert, a leering red-haired boy of eleven who had pushed his way through the children on the school bus to sit beside her. He had squeezed himself over onto her side of the cracked leather seat as the bus made its familiar and halting way down the highway, extruding children at each stop like some demon machine that had had its fill and now was belching out the leftovers.

Herbert had never actually put his hands on her. But he had leaned on her, and he had *looked* at her. It was frightening. It was exciting. Not like Jimmy Mason who had chased her through the orchard and knocked her to the ground to deliver a hasty kiss, his lips slamming to a halt on her cheek. The way Herbert had shoved and bumped her had made warmth start between her legs and roll up her body until she could feel the heat turning her face red. It was uncomfortable. She hoped he wouldn't stop.

"Carole."

Carole had been her best friend in grade school. When the weather was too wet for the nuns to scatter the schoolchildren onto the playground, they would gather them together, march them into the auditorium, and show them a religious film. The ones that weren't about the Virgin Mary hovering over some foreign meadow starred pretty nuns and handsome priests—none of them had warty cheeks like Sister Octavia or the smooth hairless skin of Sister Joyce, whose eyes had been popped naked into a face that lacked both lashes and brows. Mostly the movie priests were Irish and adorable. Not like Father O'Toole, the arrogant pastor who strode each week into every classroom to bellow damnation at any child who had been seen talking to a Protestant.

She and Carole sat next to each other in the dark, while a wavy shaft of light cast pictures on the screen. The big, bare room smelled of chalk and wet socks, and above the faint hum of the projector you could hear the constant rustle of children forced to sit still. The darkness, the muffled noise, the shadows of people you no longer knew turned the barren room into a private place.

For the first half of the film, Mary would trace a delicate line up and down the soft skin on Carole's arm. When they changed to the second reel, it would be Mary's turn. She would stare entranced at the screen while Carole's fingertips returned the delicate, feathery stroking.

That wasn't really erotic, Mary admitted. Not like Herbert. But Mary decided that sensual also had a place on her list. She left Carole's name on it.

"Mr. Maxwell."

Mr. Maxwell was an older man in his twenties. When Mary was

sixteen, he had hired her older sister, Helen, as a file clerk. Whenever she went to pick up Helen, Mr. Maxwell would call Mary into his office and flirt with her. One day he had leaned over and run his finger up her leg.

Mary pretended not to notice, but after that, whenever Mary came to get Helen, Mr. Maxwell invited her to come into his office. Sometimes he asked Helen to work overtime, and while she busied herself outside, trotting back and forth down the hallway with full file folders, Mr. Maxwell asked Mary about her boyfriends and tipped himself forward in his chair so that, as he talked, he could run his fingers lightly up and down, up and down her leg.

"Wesley Sutcliffe."

She still thought of him occasionally when she saw the moon lying low, pouring light onto water as it had at that beach party the year she was thirteen. She had barely known Wesley, but when everyone had gone for a final swim, he had waded through the water and picked her up. Holding her wet body against his chest, he had carried her up the moon's line of light, walking into the darkness of the sea. The silky, clinging wetness of her bathing suit was all that was between her breasts and his chest, and her nipples had hardened at the touch of his skin. He had carried her farther and farther into the silver light until at last they vanished in the moon.

The phone again. A neighbor was calling to give warning. The raspberries were going by. If Mary wanted any, she must pick them now.

There was enough of a breeze to keep the bugs away, but also enough to send her notes skating off the kitchen table and across the floor. And out the window. And into the hands of a neighbor child who would later ask, "Mommy, what does 'fuck' mean?" She picked up a brass candlestick and placed it firmly on the papers before taking a basket and heading for the raspberry patch.

She picked for an hour. Someone was practicing the piano—"In the Good Old Summertime"—and the ponderous notes came to her over the buzz of bees. It was all the summers that ever were, and Mary began to miss the moment even as it was happening. Next January, pulling up close to the wood-stove, she would be able to close her eyes and remember the clean feel of sun and the pleasure of licking a finger smeared red with raspberry juice. A mosquito danced across her back, and she straightened up to swat it. Drops of sweat slid down between her breasts.

How nice it would be to strip off her blouse, to unhook her bra and let the breeze lick the sweat from her skin.

She reached absentmindedly toward a dark red raspberry, but stopped at the sight of a small white worm humping and sliding its way down the cane. Mary brushed it off, decided she had picked enough, then saw one more ripe berry, then two just a few steps farther on.

"Picking raspberries is like orgasms," she said to Paul later that evening as they lay in bed together.

"You think everything is like orgasms," said Paul, who had only been half listening to her account of the raspberry patch. He had been smooching around her body, planting sweet, silly kisses on her elbow, her wrist, licking the place where her waist lowered itself onto her hips.

"I always think if I wait a minute there'll be a better one. Sometimes I don't want to come."

"We all think that," said Paul complacently. "Prolonging the pleasure. It's why eighteen-year-old boys aren't all they're cracked up to be."

Paul was fifty-two. Much better than an eighteen-year-old, Mary agreed. Although now that she thought about it . . .

"I've never been to bed with an eighteen-year-old," she said. "By the time I lost my virginity I was too old for someone eighteen. What were you like then?"

"Fast," said Paul. "It didn't occur to me to try to please a woman. It was me who was pleased just to have one; I didn't dare take any time for fear she might get away. Hop on, vrooom, hop off. Poor woman."

"Poor woman," Mary agreed, feeling the pleasure of his weight as he slid on top of her, rubbing himself against her inner thigh before pressing inside of her and beginning to move slowly back and forth, finishing at last what had started their day.

Obsessed was too strong a word, but Mary admitted she had spent a lot of time the last few days adding names to her erotic memoir. Partly it was because Paul had fastened on it. Whenever he saw her writing, he tried to look over her shoulder, pretending to believe it was a shopping list. All his insecurities had snugged down into her past. She rather liked the past he gave her, all glamor and carelessness. The real one had been much more painful.

She, in her turn, had no fear of his past. She shied at his future. She kept herself ready for the day he would announce that being together had become more difficult than being apart.

She knew that for both of them, these were protection myths, like the Indian legends of creation. You were ready with a cover, a story which would explain how strange and terrible things that could not happen sometimes did.

"Tim."

Her first lover. She had been devastated at his loss. It had never occurred to her that one would go to bed with a man and *not* marry him and live happily ever after. She had. They had not. It had been sex, but had it been erotic? She was too full of trying to please him, her mind poking itself into everything, wondering if it was all right to do this. And what he would think of her if she did that. Never in the few years they were together had she relaxed in bed and listened to him with her skin. But the first man you ever fucked, surely he had to be in your erotic memoir.

Erotic was not just a hand on your body, or she would have been swept away by the strange man who came up to her at a dinner party, gave an enchanting smile, and reached out and cupped his hands around her breasts. The Masons' secret handshake, or was he Mr. Magoo? It had been as erotic as watching a nurse plump up a pillow. Erotic wasn't the motion, or the mechanics, it was what had gone before, even if before was only a brief connection. It was the connection that counted. The mind knew not to be wary and allowed the flesh to have its say.

The phone. It was Paul.

"Are you busy, or would you like to go on a picnic?" he asked.

She met him at the town wharf, passing him the picnic basket and taking his hand. She rocked for a moment on the edge of the dock, so that she could say before she stepped into the boat, "If you were the kind of man who looked up a woman's skirt, you'd notice I don't have on underpants."

She jumped lightly into the boat, dropping safely down amid the piles of slickers, sweaters, boots, and lines.

"Aha!" he gave her a quick grin, but he was coiling the painter as he talked and she knew better than to pursue the conversation. He drifted off when they were on the water, his mind going ahead in search of rock or wind.

They ate on the shore and then walked the edge of the island. In the distance they could hear the bleating of an island ewe, anxiously calling back a wandering lamb. They walked to the top of the hill, past low bushes of sheep laurel, whose brilliant pink flowers looked innocent and enticing. "It's also called lambkill," Paul said, poking at a bush with his toe. "It doesn't seem to have hurt this batch." Another mother with her two lambs scampered off in front of them.

"They probably don't eat it unless there's nothing else," Mary said, her eyes straining ahead to pick out the gray sheep from the gray rocks that jutted out of the meadow. At the top of the hill they stood for a minute, looking down on the ocean below. Then Paul lay on his back, and she leaned on one elbow above him. His shirt was open, and she walked her fingers across his chest, lightly like a spider. She kissed the place where his neck hollowed into his shoulder and then ran her fingers around the edge of his mouth.

"You are erotic," she said. "You are the last entry on my list."

"Sure I am," he said, lost again in his vision of her past. "Number 27."

"227," she corrected him. "Do you take me for a slacker?"

He smiled and unbuttoned her blouse. He pulled the sleeves carefully down off her shoulders, and then, impatient, he gave a yank so that the whole thing dangled around her waist. He unfastened her bra and pulled her breasts free.

"I think I'll just take you."

His own pants were off, and he put his hands under her skirt. She raised her hips, and he pulled the skirt up, a clutter of clothing wrapped around her waist, her top and bottom bare. He put his fingers in his mouth, moistening them with his tongue as she watched him, then he leaned over and kissed her, putting his wet fingers between her legs.

His lips touched hers, his tongue sliding softly into her mouth so that as she inhaled she breathed him deep down inside her. His tongue in her mouth, the hardness of him pushing in between her legs, the spirit of him sliding deeper and deeper into her life.

AUTHOR'S NOTE

I've read a great many mediocre novels where the author was desperate to present sex in a shocking light—jamming people into clothes closets, conference rooms, and company. Sex in odd places and sex with odd groupings seemed to me to be like aerobics, something people do when the flab sets in. Thinking about it, I decided it was not simply flesh on flesh that awakens desire; it is the pasts that people bring to each other and the hope with which they merge.

LEAPER

By Jenny Diski

In contrast to the sensuous ease of the familiar, presented with such spirited warmth by Susan Dooley, other stories in this book, of which "Leaper" is one, take a look at chance encounters. It is quite clear to me from the many submissions I read, though in itself hardly a new idea, that the element of "unknowingness"—of unfamiliarity with another body or its history—can strongly enhance the erotic quotient of a sexual episode, whether real or imagined. But Jenny Diski and every other writer selected for this collection who has taken the sexy-stranger theme has made it her own.

Known for her daring, Diski here examines the coming together of two people whose needs and vulnerabilities match up for only a very brief moment.

He phoned at completely the wrong time, my lover. "Write me a story. A man and a woman, fucking. Keep it short and dirty."

"Fuck you," I said. "If you want a story, speak to my agent. The going rate is five hundred pounds a thousand words. If you want a fuck, speak to me. The going rate is . . . what is the going rate?"

"Do as you're told," he said, just the tiniest bit menacing.

"Fuck you," I said and put the phone down.

I'd spent the morning struggling with a never-to-be-published story and was sunk in a kind of slime of incapacity. What I lack is confidence. Much good it does to know what's lacking. I've written quite a lot:

short stories and articles for magazines, most of them published. Looked at from the outside, the writing's going quite well. I've made a small but significant reputation with a number of editors, and it's only a matter of time now, before I attempt The Novel that will, I hope, fulfill the promise I've shown.

If that sounds like an efficient piece of PR, it is, because I know, in that place where you really *know* things, that I can't write at all. That fact, that I have produced decent stuff to murmurs of quiet appreciation, doesn't affect this knowledge I have about myself. Something to do with my childhood, I suppose. Anyway, although things turn out more or less all right in the end, it doesn't change anything, and I face every blank piece of paper in a state of panic. This time, I know for sure, they'll find me out.

Things could be worse. That bone-deep knowledge of my own inability doesn't, as it might, pervade my entire life. Not any more. At least it's contained in the writing department, realizing, I suppose, that there is where I've decided I can live. I see this now as part of my internal structure; just as there is a language center in the brain, so I have a worry center which fills with anxiety and has to find something to worry about. It used to attach itself to anything available: money, sex, shopping, the daily news, the condition of my flat. For no reason connected with anything that was happening, anxiety would erupt. Suddenly, it would occur to me that there was dry rot under the floorboards, or perhaps, since I didn't know one from the other, it was damp rot; and the gnawing worry would infest the day. No matter what sensible things I told myself, that it probably wasn't true, or, if it was, so what, or I could do something about it, the ache would thrum away, coloring the day with anxiety.

The damp/dry rot was *desperate* all of a sudden, festering and rotting the fabric of my flat. I would go about my business, efficiently enough, but accompanied always in some small space inside me by my fears. By the following morning, the certain knowledge of rotting floorboards beneath my feet would have faded, but something else would take its place, filling up the worry gap before I had a chance to be relieved. A bank statement would arrive, and now the money situation, no different from the situation a day or a week before, would be terrifying, and I'd spend every free moment listing and relisting my income and outgoings, coming up each time with the same answer, forgetting almost what the problem was, but knowing there was some solution it was essential to arrive at. Sometimes, it made life very difficult to live.

All the time, even in the midst of the panics, I knew it to be free-floating anxiety, its source a well of terror in me that had nothing to do with my chosen concerns. But this information wasn't much help. And sometimes, exhausted by it all, I wanted someone around who would tell me none of it was real, and take away from me the problems that seemed, now and then, to threaten my sanity. But, in fact, I managed, and things have improved. The anxiety is contained.

Now, as I say, since I decided that writing is the only route I've got through life, the worry had latched on to that, like a cattle tick, and gains sustenance from my fears.

What I've learned about this is to ignore it. Most of the time, I write through a miasma of terror, and something decent comes out the other end. I don't know how. I think of it as "The Process" and leave it at that. It's like swimming in mud; not pleasant, but you get to the other side if you just keep going.

Usually, I can live with the discomfort. Why should things be easy? But occasionally I get exhausted by it, with having to contain my insecurity and generate enough energy to just bloody well get on with it. And still, sometimes, I wish someone else were here to do it for me.

I imagine the conversation with this paragon who will devote his energy to keeping me at it.

"I can't do this. I can't write," I wail, a formless heap.

"Of course you can." The voice is practical, not comforting, even a bit impatient. "What about all the things you've written? You did them, and they were all right. Now, do it again."

"I can't," I howl angrily. "I don't know how those other things happened. They weren't anything to do with me. *This* is the real thing, and I can't do it."

"Well, you're just going to have to try harder, aren't you?"

That's what I'm after. Not soggy comfort, but a hard line. A brusque assumption that I can and will do it, that I don't have any choice. And that, I suppose, is what I do for myself most of the time. But, as I say, sometimes it's hard to make that other voice, and I wish someone else were here to help. Which is foolish, I know, and I get over and on with it. But it doesn't help one bit when Dan calls to play games in the mud I feel I'm drowning in. It doesn't make me feel—I don't know—valued.

I decided it was a good moment to take some exercise. Sometimes I can disperse the panic by working up a physical sweat. I go to a gym just past the local underground station.

As I approached the station, trying to contain my annoyance at Dan by promising it a monumental expenditure of energy on the work-out bench, I noticed that something was going on. Too many people on the street for a weekday afternoon; the bus queue a long, rush-hour line;

and small, static groups outside the station itself, standing around in *that* way, signaling an event. An ambulance waited throbbing in the road, traffic building up as cars skirted carefully and curiously around it, its back doors open, red blankets folded neatly on the beds. The entrance to the station, normally a corridor of warm air, a dark gloomy cave into which travelers disappeared, was closed, heavy iron gates pulled across, and behind them, a handful of uniformed figures milled about. Two middle-aged men sat in pale silence on the stone step in front of the gates, neither of them looking as if this was their normal way of being on the street.

I allowed myself the luxury of imagining an electrical fault, an unattended carrier bag, a heart attack, even, while I walked through the small crowd and beyond the locked gates toward the gym. Where, no longer needing willed ignorance to get past the spot uninvolved, I gave my brain permission to interpret the signs.

There had been a leaper. Some poor but efficient sod had jumped under a passing train.

It's the drivers that call them leapers. My ex, who likes to know this kind of technical, inside information, met an underground driver in a pub who told him. Also, that leapers are a bit of a blessing among the lads, since any driver it happens to is given two days compassionate leave, with pay. It always sounded to me like front-line bravado, the brutality of the stomach-sick medical student, the ho-ho-ho of the intolerable. Anyway, "leaper" had stuck with us as a generic term for this particular kind of no-kidding suicide, and that was the word I thought.

I exercised viciously on the sloping bench, jerking the pulleys with muscles that surprised me, so that the weights clanked noisily when they came to rest, and the sliding bench screeched as it rolled up and down the gradient. But no matter how hard I pushed and pumped at the weights, I couldn't drown out the conversation. Two other women had stopped exercising and were standing at the window that looked out on to the station.

"What a terrible thing to do."

Right, that's the word, "terrible," I thought.

"Why do you think it's taking them so long to bring the body out?"

Jesus Christ, think about it. Think hard.

"You know, my sister was on a train when someone jumped in front of it. They don't let you out. *And* he wasn't killed, the bloke. Not outright. She had to sit there and listen to these awful screams. He screamed and screamed, apparently. She says she won't ever forget it. Can you imagine?"

Can't blame him, can you? A voice was probably all the poor bastard had left.

"Terrible. Terrible. Such a terrible thing to do."

I kept my end of the conversation silent and worked on grimly at the bench.

But the conversation continued.

"I suppose we shouldn't be . . . but killing yourself like that, you'd have to really mean it. I can't imagine what it must be like to feel so . . ."

"No. How could anyone imagine it. The poor driver . . ."

When I'd finished my routine I sat in the sauna for as long as I could stand, trying to sweat it all away. Which wasn't long, saunas being intolerable. A Swedish Protestant plot, I think, a stab at hell-on-earth, a dire warning of the discomforts to come. Unsuccessful, actually, since it makes hellfire attractive by comparison.

Out in the daylight, dehydrated and aching, I looked to my left, in the direction of my flat, on the far side of the underground. Small groups of people still stood outside the station, some in shock, others merely showing a passing interest, a few professionals looking as if this was all in a day's work, some of them succeeding better than others. The ambulance throbbed and waited. I turned right and sat at one of the tables outside the cafe on the other side of the gym.

Recuperate a bit, I decided. You don't have to walk back through and over that drama until you've had a cup of coffee. Sometimes, I'm good to myself.

The woman sat down at my table a few moments later.

It doesn't seem to make much sense, but there's a difference between tables inside a cafe and those on the street. Inside, unless everywhere else is taken, it's very unlikely that anyone will ask to share a table that is already occupied. It's a virtual act of aggression, the mark of men on the make and the mildly mad. But it's different in the open. Even if there are empty tables elsewhere, it's an easy, insignificant act to sit with a complete stranger. It must be that people feel they can escape more easily where there are no walls to contain them. And the bright daylit street seems to exclude the likelihood of whatever it is we fear. Streets are everybody's. Indoors, in the darker interior of the cafe, the table becomes defensible space, and the approach of another a threat.

I mean to say that I wasn't made uncomfortable by the woman's approach, nor did her presence impinge until she spoke.

She was tall, well-built, and sleek, in her elegant middle age, with a face that was all bone structure, and dark spherical glasses. Smooth, dark hair, cut to a heavy, architectural bob, and the clothes tailored (and not in England) to match her perfectly manicured fingernails. Not English. Diane, I was to learn, but think it with a Mediterranean accent: Dee-ahn.

She sat at the table, facing the station in silence for a little while, and then lit a long, dark cigarette.

"Are you watching or avoiding walking over it?" she asked, releasing smoke as she spoke and moving her head slightly to indicate the underground.

"Both, I suppose."

"It will ruin your day if you watch the stretcher come out."

"It's not much of a day, anyway. And a worse one for him or her down there. Or better."

She shrugged lightly.

"Yes. Or no. Her. I understand it was a woman."

There was a quality of utter detachment about her, as though she looked out on the world and saw, but was untouched by it. Everything—her clothes, makeup, the way she sat poised and posed in her chair—looked deliberate, and yet, it was all so well done that nothing seemed artificial. I hadn't seen her eyes under the sunglasses, but I knew they would be steady whether they looked at me across the table or at the scene along the road. Now she lifted the glasses away from her face and looked me over, running her eyes up and down my body in a slow sweep. Her cool, emerald appraisal was electrifying; the air filled with the static of possibilities.

"Does it excite you, the death down there?"

I took one of her mysterious cigarettes and leaned forward to catch the light she offered. I'm a believer in balance, a serious work-out requires nicotine as ballast.

"I'm thrilled. It astonishes me. I'm bowled over with admiration." Her brow creased in a question. "At the certainty that's been acted on," I explained. "I like a person who knows what they want and leaves no room for indecision or an accident of salvation."

"But what if it were a whim?" she queried. Her deep eyes were amused beneath their steady gaze. "A momentary thing? Irretrievable once acted on?"

I shook my head briskly.

"That's a thought the living use to comfort themselves. *He didn't really mean it*. So that the next time we stand on a station platform we don't have to choose between getting on the train or throwing ourselves under it. We wouldn't mean it, we tell ourselves, we'd be sorry afterward. What afterward? The only thing to be sure of is that we wouldn't be sorry afterward. In any case, what makes a momentary whim less true than the thought we've continued to have for twenty years because we haven't bothered to change it?"

She sat back in her chair, resting the coffee cup lightly on her silk shirt.

"The only thing that's true now is the physical end of a life," she said quietly.

I heard my voice clipped, angry.

"Is anything more important in a life?"

"No," she agreed calmly. But you are a romantic. You will be angry at being told so, but it's true. The fact is that to kill yourself in such a way is childish and aggressive. And stupid, for the corpse down there cannot reap the benefits. Look at the disruption that has been caused. Trains are held up all along the line, people are made late for appointments. Perhaps some of them are important. The traffic is slowed down, and passersby going about their everyday business are drawn in, they cannot avoid being aware of what has happened beneath their feet. Now they feel foolish and petty to be buying a bunch of flowers and a quarter pound of cheese. So much power, so much effect."

But there was no real anger in her voice. It remained distant and melodic. Even a little pedagogical. She continued.

"It makes people think thoughts they do not have to have. That person a few moments ago was living, they think, I might have passed her on my way to the grocer. Was alive, is dead. Only moments in between. A matter of a moment one way or another, they say to themselves. As I am alive now, this moment. What is to become of me? What right has someone ending their own life to impose such thoughts on others who may not choose to have them?"

This conversation pleased me. I liked her matter-of-fact, practical assessment of the anonymous death. There was a hardness in her voice that made me listen. And it was a relief to hear those things said. She echoed the thoughts I hadn't allowed myself to have, describing exactly my resistance to walking back over the scene.

I think about death a lot, in a general sort of way. I have a tendency to see it as heroic, a feat. I know we can't help dying, but it's such a serious and solitary thing. Death seems to me to ennoble the most frivolous and incompetent of lives. And voluntary death awes me with its absolute refusal to tolerate the intolerable. I admire the cold calculation, the rejection of a life of fear and panic in favor of decision.

But as I walked past the underground station on my way to the gym, what I had actually thought was: "I can't stand this."

I couldn't bear the idea of that person's misery as she walked along the street, moments before me, and the terror she felt as she stood on the edge of the platform waiting for the incoming train. I hated her for making her pain and her death so evident and imposing it on me. It angered and frightened me that she had advertised her safely anonymous unhappiness and required me to imagine that appalling death beneath my feet.

The truth was that I'd had precisely the same thoughts that underlay the conversation I contemptuously dismissed between the women standing by the window. But wouldn't permit myself to say aloud. I couldn't bring myself to admit the common thoughts, banal, true, automatic, human, inevitable, that were being spoken carefully so that the unease could be dispersed by the sound of the words. I prefer to let those thoughts, pointless as I know they are, roll around in the silence between world-weary shrugs. I want them to stay hanging in the air, recognized by their absence. I am, I must admit, ashamed to be on the side of the living.

The woman sitting opposite me with her brisk tones and coolly interested eyes voiced my real thoughts and made them seem acceptable. She spoke knowingly, in the manner of a distant observer, of the uncomfortable effects of death on our doorstep. And always her eyes held me in their gaze, faintly humorous, as if commenting, though not unkindly, on my self-deceit.

I heard myself say, "I'm trying to write something. But I can't. I just can't do it."

And held my breath, horrified to hear the words out there in the world, but certain, now that they were said, that she could give me the right answer. I hadn't thought of that harsh, reassuring voice of my imagination belonging to a woman; it hadn't occurred to me, but it didn't seem to make much difference now that I saw it was.

She stubbed out her cigarette with a sudden urgency, as if she had been waiting for a signal and now, having received it, could get on. Putting her glasses back, she smiled, but so slightly it was hardly there.

"Do you have to be somewhere?"

With you, I thought.

"No, not really."

"Then why don't we go back to my flat and have a drink? I live just around the corner. It's too depressing sitting here. Why don't we turn our back on this melodrama? Refuse to allow it any power."

She gathered her black leather bag from the table and stood, inviting me to join her.

"My name is Diane."

We crossed the road at the traffic lights in front of the cafe, and she led me to a street directly opposite the station. If we had turned to look in the other direction, we would still have been able to see the entrance to the underground. But neither of us did.

The flat was as well-manicured as her fingernails. She made me a drink.

"So you find death exciting?" she said, handing me a large Scotch.

"I suppose so."

"And does going home with a strange woman excite you, too?"

"Yes, that also excites me."

She smiled.

"Death has a way of sharpening our desires. It makes us want to eat good food or listen to a sublime piece of music. Or make love. To lie in someone's arms and feel warm flesh respond to our touch. Death is very sensual, don't you think? The dead have a secret we can't grasp. The secrecy of sex is as near as the living can ever get to it."

Did I say she was beautiful? Apart from all those other things, she was beautiful. Her face was a carved frame for the long, green eyes that looked and looked. Her body was beginning to show its age, loosened a little, but full, ripe, and round. I haven't ever rejected the idea of women as lovers, but the event had never occurred.

She undressed me slowly, looking carefully at my body and then checking back with my face. Whatever she saw in it seemed to give her permission not to hurry. When she had finished her slow examination she took off her own clothes, just as leisurely, giving me as much time for taking her in as she had given herself. Then she took me in her arms with as much passion as Dan would show, but it was different. Not his fast, harsh, funny fuck, but a long, slow pleasuring, a drawing out of desire. It was a lesson in timelessness. By the time she led me to the bed she had woven a veil around us with her intricate caresses that seemed to exclude the light. She made the world contract to a capsule containing only the two of us on the white expanse of her bed. And I knew that that was what we were there for: to create that veil that confused time and light.

All the time, the green eyes watched with the same humor and detachment I'd seen at the cafe. But I didn't mind. It exhilarated me that she was in control, building my excitement with careful touches and stroking, checking my response as she increased or decreased the pressure of her elegant fingers and beautiful mouth. Then she took my hand and guided me toward her pleasure. And all of it was more than sensual delight, it was also a promise that she could respond to my *cri*. That she could give me the energy and certainty that I couldn't find for myself. Everything she did corresponded to that person in my head who seemed too weary now to help.

I lay naked in her arms, waiting. There was no urgency. I drifted in and out of sleep listening to the buzz of traffic in the distance, content with the memory of the tone of her voice and the touch of her hands. I knew nothing about her beyond her name and the style in which she lived. But that, along with her capacity to guide me through desire, was enough information, and I had no real curiosity then about her past. Now that I was sated, it was my solved future that interested me. She would, I knew, encourage and insist I work, understand my necessity, wrap my insecurities in a blanket of her strength. At that moment I thought I had everything. Found, at last, the solution to the panic that threatened to swamp me. I remember the quality of that moment, even now. It was, I think, the first and only time I really felt that everything was going to be all right.

"So you write?"

Her voice was languid and deep, the scent of sex seeped into her low murmur.

"What do you write?"

I lay pillowed in the angle between her arm and breast, smelling the sharp mix of expensive perfume and satisfied desire.

"Stories, articles," I told her, whispering. "I think soon a novel."

I held my breath at the power of the moment, those seconds before one's life comes right.

"You must show them to me," she said and stroked my hair gently. "I'm sure they must be very good."

And the moment was gone.

I sat up and looked about the room. The afternoon sun poured in through the long windows, washing the beige tones of the furnishings with a warm pink. But I was cold. I wondered for a second if they had brought the stretcher up.

"You met me two hours ago, you can't possibly know whether I can write or not."

I was as confused by my chilly reply as I suppose she was. She sat up beside me and rubbed the side of her face against my hair.

"Well, then, you must show me, so I can judge. I'd like to see the story you're working on at the moment. The one you're having trouble with. We'll have dinner tonight, and you can bring it."

I swung my legs out of the bed and stood up.

"I don't show unfinished work. Unfinished work is nothing."

"Then perhaps something you've completed. Bring that so I can see what you do."

She lay back in bed, and I began to dress. Everything, suddenly, had slipped from my grasp, and I watched as reality wrenched at my fantasy of reassurance and tore it to shreds.

"I don't want to talk about my work," I heard myself say. "It's not something anyone else can be involved in. You have to do it alone, or it's not yours."

And this, also, was something I knew bone-deep but had forgotten in the surprise of death and sex and comfort. There is no alternative to the panic and the fear, because it is the panic and fear—and the isolation—that *are* the writing. The desperation created the necessity that made me write. I fed on it.

I was only ever half a romantic, the rest of me, the part that keeps on going, knows how things are and would not swap the final satisfaction of a finished piece for the easy comfort of that voice in my head. I had forgotten that voices in the real world have bodies and intentions of their own—and flats and furnishings and make dinner, and need.

I looked at her lying on the bed. She looked to me tired, terribly weary, worn, but her green eyes shone bright and hard still.

"All right," she watched me tie the laces on my shoes. "Dinner without your work. We must get to know each other better. When you're ready I may be able to help you. I have contacts. I can help in various ways. But tonight, just dinner."

She didn't want to be alone, I realized, although there was nothing of that in the tone of her voice which remained cool and steady. And not just tonight. I wondered, at last, about her life.

"Do you live here alone?"

"Yes. I do now. There was someone living here with me, but she's gone."

Her voice was so vague it was impossible to place this information in time. She could have been talking of decades or moments. I felt as if one of us was no longer in the room.

"I must go," I said, turning to the door. "I've got to get back to work. I don't know about tonight. It depends on how the work goes. Shall I ring you later on?"

She reached for a cigarette. The phone rang as she drew on the flame from her lighter, but she made no attempt to answer it.

"Yes, call me later," she said airily and lay back on the bed watching the smoke spiral through the light beams. The phone continued to make its mechanical bird call.

"Your phone . . ."

"I'm not going to answer it."

"But it might be imp—"

"I know what it's about."

She got out of bed, slipped on a faded silk kimono, and moved away from the phone to stand and look out of the window. There was nothing to see except the houses across the road. The phone went on ringing.

"It sounds important."

She inhaled deeply on her cigarette and turned her head slightly in the direction we had walked. From this angle, the station was out of view.

"They will have found this address on Helen. She must have had a letter or something in her jacket, because she didn't take her bag with her."

She turned and glanced at the chair by the door where a tan shoulder bag lay open.

"I suppose they're calling to find out if a relative lives here. They'll be wanting to inform her next of kin."

She spoke more to herself than me, her cool unchanging voice almost inaudible beneath the insistent squeal of the telephone.

"Are you sure you won't come to dinner this evening?"

She looked at me questioningly, her face an impassive sculpture of angles and planes.

"You lived here with Helen?"

The room for all its elegance was a desert, suddenly, an empty cold place being worn away by time.

"Helen lived here for two years. She left this afternoon. She wasn't a happy girl. I tried to look after her, she needed to be taken care of. But some people just won't be helped."

The telephone stopped ringing as she spoke. We both stared at it for a moment. The silence was shattering.

"I must go," I said. "I'm sorry but I can't stay."

She smiled.

"We must meet again soon. I would very much like to read your work."

But I was already closing the door behind me.

AUTHOR'S NOTE

Levi-Strauss has said, about totemic animals, that "animals are good to think with." I feel the same about sexual writing: sex is good to think with. Although it goes against the current of Freudian thought we seem to be stuck with in this century, I don't believe that anything is *about* sex, but that sex is *about* something. It is, if you like, a metaphor, for how we are as human beings in the social world. So writing about people doing sex, having sexual encounters, is a way of discussing something else about individuals and their relations with others. It's as if sex were a child's playground, an available space we all use both for pleasure, and for working out our other obsessions, fears, and desires. Sexual desire and its fulfillment is, of course, pleasure, but I don't believe it is only that. At least, I hope not, because it wouldn't be nearly as interesting to write about.

This particular story came out of my passing my local underground one day under the circumstances described. The rest, with its mix of death, sex, and insecurity, came from God-knows-where, as the rest usually does.

DROUGHT

By Wendy Law-Yone

Wendy Law-Yone herself comments on the (for her) natural juxtaposition of the erotic and the exotic; in this synergy was the inspiration for a unique creation, a sexual coming-of-age story that takes "what if?" for its spur and then proceeds single-mindedly to describe an answer. Bold, clever, and also, ultimately, wise, "Drought" is a fable that will be difficult for any reader to forget.

It was wartime, with its crazy misplaced fears—a time when suddenly it wasn't the bloodshed I dreaded as much as drought.

Maybe it was the Red Reservoir incident that sparked these new threats. In the north, where the fighting was fiercest, the rebels had run amok and wiped out an entire European compound, hacking up the bodies of the whites and throwing the parts into the private reservoir until the water turned red. It must have been the rumors that followed—rumors about poisoned wells and severed water lines—that brought on my nightmares about a water crisis.

But as though in a rush to make the nightmares come true, I became wasteful, not sparing, with water—especially once Auntie was gone and I was left alone with him. Amazing, how quickly I took to stripping and washing him as I pleased, using up water heedlessly. And to think how scared I'd been at first: scared to touch, even to look at him.

A white man! In those days—the early days of the Liberation—we all knew what they were doing to the whites on the mainland. We'd all heard about the Red Reservoir. Things were different, of course, on our island, where no one seemed to feel strongly about whites, or about much else. Still, the war had spread to other islands in the archipelago, and some said it was just a matter of time before we too would be caught up in it.

But I was afraid for another reason. I couldn't cast off the uneasy sense that I'd somehow caused an accident to happen.

Because I'd seen it happen. Standing on the veranda that morning, I had watched the plane go down. I didn't know it was a plane, then. It looked like a hawk, diving and disappearing in a flash from its straight-arrow course. The crash was that silent and graceful and swift. In the split moment before the sudden dive, I foresaw the whole thing. *Fall!* I'd said to myself even. And—just like that—the hawk had fallen.

I gave it no more thought until hours later, when they brought the survivor to our bungalow. It was only then that I put it all together. That hawk had been a small plane plunging headlong somewhere into the rubber plantations.

They carried him in on a makeshift bamboo stretcher. Our bungalow was on the hill overlooking the *kampong*, the village, below. From the veranda I could see the small procession snake up along the path that led from the plantations past the *kampong*—and through the gates at the foot of the hill.

"He fell out of the sky!" one of the *kampong* boys was shouting. "Like a god!"

They set him down underneath the monsoon-flower tree. He might well have been a god—large and dead to the world, but radiant. The tree was in full flower—a sign that the monsoons were close—and gold blossoms hung in clusters above him like ceremonial lanterns. His hair was gold too, though darker than the flowers; very thick and straight. A slight breeze plowed this way and that, revealing bits of scalp that looked as tender as wounds. He was wearing a short-sleeved khaki jacket—the kind with many pockets—and khaki shorts. In the glow of the flowering lanterns he shimmered all over as though dusted with mica or powdered glass.

I felt unworthy, staring at such radiance.

The man in charge of the rescue—a fast-talking Chinaman—explained things to Auntie, who was playing deaf. Her face was clenched; it was her ploy when things got difficult. And here was a difficult situation suddenly—an accident involving a white man at a time when whites were being slaughtered in the north. Not to mention all her other worries about the war.

The Chinaman was almost shouting, annoyed at having to repeat himself. The man lying unconscious on the stretcher was someone important, he kept saying. An adviser. He had flown in to help out the local militia. The Chinaman seemed to be implying that it was our duty—Auntie's and mine—to take him in. I understood why. I was the only half-caste in the area, the only blood relation to the stranger, so to speak. Naturally, they'd bring the European to our bungalow and expect us to lodge him.

"Bring him inside; you can leave him here," Auntie said at last, pointing her chin at me to indicate I should show them the way. I knew from the chin that she blamed me for this burden.

The men picked up the stretcher and followed me inside. I led them to my room. I turned down the thin blanket covering the thin mattress, and as they half-lifted, half-tilted him onto it, the jolting thought crossed my mind that maybe this was my father, come in search of me—although in the next instant I knew of course it couldn't be.

When the men had left, Auntie stood in the doorway, keeping her distance, while I looked the stranger over. A discolored swelling at the side of a knee and a cut at the temple above the right ear—the source of dried blood along one cheek—seemed to be the worst of his visible wounds.

Auntie felt I should try to wake him. This required my touching him. I put my palm down on the slight frown creasing his brow. How dark and dull the back of my hand appeared next to the pale gleam of his hair! I shook his shoulders and even slapped his cheeks. "Harder," Auntie said, quite spitefully I thought. I shook harder but couldn't bring myself to slap harder. Every smack left a stripe on his skin. Some time later, he did move an arm and a leg as though in the course of normal sleep—and by the time the doctor came, there were other small improvements: he stirred, he twitched, he turned from side to side in a delirium, he even opened his eyes for brief periods; and when I lifted his head to feed him the first spoonful of rice porridge, he swallowed. But mostly he slept.

The doctor was an old Moslem with a limp and a wheeze. With the war going on, doctors were scarce and getting pressed into service even in the islands. This old man had made the hike from the southern end and looked ready to pass out from the exertion. He put one hand on the patient's chest, tapped it with his other hand, bent the patient's elbows and knees, stuck a thermometer under his armpit, pried his eyelids apart. (Once more I was struck by the expensive color of those eyes, the color of a ring I'd seen on a Chinese merchant. A pale sapphire.)

"Coma," the doctor pronounced at last, scratching absently at the mold on his stethoscope.

"Coma?" Auntie said. "But he wakes up sometimes. He even takes soft rice."

"Sort of coma," the old man said. He handed Auntie a bottle of Gripe Water, usually prescribed for baby's wind. When she asked about the dosage, he hedged. "As needed," he said. "But not too often." He went down the stairs uncertainly, clutching the stair rail with something like panic.

In the beginning it was Auntie who decided what had to be done. *Give him a spoonful of coconut juice. Now wait. Now try a spoonful of rice. Now turn him on his side. Fold the rubber sheet under him. Now turn him back this way. Unfold the sheet from behind. Get the cloth and the basin.* She looked on squeamishly while giving the orders. But she wouldn't touch him.

And why should she? For as long as I could remember, she'd spoken of white men as an unsavory breed. They were bullies, always taking, always wanting more; they were liars, saying one thing, meaning quite another, telling the truth only if the truth was what it took to get them their way. And they were smelly.

In fact there was only one European she had known up close: my father. But the mark he left was enough to stain a race, apparently.

The thing he'd done was to leave my mother pregnant with me, forcing her into service with his lies. Lies about taking her back with him to a place called Antwerp, then—as he took off, solo—more lies about sending for her later, after he was settled.

My mother was not an island girl. Her home was on the mainland, in the dry zone, where her father worked in the oil fields run by Dutchmen like my father. It was only after my father went away that she came to this island—where Auntie, her sister, lived—to have her baby.

I was not yet weaned when she left me in a wicker basket on the floor one full-moon night to drown herself in the sea.

But along with Auntie's rancor I sensed a grudging pride in my half-white origins. "Mixed!" she crowed, when anyone remarked on my volume of curly hair. And the books were another concession. It was only English and Dutch that she wanted me to read.

It wasn't the first time I'd had an invalid on my hands. It was less than two years before that Auntie's father, Old Papu, had required around-the-clock care in the last bedridden months of his life. I had the night shift then (Auntie having collapsed for the day) and had got used to the bedpan and other unpleasant intimacies.

But this one was different. Even in his wakeful states, he wasn't alert enough to cooperate except to open his mouth for feedings or move his limbs for changings. Nor was feeding him always successful.

Auntie's close watch didn't make things any easier. And just sponging him was an ordeal that put me in a sweat, though I was generally on my own for that—Auntie didn't care to supervise.

But things did get easier with practice. I learned what to do about the messes (I'd even rigged a sort of loincloth that made the cleanup easier); and I became more adept at feeding and sponging.

The spongings were partial and routine at that point. And necessary. Despite the promise of the monsoon-flower trees, the rains still hadn't arrived and the heat festered and itched like a boil about to burst. Inside, even with all the windows open, the occasional cross breeze blew in a hot vapor that caused the floorboards to steam. Outside, the heat hit you with a force that took the breath away.

I was beginning to understand what Auntie meant about the European body odor. Strong and sour, it smelled like fermenting palm toddy. Even if you liked the smell of toddy, as I did, it wasn't something you could let run rampant.

The hotter it got, the more spongings were called for. By the time Auntie left for her monthly shop on the mainland, the rains were long overdue and the heat had become so intolerable that I was relieved to be able to swab him off at will, unobserved, with a frequency that might have alarmed her.

In truth I could hardly wait for her to leave. No sooner had she caught the ferry than I got down to business. I filled the zinc basin with warm water and brought it, with the washcloth, to his bedside. Early on, I had taken off his clothes—the khaki shorts and shirt—and replaced them with one of Papu's old sarongs, leaving it loose, like a sheet, around his middle. It made the cleaning and changing easier. I took the sarong off now and saw for the first time what he looked like, lying there on the rubber sheet, stripped utterly naked.

Huge. And very hairy. Tangled skeins of gold thread covered his chest, belly, arms, and legs; the threads were darker in the armpits and darkest at the crotch, forming a thick nest there, around the most startling part of his body. Unlike Old Papu's privates, shriveled and discolored all over like fruit gone bad, his seemed to blossom firm and ripe, with a good healthy color to the skin: thick through the scrotum but so fine on the penis that the veins showed up like lines drawn in ink.

A thorough soap and scrub was what I had planned. Auntie was gone, I was alone, and it was safe. But just standing over his exposed body, free to inspect any and all parts to satisfaction—just taking that secret liberty put me in a state. What if he came to, and his blue eyes were to shed their confusion and turn like searchlights on me?

I gave him the sponging; I even took care not to avoid the nest. But I didn't linger; I went about it as always—briskly, hardly looking, almost entirely by feel.

Auntie was to have returned on the last ferry late that evening. When the boat arrived, letting off its few passengers, and she wasn't among them, I knew something serious had happened. With the war getting closer—now we could hear the crackle of gunfire across the waves—she'd been overly anxious about leaving me even for the day. She would hardly have wanted me to spend the night alone.

I went home to wait. I thought of going down to the *kampong*, but soon it was dark and I was afraid—though not because I felt unsafe. No one in the *kampong* would have touched me—not even the older boys who came back to visit from their mainland jobs. One of them—a mocker and a strutter with too much coconut oil in his hair—once told me the reason why.

"Don't worry," he'd said when I mentioned my fear of taking the road to the *kampong* in the dark. "No one would dare touch you."

"I'm not that great," I said, thinking he was flattering me.

"Not that great, no," he laughed. "I mean no one would touch you because you're cursed."

I sat on the front steps looking down at the swarm of flickering lights in the *kampong*, waiting for my aunt long after I knew it was too late to expect her that night. When the lights were snuffed out one by one, I went inside to Auntie's room where I had slept on a bedroll on the floor since the day of the crash, when I'd given up my bed to the man in it now. With Auntie gone I lay on her bed, not bothering with the bedroll. The *kampong* noises had died down for the night; the palm trees rattled, but gently, in the breeze that had picked up finally after the breathless heat of the day. Still, it was not a night for sleep. I got up and went into my room, where the large, motionless figure filled my bed. Moonlight flooded through the open window and turned the hair on his head and chest to phosphorescence, like the surf on certain nights.

I sat at the foot of the bed, weary but bolt awake. The moon made me think of my mother. It was on a night like this that she had walked into the sea. Auntie had told me a story that came back to me now.

When my mother was pregnant, there was a drought in the dry zone, where the oil fields were concentrated, and where she kept house for my father at the time. It was the worst water shortage in years, and even the Europeans were under ration. That's when the first of the strikes began in the refineries, followed by the riots. In the turmoil of the next days the faucets in the European quarter were stone dry, and even the odd water-seller was nowhere in sight.

My mother had saved just enough drinking water to last a few days.

"For three days she took just enough from the canteen to moisten her lips," said Auntie. "While your father guzzled, thoughtless. And there she was, a child in her belly, herself not much more than a child. Later, when he went off and left her, she told me about the drought. I yelled at her. 'Stupid thing! Suppose the drought had gone on? What then?'

"Then, she said, she would have cut open a piece of her flesh to give him her blood to drink."

My mother—dead at sixteen—must have been exactly my age at the time of the drought. And my father? How old was he then? The same age, could it be, as this wounded man lying in front of me? "How old are you?" I whispered, although there was no need to. Suddenly, the moonlight felt cold on my skin, and my head swam from fatigue. I lay alongside him, pressing myself very close. After a while I loosened the sarong around his waist and crawled in until we lay side by side, cocooned.

I woke with the sun in my eyes and a bitter taste in my parched mouth. I had been dreaming of drought. The rebels, in the dream, had cut the water lines, and I was stranded on a beach, gagging on mouthfuls of saltwater.

My head was still on his chest. My neck was stiff, and when I started to rub it I found my fingers were wet. But what from? I swept my hand down across his belly—and there near his crotch was the wet patch. The moisture trailed out of the tip of his sex which lay horizontally—fuller than I remembered—across his thigh. I touched the moisture, which was clear and a little slippery. There was no odor to it. But it tasted slightly salty.

Someone from the *kampong*, one of the headman's sons, brought me the news about Auntie later that day. On the mainland, where she had been shopping, the police had made a sweep, arresting people by the lorry load. She was among those detained.

Detained. What did that mean, exactly? How long would they keep her? The headman's son couldn't tell me. "Not too long," he said, vague like the doctor. But the next bit of news hit me even harder.

"How's the Tuan?" he asked, cocking his head in the direction of my bedroom. I had forgotten that he was one of the men present on the day of the crash—was it just two weeks ago?

"Better," I lied, "much better." That wasn't a lie exactly. At least he had come to; at least we could feed him; at least he was alive.

"Not to worry!" said the headman's son; "day-after-tomorrow they're coming to take him to hospital."

The news made me dizzy, and for a moment I couldn't see straight. Looking over the shoulder of the man facing me, I fancied that the thin palm trees beyond were growing at even crazier angles than the ones along the beach, where they were almost horizontal.

"He's not ready!" I almost cried out, but knew better. The man would have wondered.

I wasn't ready. I wanted to keep him with me, as he was, without improvement if necessary. Once he was gone, nothing would stand between me and the void just waiting to swallow me whole. War would come to our island, I had no doubt of that now. The streams would run red, just like that reservoir up north. My aunt—like my mother, like my father—would never come back for me. And there would be a drought.

Just two more days! I couldn't leave his side. I couldn't bear it. Nothing seemed pressing anymore save the need, the urgent need, to hold him hostage. I didn't neglect to feed him the boiled rice—or to sustain myself on the remains. I didn't neglect the spongings, either. Nothing else mattered to me. Nothing.

When night came I got into bed with him, crawling into his sarong once more. I wanted rest but not sleep. Yet it was hard to fight the drowsiness brought on by the steady shushing of the sea. Trying to stay awake, I rummaged between his legs. Almost immediately, my fingers were wet.

By daylight, when I could see, all I wanted was to keep the liquid flowing—the little bit of liquid that emerged bead by bead at the nick of the crown on his mushroom-shaped sex. The first time I bent over to taste it at the source, I did it with utmost care, as though licking nectar off a thorn. But soon I grew reckless from a kind of greed, kneeling to face him as I continued the milking. I'd never known such power over another being—there he was, at my feet, exposed, unknowing, wholly at my mercy. So what if his eyes flared open without warning, and he watched me with that roaming gaze, a gaze less than pleasurable, less than human really? So what if he made those gargling noises? It would have taken a lot more to wrest me from my task, my dogged extraction of the juice that kept coming—only by the eyedropperful, it's true; but the miracle was that it kept coming.

No sooner had I licked up a droplet than another would seep through the nick in that tender flesh like a runnel of sap. A little kneading, a little rubbing, and out it oozed. Was it the slight saltiness that set off the thirst in me—a thirst that drink alone couldn't slake? Again and again I got up from bed for air. And for endless sips of water. I gave him to drink too—the thirst had seized him as well for all I knew: his lips were dry and white at the corners. No, I didn't deprive him. I even remembered to feed him his rice, a mouthful or two at a time. But being on my feet was a strain. Lightheaded, heavy-footed, I moved as in a delirium, craving only to return to bed, and to that little spot of moisture seeping through his sex. That was what gave me satisfaction. That. Not the tepid, tasteless water I drank and drank.

Is it surprising that by now I was rubbing between my own legs as well, in rhythm with the steady tapping of his sap? Pleasuring myself was hardly new to me. Maybe if things had been different, if someone—anyone—in the *kampong* had dared touch me, I might not yet have learned to touch myself so capably. But no one did; and so I did. How many times had I stood squarely in front of the window of my room, fingering myself with my sarong hitched up in front, while an unsuspecting male, the object of my heated fancy, went about his business in the *kampong* below! Even when they—for there were many such males—happened to look up and catch me framed at the window, whatever they saw of me from the chest up revealed nothing of how I busied myself below the window line. Skinny boys in their teens, paunchy men—I wasn't choosy about these targets. Once, it was an old Hindu in a ragged loincloth, bending over to stack cordwood. That time I was somewhat more ashamed than usual afterward. But shame is not unlike a lump of ice: painful to swallow, but only for a stinging instant. Then it melts, it goes away.

Given what I knew already, it wasn't so hard to finger myself with one hand, coaxing the drip out of him with the other—while also managing to lick. All the while I marveled at the slick rosy tip of his strange, strange growth, rubber-soft one minute and hard enough the next so that the veins beat against my fingertips. At last my licking gave way to outright sucking, in time to the sucking that pulsed between my legs just before the long tremor kicked in.

By night I was wild with abandon. I shed all my clothes—a thing I'd never done in his presence—dropping my sarong on top of his, which lay on the floor, in a coil, where I'd flung it. I bent down to look into his face and saw that his eyes were open, fixed just past me with the shock of a man gazing at a ghost. Was it my hair, I wondered—my neglected mass of frizz? He closed his eyes then, as though to shut out the disturbing vision, whatever it was.

I got up onto the bed and knelt beside him, facing his feet. The air in the room was so warm and close that I could smell my own sweat—a sour, sickly smell—along with the familiar fumes given off by his body. It felt no different from a fever—the sweating, the shortness of breath, the thirst. Naturally, I went for the liquid. Like the water I squandered while fearing drought, I kept returning to this salty, thirst-making moisture to quench my thirst.

As I squatted over him on the bed, facing his feet and bending over to drink at the source, I happened to lower my crotch onto his hand, which lay with its fingers curled, palm up, by his side. That touch, so slight, grazed me to the quick, and all I had to do—without interrupting the sucking—was to rock back and forth, back and forth, over his open hand while I climbed to that edge from which the body aches to plummet. I plummeted. I shot forward until my head came to rest at his feet. After a while I turned around and nuzzled his hand, only to discover a slickness on his fingers, so like the slickness on mine. Did our liquids also taste alike?

They did. I wanted him to taste them both. I wiped his wet hand on one of my breasts and brought that nipple up to his mouth, where I pressed it against his lips. Then I lowered my other breast down to the moisture at the tip of his sex, rubbing it around before doing what I'd done with the other breast.

The thirst was so acute now I could barely swallow. I placed my mouth over his, probing deep with my tongue—over and under his, all along his teeth, between his gums and lips. His breath was musty, his taste sour-sweet. The combination made my mouth water. I went for his ears now, first one and then the other, licking along the curves and dents and into the hole, to fetch up the bitterish taste of wax. I moved down to the armpits, burying my nose in the pungent thicket of hair; down over his chest and belly to lick his navel; and down into the depths of his genitals.

I'd never stopped to lick the sac before. I trailed my tongue over it now, over the ridged hairy skin, before lifting it to lick under as well, down the line running into his crack. I stopped at its rim, to catch my breath; then, lifting his legs at the knees, parting the cheeks, I plunged my tongue right down into the recess, as deep as it would go.

A dark bitter taste exploded through my palette; the taste of a poisonous plant, perhaps—some wild, inedible onion. The discovery was dizzying. I wanted to subject him to something comparable. That's when I moved up to straddle his face. I faced him on my knees, shifting them farther and farther apart until the very core, the very heart of that hidden cleavage between my legs was split wide open and planted squarely on his mouth. Now we were engaged in a long wet kiss; it was my lips, I should say—those other lips—that were doing the kissing as they smeared their saliva onto his. *Taste!* I said, pressing down harder on my haunches, circling faster, kissing deeper. I was dying of thirst. I was dying, dying . . . and in the throes of the shudders that sent me sprawling across his face, I glimpsed what it was like, that letting go and slipping away from the surge of inseparable pleasure and pain.

After a while my skin prickled and I sensed, before I saw, the light I was lying in, a light that chilled rather than warmed me. I opened my eyes onto the full face of the moon, filling my window, staring me down.

I picked up my sarong and tied it around my chest. Outside, I stood on the veranda briefly to absorb the night: the indigo shadows and shapes of the *kampong* roofs, the crooked palms and fuzzy shoreline of the sea. How still it was—not a breeze, not a drizzle to break the spell and let the monsoon in. Those yellow flowers had bloomed and withered in a burst of false promise.

The moon was not so close now; it had retreated to a distance from which it shed its path of light. The path led directly from the stairs of the veranda, down the incline, in a straight line to the sea. I set out without the slightest hesitation; nothing seemed more natural or more inevitable than walking its beam. I followed it until the sand turned wet underfoot. From there the path glittered like a welcoming carpet rolled out, in my honor, across the surface of the sea. I took my first step into the waves. It was easy, it was nothing, I could feel the slightest undertow pulling me in.

But on the threshold of that walk into the waves I turned—I don't know why—to take a few steps along the beach . . . and found the beam trailing me. I stopped and turned in the other direction—and there was the moonbeam, still at my side. Back I wheeled once more, breaking into a run; and back it tagged alongside me.

Whichever way I went, up and down the beach, the path of light was doggedly at my heels.

It wasn't the moon that was doing the bidding; it was taking the lead from me—it was I who was guiding the beam! I darted this way and that, stopping and starting, giddy from running circles round the moon.

When I could run no more I headed home, the sea behind me, the moon in tow.

There was time to give him a sponging. I hadn't planned on it; I hadn't thought I'd be returning. Yet here I was back home, in time for one last wash.

I hadn't thought I could do the other thing either. But that too I did. I let him go.

AUTHOR'S NOTE

When I began this, it was the setting I had to think about; the action in an erotic story, after all, is a given. I grew up in the tropics, but that's not entirely why I came to select them as the background here. Rather, it was also because of a powerful construct of the tropics shaped by the likes of Conrad, Orwell, Melville, Malraux, et al. All of them captured—and sometimes brilliantly misrepresented—this region as a zone of mythic heat and torpor that destroys decorum, breaks down morality, and erodes the will. It is to them that I owe my having settled on a tropical island as the backdrop for my story. Where else but in a steamy jungle could such a switch in rules take place? Where else could exploitation occur so illicitly?

The old tropical stereotypes, yes. But why fight them, if instead you can stand them on their head? "Drought" is my version of what happens when a restless native tends a wounded knight.

OH, BROTHER

By Bea Wilder

The lively comic charm of this monologue beautifully complements its vision of the tenderness that can spring up even between two new lovers whose erotic impulses are helped along by propinquity. Bea Wilder, like Susan Dooley, gives us a portrait of a woman at home in her body, who knows and cherishes her own ability to give and receive pleasure . . . and her relish is, I think, infectious.

I was deflowered in the City of Brotherly Love twenty-five years ago. Perhaps this explains my penchant for friends' brothers, or maybe it's because I never had one, growing up as I did in a one-gender family of three younger sisters, a domineering mother, and a large cranky female cat. I've simply always been completely fascinated with the idea of having boys around the house—boys you could touch, hug, and kiss, but never screw, of course. So when Carolyn invited me out of the city in the middle of August, my first inclination was to say no. (I already had plans to go to a Red Sox game on Sunday with an old lover and friend, and who needed extra traffic hassles?) But then she let drop that at this birthday party for her, at her family's summer house, her New York-dwelling brother Jonathan would be in attendance; not surprisingly, although she didn't know it, this turned out to be the very incentive I needed to tank up my car and hit the road early that Saturday morning.

In Cambridge, recycling old boyfriends and husbands and coming across with brothers and other relatives is de rigueur, but Carolyn had only been forthcoming to the extent that I knew Jonathan was in his midforties and unattached. That was enough though, and the promise of a "live one" fresh off the train from the Big Apple remained a tantalizing prospect all the way up the highway north to New Hampshire. Anyway, her directions were good, and in exactly the time she said it would take, I was turning off Route 69 onto the bumpy dirt road that led up a hill to her mother's driveway. No other cars were in evidence, and I remembered hearing something about how they'd be grocery shopping if they weren't there when I arrived. Hordes of daunting relatives were promised for the birthday soiree, so these peaceful moments were fleeting and precious. I unloaded my tote bag, birthday present, and tennis racquet and pushed open the front screen door to the kitchen. I put my stuff down and looked through the living room to a nice deck with a spectacular mountain view, and then I realized I was not alone. Card-shuffling noises emanated from the breakfast nook, and there was a large bearlike creature intently playing solitaire. I coughed nervously, and it got up and smiled. He had opaque brown eyes and a tender smile. "Oh, you must be Carrie's friend. I'm Jonathan."

He seemed tentative and shy, and I was a bit taken aback, but I managed a "Yes, I'm Jean. What shall I do with my stuff?" Now he looked confused, and he sort of pointed at the living room and said to stick it there for the time being. Then he went back to his card game, and I stammered about the nice view and he agreed, and then I said I was going out on the deck to look. He showed up a few minutes later, and we made desultory conversation about Carrie and mother gone shopping and would be back soon and about what an easy trip up it was and about how I hoped we would play tennis and about his documentary on a famous deceased Democrat and my Suburban Hunger study. He seemed kind and sensitive and self-effacing, different from his sister, and just as I sensed the beginnings of sweet sexual tension a noisy car jarred my mood. Carolyn and their mother had arrived.

We all converged in the kitchen, and Carolyn gushed over my early arrival and Mrs. Steele said she hoped I was ready for some tennis before it got too hot as we all put the bottles and cans and jars away. No one introduced me to Jonathan. Mugs of coffee were filled, and we sat on the deck with various newspapers commenting on interesting items here and there. I felt a bit strange and distinct from this family unit. Jonathan was very quiet but pleasant in a sort of detached way that made me curious about and interested in him. We made eye contact a few times and laughed together about a pun Carolyn didn't get. After a while, Carolyn announced that I should bring my tote upstairs to a room down the hall from Jonathan because she preferred a sort of finished basement room with only one bed. She took me on a brief tour and showed me where to drop off my bag, and then we all changed for the tennis game and met at the court nearby. Jonathan and his mother teamed up against Carolyn and me.

The woman is almost eighty, after all, and Jonathan said he rarely played, but they beat us handily. I played poorly, which is unusual, but I was thinking much more about how I hoped Jonathan liked my long tan legs in my short tennis dress than about watching the ball. Luckily it was too hot to play for too long, and we went back to the house for bathing suits because Carolyn wanted to show me the swimming hole. Her mom opted to stay and mix up chicken salad, and Jonathan came with us to swim. Despite the heat, the water temperature was subfreezing so Carolyn and I only jumped in and out and then sat on a rock in the sun and talked. Jonathan stood in the water stomach-deep and cooled off his oversized physique, and I pretended to be engrossed in Carolyn's boring tales of their childhood summers.

The hot day wore on till it was time for an agreed-upon nap. It was about 2:00 P.M., and the guests were due at 5:30. Carolyn went downstairs to her bedroom, and I went upstairs and fell on my bed naked. I couldn't really sleep wondering where Jonathan was and listening for signs of him on the stairs. It crossed my mind that masturbating would relieve some of the tension I felt, but I didn't know if I really wanted to let go of it and besides the bedsprings were so creaky. Instead I fantasized about what it would be like if he walked in and took me in his arms and licked me all over. I became so aroused, I had to have some relief, so I licked my fingers and tweaked my straining, diamond-hard nipples, then ran them down my front to the moist fuzzy outskirts of my clit. I pressed it hard then in gentle circles. Within seconds I felt the wonderful spasms of relief all through my body to my toes. I hoped I hadn't gasped too loudly. I rolled over pressing my breasts to the cool cotton sheets, happy that I could make myself feel so good, and fell asleep.

When I awoke I was sweating and disoriented. I was worried I had slept through the party. I pulled on my bathing suit and went downstairs to look for a clock. The one on the mantle said 4:30. Jonathan was in the far corner of the living room reading, and he looked up. "Aren't you ever going to get dressed?" he said smiling. "Oh, yes, I mean I just came down to see what time it was. I fell asleep, and I thought it might be later," I managed. "Why SHOULD she get dressed?" his mother, unexpectedly charging around the corner, boomed. "If I looked that good in a bathing suit, I'd never take it off. She isn't chubby like you and me, Jon," she added. Jonathan blushed visibly and mumbled something about taking a shower. He brushed by me, and I wanted to hug him and show him that we were allied against rude mothers and tell him I would never embarrass him like that, but, of course, I just stepped out of the way. Then Mrs. Steele started again, "Come help me put out the hors d'oeuvres, my dear. Carolyn's out looking for my cat who has been missing all day. She'll be back when she's found her."

I grabbed a vegetable platter and some Boursin and crackers and put them on coffee tables, and then I fraternized with the enemy a bit, she was after all my hostess, and went upstairs to dress.

I came down in my black and white polka-dotted jumpsuit (once, someone at another summer place had called it a "clown suit," but I thought it very chic) and gold sandals. Carolyn's uncle, who's a preeminent Chinese scholar and his wife had arrived. Carolyn was with them on the deck in a wonderful rust-colored handkerchief dress (she did have style), and she introduced us and told us to help ourselves to drinks. I was getting ice cubes out of the bucket when a large group of cousins came in the door shrieking and kissing. I reached for the vodka and tonic and went out to the Chinese scholar who recently had a building at Harvard named for him. He was very old, and his wife was ensconced with the cousins, so I sat near him and asked him questions about our surroundings. We talked at great length, and Mrs. Steele came by on several occasions and whispered offers of replacing me so I could "mingle," but I was very content.

I could see Jonathan across the crowded deck, and he looked uncomfortable even though it was his chance to shine about his documentary, with its initial broadcast on public television due in a month. Carolyn herself was madly mingling and soon started opening cards and gifts. The aged Chinese scholar talked about how he missed Carolyn's father because he had had such a good mind, which would be refreshing at occasions like this. Then he started to nod off, and I decided to find a bathroom. When I emerged the party was delightfully dispersing except for one maiden aunt who was invited to eat duck and play bridge with us later, "because Carrie never likes to play." I guess it was assumed that Jonathan and I would. Carolyn seemed locked in conversation with a Connecticut cousin, so I scurried around the kitchen and helped get the meal set out on the dining room table.

The duck was superb, which was surprising. Mrs. Steele was a good artist, but her kitchen here, and in Cambridge, had none of the inviting signs of an accomplished cook. The bridge was fun, too, and we all fell into an amusing round of harmless gossip while Carolyn cleaned up.

Then, just when I was starting to feel at ease with Carolyn and her family, she announced she was retiring. It was only about ten, but she said she hadn't slept well the night before, thanked us again for our birthday efforts, and descended to her bedroom. When the rubber ended, Mrs. Steele also retired, and Jonathan was asked to walk the aunt home. I wasn't at all tired, but I did feel a chill of isolation and abandonment. I walked out on the deck and made a silent prayer that Jonathan would come home and keep me company. After a few very long minutes, the front door opened and shut, and I could hear him in the kitchen rustling around. The sliding door to the deck opened, he came out, sat down behind me, and lit a joint. I turned my chair around, and we stared at each other.

"Want some of this?" he offered as he held out the rolled cigarette. I hadn't smoked dope in ages and I didn't usually like it, but I didn't want to offend him in any way so I reached for it and inhaled. "How did you like the Jesus freaks?" he asked. I looked confused, so he regaled me with a tale of cousins I had met earlier who had discovered the ways of Satan and had joined the First Assembly of God. I laughed and said I hadn't noticed, but that I had that in my family too, and he laughed and we toked some more. He pointed out their house across the meadow, and we pretended to hear Satanic rituals being performed and laughed some more. He told me we should try to talk softly because his mother's room had a window on the deck. I felt like we were naughty children sneaking around after the adults had gone to sleep, and it was forbidden and fun and the way I imagined it would be with a brother in the house. I had a sudden urge to lie down on the bench near his chair and put my head in his lap, but instead I asked if I could sip his ice water.

I drank it all, then offered to get some more from the kitchen. I was a bit tipsy, but I managed to get to the kitchen and had just opened the refrigerator door when I felt him behind me. He put his hand over mine and closed the fridge door. I turned around, and he sort of pinned me with his arms against it and kissed me in the most unforgettable way. First it was tentative and probing, then as we relaxed into it and found our rhythm we simultaneously hugged and rubbed each other with our arms, still sucking on each other's tongues and exploring for what seemed like a very long time. I guess some of it was the dope, but I honestly can say I had never kissed like that before. Jonathan took my face in his hands then my hand and led me over to a large comfortable chair in the living room. We collapsed into it and kissed more and more, and I could feel my whole body responding and aching for more. I took his hand and placed it on a breast, and he stopped kissing and looked to see where to put it. Then he gently pinched my nipple and stuck his tongue in my ear.

"You're beautiful," he groaned. I was panting, and I grabbed for his shirt and felt his smooth soft skin, and he moaned softly. Then he whispered in my ear: "You go upstairs first and open your door and close it and listen for me to come up and then sneak into my room." I tried to sit up straight and unconvincingly said, "But, Jonathan, I don't think we should do obscene things in your mother's house."

"We don't have to," he whispered, "but don't you want to kiss some more?"

"Oh, yes," I agreed. "Let's."

I followed his instructions about entering my room and listening for him, and then I quietly opened my door and crept down the hall to his room. He was lying on his bed with his shirt off, and I longed to rest my breasts on his chest. As if mind reading, he fumbled at the large buttons on the front of my jumpsuit until they opened. I was bra-less, and he rubbed my breasts, and we lay chest to chest for several minutes. Then he said rather naively, "Did you ever expect that today would end up like this?" "I was hoping it would, weren't you?" I asked. "Yeah, it's just that Carrie and I don't usually like the same people," he explained. "It's not as if she's been particularly friendly today, so it's nice that you are," I murmured, as I reached down to rub his cock. "Mmmm," he grunted as he helped me unzip his fly and put my hand on his throbbing erection. Then he took my hand off and said, "I might finish too soon, so let's concentrate on you for a bit."

He encircled my breasts and very slowly and softly stroked my stomach and thighs. I felt very wet and juicy and almost cried out when he found my clit with one finger and put another up my vagina. He took that finger away and put it up to my lips to remind me to be quiet, and I could smell my female juices on his finger, which turned me on even more. He stuck his tongue in my mouth and we kissed some more, then his tongue followed the path his finger had made around my breasts and down my stomach to my overflowing cunt. He gently sucked on my clit and reinserted his finger, and I held onto his head while I lurched in an orgasm unknown to me. Waves of chills all the way to my toes seized my flailing body over and over again. When I was spent, I felt relaxed and happy and warm all over. He grazed gently on my front some more and rested his hand on my moist bush, and I reached over to his semi-hard penis. He took my hand and licked it and then put it back on his cock and I rubbed it slowly. "Touch my balls," he requested softly, and he moaned when I grabbed them.

His cock was glistening with a few drops of sperm, and I could feel my excitement rising up again. I licked him the way he had me all down his front, and then I teased his tip until he begged me to take him. Still I ran my hand up and down his shaft and licked only the tip of his cock while he thrust himself into my mouth. I removed the penis and coddled it in the cleavage of my breasts. "Please, please," he groaned, as I held him and rubbed him across my hard nipples, then put him back in my mouth, sucking up and down and carefully keeping my teeth out of the way. He found my clit again with a spare hand, and we writhed around together until I could taste his sperm. He was delicious, and I loved the Chinese food taste of him. We lay all wrapped up in each other for a very long time until I felt him reach for a clock. We looked at the glow-in-the-dark hands together. It was 3:30. I would be an utter wreck at the baseball game if I didn't try for a few hours of sleep, but I couldn't let go of him. He kissed me again, and we entwined tongues. Then he gently lifted me up in his arms and crept down the hall to my room. He lay me down on the bed and kissed my bush. "You have a beautiful pussy," he said. I wanted him again, but I knew we should stop. "So much for not doing obscene things in your mother's house," I whispered. "No penetration," he said smiling. Then he was gone. I fell into deep satisfied sleep.

The next morning was a rush of showering, dressing, packing, morning salutations, thank-yous, and English muffins, with everyone at the breakfast table when I got there. Jonathan and I had our furtive exchanges, and when it was time to go, he walked me out to the car with my bag. He put the bag in the trunk and stood staring at me as I started the car. I rolled down the window and winked at him. "I sure hope you're in the book," he said. "Have a safe trip."

"I am," I replied. "Oh, brother," I thought as I drove down the road.

AUTHOR'S NOTE

I wrote this story one year after the weekend on which it is loosely based. It is an anniversary reflection on the beginnings of a memorable affair of the heart, with a few adjustments for fantasy, though it was a genuinely good time. I have enjoyed several of my friends' brothers over the years and remain fascinated with the brother-sister relationship, which I am only starting to understand.

NINETY-THREE MILLION MILES AWAY

By Barbara Gowdy

There are relationships with strangers, and then there are strange relationships. In "Ninety-Three Million Miles Away" Barbara Gowdy mixes the two, adding, as well, a paradox: the intense intimacy of distance. It is across this space, she suggests, that we might find a singular opportunity to be most ourselves. While certainly an intriguing notion of itself, it is accompanied by another, equally provocative one—that most women have in them an instinctive streak of exhibitionism, which is, Gowdy posits, "a side effect of being the receptor in the sex act." However, her concluding message, reminding us as it does that the sensation of feeling desire always carries with it the potential for surprise, is unassailable.

At least part of the reason Ali married Claude, a cosmetic surgeon with a growing practice, was so that she could quit her boring government job. Claude was all for it. "You only have one life to live," he said. "You only have one kick at the can." He gave her a generous allowance and told her to do what she wanted.

She wasn't sure what that was, aside from trying on clothes in expensive stores. Claude suggested something musical—she loved music—so she took dance classes and piano lessons and discovered that she had a tin ear and no sense of rhythm. She fell into a mild depression during which she peevishly questioned Claude about the ethics of cosmetic surgery.

"It all depends on what light you're looking at it in," Claude said. He was not easily riled. What Ali needed to do, he said, was take the wider view.

She agreed. She decided to devote herself to learning, and she began a regime of reading and studying, five days a week, five to six hours a day. She read novels, plays, biographies, essays, magazine articles, almanacs, the New Testament, *The Concise Oxford Dictionary, The Harper Anthology of Poetry.*

But after a year of this, although she became known as the person at dinner parties who could supply the name or date that somebody was snapping around for, she wasn't particularly happy, and she didn't even feel smart. Far from it, she felt stupid, a machine, an idiot savant whose one talent was memorization. If she had any *creative* talent, which was the only kind she really admired, she wasn't going to find it by armoring herself with facts. She grew slightly paranoid that Claude wanted her to settle down and have a baby.

A few days before their second wedding anniversary she and Claude bought a condominium apartment with floor-to-ceiling windows, and Ali decided to abandon her reading regime and to take up painting. Since she didn't know the first thing about painting or even drawing, she studied pictures from art books. She did know what her first subject was going to be—herself in the nude. Several months earlier she'd had a dream about spotting her signature in the corner of a painting, and realizing from the conversation of the men who were admiring it (and blocking her view) that it was an extraordinary rendition of her naked self. She took the dream to be a sign. For several weeks she studied the proportions, skin tones, and muscle definitions of the nudes in her books, then she went out and bought art supplies and a self-standing, full-length mirror.

She set up her work area in the middle of the living room. Here she had light without being directly in front of the window. When she was all ready to begin, she stood before the mirror and slipped off her white terry-cloth housecoat and her pink flannelette pajamas, letting them fall to the floor. It aroused her a little to witness her careless shedding of clothes. She tried a pose: hands folded and resting loosely under her stomach, feet buried in the drift of her housecoat.

For some reason, however, she couldn't get a fix on what she looked like. Her face and body seemed indistinct, secretive in a way, as if they were actually well-defined, but not to her, or not from where she was looking.

She decided that she should simply start, and see what happened. She did a pencil drawing of herself sitting in a chair and stretching. It struck her as being very good, not that she could really judge, but the out-of-kilter proportions seemed slyly deliberate, and there was a pleasing simplicity to the reaching arms and the elongated curve of the neck. Because flattery hadn't been her intention, Ali felt that at last she may have wrenched a vision out of her soul.

The next morning she got out of bed unusually early, not long after Claude had left the apartment, and discovered sunlight streaming obliquely into the living room through a gap between their building and the apartment house next door. As far as she knew, and in spite of the plate-glass windows, this was the only direct light they got. Deciding to make use of it while it lasted, she moved her easel, chair, and mirror closer to the window. Then she took off her housecoat and pajamas.

For a few moments she stood there looking at herself, wondering what it was that had inspired the sketch. Today she was disposed to seeing herself as not bad, overall. As far as certain specifics went, though, as to whether her breasts were small, for instance, or her eyes close together, she remained in the dark.

Did other people find her looks ambiguous? Claude was always calling her beautiful, except that the way he put it—"You're beautiful to me," or "I think you're beautiful"—made it sound as if she should understand that his taste in women was unconventional. Her only boyfriend before Claude, a guy called Roger, told her she was great but never said how exactly. When they had sex, Roger liked to hold the base of his penis and watch it going in and out of her. Once, he said that there were days he got so horny at the office, his pencil turned him on. She thought it should have been his pencil sharpener.

She covered her breasts with her hands. Down her cleavage a drop of sweat slid haltingly, a sensation like the tip of a tongue. She circled her palms until her nipples hardened, and imagined a man's hands . . . not Claude's—a man's hands not attached to any particular man. She looked out the window.

In the apartment across from her she saw a man.

She leapt to one side, behind the drapes. Her heart pounded violently, but only for a moment, as if something had thundered by, dangerously close. She wiped her wet forehead on the drapes, then, without looking at the window, walked back to her easel, picked up her palette and brush, and began to mix paint. She gave herself a glance in the mirror, but she had no intention of trying to duplicate her own skin tone. She wanted something purer. White with just a hint of rose, like the glance of color in a soap bubble.

Her strokes were short and light to control dripping. She liked the effect, though . . . how it made the woman appear as if she were covered in feathers. Paint splashed on her own skin, but she resisted putting her smock on. The room seemed preternaturally white and airy; the windows beyond the mirror gleamed. Being so close to the windows gave her the tranced sensation of standing at the edge of a cliff.

A few minutes before she lost the direct sun, she finished the woman's skin. She set down her palette and put her brush in turpentine, then wet a rag in the turpentine and wiped paint off her hands and where it had dripped on her thighs and feet. She thought about the sun. She thought that it is ninety-three million miles away and that its fuel supply will last another five billion years. Instead of thinking about the man who was watching her, she tried to recall a solar chart she had memorized a couple of years ago.

The surface temperature is six thousand degrees Fahrenheit, she told herself. Double that number, and you have how many times bigger the surface of the sun is compared to the surface of the earth. Except that because the sun is a ball of hot gas, it actually has no surface.

When she had rubbed the paint off herself, she went into the kitchen to wash away the turpentine with soap and water. The man's eyes tracked her. She didn't have to glance at the window for confirmation. She switched on the light above the sink, soaped the dishcloth, and began to wipe her skin. There was no reason to clean her arms, but she lifted each one and wiped the cloth over it. She wiped her breasts. She seemed to share in his scrutiny, as if she were looking at herself through his eyes. From his perspective she was able to see her physical self very clearly—her shiny, red-highlighted hair, her small waist and heart-shaped bottom, the dreamy tilt to her head.

She began to shiver. She wrung out the cloth and folded it over the faucet, then patted herself dry with a dish towel. Then, pretending to be examining her fingernails, she turned and walked over to the window. She looked up.

There he was. Her glance of a quarter of an hour ago had registered dark hair and a white shirt. Now she saw a long, older face . . . a man in his fifties maybe. A green tie. She had seen him before this morning—quick, disinterested (or so she had thought) sightings of a man in his kitchen, watching television, going from room to room. A bachelor living next door. She pressed the palms of her hands on the window, and he stepped back into shadow.

The pane clouded from her breath. She leaned her body into it, flattening her breasts against the cool glass. Right at the window she was visible to his apartment and the one below, which had closed vertical blinds. “Each window like a pill’ry appears,” she thought. Vaguely appropriate lines from the poems she had read last year were always occurring to her. She felt that he was still watching, but she yearned for proof.

When it became evident that he wasn’t going to show himself, she went into the bedroom. The bedroom windows didn’t face the apartment house, but she closed them anyway, then got into bed under the covers. Between her legs there was such a tender throbbing that she had to push a pillow into her crotch. Sex addicts must feel like this, she thought. Rapists, child molesters.

She said to herself, “You are a certifiable exhibitionist.” She let out an amazed, almost exultant laugh, but instantly fell into a darker amazement as it dawned on her that she really was . . . she really *was* an exhibitionist. And what’s more, she had been one for years, or at least she had been working up to being one for years.

Why, for instance, did she and Claude live here, in this vulgar low-rise? Wasn’t it because of the floor-to-ceiling windows that faced the windows of the house next door?

And what about when she was twelve and became so obsessed with the idea of urinating on people’s lawns that one night she crept out of the house after everyone was asleep and did it, peed on the lawn of the townhouses next door . . . right under a streetlight, in fact.

What about two years ago, when she didn’t wear underpants the entire summer? She’d had a minor yeast infection and had read that it was a good idea not to wear underpants at home, if you could help it, but she had stopped wearing them in public as well, beneath skirts and dresses, at parties, on buses, and she must have known that this was taking it a bit far, because she had kept it from Claude.

“Oh, my God,” she said wretchedly.

She went still, alerted by how theatrical that had sounded. Her heart was beating in her throat. She touched a finger to it. So fragile, a throat. She imagined the man being excited by her hands on her throat.

What was going on? What was the matter with her? Maybe she was too aroused to be shocked at herself. She moved her hips, rubbing her crotch against the pillow. No, she didn’t want to masturbate. That would ruin it.

Ruin what?

She closed her eyes, and the man appeared to her. She experienced a rush of wild longing. It was as if, all her life, she had been waiting for a long-faced, middle-aged man in a white shirt and green tie. He was probably still standing in his living room, watching her window.

She sat up, threw off the covers.

Dropped back down on the bed.

This was crazy. This really was crazy. What if he was a rapist? What if, right this minute, he was downstairs, finding out her name from the mailbox? Or what if he was just some lonely, normal man who took her display as an invitation to phone her up and ask her for a date? It's not as if she wanted to go out with him. She wasn't looking for an affair.

For an hour or so she fretted, and then she drifted off to sleep. When she woke up, shortly after noon, she was quite calm. The state she had worked herself into earlier struck her as overwrought. So, she gave some guy a thrill, so what? She was a bit of an exhibitionist . . . most women were, she bet. It was instinctive, a side effect of being the receptor in the sex act.

She decided to have lunch and go for a walk. While she was making herself a sandwich she avoided glancing at the window, but as soon as she sat at the table, she couldn't resist looking over.

He wasn't there, and yet she felt that he was watching her, standing out of the light. She ran a hand through her hair. "For Christ's sake," she reproached herself, but she was already with him. Again it was as if her eyes were in his head, although not replacing his eyes. She knew that he wanted her to slip her hand down her sweatpants. She did this. Watching his window, she removed her hand and licked her wet fingers. At that instant she would have paid money for some sign that he was watching.

After a few minutes she began to chew on her fingernails. She was suddenly depressed. She reached over and pulled the curtain across the window and ate her sandwich. Her mouth, biting into the bread, trembled like an old lady's. "Trembled like a guilty thing surprised," she quoted to herself. It wasn't guilt, though, it wasn't frustration, either, not sexual frustration. She was acquainted with this bleached sadness—it came upon her at the height of sensation . . . after orgasms, after a day of trying on clothes in stores.

She finished her sandwich and went for a long walk in her new toreador pants and her tight, black, turtleneck sweater. By the time she returned, Claude was home. He asked her if she had worked in the nude again.

"Of course," she said absently. "I have to." She was looking past him at the man's closed drapes. "Claude," she said suddenly, "am I beautiful? I mean not just to you. Am I empirically beautiful?"

Claude looked surprised. "Well, yeah," he said. "Sure you are. Hell, I married you, didn't I? Hey!" He stepped back. "Whoa!"

She was removing her clothes. When she was naked, she said,

"Don't think of me as your wife. Just as a woman. One of your patients. Am I beautiful or not?"

He made a show of eyeing her up and down. "Not bad," he said. "Of course, it depends on what you mean by 'beautiful.' " He laughed. "What's going on?"

"I'm serious. You don't think I'm kind of . . . normal? You know, plain?"

"Of course not," he said lovingly. He reached for her and drew her into his arms. "You want hard evidence?" he said.

They went into the bedroom. It was dark because the curtains were still drawn. She switched on the bedside lamp, but once he was undressed, he switched it off again.

"No," she said from the bed, "leave it on."

"What? You want it on?"

"For a change."

The next morning she got up before he did. She had hardly slept. During breakfast she kept looking over at the apartment house, but there was no sign of the man. Which didn't necessarily mean that he wasn't there. She couldn't wait for Claude to leave so that she could stop pretending she wasn't keyed up. It was gnawing at her that she had overestimated or somehow misread the man's interest. How did she know? He might be gay. He might be so devoted to a certain woman that all other women repelled him. He might be puritanical . . . a priest, a born-again Christian. He might be out of his mind.

The minute Claude was out the door, she undressed and began work on the painting. She stood in the sunlight mixing colors, then sat on the chair in her stretching pose, looking at herself in the mirror, then stood up and—without paying much attention, glancing every few seconds at his window—painted ribs and uplifted breasts.

An hour went by before she thought, he's not going to show up. She dropped into the chair, weak with disappointment, even though she knew that, very likely, he had simply been obliged to go to work, that his being home yesterday was a fluke. Forlornly she gazed at her painting. To her surprise she had accomplished something rather interesting: breasts like Picasso eyes. It is possible, she thought dully, that I am a natural talent.

She put her brush in the turpentine, and her face in her hands. She felt the sun on her hair. In a few minutes the sun would disappear behind his house, and after that, if she wanted him to get a good look at her, she would have to stand right at the window. She envisioned herself stationed there all day. You are ridiculous, she told herself. You are unhinged.

She glanced up at the window again.

He was there.

She sat up straight. Slowly she came to her feet. Stay, she prayed. He did. She walked over to the window, her fingertips brushing her thighs. She held her breath. When she was at the window, she stood perfectly still. He stood perfectly still. He had on a white shirt again, but no tie. He was close enough that she could make out the darkness around his eyes, although she couldn't tell exactly where he was looking. But his eyes seemed to enter her head like a drug, and she felt herself aligned with his perspective. She saw herself—surprisingly slender, composed but apprehensive—through the glass and against the backdrop of the room's white walls.

After a minute or two she walked over to the chair, picked it up, and carried it to the window. She sat facing him, her knees apart. He was as still as a picture. So was she, because she had suddenly remembered that he might be gay or crazy. She tried to give him a hard look. She observed his age and his sad, respectable appearance . . . and the fact that he remained at the window, revealing his interest.

No, he was the man she had imagined. I am a gift to him, she thought, opening her legs wider. I am his dream come true. She began to rotate her hips. With the fingers of both hands she spread her labia.

One small part of her mind, clinging to the person she had been until yesterday morning, tried to pull her back. She felt it as a presence behind the chair, a tableau of sensational, irrelevant warnings that she was obviously not about to turn around for. She kept her eyes on the man. Moving her left hand up to her breasts, she began to rub and squeeze and to circle her fingers on the nipples. The middle finger of her right hand slipped into her vagina, as the palm massaged her clitoris.

He was motionless.

You are kissing me, she thought. She seemed to feel his lips, cool, soft, sliding, and sucking down her stomach. You are kissing me. She imagined his hands under her, lifting her like a bowl to his lips.

She was coming.

Her body jolted. Her legs shook. She had never experienced anything like it. Seeing what he saw, she witnessed an act of shocking vulnerability. It went on and on. She saw the charity of her display, her lavish recklessness and submission. It inspired her to the tenderest self-love. The man did not move, not until she had finally stopped moving, and then he reached up one hand—to signal, she thought, but it was to close the drapes.

She stayed sprawled in the chair. She was astonished. She couldn't believe herself. She couldn't believe him. How did he know to stay so still, to simply watch her? She avoided the thought that right at this moment he was probably masturbating. She absorbed herself only with what she had seen, which was a dead-still man whose eyes she had sensed roving over her body the way that eyes in certain portraits seem to follow you around a room.

The next three mornings everything was the same. He had on his white shirt, she masturbated in the chair, he watched without moving, she came spectacularly, he closed the drapes.

Afterward she went out clothes shopping or visiting people. Everyone told her how great she looked. At night she was passionate in bed, prompting Claude to ask several times, "What the hell's come over you?" but he asked it happily, he didn't look a gift horse in the mouth. She felt very loving toward Claude, not out of guilt but out of high spirits. She knew better than to confess, of course, and yet she didn't believe that she was betraying him with the man next door. A man who hadn't touched her or spoken to her, who, as far as she was concerned, only existed from the waist up and who never moved except to pull his drapes, how could that man be counted as a lover?

The fourth day, Friday, the man didn't appear. For two hours she waited in the chair. Finally she moved to the couch and watched television, keeping one eye on his window. She told herself that he must have had an urgent appointment, or that he had to go to work early. She was worried, though. At some point, late in the afternoon when she wasn't looking, he closed his drapes.

Saturday and Sunday he didn't seem to be home—the drapes were drawn and the lights off . . . not that she could have done anything anyway, not with Claude there. On Monday morning she was in her chair, naked, as soon as Claude left the house. She waited until 10:30, then put on her toreador pants and white, push-up halter top and went for a walk. A consoling line from *Romeo and Juliet* played in her head: "He that is stricken blind cannot forget the precious treasure of his eyesight lost." She was angry with the man for not being as keen as she was. If he was at his window tomorrow, she vowed she would shut her drapes on him.

But how would she replace him, what would she do? Become a table dancer? She had to laugh. Aside from the fact that she was a respectably married woman and could not dance to save her life and was probably ten years too old, the last thing she wanted was a bunch of slack-jawed, flat-eyed drunks grabbing at her breasts. She wanted one man, and she wanted him to have a sad, intelligent demeanor and the control to watch her without moving a muscle. She wanted him to wear a white shirt.

On the way home, passing his place, she stopped. The building was a mansion turned into luxury apartments. He must have money, she realized . . . an obvious conclusion, but until now she'd had no interest whatsoever in who he was.

She climbed the stairs and tried the door. Found it open. Walked in.

The mailboxes were numbered one to four. His would be four. She read the name in the little window: "Dr. Andrew Halsey."

Back at her apartment she looked him up under "Physicians" in the phone book and found that, like Claude, he was a surgeon. A general surgeon, though, a remover of tumors and diseased organs. Presumably on call. Presumably dedicated, as a general surgeon had to be.

She guessed she would forgive his absences.

The next morning and the next, Andrew (as she now thought of him) was at the window. Thursday he wasn't. She tried not to be disappointed. She imagined him saving people's lives, drawing his scalpel along skin in beautifully precise cuts. For something to do she worked on her painting. She painted fishlike eyes, a hooked nose, a mouth full of teeth. She worked fast.

Andrew was there Friday morning. When Ali saw him she rose to her feet and pressed her body against the window, as she had done the first morning. Then she walked to the chair, turned it around and leaned over it, her back to him. She masturbated stroking herself from behind.

That afternoon she bought him a pair of binoculars, an expensive, powerful pair, which she wrapped in brown paper, addressed, and left on the floor in front of his mailbox. All weekend she was preoccupied with wondering whether he would understand that she had given them to him and whether he would use them. She had considered including a message: "For our mornings" or something like that, but such direct communication seemed like a violation of a pact between them. The binoculars alone were a risk.

Monday, before she even had her housecoat off, he walked from the rear of the room to the window, the binoculars at his eyes. Because most of his face was covered by the binoculars and his hands, she had the impression that he was masked. Her legs shook. When she opened her legs and spread her labia, his eyes crawled up her. She masturbated but didn't come and didn't try to, although she put on a show of coming. She was so devoted to his appreciation that her pleasure seemed like a siphoning of his, an early, childish indulgence that she would never return to.

It was later, with Claude, that she came. After supper she pulled him onto the bed. She pretended that he was Andrew, or rather she imagined a dark, long-faced, silent man who made love with his eyes open but who smelled and felt like Claude and whom she loved and trusted as she did Claude. With this hybrid partner she was able to relax enough to encourage the kind of kissing and movement she needed but had never had the confidence to insist upon. The next morning, masturbating for Andrew, she reached the height of ecstasy, as if her orgasms with him had been the fantasy, and her pretenses of orgasm were the real thing. Not coming released her completely into his dream of her. The whole show was for him—cunt, ass, mouth, throat offered to his magnified vision.

For several weeks Andrew turned up regularly, five mornings a week, and she lived in a state of elation. In the afternoons she worked on her painting, without much concentration though, since finishing it didn't seem to matter anymore in spite of how well it was turning out. Claude insisted that it was still very much a self-portrait, a statement Ali was insulted by, given the woman's obvious primitivism and her flat, distant eyes.

There was no reason for her to continue working in the nude, but she did, out of habit and comfort, and on the outside chance that Andrew might be peeking through his drapes. While she painted she wondered about her exhibitionism, what it was about her that craved to have a strange man look at her. Of course, everyone and everything liked to be looked at to a certain degree, she thought. Flowers, cats, anything that preened or shone, children crying, "Look at me!" Some mornings her episodes with Andrew seemed to have nothing at all to do with lust; they were completely display, wholehearted surrender to what felt like the most inaugural and genuine of all desires, which was not sex but which happened to be expressed through a sexual act.

One night she dreamed that Andrew was operating on her. Above the surgical mask his eyes were expressionless. He had very long arms. She was also able to see, as if through his eyes, the vertical incision that went from between her breasts to her navel, and the skin on either side of the incision folded back like a scroll. Her heart was brilliant red and perfectly heart-shaped. All of her other organs were glistening yellows and oranges. Somebody should take a picture of this, she thought. Andrew's gloved hands barely appeared to move as they wielded long, silver instruments. There was no blood on his hands. Very carefully, so that she hardly felt it, he prodded her organs and plucked at her veins and tendons, occasionally drawing a tendon out and dropping it into a petri dish. It was as if he were weeding a garden. Her heart throbbed. A tendon encircled her heart, and when he pulled on it she could feel that its other end encircled her vagina, and the uncoiling there was the most exquisite sensation she had ever experienced. She worried that she would come and that her trembling and spasms would cause him to accidently stab her. She woke up coming.

All day the dream obsessed her. It *could* happen, she reasoned. She could have a gall bladder or an appendicitis attack and be rushed to the hospital and, just as she was going under, see that the surgeon was Andrew. It could happen.

When she woke up the next morning, the dream was her first thought. She looked down at the gentle swell of her stomach and felt sentimental and excited. She found it impossible to shake the dream, even while she was masturbating for Andrew, so that instead of entering *his* dream of her, instead of seeing a naked woman sitting in a pool of morning sun, she saw her sliced-open chest in the shaft of his surgeon's light. Her heart was what she focused on, its fragile pulsing, but she also saw the slower rise and fall of her lungs, and the quivering of her other organs. Between her organs were tantalizing crevices and entwined swirls of blue and red—her veins and arteries. Her tendons were seashell pink, threaded tight as guitar strings.

Of course she realized that she had the physiology all wrong and that in a real operation there would be blood and pain and she would be anesthetized. It was an impossible, mad fantasy; she didn't expect it to last. But every day it became more enticing as she authenticated it with hard data, such as the name of the hospital he operated out of (she called his number in the phone book and asked his nurse) and the name of the surgical instruments he would use (she consulted one of Claude's medical texts), and as she smoothed out the rough edges by imagining, for instance, minuscule suction tubes planted here and there in the incision to remove every last drop of blood.

In the mornings, during her real encounters with Andrew, she became increasingly frustrated until it was all she could do not to quit in the middle, close the drapes, or walk out of the room. And yet if he failed to show up, she was desperate. She started to drink gin and tonics before lunch and to sunbathe at the edge of the driveway between her building and his, knowing he wasn't home from ten o'clock on, but laying there for hours, just in case.

One afternoon, lightheaded from gin and sun, restless with worry because he hadn't turned up the last three mornings, she changed out of her bikini and into a strapless, cotton dress and went for a walk. She walked past the park she had been heading for, past the stores she had thought she might browse in. The sun bore down. Strutting by men who eyed her bare shoulders, she felt voluptuous, sweetly rounded. But at the pit of her stomach was a filament of anxiety, evidence that despite telling herself otherwise, she knew where she was going.

She entered the hospital by the Emergency doors and wandered the corridors for what seemed like half an hour before discovering Andrew's office. By this time she was holding her stomach and half believing that the feeling of anxiety might actually be a symptom of something very serious.

"Dr. Halsey isn't seeing patients," his nurse said. She slit open a manila envelope with a lion's head letter opener. "They'll take care of you at Emergency."

"I have to see Dr. Halsey," Ali said, her voice cracking. "I'm a friend."

The nurse sighed. "Just a minute." She stood and went down a hall, opening a door at the end after a quick knock.

Ali pressed her fists into her stomach. For some reason she no longer felt a thing. She pressed harder. What a miracle if she burst her appendix! She should stab herself with the letter opener. She should at least break her fingers, slam them in a drawer like a draft dodger.

"Would you like to come in?" a high, nasal voice said. Ali spun around. It was Andrew, standing at the door.

"The doctor will see you," the nurse said impatiently, sitting back behind her desk.

Ali's heart began to pound. She felt as if a pair of hands were cupping and uncupping her ears. His shirt was blue. She went down the hall, squeezing past him without looking up, and sat in the green plastic chair beside his desk. He shut the door and walked over to the window. It was a big room; there was a long expanse of old green and yellow floor tiles between them. Leaning his hip against a filing cabinet, he just stood there, hands in his trouser pockets, regarding her with such a polite, impersonal expression that she asked him if he recognized her.

"Of course I do," he said quietly.

"Well—" Suddenly she was mortified. She felt like a woman about to sob that she couldn't afford the abortion. She touched her fingers to her hot face.

"I don't know your name," he said.

"Oh. Ali. Ali Perrin."

"What do you want, Ali?"

Her eyes fluttered down to his shoes—black, shabby loafers. She hated his adenoidal voice. What did she want? What she wanted was to bolt from the room like the mad woman she suspected she was. She glanced up at him again. Because he was standing with his back to the window, he was outlined in light. It made him seem unreal, like a film image superimposed against a screen. She tried to look away, but his eyes held her. Out in the waiting room the telephone was ringing. What do *you* want, she thought, capitulating to the pull of her perspective over to his, seeing now, from across the room, a charming woman with tanned, bare shoulders and blushing cheeks.

The light blinked on his phone. Both of them glanced over at it, but he stayed standing where he was. After a moment she murmured, "I have no idea what I'm doing here."

He was silent. She kept her eyes on the phone, waiting for him to speak. When he didn't, she said, "I had a dream . . ." She let out a disbelieving laugh. "God." She shook her head.

"You are very lovely," he said in a speculative tone. She glanced up at him, and he turned away. Pressing his hands together, he took a few steps along the window. "I have very much enjoyed our . . . our encounters," he said.

"Oh, don't worry," she said. "I'm not here to—"

"However," he cut in, "I should tell you that I am moving into another building."

She looked straight at him.

"This weekend, as a matter of fact." He frowned at his wall of framed diplomas.

"This weekend?" she said.

"Yes."

"So," she murmured. "It's over then."

"Regrettably."

She stared at his profile. In profile he was a stranger—beak-nosed, round-shouldered. She hated his shoes, his floor, his formal way of speaking, his voice, his profile, and yet her eyes filled and she longed for him to look at her again.

Abruptly he turned his back to her and said that his apartment was in the east end, near the beach. He gestured out the window. Did she know where the yacht club was?

"No," she whispered.

"Not that I am a member," he said with a mild laugh.

"Listen," she said, wiping her eyes. "I'm sorry." She came to her feet. "I guess I just wanted to see you."

He strode like an obliging host over to the door.

"Well, good-bye," she said, looking up into his face.

He had garlic breath and five o'clock shadow. His eyes grazed hers. "I wouldn't feel too badly about anything," he said affably.

When she got back to the apartment the first thing she did was take her clothes off and go over to the full-length mirror, which was still standing next to the easel. Her eyes filled again because without Andrew's appreciation or the hope of it (and despite how repellent she had found him) what she saw was a pathetic little woman with pasty skin and short legs.

She looked at the painting. If *that* was her, as Claude claimed, then she also had flat eyes and crude, wild proportions.

What on earth did Claude see in her?

What had Andrew seen? "You are very lovely," Andrew had said, but maybe he'd been reminding himself. Maybe he'd meant, "lovely when I'm in the next building."

After supper that evening she asked Claude to lie with her on the couch, and the two of them watched TV. She held his hand against her breast. "Let this be enough," she prayed.

But she didn't believe it ever would be. The world was too full of surprises, it frightened her. As Claude was always saying, things looked different from different angles, and in different lights. What this meant to her was that everything hinged on where you happened to be standing at a given moment, or even on who you imagined you were. It meant that in certain lights, desire sprang up out of nowhere.

AUTHOR'S NOTE

"Ninety-Three Million Miles Away" was conceived as a response to Alberto Moravia's novel, *The Voyeur*. I wanted to turn the perspective around and write from the viewpoint of the object rather than the subject, although in so doing I made the (perhaps obvious) discovery that the object of desire is simultaneously the subject.

I also wanted to write a story about teetering on the edge, so I let my exhibitionist take her fantasy right to its logical extreme.

THE SHAME GIRL

By Carolyn Banks

When one speaks of erotic fantasy, it is not normally the supernatural to which one is alluding. However, as we all know, there are certain potential drawbacks to any earthbound human lover—dandruff, say, and the ability to forget important anniversaries being only the least of them. And so Carolyn Banks imagines a young girl's sexual awakening not as just the prosaic or ultimately disappointing occurrence it so easily can be but rather as a moment that magic moves out of time. What we sense is the contentment felt by Banks' narrator, the awareness of her sexual self ignited so long before and still brightly alive within her.

Daddy says our creek is where the mer-maids come to rest." My grandchild Miranda's voice, bright and shrill.

Then that of her father, Ed, my son-in-law. "To hear your mother talk," he says, "mer-men as well."

I watch my daughter blush. "Edmund," she says, stepping in toward him, bumping his hips with her own.

My heart leaps at this, at their intimacy, and at the possibility . . . "Anything can happen," I say.

Miranda reaches both arms up, and I bend into her embrace. She smells like popcorn and wool. How old is she now? I think five. "Hello, Grandma," she says, her lips fall wet against my cheek.

"Isn't it kind of cold for you to be out here like that?" Ed gestures at my sweater. He and Jill wear matching sheepskin jackets. Their cheeks are red, their breath is visible.

"I suppose." I take Miranda's mittened hand, but she pulls away, runs down the path and past the house, out onto the edge of the lawn where the creek can be seen.

"What about the mer-maids?" she turns and asks.

We have all three stumbled behind her. I look over at Jill. She is flushed again. Ed's eyebrows arch, as if to ask what he should answer now. "Well," I remind the little girl, "this is a bywater, a salt creek that lifts and falls with the tide. It might harbor mer-folk."

"Mer-folk," she repeats, laughing. Then she shifts her focus abruptly, as children often do. "Is it true that all your friends wear pantyhose under their bathing suits?"

Her parents rush at her, shooshing. They tell me not to mind. "I don't know where she gets these things," Jill says. She glares at her child, takes her shoulders, and nudges her toward the house. "Enough of this," she says. "Inside."

But Miranda doesn't take this seriously. She laughs with every stride. And the minute that she's indoors, while, in fact, she's yanking off her cap and mittens, she asks about the pantyhose again.

I wave her mother off. "The truth is," I tell her, "one or two of my friends do. Wear pantyhose, I mean. Nude pantyhose. They think it makes their legs look better, and actually, from far away, it does. But the wonder is that they wear bathing suits at all."

Ed laughs uncomfortably and looks at Jill.

I realize what he thinks I mean. I correct myself. "I mean most women their age don't swim," I say.

"Oh!" Ed is relieved.

Miranda is bored with my answer. She is scouting what my husband called Our Great Room. Here the ceiling is two stories high and huge fish—tarpon, blue, and sail—arc in taxidermic splendor on the walls. Here, too, tarnished silver cups hold things they shouldn't: pencils, a ruler, some receipts, and maybe even bills. There are paintings, also—shipyards, yachts, the sea. And there is "The Shame Girl," an almost photographic painting that our cook—long ago, back when I was small—once named.

The Shame Girl sits naked on a rock, her privates hidden discreetly by the way she wraps herself with her arms. The water that surrounds the rock, still as a mirror, offers the same demure reflection. There is something very formal about that water. Not just its stillness but the sculpted vegetation on its shore. Not like the vegetation here at waterside: thick, impenetrable, unruly.

"Mer-maids," I say, "Indeed. And mer-men! What an astounding thing." I look at my daughter with new eyes. If I asked her, would she tell me? I rather doubt it, for what would she say?

I told someone once—my roommate at school—and I wasn't believed. Our theme for the day was First Sexual Encounter, and I'd already heard hers, a tawdry scuffle in the backseat of her boyfriend's parents' car.

"I remember it so clearly," I began. For my turn, I had made my roommate sit within a nest of throw pillows I'd collected from the dayroom. I had wanted the mood to be right and had chosen something in the pasha mode.

"Wait, wait!" she'd said, arranging the pillows another way, some beneath her knees, others behind her head.

I was, by now, eager to go on. "Ready?" I asked.

I set the scene quite carefully, as I will now:

My parents were having their annual summer party. As usual, there would be no young people there. For me the excitement was in the preparation, the hanging of the lanterns, especially.

My father would stand on a ladder beneath a line of bare bulbs he'd earlier strung. Cook would be on the ground, at the ladder's side. I would punch each lantern open—they were boxed and folded flat, but when you pressed them, they'd expand into bright ribbed bells made of the thinnest paper. I would hand the open lantern to Cook, who would then give it to my dad. And my mother, she would stand off to the side saying, "No, it leans a bit to the left," or "Ah! Just so."

And every year it would be the same. My father would come down after hanging the last lantern, hug my mother, and say something quietly in her ear. Then he'd boom again, "What an assembly line we make, eh?" And he'd thank me and thank Cook, and he'd take my mother away.

Cook would fuss over me lest I feel excluded, but the fact was, I never minded any of this. One year I even repeated to Cook what I had been told—that Daddy had only heard the mer-maids sing. I knew already that this was the euphemistic—or so I thought—phrase that he often used to signal his desire.

But this time I was sixteen, old enough to move among the party guests as an equal, I thought. When I said so, however, my father had smiled his indulgence and my mother had feathered her fingers through my hair. I still burned beneath my sense of insult.

So, when the party was well under way and darkness had taken hold, I donned a hooded jersey and a pair of blue jeans and decided to swim out to a large flat rock and sprawl there, looking back at the colored lights and spying on the guests.

I had never gone into the water at night. Nor had I swum in other than a one-piece suit. Three strokes in, the clothing I'd selected grew so cumbersome and heavy that I found myself near panic.

I gained the rock and pulled myself up on it. Then I began, with difficulty, shedding what I'd worn. When I was naked, however, I was also quite cold. Without thinking, I assumed "The Shame Girl" pose.

On shore, the colored lights were turning the people beneath them tints of fuchsia and green. I somehow grew cynical and thought the partygoers clumsy and silly and not worth observing after all.

I was sorry that I hadn't stayed in my room. I had things to do, books to read. It seemed to me then that grown-up parties relied more on laughter than words, but I thought the latter were far superior and so was scornful.

I slipped into the water; it was time, I knew, to leave this childish business of spying behind. The water was warmer, more welcoming than air. I dawdled near the rock, my legs waving as I reached to touch the soft beard of moss on the granite underside.

It was then that someone's fingers flashed against my own.

I gasped and attempted to lift myself onto the rock again, but the strength in my arms failed me. I tried again with the same result. I clung to the rock, panting, and attempted to coax myself back to a state of calm.

I did this by concentrating on the onshore colors and sounds, the jazzy lyric that floated out over the water from my parents' wind-up phonograph: "Oh, honey wait for me, oh, honey wait . . ."

Was *I* waiting? And for what?

While I wondered, a warmer swirl of water began to play at my hips and thighs. I felt that everywhere it touched me I was glowing.

Glowing! I would be seen from shore! I let go my hold on the rock, curled, and let my body plummet down.

It was black down there. I hadn't been glowing at all, at least not in any visible way. But when I felt a hand snake between my legs and across my buttocks, the radiance, the glow, the *heat* increased.

I gave myself to the water and its sensations, gave myself to what was now a cool and steady pull of current against my knees and calves and toes.

Soon something very like hair brushed against my belly and then moved away. Seconds later, it brushed yet again, my belly, hips, thighs. I reached down, my fingers floating, and I touched, though fleetingly, what seemed a human face: forehead, nose, lids and lashes, lips.

I surfaced like a shot and looked for the rock, the shore, the things that kept me earthbound. Just then, they seemed so far away. In the same breath-stopping instant, legs pressed and even wrapped around my own.

It was at this point that my roommate interrupted me. She sat straight up and hollered "Foul," as if this were a game. I was irritated and demanded to know why I had been stopped. "Because you said his *legs*. If this is about a mer-man, he *can't* have legs."

"But he did have legs. He did. He just didn't have feet."

"All right," she said, "Suspension of disbelief." She assumed her former pose. "Go ahead."

"Thank you."

The legs again.

"No, no! Don't!" someone, a woman, said from shore. Did she mean me? I looked back toward the house, the lawn. At this distance, the lanterns made the water wink and gleam. The same woman was laughing now. "Well, all right," she said.

With that, a tendril of fear began to coil within me. I thought of my parents' friends, of the fuchsia and green people, of the men. Was this one of them? The thought of it, of someone so old, made me thrash and pull away.

I made for shore as purposefully as I could, though all the while I swam, a sinewy body kept sweeping past me—back and forth and around—in the water.

This was no one that I or my parents knew.

"Were you still glowing?" my roommate asked sarcastically.

"Yes," I answered, beyond impatience.

As I stroked, the body in the water began to touch and play against my own, against my shoulders and my breast and along my neck, my spine, against my buttocks, between my legs. My will to reach the shore began to fade. I let the water buoy me.

"You wouldn't dare," a woman shrieked from shore.

"Don't bet on it," a man's voice replied. Then there was the sound of glass breaking.

"Well, last year . . . ," I heard my father begin. He pronounced "last" as if it were "lust."

Meanwhile, I had the distinct feeling that I was being held and carried. I began to move through the water with a force that was not my own. I plunged and rolled and bobbed as if I were a dolphin in an open sea. And whenever I felt my lungs would explode, I would be lifted through the air for an instant or two. I was still very near my parents' home, I noted, for I saw ribbonlike streaks of green and of fuchsia every now and again.

And then whatever gripped me arced and took me deep and deep and deep. Shells crushed against my shoulders and my back, and bits of furry weed caught in my nostrils and my hair. I caught hold of whatever it was that held me—in that moment, I did so need to—and, in answer, a sharp fin lashed out, slicing into the flesh of my hand.

And then there was nothing, no one, only the roar of my heart.

I surfaced and paddled toward an eroded part of shore. Once there I pressed my face against the earth. I was alone and hurt, the blood from my hand mingling black with the water of the creek.

Then someone softly reached from below, took my hand, licked and sucked at the edges of my cut until the bleeding stopped. I closed my eyes and tried to conjure him: his face, his jaw, his seaweed-tangled hair.

"The Mysterious Stranger motif," my roommate offered. I was silent, angry. Then she relented. "Come *on*," she said, "get back to the good part." (She later went to New York and became an important editor.)

Afterward, the water lapped at me. I swayed to its lilt. The whole of my body felt its kiss, as though all of me had been wrapped in inky, liquid silk.

"Oooh, inky silk!" my roommate cooed. "That's good."

On shore the lanterns had been doused. I knew that it was time. I slipped beneath the water, floated with the presence somewhere near me in the night. There was no urgency now, no fervor. When we neared the pilings of our dock I let my head and shoulders break the surface.

Beyond the steep roof of my parents' house, a car door slammed and then another. An engine fired into life.

"Is someone out here?" My mother's voice was so close, too close.

"And then?"

"And then he swam away. He was a mer-man. I'm sure of it."

My roommate sighed. "Good story," she said, in a languor. "Even if it's stupid," she went on, "it's good."

"But it could be," I told her, remembering what my father had once told me. I even used his words: "For ours is a bywater, subject to tides. It's connected to the bay and then the sea."

She raised her arm, laid her hand across her forehead, raised her head with great drama, "For ours is a bywater," she intoned.

I lifted a pillow and clapped it down upon her head.

I still had the scar on my hand where the fin had cut me. I mentioned this, so wanting my roommate to believe. I reminded her of my father's seemingly euphemistic phrase. About the mer-maids.

"Quoting Eliot," she gibed.

But was it only that? My father, after all, had grown up on this tidal creek.

Eventually, I inherited it all: house, creek, paintings, trophies, stuffed fish. And "The Shame Girl," which I took to staring at, long and hard.

In a certain light, after a glass or two of port, admittedly, I could see a mer-something deep within the water. Mer-man. Of course that didn't explain why the Shame Girl clutched at herself, but maybe she was taunting him, daring him out of the water. (Now I think that maybe our cook saw him, the mer-man, after all. Saw him in the painting long before I ever thought to look. There is no way to know. Cook is long years dead, buried when Jill was younger than Miranda is now. At Cook's funeral, Father—he walked with two canes by then—summed her up, telling me, "She was fat as a goose. Her passion, all of it, went into those meals. Lord, those wonderful meals.")

At any rate, by then there was another proof, the words of my husband, whom I had never dared to tell. "You smell just like the sea," he would say admiringly. (Oh, but how I remember him, square face, soft lips, fierce daily stubble! Even now I know exactly how his breath felt in my ear, against my cheek, along my neck. Or at my navel or pubis or thigh.) Why the sea?

But now, today, there is the blush that crossed my daughter's face.

"Do you like this painting?" I asked her. I am indicating "The Shame Girl," of course.

"Frankly, mother . . . ," Jill begins, in a way that tells me, no, she does not see him there, not yet at any rate.

"She thinks it's dumb," my granddaughter says.

"I find 'The Shame Girl' rather interesting," Ed puts in. We all call it by the name Cook gave it, have for decades now, and no one bats an eye.

I stand, walk to the window, look down at the creek. With the fingers of my left hand, I trace the silvery scar on my right. "In summertime, I still swim," I announce.

I turn. Then I remember what Miranda asked me earlier about those friends of mine. "And I don't wear pantyhose under my suit when I go out there, either." I wag my finger and speak sternly to the little girl, making this a joke.

"Shame Girl, Shame Girl, Shame Girl!" Miranda accuses, giggling and stomping and wagging back.

We all laugh. We're all happy. I, here at waterside, perhaps a little more than they.

AUTHOR'S NOTE

I don't think there's anything sexier than touching underwater: it's slower and silkier. This, then, was where I wanted to set my story. But I also liked the taboo aspect of portraying the narrator's sexual coming of age within sight of her parents' party on shore. And, of course, the generational aspect appealed to me, the notion that others in the family had been or would be visited by the mer-folk.

THE FOOTPATH OF PINK ROSES

By Carol Lazare

Sometimes, especially when regarding the complex issues of sexual power/sexual pleasure, it is easy to know what to think and hard to know what to do. Or would you prefer the opposite? The fact that Carol Lazare openly and honestly confronts the rape-versus-ravishment problem ("rape is ravishment defiled") does not mean that her answers are everyone's. On "The Footpath of Pink Roses" she leads us down, however, one thing is certain: erotic sensation—soft, sharp, sweet, enveloping—mimics those flowers whose petals fall all around.

Sex was always on my mind. I was fifteen and fantasized about being overcome with desire, being taken wantonly, with no holds barred, to the point of utter, complete, absolute abandon, bliss, ecstasy, and exhaustion. In a word, ravished.

A rape had been reported down by the river near a footpath where pink roses grew. Myself, I worried over the difference between ravishment and rape, and I wrote a poem about it.

> If a stranger confronts me and I am attracted to him,
> If he is after rape and I am after ravishment,
> If the act occurs, what will it be called?

At what point does my desire to be ravished by an attractive stranger
Become rape by a horrific criminal?

I analyzed the difference. " 'She was asking for it.' 'She wanted it.' " If she was like me, ravishment was what she wanted. Perhaps the rapist thought that he was ravishing her, giving her what she wanted. Perhaps our natural instincts have become so perverted that ravishment is no longer possible. Perhaps, I will never be ravished. Perhaps my definition of ravishment is really this society's definition of rape. And rape is ravishment defiled.

A year later the rape/ravishment dilemma continued, and I was on my way home from the Deluxe Theatre. There had been a Saturday double bill, and I was feeling warm and contented after having just seen two Hollywood movies full of Paul Newman. I had to walk down Carruthers Street which is like a back lane. There are no front doors facing the street. On one side are backyards, clotheslines, gardens, and garages and on the other side of the street, the bus barn. The huge, vertical, sliding door of the barn was half open, and I could see the bottoms of the orange buses and pairs of legs engaged in chores and wordless conversation. A world of thigh-to-toe legs, half-ladders, and half-mops. What response would a cry of distress from Carruthers bring? Would whole bodies come running? Or would Dalilike legs, in worker overalls, brush under the half-open barn door and dodge around and about the empty buses on the lot? One never knew what might be crouched behind an empty orange bus. I doubled my stride as I passed them and hoped that fate would once again deal me safe passage.

It was twilight too, that time of day just before dusk when you can practically see the air, when the molecules seem big enough to push aside like a veil, when time is in limbo and unusual things can happen. I moved with anticipation and S.F.s (sinking feelings) through the molecules. In ten minutes it would be dusk, the air would be normal again, and I would be home and safe.

As I neared the intersection at the end of the block, a huge boatlike car entered Carruthers and came toward me with the driver's window down. Through it I could hear the sweet voice of Todd Rundgren singing a familiar song. I was humming along when the driver stuck his head out at me and crowed, "Hey honey, I'm lookin' for some tight, young slit." I looked at him, and the molecules of his face mixed with the molecules of car that mixed with the molecules of air, like an illusory dream mixing and moving in the twilight. For an instant I tried to answer him until adrenaline kicked me into action, and I ran toward safety and the dusk.

"I'm lookin' for some tight, young slit." How could anyone who listens to Todd Rundgren be saying that? This was new vocabulary and it filled me with fear: fear of forced surrender, to power, rape. There was no fear in ravishment, only willful surrender to ecstasy.

My sexual adventures in the past twelve years have been uneventful. There has been, thankfully, no rape, but, unfortunately, no ravishment either. I've become a woman with a potentially insatiable sexual appetite. My nipples are usually visibly erect, a strong indication, so I've read, of an aroused woman. They can be seen pushing out a T-shirt or a dress while picking out a pound of beans or scrubbing off baked-on grease or rolling twenty dollars worth of pennies. And it's not the cold weather. My nipples are erect in any season, day or night. Because I can't walk around at all times flashing my aroused-woman insignia, I have often chosen to wear the "layered look." Two or three layers over erect nipples lessens the impression that I'm a slave to carnal knowledge.

When I was nineteen or twenty, I experienced one of my more memorable uneventful sexual adventures with a young man named Marshall. He was self-assured and absolutely confident about his attractiveness to women. My mother, like many Jewish mothers, has been loving and devoted to me. I've found that with the sons of Jewish mothers the care can be more extreme. Because they are so worshiped and pampered at home, they transfer this expectation to the women they meet in their private lives. Marshall, not for one millionth of a millisecond doubted his power to excite me. He knew, like no other, that the key to my arousal was my nipples. He would lightly brush them, tug them, flick them, turn them, swirl them, kiss them, lick them. I learned many things from Marshall, but my sexual education was still limited. He may have taken my breasts to university, but the rest of me remained in grade school.

One uninspired encounter after another led me to the belief that the best sex is in the mind. Free of self-consciousness, free of guilt, free of experiment, my mind had brought me to the brink of ravishment with "him," my perfect lover. He filled all my requirements, handsome, well-built, tender, attentive, and slow, very slow. I chose my perfect lover from the Cree Nation—for his piercing black almond eyes, his long, thick, black hair, his cheekbones that could fill my palms. My engagement as a field worker for social services had brought me in contact with many native people, and I began to appreciate the traditional North American native way of life. I had many questions about the troubled state of the earth. It offered me an answer—respectful coexistence in all things including the relationship between man and woman.

It is a midsummer day just before dusk. Twilight. I am twenty-eight and walking with anticipation and S.F.s along the river near the footpath of pink roses. I think about my state of readiness and my yellow karate belt. I imagine it wound neatly around my karate *gi* and am visualizing a block to my chest, when, in that instant, I feel an actual blow to my upper back. It forces me to lose my balance and my wind. Gasping for air I try to regain my balance and am helped by being grasped at the shoulder, straightened, and held with a man's hand over my mouth and my neck squeezed into the V formed by the bicep and forearm of a man's arm. In an instant we are sharing an intimacy that can often take weeks to achieve under normal circumstances. My upper back is held tightly against his chest. I can feel the contours of his body and know that he worked at it. As he pulls me backward I can feel the muscles of his upper thighs brush against my buttocks. The elbow of the arm wrapped around my neck rests on my breast and with each movement grazes my nipple until it stiffens. Can he feel it? Will he think it is arousal? Is it?

As he drags me toward the footpath of pink roses I try for a moment to convince myself that I am having a trancelike experience. As my mother would describe, "Going to one of those windy places" I am prone to go. I attempt to follow her advice, breathing deeply from the diaphragm, chastising myself for not eating that day. As I breathe in I can smell the skin surrounding my face. He smells of the outdoors and smoke, not of cigarettes but burning cedar. One of his fingers is cushioned between my lips, and I can taste the salt from his skin and sour cream and onion potato chips. My senses are acute and trustworthy. I am not on the edge or going over it into madness. I am being dragged, by a man, into the rosebushes.

As I strain my eyes, forcing their muscles into an unnatural elongation, a discomforting downward look, I see the skin of his forearm, chestnut brown and hairless. An Indian. Despite my reason that has urged me to prepare for my defense, my instinct fixates on his brown-skinned forearm and the possibility of fulfilling my fantasy. Perhaps, in this moment, with my innate will to survive, I can convince myself that what will happen next is within my power and control. My choice. The illusion of choice is vital to me. Ravishment or rape. I choose to surrender to ecstasy.

* * *

He stopped and dropped to the ground, his hand still over my mouth and his arm in a V around my neck. His legs formed another V and my lower back was pressed against his penis, my back and head at his heart. His chest was heaving, and like a rider out of sync with her horse, my body bounced off of his. He pressed me closer to correct the bounce. Force or willful surrender. The scent of roses enveloped me. I corrected my rhythm and we rode as one.

As his breathing normalized, his penis grew erect in the small of my back. "Gimme your money," he said. I was thrown by this. I had been readying myself for one of the most profoundly rationalized experiences of my life, only to find out that I was to be neither raped nor ravished, but robbed! Mugged for money! "Gimme your money," he said again. The V of his arm tightened around my throat. I cupped my hands around the hard muscle of his forearm. His voice deceived me too. It was a whisper, a warm breeze over my forehead with a hint of fake parsley. I moved my fists into the proper karate pose, positioned them, one on each side of his rib cage, then I punched. "AAAAA-Ah!!" I growled. He fell back into a rosebush, his arms circling his chest. I scrambled away on all fours and turned to face him. Here was my perfect Cree lover, and I was looking him straight in the eye. His face was framed by tiny pink roses like the cherubic angels of seventeenth-century religious paintings. An ingenuous mugger.

"That hurt. Y' fuckin' yahoo," he said.

"Gulliver's Travels," I said.

"Whose?" he asked.

"The yahoo in *Gulliver's Travels*. Have you read it?" I asked.

"Ya sure. Two or three times," he said.

"Not my favorite," I said.

"Me neither," he said.

"What's yours?" I asked.

"The Ocean Almanac," he answered.

"I don't know it."

"It fuckin' hurts. What did you do?"

"Karate," I said.

"Like black belt."

"No, just yellow," I said.

"Probably busted my floating rib again. Fuck."

"You really frightened me," I said.

"Don't go wanderin' around here. Full moon t'night," he said.

The moon was low on the horizon. As I often would, I gave myself the challenge of a fake deadline and wondered where I would be when it was high in the sky. I could have walked away. I kept talking.

"Are you a drug addict?" I asked.

His mouth broadened into a wide, white-toothed smile, a practiced smile, one that was proven to work, a bread-and-butter smile, money in the bank.

"No," he said.

"What do you want the money for?" I asked.

"Nintendo."

"Oh." He has family. I felt foolish for my fantasy.

"What's your name?" he asked.

"Sarah."

"What's yours?" I asked.

"Eddy."

Eddy and I were rooted to our spots like fence posts about fifteen feet apart and connected by the signals of arousal our bodies had revealed.

"Sarah," he said.

"Yes, Eddy," I said.

"Sarah," he said.

"Yes, Eddy,"

He walked over to me, slowly, saying my name with each step. "Sarah. Sarah . . ." He was close enough that I could smell the cedar smoke in his shirt and the potato chips on his breath.

"You're bleeding," I said.

"Fuckin' thorns'll do that," he said.

"By your temple."

"Yeah?"

As he rubbed it, the tiny ruby of blood broke and trickled down the side of his face. Spontaneously, I reached out and wiped it away. Struck by another attack of S.F.s I quickly withdrew my bloodstained hand and suspended it like a beacon in the twilight. I stared; my molecules of skin were mixing with his molecules of blood.

Eddy, reassuringly, pressed my hand to his chest and mopped the blood onto his T-shirt. I kept my hand there. Now a reckless Land Rover, it traversed the terrain of his pectoral muscles, over the ridge of his jaw to the final crest of his cheekbone. And it filled my palm.

Reaching up, he took my hand in his and placed it by my side. Then, with the back of his hands and nails he slowly began to graze—featherlike—the inner skin of my forearms. I shivered and thrust them forward for more. Over and over. I arched my neck up and back, and it was next—over and over—then my face, my hair, his fingers, his nails—over and over.

He paused for a moment and stepped away. Eddy took off his

clothes—his T-shirt, his boots, his jeans. Lit by the moon, the contours of muscle, highlight and shadow, were hills and valleys, relief on a map. He was a journey waiting to be taken. He would guide me to new sensations, a prospector mining me, vein by vein until we struck the motherlode.

I took off my clothes, my tentlike dress, my sandals, my panties. He made a nest amid the rosebushes with our clothes, and we lay down, watching the moon as it reached its zenith in the sky. I wondered where I would be at its descent. Eddy leaned over, resting on his arm. He removed the elastic band holding his ponytail and let his black hair fall loosely over his shoulders. On all fours he straddled me, dropping his head, and his hair fell over my breasts. Like a whisk of down, his hair swept my body from head to toe, tickling my skin to the next plateau. I arched my back to meet him and met his lips skimming mine. Gliding over the surface of my skin, his warm lips teased the ache that craved him. Skimming like a schooner, gliding like a clipper over my rippling body, the ache became me. I undulated in the breeze, yearning for the hurricane.

I felt the power he could wield as he raised my torso off the ground with one hand under my back and the other nearly encircling my throat. He could have snapped my neck like a twig. I looked him in the eye, his equal, not his prey. He raised his hand from around my neck and placed it on my cheek, raising me like a platter to his lips. He kissed me. Harder and longer, harder and deeper, stronger and longer his mouth enveloped mine.

The moon like a spotlight opened our eyes, his riveting on mine, diving deeper and deeper. We grabbed hold closer and closer, gripping, licking, rubbing, squeezing, kneading skin into flesh. Crablike I clutched him, and we rolled like tumbleweed out of our nest onto the earth. Tumbling under the roses he filled me. Again and again. A mold of my buttocks in the earth. Again and again. Deeper and deeper into the lode. And the molecules of earth mixed with the molecules of flesh. And the moon became his eyes, the roses his hair, my hand his shoulder, my breasts his chest, my thighs his thighs, and he became me and I became him. Ravished.

AUTHOR'S NOTE

I wrote the story because I think, as I believe most women do, if we're really straight with ourselves, that, instinctively, on a primal level, we want to be ravished. It is tricky politically, but ravishment, as the story explores it, is not rape. It is a fine line, but the line is there and Sarah draws it.

I believe a woman can acknowledge her desire for ravishment and be a feminist. In fact, I think that a denial of these powerful instincts of female sexuality is a denial of the principles of feminism as I understand them.

THE WAGER

By Sara Davidson

Like the heroine of the previous story, Sara Davidson's Lucy is ravished. A sexual challenge, issued in the mutual excitement of new lovemaking, presents her with an excuse to indulge in the passivity for which she knows she has secretly longed. It's obvious that this self-censorship alluded to is another way many women today are forced to police themselves for an impossibly elusive correctness, caught between the exigencies of sexual politics and the actual sensations of the flesh. Although some will argue that "The Wager" and stories like it cause us to continue to believe too susceptibly in the myth of the master lover, personally, I can think of no greater barrier to fulfilled desire than any use of the word "should" and whatever lie it leads us to.

It was like falling through a chute; they sped down and around past darkened houses and moist night lawns with sprinklers running until they came out on the Pacific Coast Highway, the beach. The sand was gray and damp, the parking lots closed up. Joe shifted gears impatiently when they hit the light at Sunset Boulevard. There was tension in the car, the accelerating tension of sexual possibility, and the sweet scent of Thai grass. Lucy guided him along the foggy streets that led to her house. He put on the hand brake, opened the door of the Porsche, and helped her out.

They had the house to themselves. Pam was staying with Henry and would not be back until Sunday. Lucy poured amaretto into glasses and told Joe to pick out an album. She heard familiar chords, then Mick Jagger.

Wonderful party, Lucy thought. Her pockets were crammed with phone numbers written on scraps of paper and matchbook covers. Elated at the appearance of so many prospects after a dry few months, she slipped out of her shoes and sat down on the rug, facing Joe.

They knew little about each other. He was from Los Angeles, she from New York. Both had made films for television and had been married.

"How long have you been separated?" Joe asked.

"Two years."

"What was he like?"

"Want to see a picture?"

"Sure." He lit another joint.

She went into her study and brought back a photo she had always liked. Her former husband's face was split by shadow, so that the right half appeared sunlit and ingenuous, the left half withdrawn and dark.

Joe studied it, then frowned. "I don't like him. I'm sorry."

Lucy took the picture back. "No one feels neutral about Jerry."

"How long were you married?"

"Seven years. And you?"

He stretched his arms over his head. "Ten months. I'm afraid it wasn't serious."

"What's the longest you've been with someone?"

"Few years." He smiled, dimples coming to his cheeks. He was tall, athletic, with dark blond hair and a beard that, together with his close-set eyes, gave his face a soulful cast. "Can I help it if all the women in America are screwed up?"

"Funny, they only say wonderful things about you."

He laughed, as if to say, your point. They talked some more and listened to music, and it was 3:00 A.M.

"Want to go upstairs?" Lucy said.

He shook his head no.

Pity.

"Not yet."

"Hmm?"

In a casual tone, Joe said, "I think we should prolong this through the evening. I'm going to arouse you one small step at a time."

"What are you talking about."

He moved closer, picking up the amaretto bottle. "The rest of the evening is in my hands. You don't have to do anything. You're not going to do anything."

Something prickled in her.

"I know it won't be easy, you're the kind of woman who likes taking charge." He tilted his chin, as if to say, come on, I dare you.

Who do you think you are . . .

"I bet if you're with four people trying to decide on a restaurant, you can never just sit back and go along."

"That's true."

He set down his drink, moved toward her, and kissed her. She was aroused, he was aroused, she thought they were going to lie right back on the floor, but he broke away, leaving her beached and breathless.

"I don't like this," she said.

"Too bad." He smiled.

She threw a shoe at him. She could feel that crazy, instant intimacy—the almost palpable sense of closeness—induced by the Thai grass. He turned over the record. "I wish you had some Sting. He's the only guy around still saying something. Course, the reason I like the Stones is that they don't want to say anything, except fuck me."

"They've had some good lyrics."

"It's all fuck me, all just one lyric."

" 'Jumping Jack Flash.' "

"I can shake it good, fuck me."

" 'Brown Sugar,' no, that's obvious."

"Fuck me, black woman."

" 'Street Fighting Man.' That was about something."

"Yeah, I'm a street fighting man. When I get home from the riot, fuck me."

Lucy laughed. There had to be one. "What about that song . . . oh, what was it called? It was on 'Between the Buttons.' "

" 'Ruby Tuesday'?"

"No, that's not on 'Between the Buttons.' "

"Sure it is."

"No it's not."

"You're wrong."

"I have the album, I'm positive."

"So am I."

"What do you want to bet?"

"Let's make it juicy."

"Okay."

She lay down on her back to think. He slid over, lifted her blouse, and moved his lips slowly across the smooth, taut hollow of her stomach. She sighed, and reached up to run her hand along his back, but he took the hand off and set it on the floor.

"I can't touch you?"

"Nope. You can't do anything." He went to the record cabinet to look for "Between the Buttons."

"This is stupid."

"You'll come around."

"What shall we bet?" Lucy said. His arrogance was galling.

"Dinner at the restaurant of one's choice."

"In Paris."

"It's not here," Joe said.

"Might be upstairs."

He got to his feet, she started up after him, but he turned, pointing at her. "Sit down." She did. He walked behind her, lifted the long dark hair and kissed the nape of her neck. "Nice try."

"I'm not going to throw this."

He began unbuttoning her blouse. "You hold still."

She did.

He set her blouse on a table and sat about six feet from her. "You look better with your clothes off."

"You're blowing this, you know. When you want to, I'll have cooled."

"I'm not worried." He sipped his drink. He was wearing a blue shirt with the cuffs rolled up, and she could not help staring at his arms. They were tan, smooth, with muscles rippling under the skin and a covering of fine blond hair. She felt a shock of desire so strong it was like pain.

"Lucy, it's an act of almost superhuman control for me not to jump on you right now, but I'm not going to. Because delaying it will make the pleasure even more intense."

"No!" She twisted in frustration. "You're playing with me, and I don't like it."

"I'm not."

"Yes you are, and I want you to stop."

He crawled across the floor and put his face up to hers.

"Can you tell me exactly what you want me to stop?"

She considered how to phrase it.

"No."

They laughed. Joe rolled with her to the floor, kissing her again and again in the crook of her bare neck, but then he stopped himself.

"Let's decide what the bet will be," he said, returning to his chair.

"The loser has to be the other's slave. See how you like it."

"For how long?"

"Twenty-four hours."

"Okay, if you want to prolong the agony. Where's the album?" He started for the stairs.

"Not up there."

He turned.

"In the bookcase. Bottom shelf."

When Joe found the album, a smile came to his face.

"I'm right, aren't I," she said.

He slid the record out of the jacket, cued it on the turntable, and paused. "Still want that bet? I'm willing to let you off now, because I'm such a nice guy."

He was bluffing. "Play it."

Lucy's hands flew in the air, she was certain she had won, but at the first chord she was slumped in defeat. How could this be? She had believed with all her soul that she was right, and she wasn't. She walked to the window.

"Here are the terms. Tonight doesn't count. You'll be my slave on any day I choose."

"You really want to humiliate me, don't you."

He came up, took her by the shoulders with a gentleness that surprised her, and kissed her, a kiss like those she had dreamed of at thirteen: walking down a dappled lane in a faraway place with a strange new boy. When Joe pulled away, she burst into tears. "I'm scared."

She saw a look of alarm. He walked closer, and when his face was next to hers, the pouting, hurt look in her eyes turned to merriment. He grabbed her. "You're fantastic." Then he put one arm under her legs, the other under her arms, and, hoisting her sideways, headed for the stairs.

For the next several hours, she was not permitted to move a hand, she could not tell him where or when to touch her, but he knew.

She was not fighting anymore, she was nearly out of her mind with pleasure. It was every fantasy she had ever daydreamed. Foreplay that had no end. Lovemaking that had no objective but to tantalize and please. This was going to last all night—nights and nights and nights—and it was all being done *to* her.

She was on her back, and Joe was above her, balanced on his arms. "I want you to be my slave now. Tell me I'm better than everyone."

"You think you're better than me?"

"I'm not saying that. Tell me I'm better than everyone."

"You ain't better than me."

He slid out. "You're my slave, you have to." He began to stroke her with his finger.

"I can't say something I don't . . ."

"Is that right?"

". . . believe, and have it be . . . credible."

She loved what he was doing, she loved him, she wanted it to last forever. The finger stopped.

Looking at him earnestly, she said, "You're better than *everyone*."

The finger resumed. "Big deal." He burst out laughing. He slid down between her legs, homing in with the same instinctive accuracy he had shown all night. She could feel the climax now, swishing its tail like a fish. He was pulling it up and out of her. Up and up it came, big, this fish was going to set records, they were going to weigh it, they would pose beside it for photographs. You could see its powerful form rising up through the water, navy blue.

"Let me now, Joe," she said, "please, let me . . ."

It broke the surface, shooting into the air with spray.

She was jelly, she could not stop laughing. He plunged into her as she lay, arms flopped above her head. "Move a little," he said. "Okay, stop now." She lay still, the way she had always, secretly, wanted to lie. It felt good, oh it was good like this, she loved lying back passively with her arms flung up, but as he went on, she began to move, involuntarily at first. Her small rump began to bounce, then she was matching his movements, pulling on him, squeezing.

"Oh sweetheart."

"Give it to me . . ."

"Yes."

"Now."

"So fucking good!"

It was seven in the morning. They had been making love for almost four hours. She had not kissed him or touched him with her hands, and he had been hard the entire time.

"Have you done this before?" she said.

"No."

They stared at each other, awed and a little scared, until the room became a bubble of heightened feeling and the world outside—the people in their apartments, sleeping, eating cornflakes, turning on the television—seemed to exist on another plane that was shallow and dull.

They tried to sleep, but kept thinking of things they wanted to say and arousing each other unwittingly as they tossed.

"We've got to sleep," Joe said. "I wish I had a Valium."

She went to the bathroom and returned with two yellow pills.

Joe swallowed his, took a swig from the amaretto bottle, and kissed her, sweetness on his lips.

AUTHOR'S NOTE

I wrote this during the six-month period when, pregnant with my second child, I was forced to lie in bed and abstain from sex of any kind to avoid a premature birth. During this interlude of forced abstinence, I found myself writing the most erotic passages I've done before or since, and having a wonderful time with it.

I've always felt that the most exciting sex comes not from technical virtuosity but from the play of fantasy and emotion. The fantasy in this piece is that archetypal one best dramatized in *The Taming of the Shrew*—where a strong woman resists with everything in her arsenal and yet is overcome by the cunning of the male.

THE STORY OF NO

By Lisa Tuttle

Lisa Tuttle, a much-published writer in several genres, here shows that she's as capable of being perverse as she is of being original. Naturally, any editor's concern, when introducing such a blink-if-you-dare story, is not to reveal too much, but there are a few things I feel it's safe to mention. In "The Story of No" you will encounter a wife, a husband, a memory, and a surprise, and, oh yes, there is a copy of a certain book by Pauline Réage.

At first sight I thought I knew him and felt my blood heat, my muscles loosen, the breath evaporate from my lungs.

The imprint of his touch rose like stigmata on my skin, and the memory of his tongue hungry in my mouth aroused a need I hadn't admitted to myself for a long time, a desire for the forbidden.

"What is it?" asked my husband. Startled, I looked across the restaurant table at the well-known face and remembered who and where I was: a wife in her forties staying in an elegant, expensive English country house hotel with her husband, the vacation our anniversary present to each other. "See someone you know?"

"No." For that was in another country, and besides . . . "He wouldn't be that young, if it was who I thought. He was that age *then*." The man I remembered would be my age still and maybe would still find me attractive. That young man couldn't be much past twenty. If he looked at me, he'd see someone old enough to be his mother, someone not worth noticing, sexually invisible. He turned his head, and his clear green gaze fell on me with a shock like cold water, and he smiled.

"You're blushing," said my husband with interest. "Was he an old boyfriend?"

"No. Oh, no. Just someone I met once in Houston. Do you want to taste my salmon mousse?"

Once. A single night. Yet the memory of it was with me always. Many a dull or sleepless night I had pulled it out to comfort myself. I had used it so often it had come to seem like a story I'd read somewhere, and not something that had really happened to me. As a fantasy, I'd even shared it with my husband some nights in bed. But it was real—or had been, once.

I first saw him in a Montrose bar, drinking by himself. He had a tumble of black curls surrounding a long, clean-shaven face, with a sensuous mouth and startling green eyes. Only the overlarge, slightly crooked nose kept him from beauty, but his was a striking face and mine were not the only eyes drawn to stare at it. Nor was it only his face that attracted. He had a physical presence as disturbing as some rare perfume. His was not an outstanding body—nobody would have picked him to model for a centerfold—but it was long and slim and wiry. My husband, handsome, tall, and well-muscled, was certainly more attractive by objective standards, but I wasn't thinking of my husband as I admired the fit of the stranger's jeans.

I took a seat and ordered a drink. I wasn't looking for trouble. I hadn't been planning adultery. I was content, I thought, to look and not touch. I liked the way his lips curled around a cigarette and his eyes narrowed against the smoke. I liked his slender fingers, and the way he moved, shifting his weight or rolling the stiffness out of his neck and shoulders as unself-consciously as an animal.

I gazed for a time at his intriguing, less-than-classical profile, then shifted my stare, let it fall in a caress on his shoulders, his back, down to the ass which so nicely filled his tight, faded jeans. He turned his head lazily toward me as if he'd felt, and liked, my touch. I moved my eyes back up his body to meet his eyes, and I didn't smile. He was the first to look away. Then I did smile, but only to myself.

Someone else, a man, approached him, cigarette in hand, and he gave him a light and responded to his conversational ventures absently, his attention hooked by me. I could feel his senses straining in my direction even when his back was turned, his eyes fixed elsewhere, his ears assaulted by the blandishments of the cigarette smoker—who eventually gave up and took his need to someone else. Which was when my prey turned around and looked at me again.

I had to hide a smile of triumph. That I retained the ability to make a man desire me was reassuring. I had been feeling mired in marriage, as if my wedding ring had conferred invisibility, and his look sent a surge of well-being through me. As he straightened, flexing his shoulders and the muscles of his long back before moving away from the bar with an easy, loose-jointed motion, I imagined him naked and aroused and felt a tightening of my internal muscles.

He bought me a drink and then I bought him one. We sat and looked at each other. There were few words, none of importance. The conversation that mattered was conducted between our bodies, in minute shifts in posture and attitude, in the crossing and uncrossing of my legs as I leaned toward him and then back, in the way he stroked his own face with his long, slender fingers. He never touched me. I think he didn't dare. I tried to make it easy for him, resting my hand on the tabletop near his, moving my legs beneath the table. With every move I made I aroused myself more until finally, quite breathless and unthinking with desire, I reached out my hand beneath the table and put it on his denimed thigh.

The pupils of his strange green eyes widened, and I smiled. He put his warm hand on top of mine and squeezed.

"Can we go to your place?" he asked, his voice very low.

Confronted with reality, I lost my smile. What was I playing at? I pulled my hand away and stood up. He followed me so quickly that he nearly overturned the table.

"No," I said, but he followed me out of the dim, air-conditioned bar, into the parking lot. The hot, tropical night embraced us like a sweaty lover. Someone, in a book I'd once read, had compared the smell of Houston to the aroma of a woman, sexually aroused and none too clean. I drew a deep breath; spilled beer, gasoline, car exhaust, cooking fumes, perfume, after-shave, rotting vegetation, garbage, and, beneath it all, a briny tang that might have been a breeze wafted in from the Gulf of Mexico.

He was right behind me, following, and as I turned to tell him off, somehow instead I fell against him. And then we were clutching each other, breast to breast, mouth to mouth, kissing greedily. The need I felt when he first touched me, the intensity with which it rushed all through me was so powerful I thought I would faint. Then, slowly, resting in his embrace, I came back to myself, back to him. I had never known anything as sensually beautiful as his mouth; the soft, warm lips that parted against mine, dryness opening into wetness, a moist cave where the sly, clever animal that was his tongue lived and came out to nuzzle and suck at me greedily. His breath was smoky and dark, tasting of desirable sins, of whisky and sugar and cigarettes.

His hands, long-fingered, strong and clever, moved over my body as we kissed, at first shy, but then, as I clung to him fiercely, making no attempt to push him off, becoming bolder. He was quickly impatient with the barriers of my clothes, which were little enough: a cotton blouse, a short summer skirt and underwear, my legs bare, naked feet strapped into leather sandals. One of his hands, which had returned again and again to cup and trace lazy patterns of arousal on my bound and covered breasts, now began swiftly and without fumbling to unbutton my blouse, while his other hand, behind me, was pushing up my skirt and tugging at the elastic of my panties. In a matter of minutes, maybe seconds, he could have me stripped naked.

I wanted nothing better than to be naked in his capable hands, but not here, in public, surrounded by strangers—was he crazy? "No," I gasped and pushed him off and pulled away, struggling to refasten my buttons.

He reached for me again, and I slapped at his hands. He looked stricken. "I want you. Don't you—?"

I laughed. "Not here, be reasonable!" There were people all around us, getting in and out of cars, overflow customers from the bar and people from the neighborhood out for a breath of air, drinking beer from six-packs purchased at the convenience store across the street. This parking lot and the whole street was like a fair or a carnival, an impromptu, open-air party to celebrate summer in the city. I waved a hand to indicate the crowd passion had temporarily hidden from us, and as if I'd waved away smoke we both saw, at the same time, a man and woman locked in a fervent embrace just yards away from us. As I stared, I realized that the woman had one hand inside the front of the man's trousers.

My stranger grinned at me, a wide, white, wolfish smile. He put his hands on my hips and pulled me tightly to him. His erection felt enormous. His breath hot in my ear, he whispered, "Nobody's going to notice. Nobody'll care."

It was true nobody else seemed to notice the passionate couple, or, if they did, they politely pretended not to see. Other people had their own concerns; why should they care? Nor would it have been different if the lovers had been of the same sex. The Montrose was the most Bohemian and most sexually tolerant area of Houston, which was why I had chosen it for my escape that night. It provided a place where I could temporarily forget who and where I was and become a stranger, pretending I was a free woman at large in San Francisco, New Orleans, or Paris.

The smoky, spicy, sweaty smell of this other stranger, his body's heat and solid mass against me, the hands that caressed my hips and thighs and breasts, all wore away at my hesitation, as did his low voice, telling me a story:

"I was at a rock concert one time, thousands of people packed in close together, all standing up to see better, and moving, kind of dancing in place because there wasn't room to do anything else. I was with this girl . . . she had on a really short skirt, like yours, and one time when she dropped her purse and bent over to pick it up I saw she wasn't wearing any underpants. So . . . I got her to stand in front of me, and I unzipped, and slipped it in, and slowly, easily, pumped away. Nobody knew what we were doing. Even when we both came nobody noticed, because everybody was yelling and hopping around." He had pushed up my skirt at the back again and now snagged the elastic of my underpants—soaking wet by now—and began to ease them down.

"No."

Half of me wanted him to ignore my refusal, not to stop, to take me there among the crowds, even to be seen by disapproving, envious strangers—the other half of me was horrified. What if somebody who knew me came by, somebody I worked with, or one of my neighbors? So I said no again more fiercely, and when I pulled away he let me go.

"You're driving me crazy."

"What do you think you're doing to me?"

"Nothing, compared to what I'd like to do."

We stared at each other, hot and itchy with frustration. I grabbed his hand. "We'll find somewhere not so public. Come on."

I had nowhere in mind except to get away from the crowds. We walked away from the laughter and talk, away from the blare of amplified music and the bright blur of neon signs toward the quieter streets where there were no bars or all-night service stations, no massage parlors or convenience stores; quieter streets lined with trees where the buildings housed beauty parlors and dentists, small businesses that closed up at nightfall. On one such half-deserted street he pulled me suddenly into the embrasure of a darkened antique shop and pushed me up against the wall.

"No." I whispered the word, soft as a caress. I wasn't even sure he heard. His hands were swift and urgent. My blouse was unbuttoned, my bra undone, my breasts out, nipples teased and kneaded to an aching stiffness. I surrendered, undone, melting, and then quite suddenly I saw myself from the outside: some slut, half undressed in a public place with a stranger, letting a stranger do that to her—I woke up with a sickening shock. That couldn't be me. I'd always been a good girl, even before I married I'd only had two steady boyfriends; I'd never picked up strange men. Now that I was a married woman this sort of behavior was unthinkable. Sex was something that happened at home, in bed, not in a shop doorway.

I tensed and fought off his hands. I twisted to one side and struggled to push him away, but he pinned my wrists together effortlessly, one-handed, and stared at me, a faint smile twitching his lips.

"No," I said weakly, not meaning it. I suddenly wanted more than anything to be overpowered, to be made to do what I wanted to do, to have the guilt taken away. He gazed into my eyes and read there what I wanted as he rolled an erect nipple between thumb and forefinger. I felt fixed by his gaze, unable to fight. I stood very still, quivering. He let go my hands and tugged my skirt up to my waist.

"Take off your pants and spread your legs," he said.

I felt dizzy with desire. "No," I whispered. I didn't mean I didn't want to, and I didn't mean I did. By my word I meant a different kind of yes; meant make me do it, do it to me, I'm helpless now.

His eyes were unwavering on mine, but for a moment I was afraid he wouldn't understand. Then he said, "Try and stop me." He tugged at the waistband of my panties, and then gently peeled them down my legs. When they reached my ankles, I stepped out of them and stood passively, my sex exposed to his view.

A little sigh of pleasure escaped his lips as he looked at me. Then he became stern again. "Up against the wall and spread your legs."

I swallowed hard, then found my voice and the only word I had left. "No."

He laughed. "No? No? What does that mean? Your body's saying something else." He slipped his hand between my legs. I gasped and quivered as he found my wetness. "Your body doesn't lie. Your body says yes." His touch was as soft as his voice, delicate and perfectly judged. I moaned and closed my eyes, unable to watch him watching me as he stroked my clitoris. I let him continue until his touch was too teasing, his fingering too delicate for my much harsher desire, and then I reached down to push his hand harder against me and his fingers inside me. He gasped as if he were the one penetrated, and I cried out with pleasure, a loud and violent "No!"

The wall was hard against my back. My thighs ached with strain as I rode his hand, the clever, stranger's fingers that knew me better, it seemed, than I knew myself, knowing just how to stroke and to probe together, knowing when a teasing gentleness should become more brutal. All this time he watched me, watched my face contort and read my desire as he murmured obscenities and endearments, commands and compliments alternating with a purpose like the hard-soft touch of his hand.

And then his other hand was on my ass, fingers probing the crack, and I moaned as he began to work me with both hands, back and front, and I cried out for more, still more.

Without taking his hands away, hardly faltering, he went down on his knees and began tonguing my clitoris, breathing hard with his own excitement. The warm, wet touch of his mouth was gentle, exact, and excruciating, and it was more than I could bear. Like lightning, white-hot, jagged, and intense, the orgasm flashed as I cried and yelled and clutched his curly head. "No," I cried, and "No" again, as if I must, in my last, desperate moments of pleasure, deny the force of that pleasure, or the reality of it—as if that word would keep it from being real to anyone but me.

Later, but still too soon, while I was rocked in the afterglow, unwilling to be disturbed, he caught my hand and carried it to his crotch, pressed it against the hard, warm bulge of his cock.

"No."

I have often wondered what I meant by that. Never in my life before that night had I said no meaning yes, but that night no was my word, my only word, and he had seemed to understand.

I pulled my hand away. "No."

Maybe I'd forgotten how to say yes. Maybe I wanted him to force me. Maybe I'd just had enough and wanted to send him away. Maybe, my own desire sated, I simply wasn't interested in his. Later, when I wanted more, I couldn't believe I'd meant I'd had enough then. I didn't want to believe I'd been selfish enough to send him away unsatisfied simply because my own immediate need had been met. Most of the time I preferred to believe that when I said no at the end I still meant yes, and that it was his understanding that failed him, and me.

Whatever I might have meant, whatever I'd wanted it to mean, he heard me say no, and took me at my word and left, and I made no effort to call him back.

I never saw him again, although there were nights when I went looking, and there has scarcely been a night since then that I haven't thought of him and longed for another chance.

After dinner, my husband and I took coffee in the large, yet cozy library, seated on one of the couches upholstered in leather as soft and supple as living skin, near the fire crackling in the hearth. We didn't talk to any of the other guests—we were being more English than the English on that trip—but we didn't have much to say to each other. Maybe we'd been married too long, maybe we were inhibited by the company. Certainly I was memory-haunted, aroused by the presence of the young man who looked so much like my long-ago stranger. Guilt made me uneasy in my husband's company, made me flinch when he touched me. My eyes kept sneaking across to him, and I pretended it was the books in the floor-to-ceiling bookcases that interested me. I felt him watching me, too, usually just as I looked away, but occasionally our glances would intersect, meeting for one highly charged instant before we both hastily looked away. Was it possible that this boy found me as desirable as had his look-alike of nearly twenty years ago? I hoped my husband wouldn't notice, but maybe it wouldn't be such a bad thing for him to know that another man wanted me.

It grew late, and we left the library, passed through the great hall, and mounted the grand staircase, our feet silent on the thick, pile carpet. I gazed up at the Pre-Raphaelite beauties who adorned the brilliant stained-glass windows but hardly saw them through my memories of warm, sensuous lips, long, clever fingers, and the cock I had never known.

I undressed slowly and dreamily in our luxurious room. I was down to the black silk teddy he'd surprised me with on Valentine's Day when my husband came up behind me and pulled me to him, his hands on my breasts, his breath warm in my ear. I could feel his erection, and I was as aroused as he was, but by the memory of someone else.

Guilt, or something else, made me whisper, "No."

He kissed me gently on my neck, and I moved my silk-clad bottom teasingly. His hands tightened on my breasts while his lips sought out the pulse in my neck. Caught up by rising excitement, again guilt mingled with desire and I breathed, "No," and he let go.

I remained rooted to the spot for a few moments in astonished disappointment, feeling the chill of his departure, hearing him sigh as he got into bed.

But what else could I expect?

No had never meant yes in our shared vocabulary. I had never wanted it to until now, just this moment, when I longed for a little telepathy.

Tingling with frustration, I peeled off my useless sexy underwear and climbed naked into bed.

"Goodnight, my darling," he said, and the chaste kiss he gave me forestalled my chance of letting him know, with my mouth on his, how

I really felt. Of course I could have done something more obvious, or simply told him in words, but I couldn't think of the right words. I was in a mood to be taken, not to take, so all I could do was lie there wide awake, sulking about being misunderstood and horny, while he fell asleep with insulting ease. Surely, if he'd *really* wanted me he wouldn't have been able to sleep. Surely, if he'd really wanted me, he would not have walked away.

Time in darkness alone passes slowly. I thought again about that long-ago night and imagined I hadn't said no, but yes. Or that he had ignored my token protest, had pushed me against the wall and taken me, willingly against my will. Pleasure without guilt; I didn't want to, I couldn't help it, he made me. . . . The game I had to play if I were to remain a happily married woman. Finally I got up. I thought I'd seen a copy of *The Story of O* on the bookshelves downstairs. With a little help from my hand, it might help me to sleep. I wrapped a silk kimono around my nakedness and left my sleeping husband.

The great house was silent, although not dark. Electric lights in the form of candles burned on the walls of the hallways, illuminating all the closed bedroom doors. I imagined all the other guests paired in pleasure except the solitary stranger, who might be lying awake now, as horny as I was, and for the same reason. I wished I knew which was his door.

In the library the fire still burned, casting enough light to show me that someone was there before me.

He must have had the same reason as I did for coming here. As I entered the room he turned in surprise from the bookcase, a book in one hand. He wore a short, flimsy robe, tied with a sash. Under it, I knew, he was naked.

We stared at each other without speaking for what seemed a long time. There aren't many times in life that you get a second chance. I knew I'd never forgive myself if I didn't take this one. I closed the door firmly behind me and walked into the room. When I was only a few feet away from him, standing in the full glow of the fire, I stopped, untied my kimono, and shrugged it off, enjoying the sensation as it slithered silkily down my naked body and settled on the floor, enjoying also the gleam of his eyes as he stared at me without speaking.

He made no voluntary motion, but I saw the rising of his heavy cock, and the blood-flushed, rounded head parted the silken curtain of his dressing gown, roused by my nakedness. I had never seen it before, and it was bigger and more solid than any of my fantasies.

I smiled and licked my lips. A few steps more, and I sank to my knees before him.

"No," he said. He caught me by the shoulders and raised me up. "I'm going to fuck you—the way I should have done years ago. You won't get away from me this time."

I was stunned. It wasn't possible that this was the same young man I'd picked up in a bar almost twenty years before—he wasn't old enough, and he spoke with an English accent. But if he wasn't the same man, how did he *know?*

His hands were on me, rougher than I remembered, and greedier as he felt and fondled my nakedness. Then he pulled me hard against him, the silk of his robe like the cool fall of water against my skin. His warm, firm cock butted at my sex, and he kissed me. How I could remember such a thing with any certainty after so long a time, I don't know, but his lips felt like the same lips, and his mouth tasted still of desirable sins: of whiskey and sugar and, very faintly, cigarettes. I nearly swooned with pleasure as his tongue moved in my mouth and his hands, gripping my hips, moved to caress and explore my buttocks and finally between my legs.

He laughed, finding me so wet and ready for his probing fingers. "You're hot, aren't you? Can't pretend you don't want me."

"No," I murmured into his mouth, agreeing. I wanted him, now, hard, fast, slow, any way at all.

Without letting go of me, his mouth fastened firmly, devouringly, on mine, his cock prodding me, he walked me backward and pushed me down on my back on the very same leather couch where I'd sat drinking coffee with my husband a few hours earlier.

The shock of memory, of sudden guilt, made me struggle up and exclaim, "No—I can't—"

"Oh, yes you can."

"No." I said it reluctantly as I struggled to rise, sorry that he wasn't stopping me, outraged that I wasn't stopping myself. But my freedom was an illusion. As soon as I had regained my feet he caught me in his arms and picked me up with a strength I had not known he possessed. Ignoring my feeble efforts to escape, he turned me around and pushed me down, face first on the couch. It was warm and solid, both yielding and supporting, covered in leather so fine that I had the sensation of having been pressed down on top of some other person. Before I could even catch my breath he was lifting me by the ass, a cheek in each hand, and then I felt his lips on my labia, his hot, clever tongue raking my clitoris.

All protest, all urge to flight, rushed out of me in a low moan of pleasure. He drew his head away with a low laugh. "Yes, you'd like that, wouldn't you? Let me do anything but fuck you . . . But that's what I'm going to do, and nothing you say can stop me."

I said nothing. I didn't think about what I wanted, or what was right. I lay still and let him position me for his pleasure. I was lying nearly flat, facedown on the broad leather-cushioned couch, my legs dangling over the edge. He lifted my ass and parted my legs and the head of his cock nudged at the slick lips of my cunt. I couldn't see him anyway, this stranger my lover behind me, so I closed my eyes and gave myself up to physical sensation.

He was very big and greedy in his lust. Although I was very wet and willing, he spared me no tenderness but thrust himself inside me hard and fast, using his hands to part the cheeks of my ass at the same time, as if he wanted to split me in two. Even as I welcomed and wanted this penetration, at the same time the sensation of being forced was strong, and I cried out, half fainting with the shock of it.

"No . . . oh, no . . ."

He laughed and thrust again, this time burying himself to the hilt in me. Withdrawing slightly, he thrust again. "No?" With each thrust he repeated the word which came out sometimes as a croon, sometimes as a gasp, and I echoed him.

"No . . . no . . . no . . ."

Our denials came closer and closer together as he found a hard, driving rhythm that satisfied both of us. I lost all sense of place and time and even of self as he drove into me and drove himself, and me, finally, over the brink into a fierce, all-consuming orgasm, with a final shout in which our two voices mingled.

A little while later I felt him withdraw. I made a small sound of protest but no move, too exhausted and happy where I was, sprawled facedown and legs spread on the couch. Until I heard the door to the library open.

Annoyed that he could leave me this way, I opened my eyes and raised my head just as the lights came on. There in the doorway, coolly surveying me and my lover, was my husband.

He looked at me, lying naked and flushed, and then at the man, also naked, his still-rampant penis glistening with our mingled juices. It was very quiet. And then, shockingly, he smiled.

"Happy anniversary, darling," he said. "I hope you enjoyed yourself?"

I began to push myself up, my mind whirling.

"Oh, no," he said. "Stay there, please. Or shall I ask our friend to hold you down?"

My erstwhile lover was beside me at once, his hands on my shoulders firmly keeping me from changing my position.

"I certainly hope you enjoyed yourself, because now it's my turn," my husband continued. There was a note in his voice that I had not heard in a very long time, and I suddenly realized that he had set this up, a sexual game of a sort I had never imagined he would want to play, an unexpected anniversary gift for both of us, and suddenly I felt more excited than I would have thought possible.

"You've been a naughty girl," said my husband. "So I've asked our friend to stay. . . . I'm going to have to punish you first, before we can kiss and make up."

I began an ineffective struggle to get away, but the stranger had no trouble restraining me. "No," I whimpered. "Please. No."

AUTHOR'S NOTE

It seems like it was only a few years ago (although I suppose it must have been ten or fifteen) that I frequently came across articles purporting to detail the differences between male and female sexuality, ones which declared that women tended to be less interested in, less likely to be turned on by, pornography, whether visual or written, than men. Maddeningly, we were supposed to accept such statements as reasoned, scientific conclusions! Yet a more sensible, sensitive response to the tests and surveys that yielded this rarely questioned generalization would have been that as pornography (a term meaning, literally, writings or drawings depicting whores) was always intended to appeal to a masculine audience, women's relative indifference, or repulsion, to it was unsurprising. Whether women are actually less, more, or equally responsive to pictures and texts that aim to arouse is a question that can't begin to be answered until women have had more opportunities to create and enjoy our own erotogenic stories.

It'll be fun, but it won't be easy getting there; we're laying the groundwork now for women not yet born. Though I myself would love to find a new way of writing about sex, and a new approach to sexual fantasy, "The Story of No" is not that breakthrough. As the title suggests, it's a response to other people's stories, its inspiration literary rather than personal.

REASONS NOT TO GO TO FORT LAUDERDALE

By Liz Clarke

The exuberance of Liz Clarke's story was extremely heartening to come across, after seeing so many submissions by older, wiser—and more depressed—women closer to my own age who either lack for opportunity or who've pretty much, for the usual reasons, given up on dancing (or "scrumping") the night away. The sexuality of such nineties students as Clarke depicts, shadowed as it is by AIDS, perhaps is more highly charged, more polymorphous because *of that mortal threat. But I can't say that I felt anything other than grateful after encountering this not quite sophisticated—yet not quite innocent, either—example of their youthful energy, optimism, and zest for romance.*

So you have multiple lovers. How exciting." Joel was starting to get on my nerves. He was also lying through his teeth; he was jealous as hell.

I just smiled at him. My feet were starting to freeze. I'd taken my shoes off to run through the mud in the cornfield, but now the wind was picking up. We'd just gotten back from spring break. Or rather, he'd gotten back; I'd stayed on campus.

"Who is it?" he asked.

"We agreed not to tell. You know how people gossip around here."

"Don't you trust me?"

Not a sno-cone's chance in hell. "I'm sorry, Joel, I promised."

He sulked. Several hundred yards away, at the edge where the field and woods met, there was another het couple rolling around. I looked out across the field at Mt. Jasmine and the Gourami Range.

"Tell me about your break. How was LA?" I said. That distracted him for a while. He told me about all the parties he'd gone to.

"I missed you," he said. "You're the sexiest girl I know." Translated, that meant I wasn't beautiful but he considered me worth fucking anyway.

"Woman," I corrected automatically.

We walked back to Amphlett Place.

"Who was it?" he persisted, reaching to touch the bite-mark on my throat, which was what had tipped him off.

"Joel. I really can't tell. Don't take it personally."

"Was it Elliot?"

"*Please!*"

"Gabe or Cat?"

"What makes you think that?" I said, very very casually.

"You said you spent break in your apartment bonding with them."

I laughed. "It wasn't Gabriel or Cat." It was Gabriel *and* Cat.

Joel went back to his apartment. I went back to my apartment. As far as I was concerned, after the way he'd dissed me before break, he'd better consider himself lucky to ever see the inside of my room again.

I'd gone over to his place the night before he left to say good-bye. He was scrubbing the bathroom sinks, and he had a Crockpot of beef stew going. It was like walking into the Twilight Zone. I have hideous psychic scars from childhood Crockpot meals.

"What are you doing?" I climbed onto the counter beside where he was scraping at several semesters' worth of smeg.

"Cleaning. I mopped the bathroom floor and cleaned the kitchen and did all the dishes everybody left."

Oh, Lord. The problem was, he was rabidly attractive. He had Bambi eyes and long dark curls, and he smelled sweetly of clove cigarettes and reefer. Twenty years from now I'll catch a whiff of cloves, and it'll knock me to my knees. I reached out and traced my finger along the curve of his ear. He had his hair back in a faded ribbon ponytail holder. Stop cleaning that damn sink! I hadn't *intended* to jump him when I went over, but maybe it was the challenge, or the cloves, or something. He put the sponge down. Progress. I pulled him over and locked my legs around him, slid my tongue up from his collar to the notch behind his ear.

"I'm cooking dinner for Katya. She's coming over in about half an hour," he said.

I took hold of his hair and kissed him good and slow, grinding my hips into him. Oh, yes. That ought to get his attention. When I slid off the counter to press my whole self against him, my knees were syrupy.

"How long?" I pulled him into me, my back against the doorframe of his room. My hand down his belly to a firm hold on his crotch.

"Half an hour."

"Mmm . . ."

His head went down to the space between my breasts, and he unbuttoned the top of my shirt. Half an hour was realistic, knowing him. I could manage with half an hour. I wanted to drag him into his room and throw him down. I could hardly breathe. God, what *was* it about him?

He squeezed my thighs and pulled away from me. "Katya'll be here soon. You'd better go."

You've got to be kidding. The smells of Crockpot *au boeuf* and Comet cloaked the scene. He turned back to the sink and picked up the sponge. He wasn't kidding.

I buttoned my shirt. "Have a good break," I said, heading for the couch where I'd dropped my leather jacket.

He followed, sponge in hand. He had a lot in common with sponges. "You too."

"Have a good dinner." Die of botulism. I pulled on my jacket. My knees still felt shaky, and my cunt was screaming in frustration. Which person in this picture has the warped sex drive?

"Thanks."

I paused in the doorway, holding it open. "Tell Katya hi."

"Maybe you can come over later tonight."

"Maybe." Maybe, as in, maybe you fully deserve to eat Crockpot beef stew. He'd seen the last of that shirt I borrowed from him.

Outside the stars were ice chips. I glanced toward my apartment. Patricia had materialized and suction-cupped herself to Gabriel as soon as Alan and Sarah had left together. I wasn't in the mood to deal with that; not right this second. I wasn't in the mood to do anything except fuck. All lubed up and no place to go, I thought sourly.

Except that wasn't entirely true. Cassie had come over a couple of days earlier and told me she'd changed her mind about our ban on exchanging fluids—as we romantically phrased it. Actually, it was her ban. I failed to see the difference between her exchanging fluids with me and with the men she was fucking. If anything, my fluids were safer.

At the moment I certainly had a surplus of fluids, so I turned around and went to Cassie's. The Goddess was smiling on me; she was home.

When she'd come to see me on Thursday, Cassie had also had a suggestion involving Gabriel. And her. And me. I didn't know what kind of revelation she'd had, but I wasn't going to complain. Maybe it had to do with what was going on among the group in the apartment already. Gabe had of course expressed interest when I informed him of Cassie's little proposition. Anything sexual caught Gabe's interest. But, he said, he wasn't too into it. Mainly he didn't know Cassie all that well. And I knew Cassie all that well, but I wasn't really into the specific nature of her idea. We needed to talk about it.

It was as good a pretense as any.

Warning: this part of the story reinforces the notion of bisexuals as promiscuous scum who view same-sex recreation as a substitute for the Real Thing. If you believe that stupidity already, nothing I can say is going to change your mind and you'll get offended in a few paragraphs.

"That dipwad threw me out!" I snatched off my jacket and dropped down on her bed. Like most Serling College students, she didn't have a bedframe, just a mattress on the floor.

"He's such an asshole," she said. I didn't even have to tell her who I was talking about.

We thoroughly trashed Joel, which took a while because we wanted to extract every bit of pleasure we could from the task. When he'd been reduced to a gob of wombat slobber drying to a crust on a rock somewhere in the Australian outback, I said, "I mentioned your proposition to Gabe."

"Yeah? What did he say?"

I filled her in. She already knew my reservations.

"Well, actually, I've reconsidered that too." Apparently this was the week for Cass to totally reorder her cosmology. "What if I was more actively participating?"

"Define more."

"Everything but exchanging fluids."

"Whose fluids?"

"His."

"Hm. Okay, yeah, I'd be more comfortable with that. I'll talk to him again." All semester I kept expecting Ricardo Montalban to step out from behind some piece of furniture and hand me a drink in a hollowed-out pineapple. "Where'd you get this idea?"

She made her eyes even more huge and innocent and chocolate-brown. "Weeellll . . . Gabriel is very attractive." This was true. "And you're very beautiful." This was debatable. Cassie snuggled closer to me. "I thought it'd be fun."

"That's it?"

"Yeah."

"Okay." Gabriel saw an ulterior motive in everything.

I kissed her neck. She was lying on her back, and I was curled up beside her, her arms around me. For some reason we wound up that way a lot. I kissed her some more, and she didn't tell me to stop. I didn't stop.

"Why, Liz," she said with delight as I nibbled her earlobe, afraid to move below her neck for fear she'd tell me to cut it out, "I do believe you're horny."

I hate that word, especially in reference to me, so as a matter of course I deny any connection with it. But I didn't stop kissing her either.

"Ooh, that feels nice." *Nice?* I was about to come just kissing her above the shoulders. "I think living in that apartment has been good for you."

"Yeah? How?"

She sat up. I sat up. "Mm, more comfortable with your body. You've gotten a lot more aggressive," she said.

To prove her right, I lunged at her.

"Oh, Natasha," Cassie giggled in her sexy Russian accent. "You do such things to me!"

This is the way things were with Cass: I never knew what, if anything, was going to happen until it was in progress. It was always slow, cautious. Which made it almost painfully hot. I was afraid she'd change her mind any second. Cassie asked, "Are you okay? Are you sure?" every five minutes. Making love to her was like finding my way along the edge of a cliff in the dark. Like falling over the edge. Like spreading purple wings and catching an updraft. All at the same time.

"Hey, Natasha, want to exchange fluids with me?"

"Well, Anastasia . . . if you insist . . ."

And as I said, this was the first time we'd done more than kiss and nibble and roll around.

"You probably won't be able to make me come," Cassie said.

Ha! She obviously didn't know who she was dealing with. She'd told me, of course, that she almost never had an orgasm during het intercourse—it had been a while since she'd scrumped with a woman. Clearly her memory needed refreshing.

The first kiss on the mouth always sent a few pebbles skittering over the cliff edge. Her skin was butter-soft. She liked her nipples sucked so hard I was always afraid of hurting her. My shirt got unbuttoned and stripped off; her loose green dress and the wool leggings underneath; we struggled me out of my jeans. It's a scientific fact that women's underwear is more appetizing than men's. Anyone who's ever had a hard time keeping a straight face (or concealing disappointment) at ratty semiwhite Fruit of the Looms knows it. Of course Cassie never wore a bra—she had Teflon Tits worthy of Ripley's "Believe It or Not." Not being so blessed, my personal lingerie collection ran toward black and purple lace bras, and bikini underwear flowered like Hawaiian shirts.

Maybe it was the uncertainty of it, the feeling of being bad and getting away with it—unless I got caught. Maybe it was the unexpectedness of her deciding it was okay. For some crazy reason it reminded me of those old Impulse cologne commercials: "If a man you've never met before suddenly gives you flowers . . ." That close to orgasm, any wild thing might fly across my mind. Usually in a matrix of purple swirls, thick flocks of birds, or bursts of exploding color . . . it's very depressing to me as a writer that I have such clichéd mental images during sex.

Cunts are most often compared to flowers, to butterflies, to seashells. I'm guilty of doing it myself. You can compare labia to petals, clitori to pearls from here until next Tuesday, but trust me, kids, when you're up close and personal a cunt is a cunt. The Goddess be praised.

Everywhere she touched drew fire to the surface. I was shaking. My hands and mouth grasping—

"Oh *my*," she said, giggling.

"Shut up."

She had on a Cocteau Twins tape and three candles burning on her dresser. Oh my Lord, she felt good. She pushed my thighs open, and her tongue was hot although not as hot as the flesh it was touching. Colors and colors. How sad it would be to have orgasms in black and white.

"You taste so good," Cass said, grinning over my belly.

That had been called to my attention before.

After my eyes uncrossed I kissed my way down her stomach and up her thighs, and she reminded me again that it would take an act of God or Congress to make her come. I had a mental image of a mechanic spitting into her palms and pushing up her sleeves, a pianist cracking her knuckles with a flourish. Two fingers, tongue, and she shrieked up the scale as she came. Nine minutes flat by the clock on the dresser, at the head of the bed with the candles and box trilling "*The Pink Opaque*."

"Oh, God, stop, stop." She sat up, gasping, eyes saucered.

I'm sure I looked smug.

"Oh, my God. How did you *do* that?"

I sat up and wiped my mouth on my shoulder. "I've been worshiping at the Shrine of Cat."

"Thank her for me." She curried her fingers through her hair. It made utterly no difference. Her hair was a soft bowl-shape, the same brown as her eyes. "I can't believe you did that. Oh my God." She hooked her arms around me and kissed me with markedly more respect.

I felt like calling the *Enquirer*.

"Living with that group *has* been good for you."

"Certainly educational." I neglected to mention the oral art I had performed on Patricia when she joined Gabriel and me in bed the morning after the last dance party in our apartment. It occurred to me that Cassie had deliberately waited until I wasn't a blushing baby dyke paralyzed at the very thought of initiating sex.

When the phone rang at 1:30 that morning I was in the kitchen, gathered with Gabe and Patricia around a bubbling vat of chickpeas like the three witches in *Macbeth*. We were making hummus. *Knowing* it was Joel, I let Gabe answer.

I listened to Joel with the steam from the pot saunaing my face. ". . . and we had dinner and then we got really really stoned and watched *2001* on the VCR . . ." No more first year students, I vowed. No way. And Lord, no one else from Los Angeles. ". . . it was really really fun. She just left. So can you come over now?"

"No, I don't think so." We Southerners have politeness knocked into us from the womb. Fortunately for him. "It's late."

"I could come over there."

"Joel. It's 1:30 in the morning. I'm going to bed." Total lie. "Have a good break."

"Will you write to me?"

"Right, sure." *Please.*

I did, in fact, go to bed around three, after pounding out my aggressions into the mush of chickpeas, tahini, lemon juice, and way too much garlic, gleefully fantasizing Joel's brain squipping through the octagonal holes in the potato masher. Gabe and Patricia accompanied me, and none of us got much sleep—but despite that morning's educational and entertainment value, I'm taking the liberty here of substituting another event from later in the week. With those two I always felt like I'd been conked over the head and woken up in a bad porno movie. Also, I promised Cat she'd be in this story.

Monday and Tuesday, Gabriel and Patricia went to visit Doug in Plymouth and Alan in Boston, Gabriel oozing garlic from every pore after all the hummus he'd consumed in the intervening thirty-six hours.

Wednesday I sat in the kitchen windowseat reading *Interview with the Vampire* and watching the entrance to the Amphlett Place parking lot for his return. Just as I was positive the only thing I wanted for the rest of eternity was to be a vampire, I realized I'd deliberately sought out the sunniest spot in the apartment to read. The view of the parking lot was a factor too, of course. But naturally I didn't see him drive up. He must have walked from Greenvalley Village, where Patricia lived; they'd taken her car.

"Hi."

"Hi."

"How was it?"

"Okay." The apartment door closed behind him, and he checked the message board before hauling his stuff to his room. I put down my book and followed him.

He dropped his duffel bag and backpack onto the floor, turned, and put his arms around me. We didn't have the kind of thing where I could call him baby and tell him I'd missed him. I did it anyway.

"I missed you too," he said, looking faintly surprised.

Standing on my toes and stretching, I just barely reached his shoulder. For that reason I generally stood on his bed when I was in his room—when I wasn't lying on it. Gabriel's room tended to be a gathering place and most evenings saw at least one and up to five bodies sprawled on his mattress (no frame, and he'd added a foam pad). What form of entertainment said bodies engaged in varied. I kissed his neck, still vaguely garlicky—amazing how bodies get so familiar so fast. Much easier to get to know a body than the person living inside it. It could have been just a consequence of the living conditions that I knew Gabriel liked the web of his thumb and first finger bitten before I knew the names of his brothers and sister.

After—what, a month and a half?—I knew him by taste, smell, the texture of his skin. I knew the way he kissed and the weight of his hands. The pattern of his breathing. I could identify his step on the stairs.

Knowing the parts of him that were covered with more than clothes was a different story altogether.

Of course Gabriel had groupies on twenty-four hour call, snatching each others' hair out for the chance to kiss and bite and fuck and suck and give him backrubs. He didn't think it was at all amusing when Alexa or Cat or I suggested he put a sign-up sheet on his door.

When standing-up kissing got old, he scooped me up as easily as picking up the cat (admittedly the cat, Gandalf, was the biggest, baddest beast this side of the Pecos), carried me down the hall to my room, and threw me down on my futon—more room than his bed. One-oh-one Amphlett Place, where fantasies come true. Sometimes, at least.

"Missed me, huh?" I said, grinning up at him.

Gabe dropped to his knees beside me on the futon. "Goddamn, you are so hot."

"Why, thank you."

One arm plunked down by my left shoulder; him half bridged over me. "No problem." Slowly his face came down until our lips brushed. Just barely touched. That one point of light friction, more a tease than a kiss. I raised my head and hooked my arms around his neck to draw him to me, lips and tongue, tasted him deep as his hands at the small of my back pulled me to sitting up.

He had on that look, the one that could scrape electric fingers across the back of my neck from the other side of the room with Sarah and Alexa chopping veggies for burritos, Kyle reading aloud from a chemistry book, and Alan blasting his music from upstairs. I could never hold that gaze for long. Predatory, feline; eyes hardening from blue to green. Stone cherub's mouth. Gabriel knew how to ride the thin edge of fear, push back the borders. No one had ever done that to me before.

Slow hand outlining cheek, lips, neck. The curve of his smile. His hand rounded my shoulder as if he were drawing me in silhouette. I took one of his hands and carefully circled the index-finger joints with my tongue, the webbing of his palm, sucked his fingers. He practically purred.

"Lock your door," he said.

This struck me as mildly insane. "Nobody's going to come in the apartment except for Cat," I said, getting up to humor him, "and we'd invite her in anyway."

When my room was locked I knelt behind him, pushed aside his mane to kiss the sweet nape of his neck and rub his back, working his shirttail out and my hands underneath to warm skin. We rarely made love in the daylight. My room glowed white with sun reflecting off the snow outside.

Gabe, I had discovered, had not actually reached a Buddhalike state of Sensitive New Age Guy-dom. He merely channeled that macho energy into socially acceptable directions. Like . . . sex. He bit, he grabbed, he said "fuck." All endearing traits. Fucking Gabriel was being sucked into a cyclone headed for an Oz where Glinda is a drag queen and the Wicked Witch of the West is a hot Top in tight black leather. (Remember when all the Munchkins prostrated themselves before her?) And they don't sing that dippy "Ding-Dong the Witch is Dead" bullshit. The soundtrack is by Prince—and the Yellow Brick Road leads to Erotic City.

Like they say, getting there is half the fun. This was a cyclone of hot breath in hair, open mouths, arched back, wet fingers. Tell me you want it. Hands held over my head—

"Don't move," he murmured roughly and kissed me soft as a baby's mouth, licked the salt from my eyelids.

Cyclone of blood draining, drawing to the center. Falling in a spiral. Tell me you want it. Pulse in my cunt; when we finally stripped all my pores opened their mouths and greedily tasted air and skin. Ah, the joys of sensitive nipples.

His teeth locked firm on the side of my neck, the skin of his stomach against my back. Condoms in the top desk drawer. Gabriel could (did) pick me up and move me like a doll. As far as I was concerned, he was jungle gym, roller coaster, waterslide, and concession stand all in one.

"Oh, my God, let me look at you." His hands on my hips. I was on top of him, not minding that my right foot was starting to fall asleep.

I grinned. Struck a Madonna pose with my hands behind backtossed head.

"Very hot."

I rolled my hips in that way that popped his eyes out of their sockets, and he stopped laughing.

We were sprawled in a sweaty postcoital tangle and the light had faded some when we heard the outer door open, followed by a knock at my room. Gabriel whipped a blanket over himself so fast it created a sonic boom.

"Chill, it's locked. Who is it?" I sang in my most Little Red Riding Hood-innocent voice.

"It's Cat."

"Just a min-ute!" I got up and pulled my robe off its hook on the back of the door. It was a black rayon deal from East-West Gifts, with a red and orange dragon across the back.

"I can go away if you and Gabe are busy."

"No, we're done," I said, opening the door. "Come on in."

"Aw, I missed it?" She dropped her backpack, closed the door, and joined us on the futon.

"Mmmm, not necessarily," Gabriel said, kissing her neck. I wondered why the hell he'd bothered to make himself decent—like Cat had never seen him naked before?

I kissed the places on her neck Gabe was missing.

"Goodness!" Expressions got passed around like hickeys. I believe that one originated with Alan.

"How was work?" I asked between kisses.

"Oh, sucky," Cat said cheerfully. "I like this, though."

Gabe had said before that Cat reminded him of a snake, all sinew and grace. She could have been carved out of pearl. At Serling, if you were asked to describe a specific dyke and you said, "She's got short brown hair," the querant was likely to slap you because 95 percent of them had short brown hair. Cat, however, defied the standard kd lang DA. Her crewcut spiked naturally, without the aid of gel or Butch Wax. The three of us—as we had all commented—made a beautiful physical contrast: me an inch shy of five feet, short red curls with a green Krazy Kolor streak, pale gold skin, and curves galore. Cat perfectly lithe and androgynous, at least until you saw her naked at which point you became aware that she had killer hips and breasts; delicate Celtic features. Gabriel somehow androgynous too despite his height, broad shoulders, and perpetual three days' worth of beard; sweet soft skin, fine hair to his shoulders.

With Gabriel and Cat I wished I could observe the scene at a distance, to see those bodies fully. The two of them together was . . . Gabe had described Cat and me as live MTV, the video to "Lesbians of the Congo, in D Minor." Cat and I also agreed that watching Gabe and Alan was hot enough to make us want to be men for a couple of days. Gabe and Cat together just made me want both of them more—maybe I was the most insecure person of our circle, but when there were three of us I could never shake the fear that the other two would find each other far more interesting than they found me. We tried so hard to be all liberal and liberated.

"I think you need to take your clothes off," I suggested to Cat. She thought so too. Gabriel thought so too. We assisted her. My Chinese robe got shed as well.

"Guys," Gabe said when Cat and I were pretzeled, "I'm tired. Do you mind if I just observe?" We were his favorite spectator sport. The price of being bisexual is that sometimes all the sleazy stereotyped things about it actually happen. What makes this qualitatively different from Cassie wanting to watch me fuck Gabriel? Don't confuse the issue by trying to insert logic into it. "The two of you, goddamn. . . ."

Cat laughed into the valley between my breasts where she was kissing. We knew Gabriel well enough to translate. As long as we were scrumping anyway, it was no big deal being his live MTV. Cat's lower lip just begged to be bitten. Come to think of it, I would have sold my blood to bite any part of Cat. In my modified Land of Oz, she got the part of the Witch of the West. She was working magic on my cunt, drawing blue streaks of sparks with her tongue, when somewhere back in Kansas Gabriel groaned as he came and fell back on the bed. He stayed to watch until I sizzled and melted, and then he kissed us both and put his clothes on.

"I'm going to take a shower. You guys are amazing."

"We know," I said.

Cat, still between my legs, propped on her elbows, laughed and kissed my belly. "*You* are amazing."

Affirmation time! Everybody empower and validate the person to your left—it's group therapy with orgasms!

Gabriel left; Cat and I stayed. Weeks earlier, Elliot, accosting me outside Rogers-Nelson Hall after my 9:00 A.M. class, had suggested that I install a turnstile at my door. No wonder we broke up; the boy couldn't even come up with a creative insult.

Of course Gabriel was kidding when at the end of the week he suggested that the three of us move to Seattle and have a group marriage. Of course Alexa and Alan didn't think it was at all funny when they got home and found out. Sarah was mercifully spared, being the only resident not scrumping one or more of me, Gabriel, and/or Cat. (Except for Kyle, who'd had the sense not to get involved in the first place. Much to my and Cat's disappointment.)

Mr. Roarke never did show up with pineapple drinks, ordering everyone to smile. I don't think any of us ever got hearts or brains or courage from the Wizard. A home, maybe—the real kind, with a family you want to kill and at the same time love powerfully enough to die for.

I didn't see much of Joel after that, but I didn't tell Elliot. I let him think my turnstile was having its hinges spun off.

Also, Cassie's evening of debauchery never happened.

There's always next semester.

AUTHOR'S NOTE

The idea is, wouldn't it be fabulous to come to sex (no pun intended) without cumbersome emotional baggage? Talk about the ultimate fantasy! Even with the lovers I adore and who adore me, we carry our histories, mutual and individual. We have our issues. Of course, for a child of the age of AIDS, codependency, and Oprah, it's just to be expected: latex and therapy are facts of life.

The residents of this story have collectively survived abuse, incest, rape, alcoholism, drug abuse, eating disorders, suicide attempts, depression. In their circle, the line between "friend" and "lover" tends to blur or not exist at all. They need the closeness, the intimacy. They're discovering, too, that sex can just be fun and playful, and not such a big damn religious deal. Come on, if you can't have sex with your friends, who on earth are you supposed to have it with?

BLESSED IMMORTAL SELF: HOW THE JEWELS SHONE ON YOUR SKIN!

By Susan Swan

If one thing is certain, it is that there are no certainties when it comes to sexual attraction. And, like so many aspects of erotic awakening, the possibility for surprise is always a factor. Here, Susan Swan makes us share the unexpected sensations of tenderness a woman might feel for a lover who fits into no previous category of imagined desire and who sneaks, unbidden, into her heart.

Blessed Sankara: *Om namah sivaya!*

You say you cannot live without me—that the taste has gone out of your morning tea and a sunset has no beauty because the next day will not have me in it (*Om shanti,* Sankara! Or have you forgotten the mantra, my master, Vishna, gave you?). Every day I pray you will attain God and the thrill of holy bliss. Instead you say we belong together and that you loved me from the first day you saw me standing on the ashram dock. You said you recognized me from Padma's old photographs in our retreat brochure. You said you'd never seen a sweeter yogi than this young woman with a dark braid down her back doing cartwheels on the beach.

Those pictures were taken more than a dozen years before you stepped off Chandrashekar's ferry with the other guests, still dressed in the clothes of northern cities, as pale and apprehensive as children sent to stay with relatives they didn't know. You said I still looked youthful, leaning over the railing to watch the procession troop ashore, but you were drawn to my mournful eyes. I seemed sad and perplexed for a woman hardly older than your own daughter. And then you noticed how I limped up the path by the yoga platform, lurching slowly past the upside down bodies of the other guests doing their morning headstands. Behind me trudged the giant Narayan, my faithful shadow, swearing to himself as he pushed the old cart stacked too full with suitcases.

You are always polite, Sankara, and have made no accusations, but I know you assume I'd been sleeping with Narayan before you arrived. Believe me, my darling, nothing much had transpired although naturally we were thrown together a great deal because we were preparing the new book of our master's letters for publication. (*Siranda Upanishad*—a universal scripture in my master's own handwriting.)

That first day you said you sensed Narayan's possessiveness, but I paid no attention to him or the foolish display he made of himself each morning, chinning himself on the exercise bar in the small courtyard of the ashram. The other women liked to watch the muscles wriggling like snakes in his upper arms. But not me, not your Shakti. Despite his height and physical prowess, to me, Narayan was just a spoiled boy not long out of high school with big hands and ears like Jughead in the old Archie comics. He was the pet of the camp, you see, because he was the swami's kid brother.

It is true I did enjoy discussing our project with him. Narayan does have a sardonic turn of mind, and he'd visited my master in India, and, oh Sankara—the amusing stories he can tell about forgetful old gurus meditating in Tibetan caves and getting frostbite because they never come out of their trances! Still, I didn't take Narayan seriously. And that first day, I paid no attention to you either, Sankara. I was carrying Vishna's forbidden stash of chocolate (which Narayan had just smuggled in) and hoping my master wouldn't scold me for being late.

Of course, you had noticed my sprained ankle because you coach basketball like my father, and you've trained yourself to spot an injury. I like to believe our meeting was preordained, a necessary form of incest, but I want to circumvent my nostalgia and tell you the truth. Who else at the Siranda ashram really worried over my foot? Oh yes, when it didn't heal, some of the staff gave me remedies, but it was only to hear themselves talk. It's ironic, isn't it, that we who serve others often can't serve ourselves.

So it was you who came to my small hut carrying your blue plastic box, the first aid kit you take everywhere, like a purse under your arm. You found the ice for it in the retreat's failing refrigerator and showed me how to elevate my ankle on pillows and then tape it tightly with a tensor bandage. R.I.C.E., you said in a fatherly tone—rest, ice, compression, elevation. When the swelling didn't go down, it was you who insisted on taking me to the hospital in the capital.

For that alone, I will always be grateful. But I haven't been fully honest, even here. Because I did notice you the first day. Later in meditation. As you slouched against the whitewashed wall of the temple, not bothering to sit cross-legged like the rest of us, while my master Vishna chanted his unending *bhajans* and mantras. It was the Easter our master grew lax and let those of us with bad backs lean against the temple wall. So I sat beside you, glad of the chance to rest, and found I couldn't take my eyes off you. What an ugly, ugly old man, I thought. It was your skin. You see, there is no point now hiding how you repulsed me. I was disgusted by the spidery web of wrinkles that crawled across your face, threatening to erase your features. You looked the way my father did during his last month in the hospital—distracted and restless, a withered mummy forced to stay alive against its wishes. But then I noticed the way you'd styled your hair in bangs that fell straight onto your forehead like a Roman senator. There's life in the old boy yet, I thought. And you turned to stretch and caught me staring, and I was taken aback by your clear hazel eyes glittering like Krishna's jewels in your aging face.

Sankara, I do not wish to hurt you. But I am trying to be as truthful as I can. So you will understand why I left you that morning. You didn't deserve such an unexpected leave taking, I know. It was several months later. We were old lovers by then, and you lay naked on my narrow cot, your fingers playing with the new black hair on your chest. Once again, you were shaving twice a day, and the white hair on your face and chest had started growing in dark. Because of me, you said. Because sex with me was making you young again. Now I am being unfair. You never said "sex." You always said "love." And you weren't greedy about your orgasms. You always pleased me first, as many times as I wanted, and then you pleased yourself.

Seven for me and one for you. Even steven, you'd say. No man has ever been so easy or gracious with me. Too often lovers want to please a woman out of anxiety or vanity. Not for the thrill of it, not like you.

I remember the sight of my hands in the bowl of milk cleaning the altar beads, made of real *rudrakshi,* the expensive wood my guru admired. I remember letting the beads spill off their plastic string into my palm. They were still damp, not sticky the way our sandalwood beads get if you clean them in milk.

I sat down on the bed beside you and with one hand began to stroke your forehead. I knew every inch of you by then, Sankara, and yet I still struggled to overcome my disgust before I touched you. And then when I did, I wondered why I had to struggle. I loved the feel of your skin. It wasn't dry the way I imagined old skin would be. It was slightly oily and surprisingly pliant for a man. Wait. I lie again. Your skin was as soft as foreskin.

As I began to place the slippery beads on your body, I saw Narayan doing his chin-ups outside the window. He couldn't see me at first. How could he see in the glare of the morning sun? It turned everything except the roiling green ocean a sulphurous yellow. I sensed Narayan was looking for me. Then he swung down and heaved his knapsack onto his shoulders. When he finished buckling up the straps, he walked over to my hut, and just as I was putting the first two beads on the lids of your closed eyes, he whispered my name. Then very softly, he moved my shutter ajar. I looked up and he beckoned to me.

Frightened, I poured a bunch of beads into one of your ears whose drooping lobes I'd so often nibbled. My clumsiness made you giggle. And then I began, no longer slowly, to place the beads deep in all the silky crevasses of your sun-baked body. You were lightly brown like tulsi wood by then. I lined up four, maybe five in the creases in either side of your groin where the skin was still pale. And you accepted my little game eagerly, eyes closed, smiling. You looked as beatific as Krishna smiling on the temple altar in Vishna's pictures. You know the pictures I mean—the ones my master has me string with beads, like the garlands on Christmas trees . . . the very same beads I was putting on you that morning, our last time together.

I smiled back down at you, and you started to run your narrow tongue over your lips. Now when I think of us making love, what I remember most is the slow, gratified way you licked your lips when I sat astride you, as if you could taste me.

Tenderly, I took the biggest bead, the 109th bead of the *japamala,* the bead that's bigger than all the others so you know when you have come to the end of your mantra, and touched it to the tip of your penis. And your penis swung upward, erect again, and your glittering hazel eyes flew open, but you couldn't see Narayan who stood silently watching us at the window, only me. I placed the biggest bead in the sunken hole of your belly button, where it nested like one of my master's dark unblinking eyes.

My darling, you weren't the only one who thought I made you

young. Each time you penetrated me—stroke by stroke, slowly at first and then faster and then slowly again, ah Sankara, how I liked those slow strokes!—each time you pushed into me, you lost months and then years, decades even! And by the time you came, you were younger than me. Yes, each time we made love I rescued from death the Methusaleh I'd noticed on the first day.

That morning, as you lay before me, splendid in my master's jewelry, not knowing that Narayan watched you too, I began to grow sleepy. I had been ill several times that last month, twice with a fever and sore throat and once with the flu. That was not usual for me. And I thought for a moment, my flu had returned so tired and sluggish did I feel. I yawned . . . once, twice, three times, my eyes fixed on you so I wouldn't look at the window where Narayan stood scowling at us. You didn't notice my fatigue. You groaned and pulled me down to you, whispering that I should sit on top of you again.

Naturally, I wanted to please you. And show the doubting Narayan that you were as virile as a young man in the bedroom! So I crouched down, excited by his jealousy and prepared myself to summon up in you all your gorgeous youth.

And then an exhaustion, like the exhaustion of age, rose up in me, and I knew I had to make a choice. I could be with you or with men like Narayan who'd lack the wisdom to love with full acceptance but wouldn't exact your price.

And so my beloved, I made my dreadful choice. I live now with Narayan in——, a new spiritual community Vishna, our master, has started near the capital of——. My guru forwards your letters to me, and I read them with great sadness. Narayan says if you loved me, you would release me and not write begging for my return. He says you are a vampire who doesn't have my real interests at heart. Narayan is young and doesn't choose words judiciously, but in one respect, he is right. I gave you back what I could of your youth. Now it is my turn, my love, to have the gift bestowed on me. *Om shanti,* Sankara! You who loved me the way nobody else has. Without limits or judgment. You'd never seen anyone so supple, you said, as this young woman in Padma's photographs. You admired her bare legs bending backward into a human wheel.

Thine own self, Shakti

AUTHOR'S NOTE

As far as I'm concerned, there's a confusion between erotic realism and erotic writing that focuses on sexual or sensual feelings. *The*

Last of the Golden Girls, my novel about girls growing into women, faced obscenity charges, later dropped, because of this confusion. I was accused of promoting lesbianism because I wrote about two teenage girls pretending to make love as practice for the real thing with men. I'd be happy to promote any form of erotic love anywhere, any time, but in this case. I saw the girls' erotic awakening as part of my novelistic realism.

I'm glad to say I wrote this story primarily to describe and, I hope, evoke sensual feelings. I chose a spiritual retreat as the setting because I've spent time in these places and noticed a connection between the spiritual and the erotic. Deep erotic feelings, like spiritual feelings, are part of the mystery of the inner self. Despite what the gurus would have us believe, I think that the intense concentration that comes with meditation also heightens the awareness of the senses.

BLUE FEATHERS

By Anne Rhyd

Chance encounters and sexy strangers are staple elements of erotic writing, and it is in this tradition of the literature that reality and fiction most clearly part company. However, it is for that very reason—that fiction can improve on reality by rewarding risk-taking only with perfect orgasms—that we get such pleasure from the inhibition-shedding of others in erotic fantasy-adventures. In "Blue Feathers," Anne Rhyd also recognizes that donning a mask in a carnival atmosphere will lend a sense of freedom and enhanced possibility to even the most staid among us, yet because her author's imagination is in complete control of the situation, the results of the ensuing indulgence can be sweet rather than sinister.

Josephine squeezed herself between a lamppost and a trash can as revelers pranced and paraded and even cartwheeled past her down Chartres Street. Her niece was nowhere to be seen—which meant that she truly was nowhere on the street, because even this boisterous crowd could not conceal the horde of children with Susan. Now Josephine had more than an hour to kill before three o'clock, the time they had agreed to meet after separating.

Only an hour before, she too had been caught up in the festive mood. They had been eating beignets and threading their way through the Vieux Carré from shop window to shop window when Susan had suddenly pulled her into a dark store. "Time to get our masks," she'd announced, and each child sprang first at one of the jeweled and sequined creations crowding the walls, then at one another, each convinced that the best mask was in someone else's possession. Josephine leaned against a brick wall out of the way. "You, too, Aunt Jo," Susan had said. She turned to the proprietor. "This is my aunt's first visit during Mardi Gras," she told her. "So she needs a very special mask."

The woman eyed Josephine through the dimness. She was tall, with elegant posture and languid movements, her hair piled and twisted on her head and interwoven with sparkles catching the light. Her mask was scarlet and decorated with feathers dyed to match, as was her satin dress—a magnificent creation whose strapless and feathered bodice clung to an equally magnificent figure before billowing into a full skirt. She reminded Josephine of a ripe strawberry dipped in chocolate. A white cat on the counter rubbed against its mistress, rumbling, and another cat wove itself around her legs.

Finally, the woman had smiled. "Yes, Queen Etta has a mask for your aunt," she said, pulling one from behind the counter. "There's only one other like this one in the world." The mask was a rich royal blue, the right eye outlined in blue feathers, the left, in blue rhinestones. Two strands of tiny blue beads dipped below the mask on one side. Josephine put it on. It smelled of sandalwood, and the lining was soft. The bead fringe brushed against her cheek caressingly with each breath. Josephine looked in the mirror, then fingered her dress ruefully. The mask made its navy knit and loose fit, which had seemed so practical that morning, look dowdy.

Etta had seen the gesture and pointed to a gown. "Try that one. It's like mine, only blue." Josephine shook her head quickly, afraid that the similarity would only emphasize the contrast between Etta's full body and her own more sticklike one. But, she thought, she didn't have to come out of the dressing room; she could just see how it looked. She eased its weight off the hook.

In the cubicle, merely a closet separated from the store by a rough burlap curtain, the silky fabric slipped over her head and slid down her body. As she fastened the long row of buttons up the front, she felt the softness hugging first her hips, then her waist, then her breasts. The skirt draped in soft folds that brushed her thighs. She lifted her eyes to the mirror and saw looking back at her a stranger, a woman strong enough to meet life's challenges, a woman brave enough to take risks, a woman daring enough to wear such a dress—in short, a woman unlike she had recently felt herself to be.

She pushed the curtain aside and asked, "Can I please leave my other clothes here until later?" The children stopped fighting over the masks to stare, and the littlest boy had started crying at seeing her so transformed. "Certainly," Etta replied. Then, as Josephine paid, she heard whispered, "Strong gris-gris on that. My mother, she knew the voodoo, and her mother before her, and they taught me." Etta winked. "The dress is sure to bring you a real treat."

As they herded the children out of the store, Josephine had needed to shield her eyes from the sudden glare. The weather seemed more sultry than ever after the cool cavern of the store. "Good for you!" Susan offered her approval. "That's a beautiful dress."

"Queen Etta promises it'll bring me a treat."

"Well, you certainly deserve some joy in your life for a change," Susan told her, and then she and the children had melted into the crowd, leaving the older woman standing alone.

Now, after an hour's crowded wander, Josephine had found her way back to their meeting spot and at first thought she would just wait there. She had watched a boy try and balance steaming bowls of crawfish, then saw two yapping poodles rip each other's costumes off while their owners shrieked, then looked at a laughing woman, her dress open to the waist, tossing strands of beads from a wrought-iron balcony. So much activity, so much noise, yet Josephine felt as detached as if she were watching it all on TV. The smell of gumbo and étouffé wafting by increased her restlessness and made her stomach growl.

"Might as well get another beignet while I'm waiting," she thought. She turned and ran straight into a broad chest. A man's arms caught her. "Are you all right?" he asked.

"Oh, yes, but I'm very sorry." Embarrassed, she put up her hands to distance herself from him, but a clumsy unicyclist knocked the man toward her. He automatically grabbed her waist to keep from falling, she just as automatically leaned forward to balance his weight, and suddenly she was locked in an embrace with a total stranger. And enjoying it, too, she realized, feeling the comforting warmth of his body through their costumes and smelling his clean scent. The skin of his arms was warm and dry under her hands, and she found herself reluctant to let go. A blue feather drifted lazily between them, and she looked up.

He was wearing a mask that was the twin of her own. But how different it looked! What on her face had seemed so exuberantly feminine had the opposite effect on his; the contrast between the mask's baroque delicacy and his strong bones gave his face depth and drama and heightened his masculinity, like a pirate in bright silks and an earring, or a cavalier in lace and ruffles.

Between the mask and his pirate's costume, Josephine realized that all the clues to his identity were extinguished. She could not say whether he was young or old, professional or working class, conservative or liberal; she knew only that he had a solid body and a beautiful mouth, with lines that owed more to smiling than frowning. The idea that she could invent his identity for herself excited her, and she was embarrassed to find herself not only unable to let go of this stranger, but also wanting him, wanting to touch the cheekbones jutting from beneath the blue feathers and to pull the tightly curled hairs escaping from his shirt.

"You have excellent taste in masks," he said, his voice a rich baritone with an accent she could not place.

Reluctant to break the magic of the moment and be alone any sooner than she had to be, Josephine said nothing but continued to cling to his warmth.

Looking down at her left hand, the man let go of her waist and pulled back a little. "Aren't you afraid your husband will find us like this?" he teased her.

"My husband's dead," she responded, after a pause. The words sounded as harsh and ugly as the reality they represented. Then, she added, "I'm a little scared to take it off."

He looked at her for a long moment, then reached out hesitantly to stroke her hair. "Then that's a second thing we have in common," he said. Josephine could barely hear his words over the crowd and the thudding of her heart in her ears. "After my wife died in a car accident, I kept her toothbrush on the sink, her fuzzy slippers under the bed, everything just the way she left it. Finally, I sold it all and came down here to start over."

"That sounds pretty drastic."

"Yes."

"Was it the right thing to do?"

The man thought for a moment, then said, "I think so." He added, "It must have been. I never had mysterious and exotic strangers in slinky dresses falling into my arms before I came here." His words startled her. For the first time, she realized that when he looked at her, he was seeing the stranger who had looked back at her from the mirror at the mask store. Just as his mask and costume concealed his identity, so did hers. She could be anyone she wanted to be today. Suddenly she felt as mysterious and exotic as he saw her.

He reached up and touched his mask. "My wife loved this color. I chose this mask because it reminded me of her," he said. "Seeing it on you makes me realize I must look silly in something this feminine."

"No, it has quite the opposite effect on you," she assured him and was surprised to feel her face getting hot. She tried to gather the willpower to move away.

They stood there looking at each other until an exuberant accordion player whacked them as he pulled on his instrument. "Why don't we get out of here?" suggested the man. Josephine explained, "I have to meet my niece here at three." "Fine," he said, and she gave him her hand. The warmth of his smile made her stomach knot. He started to lead her away, then stopped and gently pulled her ring off and dropped it in her purse. "Just for now," he said softly.

Her hand snug and secure in his, she followed him away from the throng and through a maze of alleys and courtyards. The smell of food and spilled alcohol gave way to that of the flowered vines that tumbled down from balconies and clung to the crumbling walls. The modern world seemed far away, and it was easy to pretend he really was a pirate, perhaps Jean Laffite himself, newly arrived from the bayous to dispose of his booty. They would drink the most expensive port in the city to celebrate his luck, and he would give her a ruby necklace that had been intended for a Spanish noblewoman's neck. All her companion needed was a sword at his side to look the part completely.

Finally, he unlocked a door and led her down a cool dark hall and up some stairs. His room gave no more clues to his identity than his appearance; only a pair of blue jeans tossed over a chair marred its spartan neatness, and only a cuckoo clock on the wall gave it any character. The windows, bright and barely draped with white gauze that the cool breeze alternately puffed up and sucked out, looked out onto a shady courtyard.

Josephine was suddenly aware of the absence of the din. She heard no laughing, no bottles clanking, no dogs barking, only a small fountain tinkling water, and a faraway phonograph playing a scratchy record, the voice barely discernible as a twangy Cajun French, and her host's breath in her ear, warm and tickly. The contrast between his warmth as he held her and the cool of the air playing around her legs and rising between them made her shiver. The sudden chill of her underwear made her realize that she was dripping wet already, just standing in his arms.

They kissed, gingerly, masks bumping. She reached up to take her mask off, but he stayed her hand. He backed her onto the sofa and bent over her when she sat. She opened her mouth in anticipation of his kiss, but his mouth landed instead on her mask. His teeth gently plucked a feather from her mask and traced its outline on her face. He encircled her face with downy caresses, finally brushing the corner of her mouth over and over. When the wind blew that feather away, he pulled out another one, this time running it over and in her ear so very softly that she only knew she really felt it by the increased rasping of her breath. Again, the wind took his feather, and this time he pulled out two and stroked her neck and chest with them, down to the edge of her dress.

Finally, there were no more feathers in the mask. He looked at the feathers over her breasts and smiled. Kneeling in front of her, he leaned forward ever so slowly and grasped a feather—and her nipple—with his teeth. He took his time plucking some feathers, chewing more than pulling, the soft fabric bunching and twisting under his teeth, gentling their points and spreading the caress over her whole breast with his every movement.

Kneeling, he no longer needed his hands to support his weight, and he used them instead to unbutton the top button of her dress and to bury his face there with his feathers. He unbuttoned another button, then another, and spread the bodice wide. Pulling the points of the fabric taut away from her breasts, he circled one breast with the feathers, spiraling in tighter and tighter circles until the feathers were concentrated on her nipple. He stroked her nipple around and around with the fuzzy stubs until she clenched his hair in her fists and wrapped her legs around his waist.

Pulling free of her, he continued unbuttoning her dress. Finally, he had her exposed from neck to knee, and he gently tugged at her underwear until it, too, was at her knees. Spitting out his mouthful of feathers, he pulled some longer, stiffer ones from her dress and slowly worked his way down her abdomen. Then his head was between her legs and he was stroking her with the feathers. Every so often, he would paint slow, warm, wet lines down the inside her thighs, then return to the source of the moisture. An occasional feather fell from his mask, grazing her stomach before being tossed by the wind onto her arm or face. Finally, she was sobbing and bucking, and he buried his fingers in her as she came.

After a minute, she was able to loosen her fingers from his hair, and she pulled his shirt off. His skin was tan and taut over his muscles, and the curly hairs waved slightly in the breeze. An appendicitis scar—or perhaps a souvenir of a duel—peeked from under his pants. She picked up several feathers from the floor and slowly traced the white line with one, pausing to loosen his pants to follow the scar to its source.

Quickly but gracefully he kicked off his shoes and pulled off his pants, jumping a little when his bare feet stepped on a feather. Josephine's breath quickened as she looked at him, and it pleased her to hear him struggling to master the raggedness of his own breathing. She ran the handful of feathers slowly and deliberately down the inside of his thigh and calf, up the other leg, then back down again. The barbs of the feathers snagged in the hairs of his legs and resisted her pull. Trying not to tickle him, she carefully drew the feathers between and around his toes. Now it was his turn to clutch at her hair.

Twining her arms and legs around him, enveloping him, Josephine closed her eyes. Suspended from him, she felt as if she were bobbing weightless in the ocean. His thrusts would push her one way, then the sofa cushions would gently bounce her back in the opposite direction, and soon she lost all sense of time and gravity, knowing only the movement and the blackness. Finally he collapsed on her, and in the stillness she felt her awareness of her body return to her. He stroked her hair gently and whispered things she couldn't hear.

They both jumped when the cuckoo clock signaled the hour. He sighed and leaned back on his heels. "Your niece will be waiting for you," he said, and he carefully and slowly buttoned all the buttons on her dress and adjusted her mask straight on her face before putting his own clothes on. "I'll take you back where I found you."

Josephine was not at the lamppost long before she saw Susan. As they got closer, Josephine saw that all the children had lemonade, and Susan was sucking on one herself and holding out another to her. Condensation dripped down the side and splattered on the sidewalk.

"Sorry, we got separated," Susan said. As Josephine reached for her drink, Susan noticed her left hand.

"Aunt Jo, you've lost your wedding ring!" she exclaimed.

"Don't worry, I've got it right here in my purse." Josephine reached inside for her ring, hesitated, then slipped it on.

Susan now had gotten a good look at Josephine, and she eyed Josephine's denuded mask and dress. Josephine resisted the urge to check whether her buttons were evenly buttoned. Finally, Susan said, "I hope you didn't just stand here the whole time."

"Oh, I wouldn't do that," Josephine replied.

"Oh, yes, you would!" said Susan. Then she looked at Josephine's mask again with puzzlement and pulled a small blue souvenir from Josephine's hair. "I've been thinking that maybe you should stay down here with us forever. There's no sense in you going back to an empty house and all that snow."

"That sounds pretty drastic," said Josephine.

"Desperate measures for desperate times," said Susan.

Josephine sucked on her straw as she considered Susan's offer. "I'll think about it," she said. "But I doubt I'll stay." Contemplating another stray blue feather, she paused. "But who knows? Anything may happen."

AUTHOR'S NOTE

Pieces of this story grew out of several elements of my life about the time I started writing it—planning for an upcoming move to New Orleans, grieving over being forced by an illness to leave a writing job at a magazine, even having a conversation about how best to incorporate beads and feathers into a stained-glass panel of Mardi Gras masks. Also, I wanted to portray sexual attraction in a way different from that in men's magazines and romance novels, in which the heroine is usually young, beautiful, and rather simpleminded, and in which an essential element is that the hero establishes his dominance over the heroine and she accepts it.

THE AMERICAN WOMAN IN THE CHINESE HAT

By Carole Maso

If there existed a world atlas of sensuality, France would occupy at least a continent, and it is probably true that this story by Carole Maso, which unfolds with such purposeful indolence, would lose a great deal were it set, say, in Indiana. Another point, wittily made here, is that language really is just a different mode of touching and that words, whether familiar or teasingly strange to the ear, can be an important element of foreplay.

A woman, x, and a man, y, plan to meet at the prearranged coordinate, z, a fountain on the Place Antony Mars in the south of France, in some late afternoon in summer at the end of the twentieth century.

Both walk slowly, inevitably to z, embracing their common fate and now as they stop and turn, each other. Y, a man with *cheveux longs,* clearly French, kisses x twice on the cheeks. It is as if he has stepped out of some unmade film of the dead Truffaut. She looks to be German or Scandinavian, possibly English or American and is wearing a Chinese hat. The sun is very bright, so bright in fact that sometimes one or the other, and sometimes both, seem to disappear in it. He circles her slowly. She sits stationary at a white plastic table, the kind that have become *"la mode"* in France in the last few years. He circles the fountain, the periphery of z, slowly, looking at her with some exasperation.

"Il fait chaud," he says.

"Non, il fait beau."

"Il fait chaud."

"Such bright, white light."

"*Oui, la lumière*. Speak French."

"Oui, la lumière."

She conjugates *vouloir: Vouloir* is to want.

She watches him appear and disappear, appear, disappear.

"This reminds me of another savage and beautiful afternoon."

"Encore?"

"In the savage and beautiful afternoon we tried to speak. You said: 'Where do you live?' I said: 'New York.' It was a time when I was still hoping you might save me."

"Oui," he says, *"comme un prince charmant, sur son cheval blanc."* He laughs.

She claps her hands. "Are you ready? *Vous-êtes prêt?* Are you ready now?"

She stands up. *"La première position,"* she says and arranges his arms and legs into the first position of ballet. He's so beautiful.

"La deuxième."

He holds the position for a moment and then breaks it.

"You thought I could save you," he says. "You wrote it in that notebook.

"La troisième. Parfait!" He holds the pose.

"Already, you knew there was nothing I could do for you." He moves away.

"I asked: 'Where do you live?' You said: 'Near the cemetery.' I asked: 'Where were you born?' You said: 'The most beautiful coast in the world.' "

"No one understands why you have come to my country," he says. " *'L'étrangère,'* they all say."

She cries. "But I remember the beautiful forever of the perfect afternoon. The beauty by the fountain. And *les cheveux longs."*

"La femme qui pleure," he says. *"Chante avec moi."* He begins in English the song she has taught him.

Row, row, row your boat.
Gently down the stream,
Merrily, merrily, merrily, merrily
Life is but a dream.

"I was already trembling then," she says.

"Crying."

"Yes, for joy. In grief."

" *'J'ai peur,'* you said."

"Yes. Already that first day there was *une chambre blanche* . . . a black and white film. *Un ange.*"

"You were expecting maybe a miracle." He smiles.

There is a close-up of the young Frenchman. A profile. And then the slow motion turn of his head. A panoramic gaze.

"You are an angel," she says.

He laughs. Takes her Chinese hat.

She takes it back.

She remembers the dazzling, the catastrophic afternoon.

He tries to remember that first day. "Already," he says, "you knew you were doomed."

"Stop," she says, running her finger down his arm, his chest. She skims the beautiful surface of his skin.

"La dernière position," she says.

"Non," he says, *"pas encore."*

He offers his hand, and she steps into the gesture.

"I love you," she says, entering the illusion like almost everyone.

He shakes his head. "It is only a dream," he says. "A lie. I thought you were different."

He takes her hand and holds it under the rushing, brilliant stream of water and then releases it, and they stand like that.

She in her Chinese hat.

He with his *cheveux longs*.

Not touching, not saying one word.

Unaccountably there is a dizzying movement of the camera, and they are suddenly seen from high above. The camera hovers. Something else hovers. It is, we see, one of the beautiful angels of France. The angel weeps. It begins to rain.

"I thought you said it never rained in summer."

He laughs.

It is night now. They turn and walk toward the cemetery. He guides her up the steep stairway placing the palm of his left hand on her back. He moves the other arm around her waist and presses the palm of the right hand against her heart. He applies the smallest pressure to her chest and whispers *"arrête."*

"Stop," he says, in a heavily accented French.

"Ouvrez la porte," she says, giggling. The man opens the door.

In the room there is a bed, a lamp, a black book next to the bed. A strange white light shines through the window. Light the cemetery gives. It reminds her slightly of night in the great illuminated city. "Home," she says, but of course that is not it.

She thinks of her city—silent now, very dark. Inconceivably tragic. She can't imagine.

"J'ai peur," the woman says to the man, digging her fingers into his upper arm and doing a quick little pirouette so that now she suddenly faces him. There is terror in the eyes of the woman who stands on tiptoe and searches his face for some sort of explanation. *"Je ne comprends pas,"* she says.

"Tu ne comprends rien," the man smiles. She releases him. He directs her to the bed.

"Yes, this I still understand," she says.

He hovers above her. Her arms encircle him. She feels the metal of his belt buckle against her lips.

"Non." He pulls away, gets down on his knees and watches her, observes her face, the two lines in her forehead that mean she is tired, the slightly open mouth. He holds her ankles in his hands and slowly moves them apart.

"Il fait chaud ce soir," she says and lies back on the bed. Slowly, everything is slowly, he undoes the six straps of her sandals. He pulls the straps tight and then loose. Six times on one foot. Six times on the other foot. He glimpses the golden brown pubic hair beneath her skirt.

She sits up and sweeps her hair to the top of her head and then tilts the head back. He studies her carefully, intently, her forehead, nose, chin, throat. She lets her hair fall and then says again, *"Il fait chaud."* She asks him to bring—what is the word?—her pocketbook. "Where?" She flexes her dazzling body. *"Là,"* she points, and he crawls to it on all fours.

From her bag she takes a small round box of hairpins which she hands to him. She turns so that she is facing the wall. He pulls the hair to the top of her head as he has watched her do and attempts to fasten it there. Long curling tendrils escape his every effort, and he sighs.

"Do not give up so easily," she says.

"Comment?"

She unbuttons her blouse and neatly folds it. Then her brassiere. It opens in the front, the back shaped vaguely like a heart. Her breasts, released from the elastic and bone and lace, swell.

She sings the birthday song, softly, off-key. "Today is my birthday," she says. Though it is not true.

He sees that the edges of her ears are red and that she has a slight heat rash along the back of her neck. Alternately he feels tender, then hostile, then indifferent toward her.

She raises her arms to check her hair, and he takes this opportunity to place his nose under her arm, breathing deeply. He runs his mouth along the slightly roughened skin of the American, cleanly shaven. He bites her, but gently. She wants him to bite her harder, hurt her somehow—make her feel something. But he won't.

She takes a small mirror from the leather bag and fingers the curls he has fashioned with the hairpins, approving of the job he has done. "Perhaps you are *un coiffeur*," she says, laughing. He moves his mouth to her rose nipple. She observes him in the mirror, a ravenous and fragile child. When she has had enough she nudges him away with her elbow. He goes around her back over to the other breast, and it is the same thing. She watches him and then brushes him away tenderly with one white wing. She turns to face him. She tries to tie his hair in a ponytail.

"Non," he says.

"Mais, il fait chaud." She tries again.

"Non."

Slowly, she unbuttons his shirt, she counts each button: *un, deux, trois, quatre, cinq, six, sept.* "You are like a child." She outlines the rib cage with her mouth, presses where she imagines the heart to be.

She unfastens the familiar belt now and slips his penis from his pants. It has a life of its own. It is at a particularly lovely angle from his body, she thinks. *"L'explorateur,"* she calls it.

Pushing her down, he pins her hands to the bed. He is more erect now, harder. He straddles her, kneeling, putting his knees under her arms. He raises himself, slowly above her so that he is just out of her reach. Her tongue is barely able to graze his underside and then not. He sways rocking back and forth, back and forth. She struggles to get free. She tries to raise herself on an elbow. *"Non."* He watches her. She struggles to meet him. She is so wet. "Let me go," she says.

"Non."

"I want you."

"Non."

"Please."

"Speak French." And with that he releases her hands, leans back, and thrusts himself into her mouth. There's a funny dipping motion. It's getting hard to describe this anymore. It's getting more and more difficult. He takes himself out of her mouth and with one hand pulls her skirt up around her waist and begins to touch her gently. He smiles and shakes his head at her wetness. His long hair hangs over her. *"Tu es comme un petit cheval,"* she says.

She bends her knees, throwing him off balance, and he topples in mock defeat. "Do not give up," she says, "so easily." Parting her legs, muttering in French, he enters her, and she is laughing and asking, "What are you saying?" He covers her mouth with his hand.

He moves his hand down to her throat as he thrusts harder and harder. "You're choking me," she says. "You're choking me." Then nothing. And I would like to help her, but I can't.

The black book falls to the floor, and she looks up terrified. "*Non.* It has no meaning," he says in English.

He sits up, and he is deep inside her, and he is now swearing and sweating, and asking for something. She doesn't know what. She tells him, she keeps telling him what she wants. What she needs. She wants to be on top now.

"Speak French."

She finds a way to say it.

"Bon."

He watches as slowly the strands of her hair escape the pins with the violence of her motions. She takes his small surrender and rides—somewhere far away, with him. *"Tu es comme un petit cheval."*

Her dazzling body falls forward onto him. She covers him with a veil of hair and tears. She is afraid. She wants something that doesn't change. Something permanent.

She'll never go far enough.

He turns her over and with an eerie precision. Takes one foot and then the other and places them on his shoulders. He holds her ankles and steers her so that her head is touching the floor. Off the edge of the bed, beheaded as she is, only a torso now, he drives into her with new ferocity.

She tries to speak, but it is useless.

"My God," he says in English, laughing.

She curls into herself on the floor. He looks at her from the bed. Her body divides into two perfect shapes: the back, the buttocks.

She seems to be floating.

I go over to them and pick up hairpins from the floor, the drenched bed. I examine the black book.

"Look," I say to him. "She is dreaming her way home."

AUTHOR'S NOTE

This is an excerpt from my latest novel. It chronicles the decline of a young American writer who has come to France to live. In her desperate efforts to slow her own disintegration she clings to sex as some last resort. In this section she entertains the possibility of romantic love for a moment—but only for a moment. The clinical, detached claustrophobic feel to it is in part an *hommage* to Claude Simon, Robbe-Grillet, and the French *nouveau roman*, as the narrator tries to hold on to some literary identity, even if it is a borrowed one.

In the novel's many sexual scenes there is an eerie splitting-off of personality as she becomes both observer and observed. "And I would like to help her, but I can't," the one who watches says. The deliberate choice not to exploit the potentialities of language, sex, or the imagination—hallmarks of my earlier fiction—made this an extremely frightening book to write. It was written from a dark, cynical, lost place in me and confronts one of my greatest fears: the catastrophic loss of feeling.

WINDOWS

By Idious Buguise

Idious Buguise, like Barbara Gowdy and Carole Maso, finds herself writing about watching and being watched. And presented with this frustrated and harrowingly articulate narrator, we recognize her as something of a passive-aggressive voyeuse *who does, in fact, realize that the act of simply opening her psyche, even to a silent shrink, might be a way of letting in some light. At the same time, one will surely have split seconds of uneasy identification with such a character—a woman who is clamorously certain that much that is owed her is being denied.*

Every day I sit down in this artsy-fartsy, really-not-very-comfortable raffia palm chair, and you sit behind that glass and metal hi-tech desk. I talk and you listen with your eyes closed or staring out the window, and I wonder what you can see that I can't see. I talk about sex, and you shift position. I stare at you, and you squirm a bit. Are you excited when I talk about sex and sticky cunts and throbbing penises, or do you just pretend I'm reading you some trashy-fiction subplot and not rambling on about the real-life thoughts in my own flesh and blood brain? And how many of these words are really my thoughts, and how many of them are just some soft-core porn I'm inventing as a game to excite you? Do you know which is which? This can't possibly be therapeutic. I don't even tell you my dreams. I just make it up as I go along, and you, with your shoes on the desk, never looking at me, suck up the money, day after day.

Ramble time!

Today, on the way here I sat next to a man on the Number 12 bus, and he had the most beautiful hands. No rings, no hair. No hangnails or torn cuticles. And, of course, those hands reminded me of the imaginary fingers I carry with me all the time.

Oh, my God. It really wasn't so very long ago, you know—three, three and a half years ago he left me for her. I bet they do it in every room in their house. Yeah. I know it's a long time without sex. But what the fuck do you expect me to do? I can't go out and sell myself. I can't go up to just anyone—or even a special someone—and say "put your arms around me, your lips on mine, and play softly with my crotch." I mean that just isn't done anymore. At least I can't do it.

It was so much easier in the sixties. I wasn't obsessed with checking out hands and fingers and trying to mentally place them on my crotch. Back then everyone just sort of melted into everyone else, and there was no threat of herpes, pregnancy, or AIDS. Herpes wasn't even considered. We all took the pill. And HIV was unknown. We did it everywhere, in every imaginable position. Oral sex, gentle sex, harsh sex. Hammocks, floors, bathtubs! And I loved all of it. The kissing and touching and sucking and fucking, and I never demanded anything, and I did everything, and I was lost in a decade of dope and sticky bed sheets for hours at a time. And the person I was then really did love it and walked around with a buzz in her crotch for any guy who'd play games with her. Fingerfucking was only something you did on the way to losing your virginity. It wasn't the prize at the end of the day. What I want now is the good old-fashioned lying in the back seat of his parents' car, crotches touching, hands everywhere soft and stroking, and just learning how to touch and please. All that adolescence, innocence, and steamy windows: I don't want to grow old. I don't want to die.

Did you have orgies in the sixties? Or were you just getting paid to hear about the orgies? Why do I even bother to ask you questions? You never answer me. You know sometimes I hate you. 'Cause I'm having problems with my fantasies and you have such a store of other people's, you could so easily point me in the most satisfying and orgasmic way with some of those stories, and you don't. I must be a masochist, continuing to come here.

Okay, so I have to accept the present and stop living in the past. I'm almost fifty, divorced with three grown-up kids, and I can't stop the aging process. You've told me that. That's the one thing you have actually said. Words do flow from your mouth. What you haven't said is that I'm also sagging, have crow's feet around my eyes, look haggard, and probably should consider hormone replacement therapy.

I know. I'm not that girl anymore. I'm a woman now with different needs and wants and not very generous and not very caring and sharing and certainly not a child of the sixties any more. I'm divorced, bitter, distanced from and jealous of my spring-chicken kids, unable to talk to my friends, and I want to have a sweep-me-off-my-feet-affair. But I don't want to give. I'm a "gimme girl" of the eighties—gimme this, gimme that! And now it's the nineties, and I want to be satisfied. I mean really satisfied. You know what I mean. I-don't-want-it-to-end-satisfaction! Is that so terrible?

I'm so useless I can't even masturbate. I've tried, but the rhythm isn't right. I just can't seem to get the right mixture of fantasy, motion, stroking, and wetness. It all gets so dry and useless. And anyway I don't want to do the work. I want it done to me.

Before getting on the bus today I walked past the sex shops in Soho and saw all these gadgets for "quick, self-contained, easy, safe sex." How do people use them? And how could they possibly be any better than human flesh—even my own? Nope. I can't use gadgets. I want flesh. Masturbation isn't really for me, anyway. Are you a wanker? Do you do it? Do you rub your penis hard and rough until it explodes? Or do you do it softly and let it all dribble out? Do you wipe it right up with a wad of Kleenex? Or do you not do it 'cause you think it's all too sticky and smelly and you don't want to deal with it. And, in your secret mind, do you call it juice, or cum, or spermatozoa? Well, what do you call it? You're squirming again. Who's weirder? Me talking like this and paying you, or you getting paid to listen to it all?

Sometimes I think about the guy across the street. And I can see myself lying naked with him. But these thoughts are sterile: they get me nowhere. I can't see him sticking his penis in me or getting sweaty. He's got the kind of skin that doesn't sweat. It probably doesn't even tingle. As usual, I've probably picked the wrong man for a fantasy. We are always lying naked side by side in the grass behind a bush. There is no moaning or grunting, just soft stroking and lots of deep kisses with some spit dribbling out—okay—so the kisses get a bit too wet! He plays genteelly with my breasts, and I seem to spend most of my time with my eyelids half closed in a state of ecstasy. But it isn't real. And anyway I don't really have such excitable nipples. My husband used to talk about an old girlfriend who had whistling tits. He'd only to look at them, and they'd stand up and whistle "God Save the Queen." Mine just sort of roll back along my middle-aged flabby sides and wait for my crotch to wake up and sing an Otis Redding song. This guy—he's got nice hands. Not great hands, but okay hands. I think if they were just a bit better, I'd be more satisfied with my neighborly fantasies.

Really, this analysis isn't getting anywhere. I share my sexual fantasies with you, and you sit there saying "ah, ah, ah ha." I don't get any satisfaction, and I don't think you do. Although I must admit I can't see your hands, and they could be working away, jerking off left, right, and center. If that's true, then I'm paying you to jerk off. Seems a bit unbalanced. Don't you think? You know, if I had an affair, I bet I'd stop coming here.

Right now I know what I want, and I know how it should feel. Do you want to know? Don't really have any choice. Got to listen, don't you? I don't really want any more kisses and stale breath and too-hard hugs and big fat penises pushing their way inside me. A finger—the middle one with short fingernails—must run ticklingly down my naked side and around my armpits over and over and just brush the edge of my crotch and occasionally almost by accident stray into my pubic hair and then immediately move off and start again. This has to happen for about five minutes, and each time the accidental brush with the pubic hair lasts two seconds more. Over and over this occurs until the side and the armpits are forgotten and only my crotch starts to move on its own. It takes off from the rest of my body and arches, strays, and moans with each soft stroke of this one finger. Sometimes this finger actually moves in and out of me and circles my ass, but mostly it just strokes—not rubs. I keep whispering to this finger "Don't stop, don't stop." I just want this finger to go on and on forever. No rough stuff. No heavy-handed movements, pushing or throbbing stuff. Funny that. You men all think and talk about throbbing, pushing, explosions—none of that interests me. I just want softness and tenderness and an unconnectedness. You probably underrate the mouth also. I want to lie back and kiss for hours.

I don't really want to be a part of the action. I want it done to me, and I want others—the unknown others—to watch. You know, even when I talk to you and I try to shake you out of that stupor you inhabit, I talk about throbbing and juicy and use words like "cunt" and "penis." But that isn't really what I'm thinking. I don't think you could ever really know what I'm feeling when I see myself, our mouths, and this finger in a soft gray-lit room with shadows dancing outside the windows. Nope. You and I, man and woman, inhabit two different sexual spaces. We need each other, but we can't really see into each other's ecstasies. How do you do it? Do you take my stories home at night? Does my rambling help you in bed?

Take these magic fingers I'm telling you about. Unfortunately, they have personalities attached to them, and sooner or later the finger is replaced by a word or a tongue or a penis, and the rhythm is interrupted and I lose it. Everything gets mundane. Stroke one, two, three. Lick one, two, three. Suck one, two, three. And, again. Repeat. As soon as the personalities enter the scene, I dry up and pleasure rapidly changes to boredom. I start to create shopping lists, listen to the radio, hear the voices next door. I don't want to give pleasure. I don't want someone sticking their tongues and penises in me. I just want to sail away on this wet island of a soft middle finger playing with my crotch.

I suppose even better than doing this with my neighbor is to do it with a stranger in a hotel in Manchester and have the bed next to an open window so that the people (whom I don't know) living across the way can actually see what is going on. Yeah! I would like to give them pleasure so they could watch us—without my knowing they are watching me—and they start doing it also. And after a few minutes this would spread up and down the street until every window is steamy and every woman is getting a tender middle finger stroking her crotch and every bed is wet with vaginal—I bet you don't like that word—drippings. And, even now, telling you about it, I feel this drop in my stomach and whimper in my throat, my eyelids drop, and my crotch does its own version of a banged funny bone jerk, and I want to have you come over here, from behind that goddamn fucking pretentious desk of yours, clip your fingernails, and take your beautifully manicured and buffed middle finger and start to get to work and earn your money.

AUTHOR'S NOTE

I always wanted to get a job as a window cleaner but am afraid of scaffolding, so I became an anthropologist: it's the same thing without the heights. I recently thought about becoming a marriage counselor but decided it was too restricting. So now I sit alone creating my own clients and their marital problems and trying to solve them. "Windows" is one chapter out of my first client's life. She is a fifty-year-old divorcee crying out for love. She can't accept her aging body, her divorce, and her need for sex.

THE MANGO TREE

By Sabina Faye

Like other contributors to Slow Hand*, Sabina Faye uses geography as an aid to stimulation. Additionally, as anyone who has ever eaten a ripe mango knows, there are few experiences more deliciously sensuous. So, having let herself be initiated into one sort of tropical ritual, Faye's heroine is definitely ready for others. And, thanks to the author's lush imagery, this story of erotic adventure far from home could just as easily be termed armchair travel into the realm of the senses.*

Of all my senses, touch is the one that operates strongest; steering a course through my life from some deep primitive place and moving my hands to feel even before my brain registers sight. Nothing is real to me until I touch it. I choose my clothes by the feel against my skin. I recoil at nylon and have near orgasms over certain silks. At home I eat with my fingers, for nothing tastes the same off a fork—a utensil as thin and cold as its name. I think I was meant to live in caveman days, with my bed a pile of skins on rock, my feet bare to the ground, and a haunch of fire-roasted beast in my hand. I walk into a room and cannot settle anywhere until I have swept around touching each thing, the wood of the table, the fabric of the draperies. Art galleries make me nervous. Museums don't exist for me, with everything cased and distant.

But I was born in the waning 20th century, into a world of shrink-wrapped produce and climate control, in the most untouchable country on the planet, England. I came to Australia looking for wind. Free-falling into the far tropical north, I was not disappointed. I found a land where the air was plump and the ground vibrated under my feet; where it rained in heavy drops and the night sky stung my face, and there I found a man of the most incredible skin.

I cannot think of him even now without a shudder, without this sensation like butterflies in the back of my heart. I had never felt skin like this before. It was soft as a newborn's tongue, smooth as a pond. It was like chocolate and moss, violas and black ice. He was a dark-haired Swede and rarely wore more than shorts and a silver ring on one toe. Beyond that, if asked what he looked like exactly, I could not tell you, so lost was I in his pure glorious flesh. I could touch him anywhere, his arm, his foot, the back of his hand, and feel my juices start to flow. There was a current beneath the softness. I had never been so aroused by simple touch before.

I had come from England to work on a distant relative's boat, a job arranged in the proper British manner, through family connections, as a way to deal with an unruly daughter of nineteen who intended not to go on to a respectable university or at least secretarial school, but hitch-hike to Istanbul or anywhere. But my family was burdened with the lingering bondage of a respectable name in society (although like most such families, an inversely respectable fortune), and it would have meant tiresome scandal. So it was decided that father's second cousin, from the seafaring side of the family (which now consisted mostly of shipping clerks), who skippered a charter yacht on the Coral Sea, should take me on as cook.

And that is how I came to be squeezing mangoes one Saturday in the farmer's market in Cairns. It was my first attempt at provisioning the boat, and I had already finished with the ordinary. Bags of potatoes, onions, cabbages, carrots sat waiting, but now I was lost in the fruit. I had never seen half the fruits offered here, not personally I mean, and I was a little delirious with the smell and feel of them. There were whole pineapples, with their tantalizing patterns of prickles. There were hard hairy coconuts and furry kiwi fruit. There were papayas, one cut open on each stack to show the fleshy orange-pink inside.

I picked up a mango. It was a soft heavy weight, the skin like glove leather, mostly green with a deep scarlet blush on one end. I turned it over a few times.

"What is this?" I asked the woman behind the stall.

"What IS it?" She squinted at me and stepped a little closer as if looking for signs of antennae or something. "It's a mango. You never seen a mango, luv?"

I shook my head. "What's it taste like?"

She shrugged. "Like a mango! Tastes like a mango." She laughed and picked one off the stack, stabbed a side tooth through the skin and peeled it back, exposing a bright orange pulp. "G'wan, try it," she nodded toward the mango in my hand. "Y're a pom, eh?"

I had only been in Australia three days, I didn't know what a pom was, but she looked friendly enough that it couldn't have been too insulting, so I nodded. I brought the mango up to my mouth when I felt a touch on my arm. "Not that end," a man's voice said. But I hardly heard him because I was immediately taken by his touch. It was the softest touch, as if a small bird had brushed its chest against my wrist. I turned and saw the man who belonged to the touch.

"This way," he said, and I felt his fingers curve around mine as he turned the mango in my hand. The softness of the two skins around my hand sent my poor brain spinning.

"The tree sap drips down on the stem end and stays on the skin," he told me. "If you bite the wrong end it can make your lips swell and sting." As he withdrew his hand my fingers clutched harder around the fruit, and as I punctured the skin with my tooth, warm sweet juice squirted out and ran down my chin. The man laughed as drops of it landed on his chest. I reached instinctively to wipe it off and had my first real touch of Deyan's skin. It was hot but dry, smooth as the moon, like suede and caramels. He did not move away but looked at my bold palm on his chest, then I noticed my hand was covered with sticky juice and pulled it back.

"They say the best way is just to take off your clothes and eat them in the bathtub." His voice was also rich, deep, and melodic. "Come on, there's a tap over here." He led me through the stalls to a faucet on the outside of the building, and we rinsed our hands. He took off his shirt, which, in the manner of most men in this tropical place, was light cotton and hung unbuttoned, soaked it under the tap, wrung it out, and put it back on.

I am not usually struck dumb with men or anybody else, but I was having trouble getting any words out through the sensory storm in my brain. All I wanted was to touch him again, to stroke that flesh, to rub my face against that skin, to lick it, touch it, anywhere. I had never felt skin like this. Out there in the light I could see that he was older, in his thirties at least. He was slim and muscular, of average height, or maybe even less, but he had a smooth tall way of moving.

The sun was hot, shimmering through the dust of the parking lot as we sat on some milk crates and I finished the mango, leaning over to let the juice fall. We had told our names, but little else when my cousin pulled up in the truck to load the groceries.

It was a long week at sea as I learned to cook in the tiny galley, handle the sails, and chat with the guests. I swam every day in the clear tropical sea. The water was so salty I could float effortlessly, feeling the warm sun on my face and the soft water lapping against my skin, and remembering Deyan's skin. I thought of him often, gently rocking on the boat at night, or feeling the warm sun on my body. One night I sat alone on deck, eating a mango, the sweet juice dripping on my leg. I thought about what he had said, about eating the fruit naked in the bathtub. I sucked one finger clean and wiped the juice off my thigh. What did his thighs feel like?

The night breeze was cool, and I lay back and spread my legs a little, lightly stroking the soft skin between my own thighs, slowly easing my fingers up under the shorts to stroke my softest place, as the memory of Deyan's skin grew too overwhelming.

As we sailed into view of the harbor at the end of the week, I stood at the bow of the yacht and felt the warm breeze on my face. It was soft and all-surrounding, soft as Deyan's skin. A shudder of anticipation rippled down my back. I had two days off, and I would die if I did not feel him. I did not know where he lived, except on the beach north of Cairns.

I walked down the esplanade, wearing only a cotton sarong with no underwear, licking an ice cream cone—another supreme sensory pleasure. Pelicans glided in low over the mud flats as the clouds edged with the first gilt of sunset. After a week at sea I loved the feel of solid ground and cool grass, the strange buzz in my head from the windless silence—these were land pleasures.

It was late spring and the frangipani bushes along the esplanade were in full bloom, the air heavy with the scent. I sat on a bench, spread my legs a little to cool myself off, closed my eyes, and smelled. It was a unique smell, sweet but urgent, like the perfume on a gown, discarded but still warm. The ice cream was cool, and I licked it as slowly as I could, boldly imagining it was not a double scoop of strawberry but the velvet skin of Deyan's cock I was wrapping my tongue around. I was jolted from thought as a brilliant storm of lorikeets rose up from the trees, chattering and shrieking.

I opened my eyes and there he was.

"Miss Mango. I saw your boat come in," Deyan said, a hint of amusement on his face at my posture. He sat down next to me, some inches away where I could barely feel the heat of his body.

"How was it? Did you get seasick?" He still had a slight Swedish accent, and a deep rich voice. The voice matched the skin, resonant, like a drum.

"No," I laughed. "Just lonely." We sat in a comfortable silence for a while. A dog left its jogger and ran up to our bench for a petting. Our hands rummaged his ears and each other. Our legs were touching with the movement. When the dog bounded off again, Deyan made no move away, but the thin cotton of my sarong was still a maddening separation. He asked me about the trip, and I learned he was a biologist working mostly up north in the rain forest. He had to come to town today to mail off some spore samples.

"Is a rain forest the same as a jungle?" I wondered. "I mean people are always talking about the *rain forest* now, whatever happened to jungles?"

Deyan considered the question. "I think you need wild animals to be a jungle. A tiger at least, maybe a few gorillas."

"I'd like to see one."

"Which?" He smiled. "Tiger or gorilla?"

"All of them."

"I'll take you if you like," he promptly offered. I made a mental note of thanks to all those teen advice columnists who were always telling me to find out his interests. Although I actually had always wanted to see a jungle.

"Are you staying on the boat?" he asked casually. "Do you have to watch it or something?"

"I was going to, but I don't have to." A mosquito bit my knee, and I pulled the cloth up to scratch it. Why didn't I think of that before! Now I could enjoy the velvet of his knee against mine. "It's locked up." I felt a twitch in my groin. I could feel my wetness soaking through the sarong.

"I'm having a few friends over to the house for a barby if you'd like to come out." It was an easy invitation with none of the bumbling I was used to from younger men. "I could bring you back if you need to," he continued. "But there's lots of extra room to sleep if you want. And we could go up to the forest tomorrow. It's best to go in the early morning before it gets too hot."

It was already too hot as far as I was concerned. Wild animals aside—it was *jungle* drums I was feeling now.

Deyan drove with his legs apart. Everything about him seemed completely relaxed, but I knew it was a coiled repose. We turned onto the highway to Macon's beach. Deyan settled in the seat and stretched his head back, told me of an octopus he had found near Fitzroy Island that week. During the tourist season he picked up extra cash by leading nature trips for the resorts.

"They change colors so fast, you know. When everybody starts crowding in to look, it gets very excited and goes from pink to dark red, a brownish red." As I listened I wondered what colors we would be if our skin reacted to emotion like an octopus.

The beach house was a cool retreat; a small frame house right by the breakwater thickly shaded by ancient mango trees. Inside the house was sparse and clean with shabby comfortable furniture and lots of plants. There were stacks of books, mostly on plants and bugs, and underwater color photos on the walls.

"That's a clownfish," Deyan answered my thought as he came up behind me and handed me a glass of wine. "They live in those anemones."

"It looks like it would feel nice," I mused aloud as I looked at the wavy arms of the anemone.

"Only to the clownfish," he explained. "Everything else gets stung." As I took the glass I noticed a large branching scar on the inside of his elbow. Instinctively I reached to touch it.

"It's a jellyfish sting," Deyan said.

"Nasty." My hand lingered on his arm, drew back slowly, my fingers hungry for the touch. The hair on his arm was silky and fine. As I reached his palm he caught my hand and pulled me toward him. We kissed suddenly and deeply, and I could feel the bulge in his shorts pressed against my easily accessible sex. I think he knew there was nothing under the thin cloth. I ran my hand up under his shirt, drinking in the feel of him. That skin, soft as a butterfly's breath, smooth as port and twice as intoxicating; I could drown in this skin. I would gladly die tomorrow if my shroud would be so soft and warm.

I bent a little and began to kiss whatever skin I could reach. I ran my tongue around the little indentation where the collarbones meet. I felt his hands exploring my body, one finger exploring the rolled waistband of the sarong. Then a car turned into the driveway, and two guys appeared on the front porch with a case of beer and the party was under way.

The night turned into a swirl of people and music, cold margaritas and hot coals. Our eyes would meet, or he would come to me as I sat talking with his friends and put a casual hand on my back for a moment. We touched at the sink, or passing in the crowded doorway, accidental but prolonged. There were other women there with obvious interest in Deyan, but I didn't care, except that I wanted to touch him so badly. I was after his skin, not his fidelity. I was nineteen, loose in a new hemisphere, breathing the tropical night.

Soon the party would be over, soon they would all leave, and we could slip into the little bedroom, with its soft cotton sheets and louvered windows open to the sea. But at 1:00 A.M. everyone was still going strong, and I was about to collapse. I had been up since four that morning and had had plenty of margaritas. Somewhere around two, I fell asleep on a comfortable saggy couch on the back porch.

I dreamed I was diving under the water through a forest of soft anemones. I felt soft caresses. I opened my eyes and found Deyan stroking my arm.

"Do you still want to go?" he whispered, his hand still resting on my arm. I was wide awake at once. I could see a faint band of red over the sea where the sun was about to rise. We crept over other sleeping bodies, out the back door to his truck. By the time we got to the forest the sun was just starting to break through the canopy, but already the ground was steaming with heat. We walked for an hour, stopping often so Deyan could show me something. I felt delirious. So much texture! The fat-leaved plants, the mossy tree trunks, smooth shelf fungi, even the air felt unique, damp but sort of sparkly.

The trail was narrow and became more and more overgrown the higher we climbed. Suddenly my leg began to sting. I thought it was an insect bite and scratched it. A few more steps, and the pain spread and grew more intense. It was an odd terrible sting that hurt worse than it looked like it ought to. The skin turned splotchy red, and Deyan bent to look.

"You hit a stinging tree," he explained. "It must have been tiny, I've been looking out for them." It was a crazifying sting, a fierce irrational pain that made me want to stamp and cry. "It's like a stinging nettle," he went on. "But about a hundred times worse. Plus it will last a long time and hurt every time you get it wet."

"Great," I tried to be noble.

"There's another plant that will help if I can find it," he said. "Wait here."

As he rustled in the bushes I stayed on the narrow path, still amazed at the amount of pain from the sting. I could see him in the woods, his body bronzed and shiny against the sharp rays of morning sun. He was silent and engrossed with the search, moving unafraid in the thick underbrush. I was still a little shy of these woods; besides stinging trees there were deadly spiders and poisonous serpents.

But Deyan was at home here. He searched farther in. His bare shoulders glowed in the filtered light, and suddenly I had to touch him. I picked my way to his side, and rested my hand on his bare back. I felt new blood surging through my body. I stroked him lightly, with some fascinated fear, as a child might stroke a beautiful snake for the first time. He was bending to look at a plant that grew by a fallen tree. There was a huge wild frangipani bush between us, and as he turned to show me the plant his body stirred the branches.

They were still wet with dew, and the odor burst up like a cloud. Suddenly we were in a wave of perfume. "Oh, smell . . . ," I cried and forgot the pain of the sting as the fragrance rushed in a cloud around us.

"Ummmm . . ." He closed his eyes and drank the scent. I also liked Deyan because he didn't talk much in the forest. He stepped around the bush and showed me the plant so I might recognize it again if I ever needed it.

"Nothing really cures the sting," he informed me as he pulled the leaves off and began to crush them in the palm of his hand. "But this will help a little."

He squatted down and began to rub the juice on my leg. The friction made it hurt worse at first, and I bent toward the frangipani for distraction, running my hands through the blooms. The dewy blossoms cooled my skin as the juice began to work. It was cool and tingly. Deyan's hands were warm, the palms calloused, the only interruption in that velvet skin.

Glancing down I saw his thigh muscles strong and steady as he squatted on the jungle floor, the skin brown and shiny with sweat. Our eyes met for a second, and then Deyan leaned forward and licked the back of my knee.

I shifted my feet a little, spreading my legs. The sting was on one ankle but his hands caressed both, then began to rub higher. I shivered as the sap cooled the inside of my thighs. Deyan stood slowly, sliding his hands up along my legs.

He leaned against me slightly and kissed the side of my neck. Then he caught me with one hand around the waist and began to play the other around the inside of my leg. My knees felt suddenly weak, and I stumbled a half-step into the frangipani bush. Overbloomed petals shook loose and stuck to my skin. I felt Deyan's hand firm on my hip, and he steadied me. I felt the lightest touch then as he reached smooth fingers up between me and began to stroke the sensitive skin there.

Deyan bent his knees slightly so I felt his thighs firm against my own, and rubbed himself like a cat against me from behind. I could feel him, aroused and hard, rubbing slowly against my ass.

We stood there in the heavy silence, rubbing luxuriously like bears. The sun grew hotter, and the thick forest was gray with haze. Deyan ran his hands up inside my wet garment. I leaned into him, reaching my arms over my head to touch the soft skin on the back of his neck.

Moleskin, silk, marble, honey, wind in the palm trees, cello concertos; I stroked his skin. I felt him peel off his shorts, then felt his legs pressing between my own, easing them farther apart, as he pushed me toward the fallen tree.

The trunk was covered with moss, soft against my breasts, almost tickling, until he pushed me harder down against the tree, the weight of his chest pinning me. The frangipani bush was half crushed beneath me.

The light cloth fell away, and I was naked in the rain forest. Deyan ran his hands down my body, digging his fingers into my ribs, pushing me almost harshly in the moss.

I felt his hard curved cock against my swollen sex, the tip probing up and down, ready but still teasing. I was going crazy, not wanting it to ever stop but hungry to feel him inside me.

He leaned back, slipped one hand around the front of my waist, down between my naked belly and the mossy tree trunk and found my hot wet pussy. He probed between the swollen lips, caressed the most sensitive spot between two fingers. I pushed off the tree trunk, crazed with the stimulation but not wanting to climax this way. His hands were great, but I liked to feel a hard cock deep inside—that full, steely pressure.

I tried to turn but he stopped me. He held his hand there, cupped around my sex but barely touching, leaving me on the very edge of orgasm. Then suddenly he turned me around, boosting me and leaning me back so I lay across the huge trunk. I was startled by his strength, and by this new roughness. He moved closer, and I could feel his cock huge and hard against me, like a mahogany log, sliding down the juicy slope. My ache spread like thunder across the plains.

My body began to tremble. I felt the blunt weight of his teeth against my neck, then finally, the tip of his cock slowly probing, slipping just an inch inside me. I groaned and raised up higher to swallow him deeper, but he held back, teasing. It seemed like forever, Deyan sliding, probing, just barely entering, as he continued to play with my clit until I couldn't hold back. Then suddenly I felt his legs tense, and he slammed in all the way. He thrust so deep, so fast, that marvelous curved rod churning into me, his hands pressing down on my arms, pinning me to the tree as he began to thrust. I felt a convulsive orgasm sweep through my body.

I was so wet I could hear him moving, and with every stroke another quiver stabbed through me. He came seconds after I did. Deyan's sounds were small, a catch far down in his throat, a small note on the breath, animal noises. I could feel each pulse as he came inside me.

We slipped together to the forest floor, drowning in the new scents—the smell of the moss and the jungle and our own juices, the ashy smells of sex clinging low around us, pressed down by the rising heat. He wrapped both arms around my waist, catching the frangipani branches, pressing the twigs into my skin.

The silence of morning had vanished, and the forest was full of soft twittering bird noise. Deyan pulled me gently off the tree trunk and brushed the moss and broken leaf bits from my skin. I thought he might speak and so kissed him. His bronzed body was covered with the pale petals, and I brushed them away, just wanting to touch that skin.

"Let me go—," I whispered. "—I have to feel you."

He looked puzzled, but leaned back and let me feel him. It was an intoxicating greedy touch, as I felt every inch of skin on his body, carefully, completely. We sat there until we had strength enough to walk, then slowly, we started back down the trail.

My season at sea passed too quickly. Cyclone season came, and the boats were put to harbor. What I remember of the water is the silken ripples over the coral, the warm straight rain of a passing storm. What I remember of the boat is the feel of the sailcloth and ropes, the sun-warmed deck, the smooth varnished helm. And what I remember between voyages are the nights with Deyan.

I was drunk on his skin. Lying next to him I grew dense with desire, reeling with the fascination of touch as if it were a new sense, an accidental gift from the gods, a momentary secret that would be snatched away when they discovered it missing.

We made love in the wooden house, with ripe mangoes falling on the roof and Deyan's small black cat walking soft-pawed across our bodies, as we lay exhausted in the dark, sweaty, but still touching.

Touching somewhere, even just fingertips, with the waves washing over the breakwater just outside and the night wind blowing in cool off the sea. Moonlight bounced off the water, slipped between the louvers, and sparkled on his skin.

It was a suspended, flooded feeling; like morning in the jungle as the sun first penetrates the canopy and steams away the night. On the forest floor, in that pocket of heat, everything seems halted, swollen, and ready to burst. Fat-leaved plants give off their must, and the ferns tremble. The rising heat has a noise—a huge soft invisible noise.

AUTHOR'S NOTE

I discovered erotic literature in my Catholic high school English class (probably unbeknownst to the nuns) in Keats's wonderful poem, "The Eve of St. Agnes." It is a delicious story of dreaming, longing, and awakening desire. Although the closest the two lovers get to physical contact is a little hot breath on her ear, the erotic images are overwhelming.

> Anon his heart revives: her vespers done,
> Of all its wreathed pearls her hair she frees:
> Unclasps her warmed jewels one by one;
> Loosens her fragrant bodice; by degrees
> Her rich attire creeps rustling to her knees.

Eroticism, I believe, is about imagination and the power of creativity. Sadly, for many people, imagination in general is quashed early, and sexual imagination is never even allowed to blossom. Creativity, though, is the one growing thing that does not benefit from pruning.

We are sensual creatures from birth. Eroticism is just an expression, a magnification of our senses. Fantasies enhance reality by making us more alive, more creative. At five we were allowed to have imaginary friends—why, at thirty-five, can we not have imaginary lovers?

Having said all this, however, I must confess that this story is less fantasy than most of my work. I did, in fact, once have such a lover, a dark-haired Swede with skin like velvet. Even today, when I think about touching him, I get a deep hollow pain, like a drop of water had just fallen in the cave of my heart. But that was years ago and a hemisphere away. I do not long for him, I cannot really remember much about him. Instead, I have taken one small bit of reality—a man with delicious skin—and explored the sensual fantasies made possible by the creative power of my own imagination.

EROS IN OVERTIME

By Kay Kemp

There really do seem to be two distinct strains that run through any group of erotic stories, that play off either the warmth of the familiar or the heat of the strange. But what happens, asks Kay Kemp, when the familiar becomes *the strange? "Eros in Overtime" is a marvelous title for the portrayal of an all-too real, all-too poignant situation, when two people make love in a time warp of their own devising.*

SHE

He parks in front of the fire hydrant to prove he won't stay. She waves through the window. She offered him the driveway, but when she sees the red of his eyes as he rounds the front fender, she shrugs, as you wish.

Eleven years they were together; in three cities, four houses they tamed, or tried to, two children. Roughly forty thousand nights (she counted). Countless fights. Now it's finished. Blissfully, terrifyingly over. The lawyers are poised for their take. But first, tonight. It seems an opportunity, a rarity. A night outside of regular life; between lives, they could be strangers on a train.

The long loose arms, the rangy body cross the doorframe. It's as if he is a transparency; the corner is visible through him, their house. His body is different now, separate. He seems so big. Once that large animal was alert to her every move, attuned to her smaller tension. Now he is bones on hinges, a puppet without strings. A husband, once removed. Her life, the visible part, the part she could cut off.

That's what I married, she thinks, objective to the last. I just wanted to tell you, she says. I loved you.

I can't take this up and down, he says. I can't bounce back like this. Head in hands, he is crying. She watches in awe. That was her territory, the tears. She heaved and sobbed; he went grim, like a killer.

Maybe it's not a bounce, she says, maybe it's a corner. I saw what was ahead, and I don't want to go that way. Not yet.

CHORUS

For a while they sit like that, him across the room. The pained silences of all their years gather and swell the room, threaten to crush them against opposite walls. It's like some organ, dwelling there in the marital house, inflated, throbbing. What a clamor. The cruelties uttered, the dumb competing.

They sit and peer at each other over all this. It is where they sat before, dumb kids at thirty. They bought the house while the market was going up. It had thirteen rental rooms and a lock on every door. They worked so hard, the woodwork shines now, the floors are sanded. They dug holes in the doors to take out the locks, then mended them so you can hardly see. But something ugly got in anyway.

Oh sure, there were times. She had sat in that rocker so pregnant and he at her feet, his head on her stomach, listening. They lay on that rug in front of that fire as the wind came down the chimney, and it was the best place in the world to be. But, overall, marriage was a poison they took in. They leaned together, faint with the dread chore of it, being all in all.

Now he sits across the room a free man, made strange by that, and alive. The line of his cheek is leaner, he's suffered. That's attractive. Her feet are under her; she sinks into the couch. They talk of banalities, the same old story—work, money, time, lack of it.

Then.

I'm going to try to tell you how I feel, he says. She can feel the immensity, the effort, granite cracking. He finds a new language, a new place to speak from.

He is crying, between the words, getting maudlin, he says but doesn't stop.

She loves to see a man cry.

Now he is in her arms, the tattered male in all his glory. She grows moist, it's so good, the great cage of his ribs, the braid of sinews in his arms. She's pulled into a spell of his remembered scent (what is it? half-clean shirt—soap—sweat—some damp shade plant). The fine light scratch of evening whiskers on her neck.

Stay tonight, she says. I know you're tired. We don't have to make love, just sleep with me.

Oh we'd make love, he says in the conditional, if—he puts his hand on hers and guides it to his cock, obvious, ready, and strange. The part she knew so well, she thought she owned it.

Go out and move the car, she says. You can't leave it there overnight.

HE

He crosses the doorframe again, lopes down the lawn to the car, and starts it up. There's a ticket already on the windshield, forty dollars. Still smiling he hears on the radio in the ninth the Blue Jays' Alomar hits a solo homer on a 1–2 pitch to tie it up with the White Sox 2–2. This is happening in the thirty seconds it takes to put the car in the driveway. He cheers.

He's upstairs now in the bedroom, the one she walked out of a year ago telling him she had walked away from his bed for the very last time. He steps out of new clothes he's bought since. She's already under the sheets.

It's been so long since I've done this, he says, stay overnight at somebody's house.

Your house, she says.

SHE

Those clothes were different, she had nothing to do with them. But naked he is himself. They wrap together, such hunger. He's thinner, a new hardness against his belly, and the great hands cup the globes of her buttocks, cup and separate. She's so wet, she drips over him, and can't wait.

You want it now, he says, so soon? His laughter against her breast.

I want to wait 'cause it's better, but I can't, she says. She twists away, and for a while they touch, nose, rub against each other. The wanting is as big now as the pain before. She guides the warm missile out of its fur and over her skin, feeling the purplish velvet, sucking water from his pores. His hands become fingers, probes, and openers.

CHORUS

Everything comes back now, even this. He fills her like silence fills daydreams, like water fills a straw, flattens and lifts her like a drenching rain. All the points where they met before, nipple and neck, hip hollow and thigh, they meet again. Reclaiming him reclaiming her. He lifts his head, mouth like a bird's, to catch her hanging nipple, and the sweet surge goes straight down her belly; he connects her poles, now the two of them make the circuit complete.

Slower now, they breathe together, steadily rocking and holding. It is new and remembered, all at once. The very best. She notes a slight change in the way he rolls, a new use of the side of his arm, a compensation, a trick, if you like. The gesture is slight but warns her. Then another. He asks her to get on her knees to crouch a new way. He's been with someone else, she thinks. It only takes a one-minute alteration in their precise ritualized passion, and all becomes clear.

If I know it, do you know it too? If you show it, do I show it too, in my dance, my newly revitalized waltz, my jive? An inspired turn: we have each tried someone else. And no, we did not want them. The words are never said, in this instant it is forgiven, even relished.

There is that moment, halfway along, when she starts talking. It's always like that. She bleeds words, crazy, ridiculous words, ones that don't bear repeating: help me take me hurt me, stop, don't stop, fuck, cunt, and more so. But that ends before long, and his animal sounds take over. Nothing but growls now, and heaves and grunting.

Here is some moment of truth. Freed from speech now another lexicon takes over her head. Fasten to me all your loving now, that once I unbuckled, in such grief and rage.

It is for this they had each other.

The rest was extra, in the way. All that depended on this one act they have shucked off. It stands by now, alert, an audience: the last dozen years, the two children, the parents, the grandparents, the house, the bank accounts. Now all that will be divided, as they will be. But not yet. Tomorrow, each will take what is fair, what he brought, and go. It's only goods.

HE

Riches are in the meat of this nearness. He has found her now. It goes and goes, the desperate rocking, bone against bone. She becomes a vast hot channel split from the waist down, he pressing up between.

SHE

She calls out to him, every cell and pore, the old furry body, her brother, her old man, the one who seeded those children, the one who tasted her milk, who wished to nurse his children. Somewhere in all that she lost him, lost the man in him, the valued other.

CHORUS

Who's to sing the praise of this practiced love, this rewarmed corpse, who ever did? The woman novelists always cleaved desire and duty, made the passionate heroine accept the drowsy sputters of married sex. Who will discover it, claim it, the rich depth you can charge again and again with the booty of years?

In the morning the children try the bedroom door. What are you doing here, Daddy?

HE

It was only for last night.

CHORUS

The children bounce on the bed. Alomar tried it again in the eleventh, his third homer, tying the Jays up again with the Sox at 3–3. It was a form of heroism, but he couldn't do it alone. Sosa homered in the twelfth to make it White Sox 5, Blue Jays 3.

AUTHOR'S NOTE

I've always been in awe of prepositions. "Before," "after," "between", "behind": little words with huge power. They put us in the right place at the right time, or the wrong place at the wrong time—to be hit by a sniper's bullet, struck by lightning, miss the last boat. Fall in love.

I realize now that this preoccupation has the potential to turn me into an erotic writer. Placement and timing are what it's all about. This story takes something that is seldom written about—married sex—out of its place and time. Into the vacuum that is created rush memories and sensations, and the act of loving is recharged.

ANECDOTE

By Catherine S.

Many of the women I know, if queried about the sexual fantasies their lovers or husbands have confided in them, would answer, I think, that men frequently dream of having two women available to them for an erotic interlude. But turn the tables and suggest back to them a single woman pleasured by a male pair, and some of these guys suddenly get a little huffy. Actually, of course, since any amorous combination offers the potential for considerable pleasure, it's going to be the one who crafts the scenario who gets to cast the supporting players. In this case: Catherine S.

I met Caldwell first. Not that it matters. Whichever one you met first, the other soon followed. They were a set, a unit. I have tried to remember what it was like, the brief time of knowing only Caldwell, of seeing him without expecting to see Mark nearby. I have no memory of it. But then, it truly was a brief time, perhaps two hours in all.

Caldwell had moved into the apartment below mine. We met on the fire escape, where he was trying to cook an entire chicken on a temperamental grill. He invited me to dinner when I lent him kosher salt for the rims of his margarita glasses. Mark came, too. Of course. This was how it had always been, and I quickly understood this was how it would continue to be. Caldwell and Mark. Mark and Caldwell. And me, Catherine. Sometimes. As long as I understood the rules.

They had been friends almost twenty years, since second grade.

They did not remind me of other men I knew. They loved each other and were comfortable with this. If one went away for more than forty-eight hours, the other hugged him when he came back. Being with them was like being carried along by a warm breeze. I wanted to spend all my time with them. I wanted to be them.

Which one would I choose to be? Mark was tall and thin, with soft hands and the prettiest mouth. Words streamed out of that mouth, thousands of words about hundreds of things. Statistics carried out to inane conclusions. Ignominious deaths of famous people. Obscure laws and religious practices. State capitals. I called Mark when I wanted to be distracted or soothed. When I needed help with the crossword puzzle. Or when I wanted to lose control—drink too much, laugh too hard, drive too fast. I see him with a drink in his hand, his lanky height draped over a bar in some dive, making Caldwell and me laugh. I wanted to talk like Mark.

Words came easily to Caldwell, too, but so did work. He always had to be doing something. He could build a bicycle from components, tune up a car, get an eight-foot table into the trunk of a Toyota. He was broad-shouldered, with short, sturdy legs and bright eyes. I called him when things broke. I called him when I was restless. I called him to find out what had happened the night before. Caldwell was our collective memory, the one who filled in the blanks for Mark and me after a particularly hard night. Sometimes, he half carried me up the stairs to my apartment, putting me to bed. Mark trailed behind him, helpfully suggesting hangover cures.

They liked me because I shared their view that their friendship was their single best quality. I was an admirer, an audience. Unlike girlfriends, who came and went quickly, I didn't want to break them up, I wasn't enduring an evening with both in hopes of getting one. In fact, being with only one of them made me nervous and edgy. It seemed unnatural.

What I really wanted was their memories. To be in the team picture for the junior high school floor hockey team. To be there Halloween night in Madison, when they dressed as Marx and Engels, ate mushrooms, and got paranoid. To see the smoke the night they almost burned down their college apartment while trying to make a rack of lamb. Failing that, I wanted them to know me as well as they knew each other. One year passed, two years. I grew closer to them, true. But they grew closer still. It seemed I could not catch up.

It was spring, a time of heavy, drenching rains. My boss asked me to house-sit so he could go climb a mountain with some other executives. I liked the idea of living among fine things, even if they weren't mine, or to my taste. I liked the idea of being alone.

My boss lived in what had once been the guest house on a grand estate, in the rolling farm country north of the city. Developers had razed the main house and put a small subdivision on its site, leaving behind this shingled cottage in a grove of trees. Broken statues—one-armed Cupids, fawns with chipped ears, headless maidens—lined the rutted brick sidewalk that led through the trees. The house, mossy green with golden trim, was barely visible as you made your way up the path. The only sound was a small stream that ran behind the house. Polluted, my boss said, from the subdivision's runoff.

Inside, it was simple and spare, but not cold. Large, unshuttered windows stared back into the trees, leafy enough now to shut out the modern world just beyond the grove. It was a place of solid colors, inside and out: green trees, green chairs, blue sofa, red table, blue rugs, white crockery, cream walls. The effect was deliberate, I think, a way of forcing the eye to my boss's odd collections of things.

There were Mexican masks, for example. Not gourd masks, but larger, more delicate pieces, carved from soft wood. A woman's face peered anxiously from between butterfly's wings, caught at an awkward moment in her metamorphosis. A mermaid stared stoically ahead as her tail—really a serpent—swallowed her. A bird's face smiled with a woman's bow lips. A jaguar had breasts and long, black hair, real hair, to judge by the feel of it.

In the kitchen, bird cages and bird houses lined the walls and counters. An egg had been placed in each. A Ukrainian one in a pseudo-Victorian cage. A black glass egg in a cage made of old coat hangers. A sugary diorama locked in a cage of twigs. A real robin's egg in a house that was an exact replica of the cottage. I was convinced there was yet another replica within that bird house, and another within that, on and on to infinity.

Finally, in every room, there were oil paintings, vivid canvases of women draped in veils, crouched behind walls, hidden in courtyards, locked in towers. The women had purple faces, red hands, green hair. It was unnerving, especially in the bedroom where there was no other color, just a white iron bed and a white spread, and those women on every side of you.

I sat by the window in this lovely and disturbing place, watching the rain come down, waiting. The idea of being alone had been attractive. The practice was unbearable. I knew Caldwell and Mark would miss me eventually, would find me somehow. The odd little house would be my gift to them, one of my ongoing bribes to keep in their good graces. Chocolates. Good wine. My ears. My laugh, which is what they liked best, spilling out at their weakest jokes and stories. I sipped brandy and stared into the dense green leaves, casting a spell. I drew them to me. It didn't take long. After all, I had left the directions on Caldwell's answering machine, along with promises of expensive liquor and a large-screen TV set.

They were soaked to the skin by the time they found the cottage's door. I watched them run up the curving path, laughing, in the middle of their never-ending conversation. Separated from them by the window, safe and dry within my cottage, I felt as if I were seeing them for the first time. Caldwell and Mark. Mark and Caldwell. I couldn't imagine one without the other, didn't want to. I wanted to be with them both, forever and ever. Even as I made my wish, I knew how impossible it was. Others would claim us, one by one. Caldwell and Mark would manage to hold onto each other, I might manage to hold onto them. But it would not always be like this. Just the three of us. The perfect number in some ways.

I brought them coffee in white mugs, brandy in squat blue glasses. I brought them white towels for their hair, blue cotton blankets to wrap around their damp clothes. We sat cross-legged on the floor, wrapped in the blue and white light of an old-fashioned space heater. In front of us, the soundless television was turned to some out-of-town baseball game that no one cared about.

And, of course, we talked. They talked. Calculus class, in which Mark had cheated on the final and still flunked. Caldwell's chronic lateness, which kept them from a concert that turned into a riot. Trying to smoke. Learning to drink, a bad experience with Jack Daniels and orange juice that led straight to the emergency room. Story after story, joke after joke, with one constant. Caldwell and Mark. Mark and Caldwell. Caldwell's hands were like white lights rising and falling in the darkening room. Mark's stories ended with self-deprecating sighs, a cue for me to laugh, which I kept forgetting to do. I was too busy thinking of how they had looked, running up the path toward me, toward this house. Give me both of them, I asked the mermaid and the butterfly, the jaguar and the smiling bird. Just for now.

"The White Sox might actually amount to something this year," Caldwell said.

One man is easy, of course. We all know how to do one man—how to lean a little closer, how to touch a hand, or leave your fingers a moment too long on his arm. Every woman knows this. But if I touched one, the other would leave. Or perhaps, at best, wait and follow.

That wasn't what I wanted. I thought of the bird house on the kitchen counter, the cottage within the cottage within the cottage.

Mark's voice now: "So this girl behind the counter, she repeats the order back very slowly, and gets everything wrong, absolutely everything . . ."

I slid Caldwell's blanket from his shoulders, wrapped it around myself, and laid down on the rug, as if I were going to sleep. They took no notice. So many times before, I had let their conversation be my lullaby, had faded away as they kept talking. Eyes shut, I listened to their voices—Caldwell's slow rumble, Mark's quicker, lighter rush of words. Beneath the blanket, I slipped off my clothes, touching myself. The wind moved in the trees outside, the rain-swollen stream rushed over the rocks, the purple-faced women whispered to me. They approved of me. I felt as if I were a solid color, too, as if my skin were changing from purple to blue to green to red to cream. I belonged in this house.

"No, what it said in the paper was that if the new law takes effect, it would be toothless, because there's absolutely no enforcement . . ."

I thought of how I had caught them, from time to time, appraising the curve of a hip or a thigh, judging the length of my neck. Men did this, of course, even with friends. Especially with friends. What is it like, Caldwell had asked me once, to be looked at when you walk down the street? It's like being a woman, I told him.

". . . and she opened the car door, and there was this huge dog in there . . ."

Their voices now were indistinguishable. I couldn't make out words, or who was speaking. All I had was the sensation of warmth—from the space heater behind us, from the sounds moving between them. Their voices wrapped around me, familiar and beloved, endless and perfect. I didn't want them to stop. I took inventory of myself, noting how symmetrical the body was, how accommodating.

I sat up, the blanket falling to my waist. In the almost-dark room, my body absorbed all the light. It was shockingly white, the brightest thing in the room, I could no longer see their faces or their hands. And suddenly there was nothing to hear, except the rain, the wind, and the hiss of gas in the heater. They had stopped talking.

"Catherine—," Caldwell began, almost sorrowfully, as if I were drunk, as if he might have to carry me to bed as he had so many times before. He looked at me, looked away, looked at me again. He did not seem quite so sorrowful. Mark tried to pull the blanket back around my shoulders. But his hands kept shaking, and he gave up.

I wrapped my arms around myself, watching them watch me. The silence in the room was huge, deep, and wonderful. It was as if I were still watching them through a window, safe and dry, still waiting for them to find me. They still needed directions.

I kissed Caldwell, then Mark. Mark's kiss was as light as his voice, his pretty mouth worked well. Caldwell was earnest, as if he were trying out for something. I tasted brandy and amazement and something else. Competition, older than time, going all the way back to second grade. As I started kissing Caldwell again, Mark brought his arms around my hips and lifted me onto Caldwell's lap, so I was straddling him. Caldwell understood, began unzipping his jeans.

"It's okay," Mark said quietly to Caldwell, his hands cupping me, preparing to help me move up and down on Caldwell. He wanted Caldwell to go first, so he could best him, love me harder or longer. I knew this, somehow, and I knew I would not allow it.

Standing, I held a hand out to each of them and led them into the bedroom, into the center of the white-on-white bed. Stretched out between them, I undressed each of them, kissed each of them, held each of them. Naked, they were identical. They tasted the length of me, working from the ears to the shoulders, down to the breasts. But when their hands touched at the top of my thighs, they pulled away. They looked at me, almost angry, silently demanding I make it work, determined I make a choice.

Instead, I rolled toward Caldwell, fixing my mouth on his while reaching my arms back to Mark, opening myself to him. This was new to me, hot and tight. Mark stroked my belly and kissed my hair, reassuring us both, reassuring us all, even though he could barely move inside me. Caldwell's bright eyes shone brighter than ever. It was only when I brought him inside me that everything felt right, as if I were balanced between them.

They reached around me, holding on to each other's shoulders as if to steady themselves. Slowly, hesitantly, Mark started, gentle and easy within me, pushing in as far as he could, then pulling out again. Then Caldwell, picking up his rhythm exactly, did the same, stroking me gently and slowly, all the way in and out. Mark repeated himself. Caldwell answered back, deeper and more insistent, moving in as Mark moved out. They grew more sure of themselves, there was almost no lapse as they passed me back and forth. This, Mark seemed to say, pressing in until I cried out. No, this, Caldwell replied, thrusting deeper still. I could not tell them apart, could not tell us apart, could not separate one sensation from the other.

They quickened, as if they were arguing about something they cared about, became strident and passionate, their voices overlapping, interrupting. Yet the only sounds were the wind and the rain and the stream—and, for once, my voice, just my voice, until Mark groaned into my ear and Caldwell shouted into my breast, and one sensation ran through all of us and back again.

Silence. For a long time, no one moved and no one spoke. I had given them, given us, something new: a story we would never tell, not even to each other. We would leave the cottage and leave this behind, an intangible addition to my boss's collection of wild and beautiful things. Our best anecdote.

We fell asleep, still joined, but in sleep our bodies separated of their own accords. No longer entwined, we were too much for the bed. I ended up crawling away, making my bed on the pile of blankets we had left in the living room. In the morning, when I went to check on them, they were still asleep, clasping one another's hands, closer than ever. But this time, because of me.

AUTHOR'S NOTE

An old college friend gave me the basic elements of this story—two men, one woman, an isolated house. Everything else is invented. While I was writing it, I talked to my male friends, and they had little interest in such a combination. This attitude made me curious. I had to ask myself: how do you seduce two men simultaneously, instead of sequentially?

The traditional view of such situations is that they have to result in a choice—one lover over the other, or one before the other. Or neither. Or both, then suicide. Or murder. But given the right time and place, why shouldn't three people make love to one another? And why shouldn't they be two men and one woman?

I do find strong male friendships enormously sexy, all the more so because men ignore the sexual content of their friendships. Recently, one man was giving me a detailed description of going home to visit one of his closest friends.

"Landed at the airport, saw M., shook hands—," he began.

"Do you really shake hands when you see each other?" I asked.

"Well, we hugged," he admitted. "But I only do that with him."

TREATS

By Rebecca Battle

*In "Treats," Rebecca Battle takes a vivid, angry look at a sexually awakened teenager's unwillingness to play the demure role scripted for her by unseeing parents. As a narration, it reads like part-*cinema verité, *part-catharsis, and it seems to me calculated to remind us that in every household there are always several coexisting but very separate worlds.*

It's always around midnight when you hear them doing it in the next room. You are usually into your second package of saltines by then, slopping on peanut butter and honey with reckless abandon. When you can't even force yourself to take another bite, your hunger—that other hunger—is finally, if temporarily, satiated.

You reach over to the bedside table, actually a light blue plastic crate with "Farmfresh" printed on the side, and push in the button to turn off the little black and white TV. The sounds from your parents' bedroom are much clearer now. With all the furtive whispers and frantic shuffling, they could be disposing of a body or hiding a stash of stolen money. But having discovered your father's dirty magazines some time ago, you know exactly what they are doing.

Pick up the sticky remains of your nighttime treat and walk toward the kitchen.

The hall is dark, and this makes you nervous, even though you are not alone in the house. It is midnight, the witching hour, and what good is your father or brother in the face of the evil that may be out there, that *must* be out there; otherwise why would you feel so unsafe? But it is a feeling you have gotten used to. Insecurity is the norm, and turning on a light would expose you. There is power in the dark and the quiet, as much as there is fear. You see others, but they do not see you.

It frees you to listen there by the door as your father and his wife stifle their moans. You stand on the balls of your feet, poised to dart into the kitchen if anyone should come out. You check for a light under the door of your brother's bedroom. Nothing. You turn back to the clandestine activity behind your parents' door, straining desperately for more sound, more stimulation. But usually the rustles and squeaks and murmurs are all you can grasp. Usually, they are enough. You feel the involuntary twitch between your legs, and the dull, low ache that begins in your crotch and twists a path into your gut.

Rush into the kitchen to hide the evidence of your binge. Quickly, so that you can get back to the cavern of your sheets and the treat waiting for you there. Once in bed, reach under the pillow and pull out the bottle of baby lotion. It is your teddy bear.

The lotion is cool as it touches your fingers, and you pause for a moment, anticipating the sensation when you reach between your legs. It is even colder there. It is wonderful. You spread it around eagerly between the folds of skin and over that one most sensitive spot. The clit, but you don't like calling it that. No, don't think. Right now, at long last, you don't have to think. Just let go, just imagine—*him*. Tall and athletic and a little dirty, always spitting tobacco juice by the side of the road at the bus stop. A hick, but they're all like that around here. What matters is that he pays attention to you. It makes going to school in this chicken farm, chicken shit county almost bearable. Just to greet him in the morning, perhaps bring him some cookies, have him sit with you at the back of the bus and reach up your skirt, between your knees.

Close your eyes and imagine him now, being with him in a way you have never been. Think what it would be like if he were swirling his tongue where his hand has been, and you clutching the sides of his head with your thighs, his shaggy brown hair wet against your skin. He is licking slowly from bottom to top, in long ice cream cone swipes. Your own tongue goes out to lick the air as you envision his, searching through every crevice. Your hand is his mouth, and then his lips, sucking around that unnamed spot, nibbling, seeking, devouring, around and around so warm and wet until you burst and writhe and whisper, almost too loud, "Fuck me! Yes, fuck me now!"

* * *

The distance from pleasure to pain is too short. First, the fear: that someone has heard your little outburst. Perhaps Lois, the stepmonster so adept at eavesdropping. Or worse, your father.

Then, the guilt. At having fantasized so recklessly. At not being normal. At not fitting in with anyone in this town. Your "new home," so they say, but really just another stop in a string of wanderings, of Dear-Old-Dad-Trying-to-Find-Himself-Wanderings. You don't know anyone, except your back of the bus buddy, and no one, especially not your parents, knows you. Knows what you do. The lotion and the food every night.

When did you learn to do this? A year ago? Two years? About when you learned to throw up. About when you learned to hate them.

It is a thrill to hide these treats. There they sit, in the very next room, as you sneak food from the kitchen to the bathroom, gorge on giant-sized Kit Kat bars or whatever it is, lean over the toilet, and then throw it all up. You know just when to flush so that it drowns out the sound as you gag on your own finger. Eating your cake but not having it.

You never know when you will get caught. When your father, grown sullen at the dinner table after too much to drink, will say, "Come sit on my lap" in his all too friendly dirty old man pathetic son of a bitch kind of way. And you will sit, to avoid his anger. Then perhaps he will say, "I know what you've been up to with the lotion." And he will look at you, rosy-eyed, rosy-cheeked, with that mocking smile of his: "You know, the Incas used to burn women at the stake who disgraced themselves that way." Or some other similar nonsense. But part of you will believe it, or at least the implication that you are dirty and deserving of a terrible death.

But you cannot give them up, your treats. They are the only pleasure you know. They get you through these dinners, for one thing, when you are forced to be with your father and Lois. They get you through the exhaustion of pretending.

Sit up straight and wait for your father to take his first bite before you begin. Then smell it and say, as genuinely as you can, "Mmmmm."

Take a mouthful, and then another, as if you can't get enough, and then: "Lois, this is really delicious."

"Well thanks. It's cassoulet, the national dish of France."

Your brother plays the game too: "What's this meat in here? It's really good."

"That's goose."

"Mostly the gizzards," your father amends. He has decided to take this opportunity to further your education. "This dish originated with the French peasants. They couldn't afford to waste, like some of us can" (a deliberate look to both kids), "so they used every part of the bird. They ate the meat off, then cooked the bones and the insides."

He takes another bite with hands made shaky from drink. He is very self-conscious about it so you try not to stare. But it is a natural attention grabber, the way he scoops up the beans in the spoon and carries them painstakingly toward his mouth, and all the while they are spilling back into the plate, so at the end he must lurch forward to grasp the last few before they too fall away.

He looks up, suddenly, as if he has caught everyone staring at him. You purse your lips in expectation of his wrath. But he says instead, "Lois and I have to go on a trip this weekend. Her father isn't feeling well, and we thought it best to look in on him. We figured it would be a drag" (he is always trying to use a "hip" expression for your benefit) "for you two, so if you promise to be good" (and here he looks at you and your brother both, one at a time, with a long meaningful glare) "then we'll let you take care of yourselves overnight."

Stay calm. Take care not to reveal your delight.

Smile and say okay, we'll be fine, I'm sorry for your father, Lois. Shall I clear the table now? Thanks again for dinner.

Go into the bathroom and vomit. It soothes your nerves, your excitement.

This is better than you ever hoped.

Finally! you think, as you flush the majestic national dish down the toilet.

You've got it all arranged. You will meet *him* at the end of the driveway the night your parents are gone. You will keep the porch light off so the neighbors don't see him and report back to your father. He may have asked them to spy. Your brother is going out at eight o'clock. He is planning to spend his night of freedom drinking Beam with his friends outside the Tastee Freeze. He is not so innocent either. You have agreed to stay home and cover the phone, among other things.

When you go to meet *him*, you are wearing your shortest dress, pantyhose, and heels. He knows what he is here for. Though you have not had the opportunity to take things further than the back of the bus, he has hinted from the beginning about his intentions. From the time when you first let him kiss you outside the rear exit door of the school. He had taken your breasts in his hands, as if it was the most natural thing in the world, as if they belonged to him. At first, you thought maybe you should object, but you didn't. You let him. You even let him reach down the front of your jeans as far as he could squeeze his fingers, where he took one slow circle with his hand and came up with a finger covered with wetness. You watched as he brought his hand up to his nostrils and breathed in, sniffing deeply and with relish.

He is older.

Now, as you approach him, walking carefully over the gravel, you hardly have time to make out his face in the dark before you feel his breath on your forehead, his hands clutching your buttocks, his penis thrusting out through the thin fabric of his shorts.

Make him wait. This is your night, your territory. You are not a woman, but for now you can pretend.

Take him by the zipper and lead him silently back into your bedroom. Make him stand apart from you, watching but not touching as you undress, staring him down with the bravado of a whore.

Make him get down on his knees and engulf your sex with his mouth.

Make him work hard, harder, not coming up for air. Keeping his head in place, forcing it to stay, both of you needing air, but holding on for more. This is so much more than you had imagined and almost too much all at once, so you push him away. He too seems a little off-balance. You stare at him shamelessly, there down between your legs, and you realize that maybe he hadn't done that before. That his finger smelling had been a bit of machismo which he wasn't planning to follow up on.

You have shaken him up.

You are the stronger one here.

Take his clothes off, slowly, so slowly, making him wait as you lightly brush each patch of skin with your lips. Stay a long time around his stomach, knowing he aches for you to go lower. You blow lightly on his penis, seeing it twitch uncontrollably in response.

The power.

Kneeling before him, you take him by the hips and spin him around, forcing him to his hands and knees. Before he can protest, you shove your tongue between his buttocks, all the way up, reaching for that bit of flesh behind the two sacs lying so helplessly there. That obscure, out of the way area you have seen in the pictures and have always been curious about.

Is he saying something now? It doesn't matter. Push him down onto the bed and order him to wait there, on his back, as you walk slowly to the kitchen to retrieve the bottle of honey. There is something else you've always been curious about.

"What're you up to?" he asks, looking both a little afraid and a little thrilled.

You flip open the cap of the honey. It is a silly little plastic bottle shaped like a bear. You squeeze it hard, so the honey gushes out over his penis, onto his thighs, shining thick in the patches of hair. He has stopped questioning.

Keep his eyes locked to yours as you go down slowly, purposefully, and he groans in anticipation, much like the groans you have heard from that other room on so many nights.

You taste the slimy sweetness of the honey, and the salty flesh beneath. You grope messily around with your tongue, licking it all up. And suddenly you taste the rush of fluid escaping from him, along with his gasps. It comes half on your tongue and half on his stomach, swirling with the honey like saltwater taffy. You lick it up, all of it, with the ache between your legs growing more intense.

This you won't throw up. This is a treat all your own.

As you slurp the last of the liquid from his belly button, you reach behind and slap him hard, too hard, on the ass.

"Now," you say, "fuck me."

AUTHOR'S NOTE

There are few worlds as painful and isolated as that of adolescence. And many of us try to put it behind us as quickly as possible, by either forgetting or ignoring. However, sometimes such pain can be a springboard to anger, and anger, in turn, often fuels creativity and freedom. If it weren't for my own anger, I would not have been able to push past the inhibitions I continue to have about dealing so candidly with sexuality. As with the young girl in this story, it was anger that compelled me to decide for myself what I needed to say and, thus, to defy the image of a judgmental finger being wagged in my direction.

TOO TALL FOR GRACE

By Susan J. Leonardi

"Too Tall for Grace" was the first story I accepted for Slow Hand, *and, after you read it, it should be easy to understand why it gave me an extra measure of confidence. Radiating strength and careful originality, it is set in a community of women whose everyday lives are spent in the sort of examination most of us prefer to avoid. The questions Susan Leonardi raises are about love, about sexual desire, about body and spirit, and she recognizes that in any human being conflict is both natural and inevitable. Observing the serenity and the pain inherent in difficult choices, Leonardi passes no judgment, only showing us how lovers with different needs adjust to one another, striving always to fine-tune their responses and express their devotion.*

Karen had started to run on the day after the end of the world. She ran even though only recently she had been very ill, with a mysterious liver ailment, and almost died. She ran even though she hadn't run since her last high school track meet ten years before. She ran even though the mountain roads knocked the breath out of her before she had gone a quarter of a mile. And she kept on running for five years, though not with the determination or desperation of the first day, the first week, the first month. She ran in the early seventies, before runners became (even in the mountains where you'd think just living would be exercise enough) familiar figures and before the books appeared telling you how to maximize your endorphin high and minimize the damage to your limbs. She ran until her right knee gave out, whether from the running itself or from what she heard as she ran by Lisa's open window, she didn't know.

What she did know was that half a mile into her run that day, her knee buckled and she fell. She limped home, cried—whether from the pain in her knee or from the pain of hearing what she heard as she ran by Lisa's open window, she wasn't sure, though she had a pretty good idea and she didn't like it—until her eyes were swollen shut. She was afraid to cry anymore, so she lay on her bed and willed away the pain so successfully that by morning she could walk without limping. The areas around the knee and around the heart, however, felt tenuous and sore, and her eyes were still swollen. The swelling was ugly and uncomfortable but hid the angry, disgusted, pleading looks she directed, against her will and better judgment, at Anne all through matins and lauds. She spent the afternoon alone, tending the flowers in the greenhouse, taking special care of the lavender roses, whose skins she touched, whose outer petals she blew gently, whose inner petals, though she could not see them, she sang to in a low quiet voice. Eventually she sang their favorites, "Lavender's Blue, Dilly, Dilly" and then "Purple People Eater" in reparation for the folksy laments she started with. They suited her mood but might, she feared, make the roses droop.

She skipped vespers and dinner again, telling herself aloud that she should lay off her knee as much as possible, not telling herself but knowing that she did not want to see Anne or Lisa. She wrapped the knee thickly in winter wools and wished she had hot water to soak it in. As she feared or as she hoped, Anne came knocking on her cabin door about seven. Karen didn't answer the first knock or the second. She knew Anne was there, of course; she knew Anne wouldn't come in unasked; she knew from the absence of footsteps that Anne was waiting and from the absence of any sound at all that Anne was waiting patiently, humbly, apologetically, wearily, and defiantly outside her door. She didn't get up from her reading chair ("I must stay off my knee," she said to herself by way of excuse) but called out, "Come in."

She hardened her heart when Anne hugged and held her. She said, "What do you want?" When Anne didn't answer, she said, "Why, Anne, why?" and looked out the window so that she wouldn't cry again.

"Because I love her."

"You're infatuated with her."

"How do you know that?" Anne asked.

"Because she's not your type" was the first thing that Karen said, and then she said a lot of other things about Lisa—how loud she was, how obnoxious, how disruptive, how careless, how intrusive, how self-centered, how lacking in self-control, how immature, how ill-suited to life at Julian Pines—before she repeated the observation "She's not your type." Karen said all these things in a measured, calm voice, all the time looking out the window. She waited for Anne's explosion, hoped for it, longed for it in some part of herself (probably in the fat that lay around her left ventricle) she thought she had melted off running.

Anne reached her neck around Karen's face so that Karen had to look at her, but she didn't yell that it was none of her goddamn business and she didn't kick the desk and she didn't pound her fists on the wall, any or all of which Karen waited for, hoped for, longed for, expected. Instead she brushed her cheek against Karen's and so forced her to pull away for the second time. She said, "Who is my type, Karen? You?"

"Of course, me. Me. Me. I love you. I've loved you for seven years. I go out every day and run you off, and just when I think I might be getting somewhere, you pull this. My God, Anne, look what you've done to my knee."

They talked late into the night, in and out of a circle the circumference of which was Anne's contention that they would be lovers still and always if Karen hadn't decided that their attachment was somehow inimical to the community life they were trying to lead and Karen's conviction that in spite of her unspeakable sorrow—it felt like the end of the world—Anne was, after all, right. Inside the circle was this new relationship which, Karen said, was equally inimical, which, Karen thought several times but only said once, was really much *more* inimical because Lisa was herself inimical to the whole spirit of Julian Pines Abbey, a place of silence, order, peace, prayer, and simple pleasures. Inside the circle, too, was Anne's desire for sex, which Anne wanted (but Karen didn't) to include among the simple pleasures, to make a congenial companion to or (when her argument became most intense and emphatic) a necessary component of silence, order, peace, and prayer. At that Karen snorted, but the conversation proceeded amicably and, it must be admitted, predictably, given the other conversations, theological, philosophical, literary, political, and psychological that Anne and Karen had had, usually late into the night, during those five years of daily runs. Conversations that were as often as not about lust, love, and community life.

Somewhere around 2:00 A.M. Anne advanced the theory (and Karen expressed skepticism of it, though later she began to think it had some merit) that the essence of life at Julian Pines, what made it different from other monasteries, what made it a place where women like she and Karen (and, yes, Lisa) could survive and flourish, was the blank pageness of it, the way you had to invent life every day and eschew the hierarchical assumption that peace is a higher good than passion or the clichéd assumption that peace and passion were mutually exclusive. Karen's refutation descended from these lofty heights to a more personal level at which point Anne accused her of seriously undervaluing Lisa, a brilliant and beautiful woman, and Karen charged Anne with so blatantly *over*valuing brilliance and beauty (Anne insisting here that "beautiful" referred not to any physical traits but to a wide spectrum of virtues) that they blinded her to the presence of serious defects.

Somewhere in the midst of all this heady (though Karen could feel it in her throbbing limb) talk, somewhere, that is, around three, came frantic knocking at the door, and, without waiting for Karen's response, Lisa threw the door open and stumbled in, face dirty and tearful, long hair wildly knotted, shoulders defeated, voice distraught. "Oh my God, Anne, where have you been? I'm a mess. I've looked everywhere. Do you have any idea what time it is? I was afraid you were lost in these fucking mountains." She took Anne in her arms. "Oh how could you do this to me? Anne, darling, what are you doing here in the middle of the night?" Karen, wondering at the extravagance of the drama, cynically admiring Lisa's convincing performance, and trying to figure out if Anne were so deeply deluded that she didn't detect the artifice, forbore repeating Lisa's question and said, quietly, calmly, as though soothing an overwrought child, "We were talking, Lisa, but we're finished now."

Anne looked a bit bewildered, from one woman to the other, then kissed Lisa on the cheek and said, "Go back home, dear one. I'm fine. Karen and I are talking, and we're *not* finished." This firmness reassured Karen that Anne smitten was still Anne, but she noted unhappily the longing in Anne's fingers as Lisa let go of them and left. "Quite a scene," Karen said.

"Did she ever tell you," Anne asked, "that her mother worked for the American Theatre Company?"

"No," Karen said, "she told me that her mother was a gypsy."

Although they talked until dawn, Karen didn't manage to convince Anne that Lisa's flamboyant immaturity was, in fact, flamboyant immaturity and hardly conducive to a decent, much less elevating, relationship. Nor did Anne manage to convince Karen that licking Lisa's labia did, in fact, contribute to her own growth, to the mission of the abbey community, to the spiritual renewal of the universe. Lisa left Julian Pines a month later that year (as Karen knew she would), wanting loudly and melodramatically to take Anne with her, but Anne, in spite of an anguish that she, too, expressed rather too vociferously for Karen's taste, stayed and Karen's knee healed, slowly, over time. Although the conversations changed somewhat—Anne's rhetoric, for example, became a bit less grandiose, and Karen's dismissal of Anne's defense of lust and love a bit less adamant—they continued dense, long, loving, and repetitive. Karen had hopes, unspoken even to herself, that Anne would settle down, embrace celibacy, and cease in general to agitate quite so severely her, Karen's life. Endorphin highs were nice, but running was dangerous.

The hopes persisted for years, seemed, in fact, fulfilled, until Teresa came. And then Karen let them go, because you couldn't make the same objections to Teresa that you made to Lisa. It was actually hard to make any objection at all except that she was sometimes vague and never raised her voice at the end of a question. She loved Teresa. Everyone loved Teresa. And Teresa's sexual relationship with Anne seemed so quiet, simple, and joyful that you almost, sometimes, might think that Anne was, at least partly, right about lust and love. You might even romanticize the relationship, you might say to yourself, well, Anne *has* settled down, to monogamy if not celibacy. Karen did all these things, and thought that she had finally come to terms with both the issues and personalities involved, when she, engaged one night with Anne in late talk and mutual comforting, felt desire, and Anne, too, wanted more than holding. And suddenly, though she walked away still longing, the hard edges of Karen's hardly won clarity blurred, and when that night she ran her hands down the inside of her thighs to stop the longing, she felt a certain blurriness there, too, and thought, for the first time in a long while, of running again.

By this time, though, Karen was the priest at Julian Pines (Beatrice had argued against using that word, so concretely did it conjure up a male human being, a hierarchy, a corrupt church, in the imaginations of all who heard it, but Anne had countered, cogently, most of them thought, and voted accordingly, that the very contrast between those expectations and the reality of *their* priest—a woman who conceived her priest part as just that, a part, no more or less important than other parts, she could play in the group—was itself salutary both for themselves and for their many visitors and correspondents) and spent the hours she wasn't painting and tending roses talking through troubles, fitting words to music and music to words, laying on hands. And in this way more time passed without Karen taking up again her weird and long-winded sport.

* * *

Late October in the Sierras can be starkly dry with pine needles and cones crunching underfoot, giving off the scent of mountain forest and holiday greens. Halloween day reached eighty-six degrees by mid-afternoon, was seventy at dusk, and plunged to forty by nine. As soon as it began to get dark, mountain friends brought children, theirs and neighbors', to the abbey's common house for tricks and treats. For treats, Jan made hot chocolate, Kathleen baked black-bottomed cupcakes, and Karen caramelized small apples from the orchard. For tricks there were witches' incantations. *Good* witches, the nuns carefully explained to the children (and hoped the parents would absorb, too), as most witches were, and are. Anne, Jan, Karen, Teresa, and Beatrice dressed the parts in costumes culled from twenty-five years' rummaging through used clothes sent, unsolicited, by supporters of the contemplative life. "Pray for me," said the letters accompanying the clothes, and so the community did, in their fashion, even as they pulled ruffled polyester blouses, barely wrinkled, out of bottomless boxes. Those they sent on, along with most of the skirts, coats, nightgowns, belts, dresses, and handbags, to local thrift stores and shelters. What they kept were jeans, wool and flannel shirts, fabric remnants, and occasionally attire suitable for dressing up, down, or different. Donna had discovered a gray bodysuit in a recent box which she wore this hallowed eve with oddly shaped corduroy ears. "Coyote," she whispered in response to a young questioner. Louise and Kathleen, having declared themselves weary of witches, wore, respectively, a dramatically colored and designed Renaissance gown, somewhat too large and badly stained, and a huge brown paper garment stuffed with cereal boxes collected from a neighbor's trash. "A bag of groceries, of course." Sharon came late and didn't dress, and Karen realized that probably no one had thought to warn the relative newcomer of the coming chaos or to point out the cupboard where accumulated costumes lay ready for play or party.

The children laughed gratifyingly at the cackling but not particularly scary women and at the overexcited dog, Kiera, who ran in circles and licked their sticky faces. They shifted in their seats in the middle of Jan's ghost story, sign not so much, Karen thought, of boredom as of longing for more conventionally sweet pastures of miniature Hershey bars and full-sized Snickers. After they left, Karen sighed at the mess made in less than an hour and took the largest broom to the common room floor while Louise and Beatrice shook crumbs out of the rugs and wiped up the brownish stains. Donna reported a puddle of pee in one corner, and Kathleen seemed to remember a small boy huddled there.

"I'll bet his mother told him not to ask to use the toilet," she said, "either because she thinks we don't have one or because it seemed to her unseemly to mention such an object in a house of prayer."

Jan drew the curtains, dimmed the lights, and chose carefully from her collection of tapes. Before her arrival at Julian Pines, the good nuns, under Louise's tutelage, did contra and Irish folk dancing on Halloween and other celebratory occasions. But Jan had brought rock music and amazing dance skills that she insisted could be easily learned, and soon she had all but Louise convinced of their cathartic capabilities. Louise she won over by incorporating lower back exercises and learning with great enthusiasm the folk steps for less raucous entertainment. Karen was not, on either contra or rock nights, a very enthusiastic dancer, but some times, Halloween usually one of them, she let herself be pulled, always by Anne, to the middle of the floor, where she abandoned herself to the pounding rhythms and lost for an hour or two that persistent sense of herself (though it was, of course, less acute now, less pervasive than it had been at seventeen) as too tall for grace.

She had used that phrase once, "too tall for grace"—it had been her Aunt Pearl's pronouncement on Karen-at-fourteen-years-and-almost-six-feet—when she and Anne were first experimenting with sex. She had felt so, well, limby and jerky next to Anne, who moved smoothly over Karen's stretched-out body and who, Karen had thought with awe and unstinting tenderness, moved like a dancer even when she came. "You may be," Anne had said, "too tall for Grace, but you're not too tall for me." In that sweet and silly pun (wordplay being one of Anne's many addictions and attractions) was, Karen recognized, the beginning of her long, slow, and sometimes painful process of standing up straight.

The witches left their costumes on and were the first to dance; Karen liked the long skirt at her calves and found softly erotic her circle of four—Beatrice seemed to have disappeared—black-outfitted women shaking, stretching, rolling, waving, and bending their witch-clothed bodies. "We look like nuns," Teresa shouted above the music, and they all laughed. Beatrice reappeared and joined the circle, which after a few minutes broke into a circle of three and a pair, Anne and Teresa. Damn them, Karen thought, oh, damn them both.

On another night she might have scolded the voice, called up her less belligerent spirits, repeated, incantationlike, the numerous virtues of the two witches dancing alone. But it was Halloween, there was mischief in the air, and she let the curse stand without censure, without comment, without even wondering what she meant by it. She just kept dancing. Both circles widened again, by the addition of the now uncostumed, though Donna left on her coyote ears. A weird woman, Karen thought, even weirder than the rest of us.

When she set out for her cabin, it was almost eleven, a late night for the good sisters. She flashed her light only when she needed it. Unlike Anne, who was night-blind, she saw well in the dark and didn't like to obscure the stars. She walked alone (having taken time to remove her witch's garb), fifty feet behind Anne and Teresa, engaged in some intense exchange that ended with a brief embrace when they reached Anne's rooms. A strange sight, Karen thought, two witches embracing in the dark, a small pool of light at their feet. She watched them. Teresa pulled away first and continued at a measured pace down toward her own cabin. The path to Karen's place diverged to the right from the road, about thirty feet before Anne's. As she turned off, the remaining witch walked toward her. She wasn't crying—Anne almost never cried—but the veins stood out at her temples and her eyelids were red-rimmed, signs, Karen knew from many years' experience, of trouble.

"Turn off that flashlight," Karen said, in an effort to ignore what brewed. "Witches are supposed to be able to see in the dark." Anne looked down at her black clothes as though she had forgotten them and pressed the button. The two women stood there for a moment, in silence, under a moon that was not quite full and partly obscured by a small cloud. "I can't see your face," Anne said. "Can we talk inside?" She fumbled for a match to light the propane lamp in her entryway and let the lamp provide the light for the bedroom as well. Dim but sufficient. Karen sat cross-legged, as was her wont, on the bed and waited without speaking for Anne to initiate the inevitable ritual of sitting backward astride her desk chair as though she were going to plunge into conversation, then, before saying anything at all, turning back to the desk, opening the top drawer, taking out a cigarette, getting up and searching for matches, which were never in the porcelain ashtray where Karen would have kept them, were never, in fact, in any predictable place. She ended up going back to the box in the entryway. After she lit the cigarette, she abandoned the chair and joined Karen on the bed, an action that would within a minute or two, Karen knew, necessitate getting up for the ashtray, now out of reach. Karen liked knowing the moves ahead of time, liked knowing, for example, that there would be only one cigarette, to get them started, and that, once started, Anne would get right to the point.

"I'm a sex fiend."

Karen laughed. "You look like some sort of fiend in that outfit, but sex fiend wouldn't be my first guess."

"I'm not trying to be funny, Karen."

"Yes, you are, or you wouldn't have said that."

"I was trying to express, in a pithy but admittedly exaggerated way, a serious problem. I mean, when I assess the situation rationally, I decide I'm just a normal woman with a normal sex drive. But here, among the saints, I feel like a nymphomaniac."

"Translation: Teresa doesn't want sex with you as often as you want sex with Teresa."

"Your translation," Anne said, "like most translations, is literally accurate but misses the subtle nuances."

"Like?"

"Like the fact that Teresa likes sex but doesn't seem to need it, like the fact that you liked sex once upon a time but seem to have transcended it, like the fact that Donna and Sharon and Louise and Jan and Kathleen and Beatrice do without it on a regular basis and never complain and never seem to fill the common space with erotic tension and never seem about to explode. What's wrong with *me?*"

Karen decided to be fair. "Maybe the question is what's wrong with the rest of us."

"I tell myself that sometimes," Anne said, "but it won't wash. You are all fine. You are affectionate and more or less sane and intelligent and fun and well, fine—not twisted by frustration, not anguished by erotic energy, not driven by the need to channel your sex drives into creative endeavors."

"You are affectionate and sane and intelligent and fun and fine, too, Anne, maybe even more so than the rest of us. Besides Beatrice."

"Then why do I feel like this? I love Teresa, I want her, I want her desperately, I want her to want me. She says yes, okay, fine, anytime, thanks, but she never *wants* me, and so mostly I've just stopped asking, and we haven't slept together in weeks."

"I'm sorry." Karen did feel sorry, rather to her surprise.

"Why should you be? You haven't slept with anyone for twenty years, and you never moan and groan about it."

"Never to you. I could hardly moan and groan about it to you, friend, when your answer would be—and it would be a fair answer—'you're the one who walked away.' "

"To whom, then?"

"Oh, to Beatrice."

"I bet you did it once, Karen, maybe fifteen years ago. Am I right?"

Karen laughed. "I think it was more like ten years ago, but yes, you're right. But . . ."

"But you still have desires. You just breathe them into your roses, sing them into vespers, paint them into flowers, send sweet loving messages with them to us all, and maybe you even masturbate once in a while. Don't worry. I'm not asking. Damn it, Karen. I like my work, too, and I love vespers, and I feel close to my sisters, and I masturbate. But I want *sex*, with another living, breathing, panting human being. Who doesn't even have to be Teresa. Who could be Sojourner, who could be Jan, who could be that journalist who came—what was her name, Marta?—who could be you. Sometimes I even think about sex with Beatrice. I'm promiscuous as well as desperate.

"Do you understand what I'm saying, Karen? I live surrounded by women I love and I *want* them, and I don't understand why they don't all want each other."

Karen took a deep breath. She didn't know where to start. She lacked Anne's eloquence and perhaps her passion, but she, Karen, had things to say to this woman who mistook control for calm, who discarded effort, who, like the fisherman's wife, wanted castle for cottage and even then wasn't satisfied. She wanted to start five minutes back and say that if Teresa said yes, it was enough, take it, love her. It was greedy to want more than Teresa's yes. She wanted to say that Donna, good, kind, dependable Donna, preferred animals to humans and had who knows what kind of secret desires or secret holiness wrapped up in her silent ways. She wanted to say that Louise was single and celibate when she arrived at the monastery, in her thirties. What, if any repressions had brought her to them virginal were as incomprehensible to her, Karen, as to Anne. She wanted to say that Sharon hadn't been there very long but was, Karen strongly suspected, going to have a lot of trouble with this very desire and that Jan, Karen knew for a fact, though she wasn't at liberty to say so, had as much trouble with it as Anne; that Jan had actually, for over a year, had an enormous crush on Anne, which she worked with touching diligence and ingenuousness to overcome. She wanted to say that Kathleen and Beatrice had desire beaten out of them at Mt. Carmel and that Beatrice sometimes seemed to beat back desire still. Once, at least, Karen thought she had seen it, alive and, yes, desperate, in Beatrice's eyes—which were, at the time, looking at Anne.

She wanted to say that she, Karen, had times of calm and times of chaos, that she *did*, when chaos came, breathe desire into her roses and into her drawings, that she did love herself with it and torture herself over it, that Beatrice had, in a most passionate and un-Beatricelike way, said once that she must never do it violence because without it this life was nothing. She wanted to say that sometimes (maybe because she had tried not to do it violence) she, Karen, wanted her, Anne, desperately and passionately, not often, but sometimes. Like, Anne, like tonight when we were dancing, when you and Teresa broke away from the circle and I said to myself, damn them, damn them. I said that, Anne, because *I* wanted you, I wanted to throw myself at you and rip off that witch's shirt and—right there on the common room floor—suck your nipples through my teeth until they bled. That's what I wanted, Anne (how do you like that?), that's what I *want*.

She wanted to say these things, and she did say them. She said them all except for the part about Jan, which she knew but couldn't say, and the part about Beatrice, which she didn't know and couldn't say and was afraid of. She said them until the tears were running down her cheeks and until Anne unbuttoned first the witch's shirt and then the witch's skirt and took off the bra and pants underneath and came at Karen naked, her nipples erect, and said in her huskiest voice, "Suck them, Karen, until they bleed."

While Karen sucked, Anne stripped her, not gently, carefully, as she had so many years before (when that her tall, thin body even breathed must have seemed to Anne a tenuous miracle), but quickly, roughly. Karen helped with her jeans, let go of Anne long enough to light a candle to replace the dimming propane lamp. "I want to *see* you," she said. She looked hard at Anne's body, different from the memories but no less compelling. She ran her hands down Anne's hips, felt Anne's hands grabbing her butt, pushed Anne to the bed. They struggled there, not for anything but the struggle itself, and Karen came out on top. She slid herself down until her mouth was again around Anne's breast, and she drew the nipples again through her teeth, in and out, in and out. At the same time she thrust three fingers inside of her and rubbed the ball of her hand firmly against Anne's pubic bone. Anne spread her legs far apart and danced wildly into Karen's hand, whispering, hoarsely, harshly, "Harder, harder," then moaning so loudly that young Karen would have let go at first sound of it, but this Karen didn't, couldn't. She only sucked and pushed and pulled harder until Anne came, almost shouting. She tasted blood.

Without transition, without letting up on the frantic pace, Anne flipped her over and took charge. Suddenly the moans were Karen's, and she felt with panicked pleasure the finger that had been aimlessly roaming her belly and cunt work its way slowly into her ass and Anne's thumb on her clitoris. And by the time Anne's mouth closed over her breast she had wrapped her legs around Anne's body and was using them to push her hips forward into the firm flesh of Anne's belly. "What *is* this," she said in a loud voice that seemed to be coming from across the room, "Oh God, what *is* this?" Anne slid her mouth down Karen's pumping body, and with her tongue traced circles in Karen's pubic hair while she pressed her thumb inside her. Karen writhed, trying to get herself into Anne's mouth, but Anne teased on. "Tell me what you want."

"You know what I want," Karen managed to say between breaths.

"Say it."

"Suck me."

"How?"

"Hard."

When she woke up at 4:30, Karen lay quietly beside the sleeping witch and wondered if what they had done at midnight was make love or do battle. She felt bruised, her thigh muscles ached. She remembered the way they had held each other down, pushed and pulled, teased and scratched, bit and shouted and dared. She remembered it as a dream and she the dreamer but not one of the breathless, violent women, teeth bared, rolling over in the bed, spitting blood out of their mouths. She wished it were light so she could see if she had broken the skin on Anne's breast. Surely not. She tried to say "Damn you" to the body at her side, but she couldn't. The words that came so easily last night were gone. And when she slid silently out of the bed and into her clothes, she longed for Anne's fingers on her flesh, not clawing but tracing. She took her shoes to the entryway, and as she bent over to pull them on, she noticed the objects on the table by the door. A glass of water, with a note taped to it: Always drink before running. Two pieces of chocolate on top of another note: Don't run away altogether. Anne must have written the notes, blind as she was, in the night, while Karen slept; Anne had known she would run, though she hadn't run for years; Anne, Anne, Anne. She loved her with every sore muscle in her body, with every drop of her blood, with every cell of her brain. She had loved her, not since the day they met, the two young newcomers, wary of the women, of each other, wondering, separately, about this strange step their lives seemed to have taken without them, not since then but since the day Anne appeared at the side of Karen's bed, though she had never nursed, and stayed through the long and frightening illness that so suddenly claimed her. Though the doctor had answered her questions patiently enough, her diagnosis of Karen's driving pain paled in explanatory power beside the dark, troubling pieces of her life that worked their way like shards of glass to the surface of her skin. It was Anne who took tweezers to them, held them up to the light for her, safely disposed of them when she was finished. Likewise the doctor's account of Karen's recovery bore too little resemblance to her own sense that cells healed under the tips of Anne's fingers, that every time Anne's hands rubbed her neck, her shoulders, her sides, they rubbed off death.

Outside Anne's door, Karen stretched and reached and fell without thinking into her old prerunning routine. It was dark and it was cold, but Karen thought that in a couple of miles it would begin to get light and she would begin, even sooner, to get warm. And so she ran, trying at first to ward off the cold by singing some of the songs, what she could remember of them, that Anne had sung to her during the weeks of nursing. Quiet, kind weeks. Anne had sung while she stroked Karen's face, blew cool breath on her hot forehead, traced soft circles on her cheeks. First there were folk songs—it was 1969—lullabies, labor songs, songs from the civil rights movement, songs from some long ago summer camp. "From the hills I gather courage / Visions of the days to be. / Strength to lead and strength to follow / All are given unto me." Karen looked out the window when Anne sang that one. "Nuns," Anne explained. "It was a camp run by the Sisters of Social Service. They wore gray wool and were into the inspirational stuff." But she sang it purely, and Karen's arms got goose bumps. They were so young.

"O gay is the garland and fresh are the roses / I've culled from the garden to bind on thy brow." Karen had liked the roses in that song. Some days she imagined them yellow and warm, other days, when her fever raged, lavender and cool. And then there was the song in a minor key, so slow and mournful. How did it go? "Come all ye fair and tender maidens / Be careful when you court young men / They're like a star on a summer morning / They'll come in view, then fade again."

"And, Sister Karen," Anne had said, after the first time she sang it, "let that be a lesson to you." Karen had been too sick to laugh. And there were days when she was so sick that she only wanted one song, but she never told Anne that, she just let her sing and hoped she'd come to it eventually. "When you wake, you will find / All the pretty little horses. Dappled and gray, pinto and bay / All the pretty little horses." Karen's mother had sung that song, but never the part about dappled and gray. Had Anne made it up?

She was already at the apple orchard when she remembered the Irish songs. Anne had thought of them late, when Karen was already mending, so she associated them with the best days of the illness, when she and Anne could talk and laugh, and she could eat, and Anne took such touching pleasure in bringing her food, always carefully arranged on the plate, trimmed with bits of parsley, accompanied by slices of apples in whose restorative properties Anne firmly believed. An apple a day.

"You may take the shamrock from your hat and cast it on the sod / But 'twill take root and flourish still though underfoot 'tis trod." Once Anne had figured out all the words, she sang it almost every day. A fighting song, she said to Karen, good for you. "And if the color we must wear is England's cruel red / Sure Ireland's folk will ne'er forget the blood that they have shed." Anne's English father hated that song, she said, so she sang it often, especially in March, especially when she couldn't get his attention any other way. He hated that song most, but he hated all Irish songs. Maybe, she said, maybe that's why she knew so many.

Anne used to say good-night with "Danny Boy," which, as often as not, she changed to "Annie Girl." After a while she'd make Karen sing the last two lines—while she kissed her: "For you will bend and tell me that you love me / And I shall sleep in peace until you come to me." The better she felt, the more lines she would sing, the more Anne would kiss her, her forehead, her cheeks, her ears, her neck. And, when the song was over, her lips. The kisses got longer, and one night they kissed so long and it was so dark and cold that Anne asked if she could stay. She could, oh yes, she could.

Karen picked up the pace, partly because she was running downhill, partly because she couldn't bear to remember what had happened that first night Anne stayed. The sweetness of it, the youthfulness of it, the carefulness of it, the wholeness of it. Whole and healed she had felt afterward, lying in Anne's arms. She didn't want to sleep because Anne was asleep, and she wanted to watch her, so small, so lovely, so delicate, so unlike the vigorous woman who had cared for her so competently, day after day, for almost three months. Sweet gum leaves were falling all around her, red and orange and yellow, she knew, though they all looked alike in the dark. She wanted to see a real fall someday, a Vermont fall, for example, a New Hampshire fall. Anne said that you had to see it to believe it but that they deserved it, the New Englanders, compensation for the cold and the dark.

By catching leaves and giving them colors—pomegranate, persimmon, pumpkin, grape, mustard, ocher, olive, chestnut, aubergine—Karen could stave off exhaustion for a while. She stuffed them into her pockets so she could see, after sunrise, if they lived up to their names. She ran and ran. It was still dark, but you could feel dawn. She knew she should stop because she'd been running an hour after years of not running and her knee ached. She knew she should stop because she had gone too far already, mostly downhill, and it would be a long hike back. She knew she should stop because she was too old for this, not the running but the running away. But she kept going because Anne's taste was still in her mouth, Anne's smell in her nose, Anne's fingers on her breasts, Anne's leg between her legs, Anne's eyes everywhere. Run, Karen, run.

In the half light of this All Saints' morning Karen started to feel her knee collapse. She cried out in irritation that her old injury had recurred, that it was so cold, that she was so many miles from Julian Pines, that she hadn't finished running. She dragged herself to a tree and sat down against the trunk. After a few minutes she had to shift her weight because her good leg was falling asleep and her tailbone ached. She thought of Anne's hands, generously covered with almond oil, cinnamon scented, starting with her feet and massaging their way up, every muscle, large and small, succumbing to their warm pressure. Thanks, she was convinced, to those daily rubs, her limbs had worked admirably when she left her sickbed.

She leaned against the tree, almost warm on her back. She listened for cars, heard nothing for a long time, thought again about crawling to the nearest house, then fell, briefly, asleep. She dreamed. A vague woman, a half seduction, a windowless room, a cup of coffee she tried to smell but couldn't, a heart—hers—beating fast, hard, loud. She caught herself before she toppled over onto the ground, dream suspended. She was cold, her bladder was full, her knee hurt. She wondered why no one came.

Finally she heard a car approaching, more slowly than she would have expected, the curve around her tree. She was relieved that it didn't sound like a pick-up. She wouldn't ask a ride from a stranger, but there were, she reminded herself, friends in the mountains. It was, however, none of the Halloween guests, still sticky from her caramel apples, who was driving the car. It was one of the witches. "Anne," she shouted. "Anne." Anne parked the abbey Toyota in a small clearing on the other side of the road from Karen's tree. She got out slowly and walked, just as slowly, across the road. She sat down next to her. "Hi," she said. "Hi there."

"Hi there, yourself," Karen said.

"You forgot your chocolate." Anne held out the wrapped balls. Karen shook her head.

"I picked an apple on my way through the orchard."

"Looks like it's still in your pocket."

"It is," Karen said, "minus a bite." She took it out along with the leaves, most of them disappointingly brown, which she tossed in Anne's direction. Several landed in her hair. "Happy fall."

"Happy fall," Anne said, "oh happy, happy fall. When did you do it?"

"Do what?"

"Fall."

"How do you know I fell? Maybe I'm just resting. Waiting for the sun to rise over the mountain peak."

"You're facing in the wrong direction."

"And what are you doing in these parts, Sister Anne Stratford?"

"Looking for a runaway nun," Anne said. "Tall, thin, brown hair, wearing jeans and a green jacket. Early forties, very attractive, bum knee, answers to 'Karen.' There's a reward."

"What is it?"

"Oh, a cup of steaming hot coffee. Scones and boysenberry jam. Me."

Karen licked her lips. "I had a dream."

"Was she beautiful?"

"Very."

"Did she look like me?" Anne asked.

"Not a bit. She was tall, elegant, dressed in some sort of smoking jacket. When she was dressed."

"Nice dream. Did you run away?"

"No," Karen said, "I woke up. And I was cold and my knee hurt."

"That's the trouble with dreams," Anne said, reaching out to help Karen to the car.

"But maybe," Karen said, "maybe that's the trouble with sex."

And so the conversation went, predictably enough, all the way home, Anne wanting, it seemed, to go over every inch of the night's territory, describing the warmth of it, delineating the loveliness of it, dwelling on the usefulness of it. "We have been talking for twenty years," she said, "arguing away our lives. I feel as though we've settled something, come together, loved each other again in some significant way." Absorbed in the eloquence of one and skepticism of the other, they missed the sunrise.

"I tasted blood," Karen said.

"How did it taste?"

"Bitter," Karen said, "and strong."

Anne one-handedly unzipped her jacket and unbuttoned her shirt and lifted her breasts, one at a time, out of her bra. "Look," she said, "whole and pink. If you tasted blood it was your own. Maybe you bit your tongue." One at a time, Karen tucked the breasts (they were soft, smooth, tempting, unmarked by teeth) back into the cups; she buttoned the shirt; she zipped the jacket. She exaggeratedly examined her tongue in the visor mirror.

"Tongues heal quickly," Anne said, as she turned into the abbey entrance and drove slowly up the dry dirt road to the common house.

"Maybe breasts do, too," Karen said, "on the feast of saints. You know, a sort of miracle in honor of Agnes, who lopped off her breast to save her hymen. Or did the Roman lop it off?"

"The Romans. And it was Agatha. Or maybe you're thinking of Lucy who plucked out her eyes," Anne said, "or Apollonia who jumped into the fire. They were bloody and savage women, our virgin martyrs."

"I smell coffee," Karen said.

"Well," Anne said, "let's drink to them: St. Agnes, St. Lucy, St. Agatha, St. Perpetua, St. Felicitas, St. Apollonia, St. Cecilia, St. Anastasia, St. Catherine, St. Bibiana, St. Christina, St. Ursula, St. Dorothy, St. Barbara, St. Emerentiana, St. Margaret, St. Martina . . ."

"Anne," Karen said, interrupting the litany, "sometimes you exhaust me."

AUTHOR'S NOTE

I have been thinking for a long time about Allan Sillitoe's story, "The Loneliness of the Long-Distance Runner" and Grace Paley's brilliant contribution to the conversation, "The Long-Distance Runner." It occurred to me that Paley accomplishes such interesting things by replacing the handsome male adolescent hero with an overweight middle-aged woman that I wondered what would happen if I replaced him with someone who differed not only in age, appearance, and gender but sexual orientation as well.

I then found a story by the English writer Sara Maitland called "The Loveliness of the Long-Distance Runner," in which the main characters are lesbian, but I didn't think the story worked very well. So, I wrote my own, using characters about whom I have been thinking and writing for several years—a group of offbeat nuns in a monastery in the Sierras. The original title was "The Nunliness of the Long-Distance Runner."

ABOUT THE AUTHORS

Some of these names are real, some invented.

Jacqueline Ariail lives with her two sons, Isaac and Jacob, and her daughter, Hannah, in Durham, North Carolina, and teaches expository writing at North Carolina State University. She has published a number of short stories and is working on a novel about Barry and Laura.

Carolyn Banks is the author of four novels, including *Mr. Right* and *Patchwork*, as well as many short stories. She and her husband raise horses on a farm near Austin, Texas.

Rebecca Battle works as an actress in Los Angeles and New York. This is her first published story. "Since I have a sublet, I had to type it at a public terminal, which turned out to be somewhat traumatic—writing about such things with all those people strolling behind you, discussing the latest fonts! Still, it definitely added to the excitement of the experience."

Idious Buguise lives in London near Paddington Station. "I have never been in therapy—except once for forty-five minutes when I was eleven years old—have two small children who know where babies come from, and hate people who wear fur coats."

I. Buguise is an anthropologist living in London. This is her second piece of fiction.

Marion Callen lives in Peterborough, England, where she is an area organizer for the Cambridgeshire literacy and numeracy program. She has contributed for five years to the Peterborough Writers' group and has recently become a member of Cambridge Women Writers.

Elizabeth Clarke is a professional erotician who writes, dances, models, and performs for men and women. She does safe sex education for lesbian and bisexual women as part of the Peer Safer Sex Slut Team. "Queer" is the first chapter of a novel in progress. Most recently, she has been living in San Francisco.

Liz Clarke is a 1992 college graduate. A native North Carolinian, she wrote her first poem at age six and began her first novel two years later. She is an alumnus of the University of Virginia's Young Writers Workshop. "I'm fascinated by sex and sexuality these days because I spent so much of my life utterly out of touch with, and terrified by, my body, and so I'm making up for lost time."

Sara Davidson is the author of the bestselling novel *Loose Change*, which was turned into a miniseries. Her other books are *Real Property* and *Friends of the Opposite Sex* (from which "The Wager" was excerpted). Currently writing for television, she lives in Los Angeles with her two children.

Jenny Diski, who lives and works in north London, has published six novels. The most recent, *Monkey's Uncle*, appeared in England early in 1994.

Susan Dooley is a writer living in a small New England village.

Francine Falk is an actress, poet, and short story writer born in Washington state and long a resident of Pennsylvania. She is the mother of a twenty-one-year-old son.

Sabina Faye is a mystery novelist who has lived in Australia, Nepal, and Switzerland; when not traveling, she makes her home in Washington, D.C. She has worked as an au pair, a manual laborer, a bartender, and as a dancing extra in an opera company.

Barbara Gowdy is the author of two novels, *Through the Green Valley* and *Falling Angels*. She lives with her cats, Jack and Emma, in Toronto, where she can be seen as one of the guest interviewers for the TV-Ontario book program "In Print."

Phaedra Greenwood is a writer and photographer living in New Mexico. In 1988 she was a finalist for the Katherine Anne Porter Award.

Laurel Gross lives in New York City. She has been an entertainment and television editor and critic for the *New York Post* and an editor at *Variety*.

Nancy Holder dropped out of high school to become a ballerina. She has published eighteen novels and numerous short stories. Two of her erotic horror novels, *Making Love* and *Witch-Light*, were written in collaboration with Melanie Tem. She lives in San Diego with her husband and three dogs.

Kay Kemp is the alter ego of a Canadian novelist and short story writer. She was born in Edmonton, Alberta, and has lived in Washington, D.C., and London. She now lives in Toronto with her husband and two children.

Wendy Law-Yone was born in Mandalay, Burma, grew up in Rangoon, and lived in several countries of Southeast Asia before settling in the United States in 1973. Her first novel was *The Coffin Tree;* she is at work on a second. Her work has appeared in *The Atlantic* and in *Grand Street*. The mother of four, she is the recipient of a National Endowment for the Arts award.

Carol Lazare lives with her daughter, Lilly, in Toronto. Her work as an actress earned her two Canadian film awards; more recently, she has concentrated on writing for theater and film. " 'Footpath' is one of a collection of short stories called *When the Cycle Ends* that I'm currently working on. All of the stories, of which there are now five, revolve in some way around the same characters, Sarah and Eddy; this one describes their first meeting and sets the tone for their obsessive relationship."

Susan J. Leonardi teaches literature and creative writing at the University of Maryland. She is the author of *Dangerous by Degrees: Women at Oxford and the Somerville College Novelists*. "Too Tall for Grace" will appear in a longer version in her collection *Nun Stories*. "I'm also working on a detective novel and collaborating on something more academic, a book called *To Have a Voice: The Politics of the Diva*. This is a project that perhaps suggests a secret longing to exchange the privacy of the page for the exhibition of the stage. In my next life, I'm going to be a performance artist."

L. M. Lippman is a writer and journalist living in Baltimore.

Carole Maso is the author of the novels *Ghost Dance* and *The Art Lover*. She has recently completed a third, *The American Woman in the Chinese Hat*. She makes her home in New York City.

Susan Musgrave, a native Californian, lives on Vancouver Island. Her eleventh book of poetry, *Forcing the Narcissus*, was published in Canada in the spring of 1994, along with her second collection of personal essays, *Musgrave Landing*.

Lawanda Powell lives in Washington, D.C. The mother of two grown daughters, she has been a social worker and an administrator.

Francesca Ross is a midwestern writer of Regency romances. She also teaches literature and composition at a state university.

Anne Rhyd is a science and technology writer who has recently moved to New Orleans.

Catherine S. is a journalist. She is from a southern family that her sister has described as one part Tennessee Williams, one part Erskine Caldwell. "As a child, I read compulsively from a cache of books beneath my bed that included *Lolita, The Valley of the Dolls, Candy*, and *God's Little Acre*."

Susan St. Aubin lives and writes in a turn-of-the-century cottage in northern California. Among the places her short fiction has appeared are the three *Herotica* collections and both the magazine and the anthology *Yellow Silk*.

Nazneen Sheikh was born in Srinagar, India, and was educated in Pakistan and Texas. She lives in Toronto with her husband, Gustavo, and is the mother of two daughters. Her second novel, *Chopin People*, was published in Canada in the spring of 1994.

Susan Swan is a Toronto-based journalist, performance artist, and fiction writer. Her works include *Unfit For Paradise, The Biggest Modern Woman of the World*, and *The Last of the Golden Girls*. Her new book, *Homage to America*, will examine the personification of ideas in the U.S. media.

Lisa Tuttle was born and raised in Houston, Texas, but now lives on the remote west coast of Scotland with her husband and baby daughter. She is the author of many short stories and several novels, the most recent of which is *Lost Futures*, as well as the nonfiction books *Encyclopedia of Feminism* and *Heroines: Women Inspired by Women*. She has also edited *Skin of the Soul*, a collection of original horror stories by women writers.

Toby Vallance was born in London and educated in Cambridge and London. She is working on a collection of short stories and a novel.

Bea Wilder has lived in Cambridge, Massachusetts, for the past twenty years, with the exception of a period when she taught in South America—"where I rediscovered my Peruvian roots." She has worked as a community activist, newspaper gossip columnist, and elementary school teacher. She is currently studying for a master's degree in counseling/psychology.

COPYRIGHT ACKNOWLEDGMENTS

"A Slow Freight." Copyright © 1994 by Phaedra Greenwood. An original story published by permission of the author.

"The Night Mare." Copyright © 1994 by Susan Dooley. An original story published by permission of the author.

"G.T.T. (Gone To Texas)." Copyright © 1994 by L. M. Lippman. An original story published by permission of the author.

"Climacteric." Copyright © 1994 by I. Buguise. An original story published by permission of the author.

"Where the Cypress Paints the Sky." Copyright © 1994 by Laurel Gross. An original story published by permission of the author.

"Love in the Wax Museum." Copyright © 1994 by Nancy Holder. An original story published by permission of the author.

"Yarn." Copyright © 1994 by Jenny Diski. An original story published by permission of the author.

"A Dish for the Gods." Copyright © 1994 by Kay Kemp. An original story published by permission of the author.

"Last Tango in Geneva." Copyright © 1994 by Jacqueline Ariail. An original story published by permission of the author.

"Polishing My Skin." Copyright © 1994 by Nazneen Sheikh. An original story published by permission of the author.

"Valentine's Day in Jail." Copyright © 1994 by Susan Musgrave. An original story published by permission of the author.

"In the Prick of Time" by Susan Dooley. Copyright © 1992 by Susan Dooley. An original story published by permission of the author.

"Leaper" by Jenny Diski. Copyright © 1992 by Jenny Diski. An original story published by permission of the author.

"Drought" by Wendy Law-Yone. Copyright © 1992 by Wendy Law-Yone. An original story published by permission of the author.

ABOUT THE EDITOR

Michele Slung's works include *The Absent-Minded Professor's Memory Book; The Only Child Book*; and the bestselling *Momilies®* books, *Momilies: As My Mother Used to Say®* and *More Momilies.* Among her successful anthologies are *Crime on Her Mind: Fifteen Stories of Female Sleuths from the Victorian Era to the '40s; I Shudder at Your Touch: Tales of Sex and Horror* and its sequel, *Shudder Again*; and *Slow Hand: Women Writing Erotica* (HarperCollins). Most recently, she has published *Hear! Here! Sounds Around the World* and coedited the collection *Murder for Halloween.*